Between Heaven and Earth

A selection of short stories

Translated from the German by Graham Twinn

The Monkswell Press
Cambridge

Between Heaven and Earth

ISBN 978-0-9555372-0-2

First published 2007

The Monkswell Press
9 Ely Place
Monkswell
Cambridge
CB2 9SS

Between Heaven and Earth

For Sophie and Charles

CONTENTS

The Earthquake in Chile

By Heinrich von Kleist

When Santiago, the capital of the kingdom of Chile, was struck by the great earthquake of 1647 in which many thousands perished, a young Spaniard named Jeronimo Rugera was standing by a pillar in the prison to which he had been committed for a serious crime, and was about to hang himself.

About a year before, Don Henrico Asteron, one of the richest noblemen of the town, had dismissed him from his house, where he was employed as a tutor, because he and Donna Josephe, his only daughter, had fallen violently in love. A secret rendezvous, after a stern warning, was betrayed to her father thanks to the malicious prying of his arrogant son. This so angered her father that he forced her to enter the Carmelite convent of Our Lady of the Mountains in Santiago. By a lucky chance, Jeronimo had succeeded in renewing their relationship there, and one quiet night the convent garden was the scene of the complete fulfilment of his desires.

It was on Corpus Christi day and the procession of nuns followed by the novices was just setting out, when the unfortunate Josephe, just as the bells rang out, collapsed on the steps of the Cathedral with labour pains. This extraordinary event caused an enormous scandal. Regardless of her condition, the young sinner Josephe was immediately thrown into prison. Hardly was her confinement over, when legal proceedings were taken against her on the orders of the Archbishop.

The scandal was discussed with such bitterness in the town and tongues wagged so maliciously about the whole convent where it happened that neither a plea by the Asteron family nor the wishes of the Abbess herself, who had come to love the girl for her otherwise blameless character, could moderate the severity with which the laws of the convent were meted out to her. All that could be done was to commute her sentence from death by burning at the stake to death by beheading, thanks to a decree by the Viceroy but much to the annoyance of the matrons and spinsters of Santiago. In the streets through which the procession would pass to the execution all the windows were hired out and the rooftops cleared, as the God-fearing daughters of the town invited their friends to watch with them this spectacle of divine retribution.

Jeronimo, who meantime had also been thrown into prison, almost fainted when he learnt of the horrible turn events had taken. He longed in vain for escape, but wherever the boldest flights of his imagination led him, he always ran up against walls and bolts, and an attempt to file through the bars of his window only earned him an even more severe imprisonment when it was discovered. He knelt down before an image of the Virgin Mary and prayed fervently to her as the only one now able to affect his escape. Yet the dreaded day arrived and with it the conviction of the complete hopelessness of his position. The bells which accompanied Josephe to the place of execution rang out, and despair gripped his mind. Life seemed hateful to him and he decided to kill himself by means of a piece of rope which chance had provided for him.

And so he was standing by the pillar fastening the rope which was to put an end to his miserable existence to an iron hook in the cornice, when suddenly a large part of the town collapsed with a roar, as if the sky had fallen in, and buried every living thing under the rubble. Jeronimo was petrified with fear and immediately, as if his consciousness had been completely erased, now clung to the pillar on which he had wanted to die, in order to stop himself falling. The ground shook under his feet, the walls of the prison were rent apart, the whole building leaned over and threatened to fall into the street and was only prevented from complete collapse by the building opposite also leaning over to form a temporary arch.

Trembling, his hair dishevelled and his knees shaking so that they could hardly hold him, Jeronimo crept across the slanting floor towards the gap which had been created in the front wall by the collapse of the two buildings. Scarcely was he in the open when the whole street, already badly shaken, completely collapsed following a second quake. Without any idea of how to escape the general destruction he hurried through the rubble and fallen timbers towards the nearest town gate, with death threatening on every side. Here another building collapsed scattering heaps of rubble and forcing him into a side street. Here flames, gleaming through clouds of smoke, were already licking up from the rooftops, driving him through fear into another.

Here the river Mapocho, forced out of its course, roared towards him and carried him into a third. Here lay heaps of dead, voices were groaning under the rubble, people were shouting down from burning rooftops, men and animals were struggling against the torrent. A brave rescuer was doing what he could to help, another, deathly pale, speechlessly stretched up his hands to Heaven.

When Jeronimo had reached the gates and climbed the small hill behind it, he sank down in a faint. He must have been completely unconscious for a good 15 minutes before he finally came to and half raised himself from the ground with his back towards the town. He felt his forehead and chest, not knowing what to make of his condition, and a feeling of unspeakable joy came over him when the west wind off the sea fanned his returning consciousness and he gazed in all directions over the blossoming countryside around Santiago. Only the bewildered groups of people everywhere to be seen made him uneasy. He could not comprehend what they or he could be doing there and only when he turned round and saw the city in ruins behind him did he remember the terrifying moments he had just lived through. He fell down on his knees, bowing his head to the ground to thank God for his miraculous escape. And as if this one terrible event had imprinted itself on his mind and driven out every other thought, he now wept for joy that he still enjoyed life and all its manifold blessings.

But then, noticing the ring on his hand, he suddenly remembered Josephe and with her his prison, the bells he had heard ringing and the moments which had immediately preceded the quake. Deep dejection came over him again. He began to regret his prayer of thankfulness and God who reigns above the clouds now seemed to him a terrible being. He mingled with the people pouring out of the town, attempting to save their possessions, and dared to ask after Asteron's daughter and whether the execution had been carried out, - but nobody was able to give him definite information.

 Then a woman, weighed down by an enormous burden of household effects and with two children clinging round her neck, told him as she went by, as if she herself had been present, that the girl had been beheaded. Jeronimo turned away and since he could not but doubt that this was true when he reckoned up the time, he sat down in a lonely clump of trees and gave himself up completely to his grief. He wished that the destructive power of nature would break over him again. He did not understand why he should have escaped death when in his wretched state he had so freely desired it as the only salvation. He determined, though, not to waver, even though the oak trees should be uprooted and crash down upon him, and now, having found relief in hot tears through which hope gradually returned to him, he stood up and wandered across the fields in every direction. He visited every hilltop on which people had gathered. On every path he went to meet the crowds of refugees who were still streaming out of the town. Wherever a woman's dress fluttered in the wind his trembling feet took him there- yet none concealed the beloved form of Asteron's daughter.

The sun was beginning to sink, and with it his hopes, when he stumbled to the edge of a cliff and looked down into a broad valley almost empty of people. Uncertain what to do, he was glancing from one group of people to another when he suddenly caught sight of a young woman busy washing a child in the stream which watered the valley.

His heart leapt when he saw her. He jumped down over the rocks full of misgivings, but cried out, "Holy Mother of God!" on recognising Josephe as she shyly looked round at the noise. With what unspeakable joy did they embrace, these two unfortunates saved by a divine miracle.

Josephe had been quite near the square where she was to be executed when the whole procession had been scattered by the buildings suddenly collapsing with a roar. Her first terrified steps had carried her out towards the nearest town gate, but recollection had soon returned and she hurried back towards the convent where her little son had been left. She found the whole convent already in flames and the Abbess, who as Josephe's last hours approached, had promised to look after her little child was standing outside the gates shouting for help to come and rescue him. Josephe rushed straight into the building which was already beginning to collapse on all sides and, as if protected by the angels in Heaven, came out again through the portals with him unharmed.

She was about to sink into the arms of the Abbess who was clasping her hands over her head, when the latter together with most of the nuns was struck down by a falling gable. At this terrible sight Josephe stumbled back. She hastily closed the Abbess's eyes and fled terror-stricken to try and save from destruction the dear child whom Heaven had restored to her. She had not taken more than a few steps when she came across the body of the Archbishop who had been crushed in the ruins of the cathedral and had just been carried out. The Viceroy's palace had collapsed, the Court House in which she had been condemned to death had gone up in flames, and on the site of her father's house the sea had swallowed everything, producing clouds of steam glowing red from the flames. Josephe had to summon up all her strength to prevent herself fainting. She strode on courageously from street to street with her precious burden, putting all thoughts of suffering from her mind and she was near the town gate when she saw that the prison where Jeronimo had languished was also in ruins. At this sight she staggered and almost fell on the corner of the street, but at that moment a building behind her, already tottering, suddenly collapsed forcing her to go on, her strength renewed by fear. She kissed the child and, forcing back the tears from her eyes, she reached the gates, no longer aware of the horrors that surrounded her.

When she was out in the open she quickly persuaded herself that not everyone who had been in a building as it collapsed must necessarily have been crushed. When she came to where the paths crossed, she stopped and waited to see if the one person most dear to her after little Philip would appear. Nobody came, so she went on. The throng of people grew so she stopped again and waited – and finally crept weeping into a dark valley shaded by pine trees where she could pray for his soul which she believed must have returned to its maker. And now this valley had become a Garden of Eden to her for she had found there both her beloved Jeronimo and perfect bliss. All this she now told Jeronimo with great emotion and offered him the boy to kiss when she had finished. Jeronimo took him and fondled him with indescribable paternal joy, smothering with endless kisses its tears at his strange face.

Meanwhile the most beautiful night had fallen, full of wonderfully sweet scents and so silvery and still that only a poet could have imagined it. Everywhere along the stream which ran through the valley people were lying down by the light of the moon and preparing themselves soft beds of moss and leaves to rest on after the distresses of the day. And because many of the unfortunate ones still suffered – one had lost his house, another his wife and child and a third everything – Jeronimo and Josephe crept behind a thick bush so as not to disturb anyone with the secret rejoicing of their hearts. They found a magnificent pomegranate tree which spread wide its branches full of sweet-smelling fruits and with a nightingale trilling its song at the top. Here Jeronimo lay down by the trunk with Josephe sitting in his lap and Philip in hers, and there they stayed covered by his coat and rested. The shadow of the tree stretched out above them diffusing the light of the moon which was already paling into dawn before they fell asleep. For they had a great deal to talk over – the convent garden, the prisons, and what they had suffered for each other- and they were very moved when they thought how much suffering had come upon the world so that they might be happy.

They decided that as soon as the earthquakes had subsided they would go to La Conception where Josephe had a trusted friend, and, with the help of a small loan which they hoped to obtain from her, to take a ship to Spain where Jeronimo's maternal relations lived and where they hoped to spend the rest of their days happily. Having decided this and after endless caresses they fell asleep.

When they awoke the sun was already high in the sky. They noticed near them several families preparing a little breakfast by a fire. Jeronimo was just wondering how he could get food for his little family when a well-dressed young man with a child in his arms came up to Josephe and asked her shyly whether she would not feed this poor mite at her breast for a short while, for its mother lay injured under the trees. Josephe was rather embarrassed, for she recognized the young man as an acquaintance. Misunderstanding her embarrassment, he continued, "It's only for a moment, Donna Josephe, and this poor mite has had nothing since the terrible events which have shaken us all." "That's not why I didn't answer, Don Fernando", replied Josephe. "In these terrible times nobody grudges sharing whatever he may be lucky enough to have." And giving her own child to its father she took the little stranger and laid him at her breast. Don Fernando was very thankful for this kindness and asked whether they would not join his party which was preparing a little breakfast at the fire. Josephe said she would gladly accept his offer and, since Jeronimo had no objection, she followed him over to his family, where she was received in a most friendly and tender way by Don Fernando's two sisters-in-law, whom she knew to be worthy young ladies. Donna Elvire, Don Fernando's wife, who lay on the ground badly injured in the foot, beckoned Josephe down beside her with great friendliness when she saw her own ailing son at Josephe's breast. Don Pedro, too, his father-in-law, nodded to her affectionately. In Jeronimo and Josephe's hearts strange thoughts were stirring. When they found themselves treated with such kindness and familiarity they did not know what to think about the past, the place of execution, the prison and the bells, or whether they had merely dreamed them. It was as if all minds had been purged by the terrible event which had so shaken them. Their memories did not reach back beyond it. Only Donna Elizabeth, who had been invited by a friend to watch yesterday's spectacle but had refused, sometimes allowed her eyes to rest dreamily on Josephe, but the account of new terrible misfortunes soon brought her mind back to the present.

Stories were exchanged of how the town had been full of women who immediately after the quake had given birth in full view of the men, of how the monks with their crucifixes in their hands had run about crying that the end of the world had come, of how a soldier who ordered a church to be cleared on orders of the Viceroy was told that there was no longer a Viceroy, of how the Viceroy at the height of the terror had been forced to erect a gallows in order to put a stop to the looting and how an innocent man who had just escaped from the back of a burning building had been precipitately seized by the owner and immediately strung up.

Donna Elvire took the opportunity offered by Josephe's tending to her wounds, while the stories flowed thick and fast, to ask her how she had fared on that dreadful day. When Josephe gave her a few of the main details with a heavy heart, she had the satisfaction of seeing tears appear in her listener's eyes. Donna Elvire grasped her hand and pressed it, making a sign for her not to speak. Josephe thought herself among the saints. She could not suppress the feeling that the day which had passed, however much suffering it had brought the world, had been a blessing such as Heaven had never granted her before. And in fact the human mind appeared to blossom like a rose during those fearful moments when man's possessions were destroyed and nature itself threatened to be buried.

Over the fields as far as the eye could see, people of all ranks mingled together, sitting on the ground. There were princes and beggars, spinsters and farmers' wives, civil servants and shop-keepers, monks and nuns, all commiserating with one another and offering to share whatever they had managed to salvage in the way of necessities of life, as if the misfortune had made all who had escaped it into one great family. Instead of idle gossip about what was going on in the world, people now discussed isolated incidents during the time of terror. People who had been very little thought of in society had shown the heroic qualities of a Roman. There were countless examples of dauntless behaviour, of exultant scorn for danger, of self-denial and Christian sacrifice, of eager disdain for life, as if it could be found again in a trice like a valueless piece of property. Indeed, since there was not one person there to whom something tragic had not happened, or who himself had not done something generous, so the pain in every man's heart was mixed with so much happiness that it could not be determined whether the sum of general well-being had not grown on the one side by as much as it had decreased on the other.

Jeronimo took Josephe by the arm, after they had exhausted themselves in these silent reflections, and led her with indescribable happiness up and down under the shady leaves of the Pomegranate tree. He told her that he had given up his plans of taking a ship for Europe, thanks to people's changed mood and the altered circumstances, and said that he would throw himself on the mercy of the Viceroy, provided he were still alive, since he had always favoured his case. Kissing her, he said he hoped now to be able to remain with her in Chile. Josephe said a similar idea had occurred to her and that she too now expected to be reconciled to her father, should he still be alive. She advised him not to throw himself on the mercy of the Viceroy, but to go to La Conception and from there negotiate for his pardon by letter. There he would be in any case near a harbour and should the matter be satisfactorily concluded could return to Santiago with the greatest ease. After a moment's consideration Jeronimo approved the wisdom of this step and they walked for a while up and down the path thinking over their future happiness before returning to Don Fernando's party.

Meanwhile the afternoon had drawn on, and the spirits of the fugitives swarming around had only just begun to calm down after the quakes when the news was spread around that in the Dominican Church, the only one spared by the earthquake, a solemn mass was to be celebrated by the prelate of the monastery, to beg God to spare them any further misfortune. People were setting out from all directions and streaming into the town, and Don Fernando's party discussed whether they should take part in the service and join the general throng. Donna Elizabeth reminded them anxiously of the unhappy event which had occurred in the church the day before, that such services of thanksgiving would be repeated and that at a later date they would be able to share this feeling with all the more joy and calmness because the danger would have been longer past.

Josephe, standing up with some emotion, declared that she had never before felt so strongly the urge to fall down at the feet of her Creator, now that He had revealed in such a devastating way His incomprehensible and sublime power. Donna Elvire supported her enthusiastically. She insisted they should attend the mass and called on Don Fernando to lead their party. Whereupon they all, including Donna Elizabeth, rose from where they had been sitting. But Donna Elizabeth made the necessary preparations for departure with great hesitation and with great emotion, and when she was asked what was the matter, replied that she didn't know, but that she had a premonition of disaster. Donna Elvire calmed her and asked her to stay behind with her and their sick father.

Josephe said, "Then will you be kind enough to look after this little mite who as you see has found his way to me again?" "Gladly", answered Donna Elizabeth and prepared to take him, but when the child began to cry pitifully at this and wouldn't go on any account, Josephe said smiling that she would keep him with her and kissed him quiet again. Then Don Fernando offered her his arm, for he liked what he saw of her charm and her dignified behaviour. Jeronimo, who carried little Philip, escorted Donna Constance, and the others followed behind and in this way the whole party set out towards the town.

They had scarcely gone fifty yards when Donna Elizabeth, who had been whispering intently with Donna Elvire, called out, "Don Fernando!" and hurried with anxious steps after them. Don Fernando stopped and turned back to wait for her, but without letting go of Josephe's arm. Donna Elizabeth stopped a few yards away, as if she was waiting for him to come to her. When Don Fernando asked what she wanted, she came up to him, though with evident reluctance, and whispered a few words in his ear so that Josephe could not hear. "Well", answered Don Fernando, "and what about the unfortunate consequences which might arise from it?" Donna Elizabeth continued to whisper in his ear with a troubled expression. Don Fernando's face revealed evident unwillingness, but "All right", he said, Donna Elvire could calm herself, and he walked on with Josephe.

When they reached the Dominican church they could hear the organ pouring out its incomparable music, and an immense crowd of people was surging in. The crush stretched right out of the portals onto the square in front of the church where the light streamed down from the chandeliers and, as evening drew on, the pillars cast mysterious shadows. The glass in the great rose window at the far end of the church glowed like the setting sun itself which lighted it. When the organ stopped playing a sudden hush fell on the whole assembly, as if not one person had a sound in his throat. Never had such a pure flame of religious fervour risen to Heaven from a Christian church as now did from the Dominican cathedral of Santiago, and no human heart added more warmth to it than Jeronimo's and Josephe's.

The solemn service began with an oration from the pulpit by one of the oldest canons dressed in ceremonial robes. He began at once, raising his trembling hands covered with the flowing surplice to Heaven in praise and thanksgiving that there were still men in that part of the world, which had been so nearly destroyed, who were capable of offering up their feeble prayers to God. The Day of Judgement could not be more terrible. And when he called the previous day's earthquake a forerunner of it, pointing to a crack in the cathedral wall, a shudder ran through the whole congregation. Next he passed in full flow of priestly eloquence to the state of morality in the town. God had punished in Santiago an abomination such as Sodom and Gomorrah had never seen and he ascribed it to the endless patience of God that it had not been completely wiped off the face of the earth.

The hearts of Jeronimo and Josephe, already affected by the sermon, were cut to the quick by this. The Canon then took the opportunity of mentioning specifically the crime which had been perpetrated in the garden of the Carmelite convent, describing as godless the sanction it had received from some sections of society, and in an aside full of venom, he condemned the souls of the perpetrators by name to the Prince of Hell.

Donna Constanza cried out, "Don Fernando!" and tugged at Jeronimo's arm. But Don Fernando replied, emphatically yet mysteriously, "Keep quiet, Donna, don't move a muscle, but pretend to faint and we will all then leave the church." But before Donna Constanza could carry out this sensible precaution, a voice called out loudly, interrupting the canon, "Keep back, citizens of Santiago, the sinners are here in our midst."

"Where?" asked a second terrible voice, as a wide circle of horror formed around them. "Here", answered a third, full of righteous malice, pulling Josephe down by the hair, so that she would have fallen to the floor with Don Fernando's son, if he had not held her. "Are you mad?" cried the young man, putting his arm round Josephe. "I am Don Fernando Ormez, son of the Commandant of this town, whom you all know!"

"Don Fernando Ormez?" shouted a cobbler standing right in front of him, who had worked for Josephe and knew her as well as knew her feet. "Who is the father of this child?" he said, turning to Asteron's daughter with obstinate boldness. Don Fernando went pale at this question. He first cast a timid glance at Jeronimo and then gazed quickly over the assembly to see if there was anyone there who might know him.

Josephe, distressed by the terrifying situation, cried out, "This is not my child, Master Pedrillo, as you seem to think." Looking anxiously at Don Fernando she continued, "This young gentleman is Don Fernando Ormez, son of the Commandant of this town whom you all know." The cobbler asked, "Which of you citizens knows this young man?" and several people standing nearby repeated, "Who knows Jeronimo Rugera, let him now step forth." Now it happened that just at that moment, Don Fernando's son, little Juan, frightened by the tumult, clamoured for Josephe to give him back into his father's arms. Whereupon a voice cried, "He is the father!", another "He is Jeronimo Rugera!" and a third "These are the blasphemers!" And the whole multitude of Christians gathered in Christ's temple shouted, "Stone them! Stone them!" At this Jeronimo interjected loudly, "Stop, you devils! If you seek Jeronimo Rugera, I am he. Release that innocent man!" The furious mob, confused by Jeronimo's words, stopped short and several hands released Don Fernando.

At that moment a high- ranking naval officer approached and, pushing his way through the tumult, asked, "Don Fernando Ormez, what has happened to you?" With truly heroic presence of mind Don Fernando replied, "It's these assassins, Don Alonzo. I would have perished had it not been for this worthy young man who pretended to be Jeronimo Rugera in order to calm the frenzied mob. Take him into custody, if you will be so kind, along with this young lady, for their mutual protection and arrest this villain (seizing Master Pedrillo) who has stirred up the whole incident." At this the cobbler cried out, "Don Alonzo, I ask you on your conscience, is not this girl Josephe Asteron?" Since Don Alonzo, who knew Josephe very well, hesitated to reply, several people enflamed to fury cried out, "It's her! It's her! Kill them."

Josephe put little Philip, whom Jeronimo had been carrying, together with little Juan into Don Fernando's arms, saying, "You go, Don Fernando. Save your two children and leave us to our fate." Don Fernando took the two children and said that he would rather die than suffer any harm to come to anyone under his protection. He offered his arm to Josephe after he had asked for the naval officer's sword, and asked the other pair to follow him. Such preparations created a certain respect and a way was made for them to pass. They succeeded in leaving the cathedral and were beginning to think they were safe.

But scarcely had they set foot on the square outside, likewise packed with people, when a voice from out of the raging mob which had followed them cried out, "Citizens, this is Jeronimo Rugera, I am his father!" And he struck Jeronimo down at Donna Constanza's side with a murderous blow from a club. "Jesus Maria!" cried Donna Constanza and fled to her brother-in-law. But a voice rang out again, "Convent whore!" and a second blow with a club on the other side stretched her lifeless on the ground next to Jeronimo. "Monstrous", cried a stranger. "That was Donna Constanza Xares!" "Why did they deceive us?" asked the cobbler. "Seek out the right one and kill her!"

Don Fernando, seeing Constanza's corpse, was overcome with rage. He drew the sword and swung it so that it would have cleft in two the fanatical murderer who had caused this abomination, if he had not escaped the furious blow by turning aside. But since he could not subdue the whole crowd which was pushing in on him, Josephe called out, "Farewell, Don Fernando. Farewell children! Here, murder me you bloodthirsty tigers!" And she rushed dauntlessly into the midst to put an end to the struggle. Master Pedrillo struck her down with the club then, stained with her blood, he cried, "Send the bastard to Hell with her!" and he pressed forward again with still undiminished lust for slaughter.

Don Fernando, like a saintly warrior, stood with his back to the wall of the church. In his left hand he held the children and in his right the sword. With every blow he stretched one of them out – a lion could not have defended himself better. Seven of the murderous pack lay dead in front of him and their satanic leader himself was wounded. But Master Pedrillo did not rest until he had torn one of the children from Don Fernando's grasp and, swinging him round in the air by the leg, smashed him against the corner of a pillar.

Then all was suddenly still again and the people moved away. Don Fernando, seeing his little son lying before him, his brains oozing out, raised his eyes to Heaven full of indescribable anguish. The naval officer made his way over to him again, tried to comfort him and assured him that he much regretted his failure to act in this tragedy, although it was justified by several circumstances. But Don Fernando said that he had nothing to reproach himself with, and merely asked his help to carry away the corpses. They were all carried under the cover of falling darkness to Don Alonzo's residence whither Don Fernando followed them, weeping copiously at little Philip's expression. He spent the night at Don Alonzo's and for several confused reasons delayed for a long time telling his wife the full extent of the tragedy, firstly because she was ill, then because he didn't know how she would judge his share in the events.

Yet, a short time later, informed by a chance visitor of all that had happened, this excellent lady wept her fill of maternal grief and in the morning fell on his neck, the tears glistening in her eyes, and kissed him. Don Fernando and Donna Elvire adopted little Philip as their own son and when Don Fernando compared him in his mind with Juan and remembered how he had acquired both, it seemed to him that he almost had some cause for rejoicing.

Clothes make the Man

By Gottfried Keller

One unpleasant day in November, a poor tailor was walking along the main road to Goldach, a small wealthy town some few hours walk from Seldwyla. In his pockets the tailor had nothing but a thimble which, for want of a coin, he constantly twisted and turned between his fingers whenever he put his hands in his pockets because of the cold. His fingers were really painful from this twisting and rubbing because, thanks to the bankruptcy of a certain master tailor in Seldwyla, he had lost all his income along with his job and had been forced to move on. As yet he had had nothing for breakfast except for a few snowflakes which had drifted into his mouth, and he had still less idea where his next meal, however small, was to come from. Begging was extremely difficult for him, indeed seemed completely impossible, for over his best black Sunday suit, his only one, he wore a wide dark-grey cloak lined with black velvet, which lent its wearer a noble romantic appearance, especially as his long dark hair and moustache were well cared for and he enjoyed pale but regular features.

Such a costume had become a necessity for him, without his intending anything bad or deceitful by it; rather he was content if people would just leave him alone to carry on his work in peace; but he would have starved rather than part with his cloak and his Polish fur cap, which he also knew how to wear with great distinction.

For this reason he could only work in the larger towns where such things did not attract too much attention. If he travelled around and took no savings with him he fell into the greatest distress. Approaching a house, the people looked at him with astonishment and curiosity and expected anything but that he would beg; so the words died away in his mouth, since he was in any case not very eloquent, and he became a martyr to his cloak, suffering hunger so dire that it seemed as black as its velvet lining.

As he was walking wearily and anxiously up a slope he came upon a comfortable new coach which a certain gentleman's coachman had fetched from Basel and was taking to his master, a foreign count who lived in an old castle he had bought or rented somewhere in Eastern Switzerland. The coach was fitted out with all kinds of contraptions for storing luggage and therefore seemed heavily laden when in reality it was quite empty. Because of the steepness of the road the coachman was walking beside the horses and, having got back up on the box when he reached the top, he asked the tailor if he would not like to get in the empty coach. It was in fact just beginning to rain and he had seen at a glance that the man on foot was wearily making his way through the world in great distress.

The tailor humbly accepted the offer with gratitude, whereupon the coach rolled quickly away with him and in scarcely an hour thundered in stately fashion through the gates of Goldach. The princely vehicle stopped suddenly at the first inn in the town called The Scales and immediately the boot-boy pulled so heftily on the bell that the wire nearly snapped in two. Then the landlord and his minions came rushing down and flung open the carriage door; children and neighbours were already thronging round the splendid carriage curious to see what sort of pearl would emerge from such a remarkable oyster; so when the embarrassed tailor at last sprang out, wearing his cloak and looking pale and handsome, his eyes cast dejectedly down, he seemed to them to be at least a mysterious Prince or Count's son. The distance between the coach and the door of the inn was short and in any case the path through the spectators was rather blocked. Whether it was from lack of presence of mind or the courage to push through the crowd and simply go on his way, he did not do this but allowed himself to be conducted involuntarily into the building and up the stairs, and he only really became aware of his strange predicament when he found himself sitting in a comfortable dining-room and his cloak, which had aroused so much awe, was obligingly taken from him.

"Would the gentleman care to eat?" he was asked. "Dinner will be served at once; it is just ready!"

Without waiting for an answer, the landlord of The Scales ran into the kitchen and cried, "Gracious heavens!" Here we are with nothing but beef and a leg of mutton! I daren't cut up the partridge-pie, that's for the guests booked this evening and is all spoken for. Isn't that just like it! On the very day when we don't expect any such guest and we have nothing in, such a gentleman has to arrive! And the coachman has a coat of arms on his buttons and the coach is like that of a Duke! And the young man scarcely deigns to open his mouth, he's so aristocratic!"

But the uncouth cook replied," Oh, get on with you, what are you making such a fuss about? Just go ahead and serve up the partridge-pie, he won't eat it all! The guests tonight will still be able to have a bit; we'll still be able to make six portions out of it."

"Six portions? You forget that the gentlemen are accustomed to eating their fill!" said the landlord, but the cook remained unshaken and continued, "So they shall! We'll send off quickly for a half dozen cutlets; we need those anyhow for the stranger, and what he leaves over I'll cut into small pieces and mix in with the pie; you just leave it to me!"

But the valiant landlord said severely, "Cook, I've told you before, that sort of thing will not do in this town and in this inn! We're respectable people here and we expect honest dealings!"

"Oh! What the Devil! All right! All right!" cried the cook, rather worked up by now. "If you can't concoct something in these circumstances, it's a pity! Here are two snipe which I've just this minute bought from the huntsman. We can surely put them in the pie, if the worst comes to the worst. I'm sure those gourmets won't object to a partridge-pie laced with snipe! Then we have trout too. I'd just popped the largest one in the boiling water when this fantastic coach arrived; and also the soup is simmering in the pan; and so we have a fish course, the beef, vegetables with the cutlets, the leg of mutton and the pie. Just give me the key so I can get out the preserves and the dessert. And, by the way, there's no reason why you shouldn't hand over the key to me with complete confidence so that I don't have to be for ever running after you and cause a lot of embarrassment!"

"My dear cook! You have no need to take offence! I had to promise my dear wife on her deathbed that I would always keep the keys in my own hands, so I've done it on principle and not out of mistrust. Here are the gherkins and the cherries, here the pears and the apricots; but we can't serve up these old petits fours. Lise must run quickly to the confectioners and fetch some pastries, three platefuls, and if he has a good tart she can bring that too!"

"But, good Lord! You can't put all that on a single guest's bill! However hard you try you can't make that much out of him!"

"It makes no difference, it's a matter of honour. It won't break me, but a great gentleman when he travels through our town ought to be able to say he's had a decent meal, even if he does arrive quite unexpectedly in the middle of winter! I won't have said of us what is said of the landlords in Seldwyla, that they eat all the good food themselves and serve up the bones to their guests! So, come on, look lively! Make haste everyone!"

During these detailed preparations the tailor found himself in a position of the most fearful anxiety, since the table was laid with gleaming cutlery. The more the starving man had longed for some nourishment before, the more anxiously he now wished to flee the impending meal. At last he summed up courage, put his cloak around him and his cap on, and made his way through the door in order to make his escape. But in his confusion he could not immediately find the stairs in this extensive building so the waiter, who was always rushing around like the Devil, thought he was looking for the conveniences and said, "Allow me, Sir, to show you the way" and led him down a long corridor which only ended in a beautifully lacquered door with a decorous inscription.

Without contradicting him, Strapinski went in like a lamb and closed the door behind him. There he leaned against the wall sighing bitterly and wishing he was back again enjoying the idyllic freedom of the open road, which, however bad the weather, now seemed to him the greatest possible happiness.

And now he embroiled himself in the first spontaneous lie because he remained for some time in the closed room and thereby set foot on the steep slippery path of Evil.

Meanwhile the landlord had seen him walking along in his cloak and cried out, "The gentleman's freezing! Light a fire in the room! Where's Lise? Where's Anna? Quickly a basket of wood in the stove and a few handfuls of chips so that it burns up well! Confound it! Are people in The Scales to sit at table in their cloaks?!"

And when the tailor came wandering back out of the corridor, looking as melancholy as the haunting ancestor of some old castle, the landlord ushered him back into the accursed room, constantly rubbing his hands and with a profusion of compliments. There, without further ado, he was shown to the table, his chair was pushed in behind him, and since the smell of the nourishing soup, the like of which he had not smelled for a long time, completely robbed him of his senses, he abandoned his scruples and sat down, dipping his heavy spoon at once into the golden-brown broth. In deep silence he refreshed his weary limbs and spirits and was served quietly and calmly with all due respect.

When he had emptied his plate and the landlord saw that he had so enjoyed it, he politely encouraged him to take another spoonful; it would do him good in such inclement weather. Then the trout was served, garnished with green leaves, and the landlord put a good large portion on his plate. But the tailor, tormented by worry, was too diffident to dare use the shiny knife, but merely picked at it shyly and gingerly with the silver fork. This was noticed by the cook who was peeping through the door to see the great gentleman and she said to those standing round, "Thank God! Here's someone who knows how to eat a fine fish properly. He doesn't hack at the tender meat with a knife as if he were slaughtering a calf. He's a gentleman from a great house, I'd swear to it, were it not forbidden. And how sad and handsome he is. He must be in love with some poor girl whom they won't allow him to marry! O yes, noblemen have their problems too!"

Meanwhile the landlord had noticed that the guest was not drinking and said respectfully, "Perhaps the gentleman does not like the table wine? Would you care to order a glass of fine Bordeaux? I can thoroughly recommend it."

Then the tailor committed his second spontaneous mistake, in that he obediently said yes instead of no, and at once the landlord went personally down to the cellar to fetch the desired bottle; for it was all-important to him that people should be able to say that there was always something good to be had at his inn. So when the guest once again with a bad conscience merely took little sips of the wine in his glass, the landlord ran full of joy to the kitchen, smacked his lips and cried, "Devil take me, he really knows what's what; he sips my good wine on his tongue as one tests a ducat on the gold scales!" "Heaven be praised!" said the cook, "I told you he knew how to behave!"

So the meal took its course, very slowly in fact, because the poor tailor continued to eat and drink hesitantly and gingerly, and the landlord, in order to give him time, let the food stand on the table a good while. Nevertheless the amount the guest had eaten so far was scarcely worth mentioning, but his hunger which was constantly so dangerously aroused now began to overcome his fear, and when the partridge-pie appeared, the tailor's mood changed completely, and a firm resolve began to be formed in him. "It's done now and can't be helped", he said to himself, encouraged and stimulated by one more drop of wine; "I'd be a fool now to go through all the coming shame and persecution without first eating my fill. So I'll make the most of it while there's still time. That enormous pile of food they've served up might easily be the last food I get. I'll get on with that, come what may! What I've once eaten not even a king can take back again"

No sooner said than done; with the courage born of despair he attacked the tasty pie with no intention of stopping, so that in less than five minutes half of it had completely disappeared and the prospects for the guests that evening were beginning to look black. Meat, truffles, dumplings, under-crust, top-crust, the whole lot he swallowed down with no respect for his person, only anxious to pack his belly full before his fate overtook him. With all this he drank the wine in mighty draughts and stuffed large pieces of bread into his mouth – in short he stowed away the food at a tremendous rate, just as the hay from the nearest meadow is stored quickly away in the barn when a storm is brewing. Once again the landlord ran into the kitchen and cried, "Well! He's eating up the pie, while he's hardly touched the roast! And he's drinking the Bordeaux by the half-glassful!" "May he enjoy it!" said the cook. "Let him get on with it; he knows a partridge pie when he tastes one. If he were a common fellow he would have kept to the roast!" "That's what I think too", said the landlord. "It doesn't look exactly elegant but the only people I've seen eat like that when I was travelling for my education were generals and canons of the Church!"

Meanwhile the coachman had seen that the horses were fed and had himself eaten a solid meal in the room where the servants sat, and since he was in a hurry he soon had the horses harnessed up again. The servants at The Scales could not hold back any longer, but before it was too late had to ask the gentleman's coachman straight out who his master was up there and what his name was. The coachman, a sly cunning fellow, answered, "Didn't he tell you himself?" "No!" was the answer and he continued, "I can well believe it. He doesn't say much all day – well, it's Count Strapinski. He'll be staying here today and perhaps for a bit longer, for he's ordered me to go on in advance with the coach." He played this dirty trick in order to get his revenge on the tailor who, he thought, instead of thanking him for his kindness and saying farewell, had made his way without hesitation into the inn and was lording it there. Taking his practical joke to the extreme he got back up on the coach without bothering about the bill for himself and the horses, swung the whip and drove out of the town, and thus everything was found to be in order and chalked up to the tailor's account.

Now, whether it was mere chance or whether the tailor had taken out his journeyman's book in the coach, had left it there and the coachman had picked it up, it turned out that in fact the tailor's name really was Strapinski, Wenzel Strapinski, and he was born in Silesia. Be that as it may, when the landlord, rubbing his hands and beaming with pleasure, appeared before him again and asked if Count Strapinski would care to take with his dessert a glass of mature Tokay or a glass of Champagne, and announced that his rooms were just being prepared for him, then poor old Strapinski went pale, became confused again and made no reply.

"Very interesting!" muttered the landlord to himself as he once again hurried down to the cellar and fetched from a special compartment not only a bottle of Tokay but also a Bocksbeutel and carried under his arm a bottle of Champagne. Soon Strapinski saw a small forest of glasses in front of him, above which the Champagne glass towered like a poplar. They all gleamed and clinked strangely in front of him, exhaling a sweet fragrance, but stranger still it was not without a certain skill that the poor but elegant man picked his way through this forest and, when he saw the landlord put some red wine in his Champagne glass, poured a few drops of Tokay into his.

Meanwhile the Town Clerk and the Notary had come in to drink coffee and play their usual game of cards to see who should pay for it. Soon the elder son of the family firm of Haberlein and Co, the younger son from Putschli-Nievergelt and the chief accountant of a large spinning mill, Herr Melchior Bohni, also arrived. But this time, instead of playing their game, they all walked round in a wide semi-circle behind the Polish Count, their hands in their coat pockets, their eyes shining and smiling to themselves. For they were those members of the best firms who had stayed at home all their lives, but whose relations and associates lived all over the world, on which account they themselves thought they knew the world pretty well.

So that was supposed to be a Polish Count! The coach they had of course seen from their office chairs, but they didn't really know whether the landlord was entertaining the Count or vice versa. Never before, though, had the landlord done anything foolish, rather he was known as a rather sly fellow and so the circle which these inquisitive gentlemen had formed round the stranger gradually got smaller until at last they sat down intimately at the same table and cleverly invited themselves spontaneously to the banquet, whereupon they began without further ado to throw dice for a bottle of wine. Yet they did not drink too much as it was still early, on the contrary the correct thing to do was to take a few sips of excellent coffee and oblige the "Polack", as they already secretly called him, with good cigars and cigarettes, so that their fine fragrance should make him even more aware of his pleasant surroundings. "May I offer the Count a fine cigar? I have received these direct from my brother in Cuba!" said one. "Oh, a Pole always likes a good cigarette. Here is one made of genuine Smyrna tobacco! My partner sent it", cried another, proffering a red silk pouch. "This from Damascus is still finer, Count", cried a third, "Our agent there obtained it for me himself." The fourth offered a great clumsy-looking cigar, saying "If you would like something really excellent, try this planter's cigar from Virginia, home-grown, home-made, and not on the market."

Strapinski smiled a sickly smile, said nothing and was soon enveloped in fine clouds of fragrant smoke which were charmingly illuminated by the sun breaking through. The sky became cloudless in less than a quarter of an hour and the most beautiful autumn afternoon set in. Everyone said that they ought to take advantage of this favourable weather since the year might well not produce any more such days and it was decided that they would go out for a drive to visit the jovial Alderman of the town on his estate, since only a few weeks before he had pressed his grapes and they would be able to taste his new wine, the red Sauser. Putschli-Nievergelt, the son, sent for his dog-cart and soon his young steel grey horses were pawing the ground outside The Scales. The landlord too ordered his carriage and the Count was politely invited to join the party and get to know the area. The wine had warmed his spirits; he reflected quickly that this would give him the best opportunity of slipping away unnoticed and continuing his journey. These foolish importunate gentlemen would have to bear the consequences themselves. Therefore he accepted the invitation with a few polite words and climbed into the dog-cart with young Putschli.

Now it was a further twist of fate that the tailor, after being as a young lad in service for a time with the squire of his village, had done his military service with the Hussars, and was accordingly fairly familiar with horses. When, therefore, his companion politely asked him if he would perhaps like to drive, he at once grasped the reins and the whip and with the correct bearing drove at a fast trot through the gates of the town and out onto the main road, so that the gentlemen looked at each other and whispered, "It's quite right! At least he's a gentleman!"

In half an hour the Alderman's estate was reached and Strapinski drove up in a splendid half circle, pulling the fiery horses up sharp. They sprang from the carriages; the Alderman hurried to greet them and conducted the company into the house and at once the table was covered with a half-dozen decanters full of dark-red Sauser. The fiery fermenting drink was first tasted, praised and then merrily attacked while the master of the house passed round the information to his household that a distinguished Count was there, a Polack, and prepared finer hospitality.

In the meantime the party divided up into two and sat down to make up for the game of cards they had missed, since in this country no men can be together long without gambling, probably because they have an in-born inclination to be always doing something. Strapinski, who for various reasons had been forced to refuse his participation, was nevertheless invited to watch, for it seemed to them eminently worth watching, since they always displayed such skill and mental agility in the game. He had to sit between the two groups and they made a point of playing cleverly and expertly and at the same time of entertaining their guest. So he sat there like an ailing Prince before whom the courtiers perform a pleasant play about the ways of the world. They explained to him the most important twists and turns of the play and when the players at one table had to give their undivided attention to the game for a moment, the other group carried on the conversation with the tailor all the more urgently. The best subject of conversation seemed to them to be horses, hunting and the like; Strapinski too was most conversant with these topics for he only needed to use the expressions which he had learned from serving officers and landed gentry and which he had taken a special liking to even then. The fact that he used these expressions sparingly, with a certain diffidence and always with such a melancholy smile, only served to produce a still greater effect. When two or three of the gentlemen got up and moved aside for a moment they said, "He's a real gentleman, all right!"

Only Melchior Bohni, the accountant, a born doubter, rubbed his hands with glee and said to himself, "I can see what's coming! There's going to be another bit of excitement in Goldach. It's already happened to some extent. About time too, for its two years since the last! That man has such remarkable fingers, full of holes like a pincushion. Perhaps he's from Prague or Ostrolenka. Well, I'll take care not to upset the way things are going!"

Both games were now over and the gentlemen's appetite for Sauser stilled and they now chose to cool themselves off on the Alderman's mature wine which was now brought in; but this cooling-off was of a somewhat passionate kind, since immediately, in order not to fall into contemptible idleness, a new game of cards was proposed in which they could all take part. The cards were shuffled and each player staked a dollar, but when it came to Strapinski's turn he could not very well put his thimble on the table. "I don't possess such a coin", he said blushing, but Melchior Bohni who was watching had already staked for him without anyone noticing, for they were all much too comfortably off for them to have suspected that anyone in the world could have no money. The next moment the whole pool was pushed across to the tailor who had won. In utter confusion he left the money lying there and Bohni attended to the second game for him, which was won by somebody else, as was the third. But the fourth and fifth were once more won by the Polack, who gradually woke up and adapted himself to the situation. He sat there silent and still, and played with varying luck. Once he got down to his last dollar which he had to stake, but he won again and finally when everyone had had enough of the game he had accumulated several gold sovereigns, more than he had ever possessed in his life before and which, when he saw that everyone was pocketing his winnings, he too put in his pocket, not without fear that it was all a dream. Bohni who had been watching him closely all the time was now clear about him and thought, "The Devil's riding on his back!"

But because he noticed at the same time that the puzzling stranger had shown no greed for the money and had conducted himself with extreme modesty and sobriety, he was not ill-disposed towards him and decided to let the affair take its course, come what may.

But when they all went out for a stroll in the open air before dinner, Count Strapinski collected his thoughts together and considered that the time had come to take French leave of them. He had acquired a nice sum of money for his journey and decided to pay the landlord of The Scales for the midday meal they had forced upon him from the next town. So he threw his cloak picturesquely round his shoulders, pressed his fur cap down lower over his eyes and strode slowly up and down in the evening sunshine beneath an avenue of tall acacia trees, looking at the delightful scenery, or rather spying out which path he should strike out on. He looked exquisite, with his domed forehead, his charming but melancholy moustache, his shiny black locks, his dark eyes and with his pleated cloak streaming behind him. The evening sunshine and the rustling of the trees above him enhanced the impression so that the company observed him from a distance attentively and favourably. Gradually he walked further and further away from the house, then stepped through a thicket behind which passed a field path and, when he saw that he was hidden from the view of the other guests, he was about to march off briskly when suddenly there came round the corner towards him the Alderman with his daughter Nettchen. Nettchen was a pretty girl, really good-looking but a bit over-dressed and richly adorned with jewellery. "We've been looking for you everywhere, Count!" cried the Alderman, "so that firstly I can introduce you to my child here and secondly to beg you to do us the honour of having a bite of supper with us. The other gentlemen are already in the house."

The tailor quickly took off his cap and bowed respectfully, even timidly. For events had taken a new turn! A female had appeared on the scene. But his bashfulness and excessive deference did not do him any harm with the lady; on the contrary the shyness, modesty and deference of such a distinguished and interesting young nobleman seemed to her really touching, not to say charming. It just shows you, she thought to herself, that the nobler you are the more modest and unspoiled you will be. Just you take notice, you wild young men of Goldach, who scarcely even bother to take your hats off to a young lady any more!

Therefore she greeted the nobleman most graciously, blushed charmingly and spoke impetuously to him, her words pouring hastily out, as is the way with provincial women who want to make a good impression on a stranger. Strapinski on the other hand in a very short time underwent a change. While up to now he had made no attempt to play the role they had forced upon him, he now began involuntarily to speak more carefully and mixed all kinds of Polish phrases in his speech, in fact to sum it up his tailor's blood began to get frisky in the presence of the lady and began to run away with its rider.

At the table he was given the place of honour next to the daughter of the house, for the mother was dead. But he soon became melancholy again when he realised that now he must return to the town with the others or else run off forcibly into the night and also when he considered further how fickle was the good fortune which he now enjoyed. But nevertheless this good fortune was very real to him and he said to himself in anticipation, "Oh well! At least for once in my life I shall have really been someone and sat next to such a divine being!"

It was in fact no mean thing to see a hand jangling with three or four bracelets glittering next to you, and to see, each time you glanced to the side, a head with a charmingly romantic hair-style, an attractive blush and a look full into your eyes. For no matter what he did or did not do, it was all construed as unusual and noble and his very clumsiness was considered to be remarkable naiveté by the amiable young lady who on other occasions was accustomed to gossip for hours about social faux-pas.

Since they were all in high spirits a few of the guests sang songs fashionable in the Thirties. The Count was requested to sing a Polish song. The wine finally overcame his shyness, although not his anxiety. He had once worked for a few weeks somewhere in Poland and knew a few Polish words and he even knew a Polish folk song by heart, parrot-fashion, without really understanding the words. So he sang nobly, but more timidly than loud, and with a voice that trembled slightly as though with secret sorrow, in Polish;

A hundred thousand oxen bellow
On Wohlynia's lush green meadow,
And Kathinka, fair Kathinka
Thinks my love for her is sure.

"Bravo, Bravo!" cried all the gentlemen, clapping their hands and Nettchen, very moved, said, "Oh! Patriotism is such a beautiful thing!"

Having passed such a peak of entertainment the company broke up. The tailor was packed into the coach again and carefully brought back to Goldach. Previously they had made him promise not to leave town without saying farewell to them. In The Scales the gentlemen drank another glass of punch, but Strapinski was exhausted and expressed a desire to retire to his bed. The landlord personally conducted him to his rooms, whose splendour he hardly noticed any more, although he was only accustomed to sleeping in the poorest rooms in an inn. He was standing there in the middle of a beautiful carpet without a possession in the world when the landlord suddenly discovered his lack of luggage and slapped himself on the forehead for being a fool. Then he ran quickly out, rang a bell, called the waiters and bell-boy to him, exchanged a few words with them, came back and said solemnly, "It's quite right, Count, they've forgotten to unload your luggage. Even the most necessary things are missing!" "The little parcel, too, that lay in the coach?" asked Stravinsky anxiously, for he was thinking of a small hand-size bundle which he had left lying on the seat and which contained a handkerchief, hair-brush, comb, a small box of pomade and a stick of cosmetic. "That's missing too, there's nothing here at all!" said the good landlord, shocked because he guessed that there was something important in it. "We must immediately send a special messenger after the coachman", he cried eagerly. "I'll see to it!" But the Count, just as shocked at this idea, stopped him and said agitatedly, "Leave it! That must not be done! I have to cover my tracks for a time" he added, himself embarrassed at this invention.

Astonished, the landlord went to the guests who were still drinking punch and told them of the case and concluded with the remark that the Count must doubtless be the victim of persecution by his family or political rivals. For at this very time many Poles and other fugitives were expelled from the country because of violent attacks. Others were watched and ensnared by foreign agents. But Strapinski slept soundly and when he woke late the next morning the first thing he saw was the landlord's enormous dressing gown hanging over a chair and in addition a small table covered with all possible toilet requisites. Thereupon there waited upon him a number of servants in order to deliver baskets and boxes full of fine linen, clothes, cigars, books, boots, shoes, spurs, riding whips, furs, caps, hats, socks, pipes, violins and flutes on behalf of his friends of yesterday, with the solicitous request to be pleased to make temporary use of these conveniences. Since they spent the morning hours regularly in their businesses, they announced that they would call on him after dinner.

These people were anything but ridiculous or foolish, but rather prudent businessmen, more cunning than stupid. But since their prosperous town was small and sometimes seemed boring to them, they were always eager for a change, an event or an incident to which they could give their undivided attention. The coach and four, the emergence of the stranger, his midday meal, the remarks of the coachman, all these were such simple and natural things that the inhabitants of Goldach, who were not used to indulging in idle suspicions, built up a whole adventure out of these incidents as on a rock.

When Strapinski saw the assortment of goods spread out before him, his first reaction was to feel in his pocket to see whether he was awake or dreaming. If his thimble was still there in its lonely state then he was dreaming. But no, the thimble lay there snugly among the money he had won at cards and was rubbing up amiably against the dollars, so its master once again acquiesced in what had happened and went down from his room into the street in order to have a look at the town in which Fortune smiled so fondly upon him. In the kitchen doorway stood the cook who made him a deep curtsey and watched him with renewed fondness; in the hall and at the doors stood other domestics cap in hand, and Strapinski strode out with dignity, yet modestly, pulling his cloak decorously round him. Fate with every moment that passed made him greater.

It was through quite different eyes that he now looked at the town from if he had gone out looking for work in it. The town consisted for the most part of fine well-built houses, each of which had an emblem painted on it or one made of stone attached to it and this emblem provided the house with its name. In these names the customs of centuries were clearly to be seen. The Middle Ages were reflected in the oldest houses or in the new buildings which had taken their places but preserved the old names from the period of warlike rulers or from fairy-tales. These houses bore such emblems and names as; The Sword, The Helmet, The Suit of Armour, The Crossbow, The Blue Shield, The Swiss Blade, The Knight, The Flintlock, The Turk, The Sea-Monster, The Golden Dragon, The Linden Tree, The Pilgrim's Staff, The Water-Nymph, The Bird of Paradise, The Pomegranate Tree, The Camel, The Unicorn etc. The period of the enlightenment and philanthropy could clearly be seen in the moral precepts which shone in beautiful golden letters above some of the other front doors, for example; Harmony, Integrity, Ancient Independence, Modern Independence, Civic Virtue A, Civic Virtue B, Loyalty, Love, Hope, Reunion 1, Reunion 2, Cheerfulness, Inner Righteousness, National Prosperity (a clean little house in which there sat behind a canary cage hung with cress a little old lady in a white peaked hood, winding yarn on a reel), The Constitution (below which lived a cooper who zealously and with a great deal of noise encircled little buckets and barrels with hoops and banged continuously). One house bore the horrifying inscription-Death. A faded skeleton extended from top to bottom between the windows. Here lived the Justice of the Peace. In a house dedicated to Patience lived the Debt Recorder, a starving picture of misery, for in this town nobody ever had debts to record for very long.

Finally on the newest houses was proclaimed the poetry of the bankers, merchants, manufacturers and their imitators in such well-sounding names as: The Vale of Roses, The Eastern Valley, The Sunny Mountain, The Castle of Violets, The Garden of Youth, The Mountain of Happiness, Henrietta's Vale, Camellias, Wilhelmina's Castle etc. The vale or castle attached to a woman's name indicated to the connoisseur that it had been acquired as a dowry from their wives.

At each street corner stood an old tower with an expensive-looking clock, brightly-coloured roof and artistic gilded weather-vane. These towers were carefully preserved, for the inhabitants of Goldach rejoiced in their past as well as their present, and rightly so. The whole splendid array was encircled by the old town wall which, although of no more use, was nevertheless preserved as an ornament to the town. The walls were completely overgrown with thick old ivy and thus encircled the little town with a garland of evergreen.

All this made a wonderful impression on Strapinski; he thought he had arrived in another world. For when he read the superscriptions of the houses, the like of which he had never seen before, he was of the opinion that they referred to the particular secrets and habits of each house and that in reality behind each front door it appeared exactly as the superscription read, so that he appeared to have come upon a sort of moral Utopia. Thus he was inclined to believe that the wonderful reception he had received was in some way connected with this, so that e.g. the emblem of The Scales where he lodged meant that there unequal fortunes were balanced and equalized and it was possible for a travelling tailor to be made into a Count.

On his walk he wandered out beyond the Town Gate, and as he was standing there looking out over the open fields, there came to him for the last time the thought that his duty was to continue on his way without further delay. The sun was shining, the road was good and firm, not too dry and not too wet, ideal for walking. He even had money for his journey now, so that he could put up with ease wherever he felt like it and no obstacle was to be seen.

So he stood there, like Hercules at the parting of the ways, at a real crossroads. From the ring of lime trees which surrounded the town rose hospitable columns of smoke and the golden balls on top of the towers sparkled enticingly through the treetops; happiness and enjoyment, but guilt and a mysterious fate beckoned there. But from the direction of the fields glittered the wide-open spaces of the distance; work, want, poverty and obscurity awaited him there, but also a good conscience and a peaceful life. Feeling this, he was about to turn resolutely aside into the fields, but at this very moment a carriage travelling very fast drove by. It was the young lady he had met yesterday, who sat all alone with a blue veil billowing behind her in a trim light carriage, managing a fine horse and driving into town. As Strapinski touched his cap and in his surprise humbly doffed it, the girl quickly blushing bowed slightly to him, but in an exceedingly friendly manner and drove on with great commotion, whipping up the horses to a gallop.

Now Strapinski involuntarily made a complete about-turn and went back to the town with new confidence. The very same day he was galloping on the best horse in town at the head of a whole party of riders through the avenue which led round the green town walls and the falling leaves of the lime trees danced like golden rain round his transfigured head.

Now he began to enter into the spirit of it. With every day that passed he changed, like a rainbow that gets noticeably more colourful when the sun breaks through. He learned in hours, in moments, what others learn in years, since it was inherent in him, like the colours in a raindrop. He observed carefully the manners of his hosts and as he watched formed them into something new and unusual. He especially sought to overhear what they really thought of him and what sort of image they had of him. This image he worked on further according to his own taste, for the pleasant entertainment of some who always liked to see something new, and to the amazement of others, especially the ladies, who thirsted for edifying stimulation. So he quickly became the hero of a romantic novel on which he worked lovingly together with the whole town and whose main constituent remained always his aura of mystery.

With all this, Strapinski experienced now, as he had never done before in his obscurity, one sleepless night after another and we must point out with due censure that it was just as much the fear of being shamefully revealed as a poor tailor as it was an honest conscience, that robbed him of sleep. His innate need to represent something elegant and unusual, if only in his choice of clothes, had led him astray in this conflict and now produced this fear and his conscience was only so far effective in that he constantly cherished the plan of finding at some good opportunity a reason for travelling away and then by means of gambling and such like to procure the means of paying back from some mysterious distance the money he had taken from the inhabitants of Goldach. He sent for lottery tickets from all the towns where there were lotteries or the agents of lotteries, staking each time a more or less moderate amount, and the correspondence which arose out of this, the receiving of letters, was again remarked as a sign of important connections and associates.

Already more than once he had won a few florins and used them straight away to purchase more lottery tickets, when one day he received from the organiser of a foreign lottery, a man who called himself a banker, a considerable sum of money which was sufficient to carry out his plan for deliverance. He was already no longer astonished at his good fortune, which seemed to be perfectly natural, but yet he felt relieved and reassured, especially with regard to the good landlord of The Scales whom he might well feel sorry for on account of the good meals he was getting. But instead of cutting things short, paying his debts straight out and taking his leave, he thought he would give it out, as he had planned, that he was leaving on a short business trip, but then to announce to them from some large town that inexorable fate forbade him ever to return. In that way he wanted to fulfil his obligations, leave behind a good impression and devote himself anew but with more discretion as well as more fortune to his tailoring, or else to seek some other respectable career. Best of all he would really have liked to stay in Goldach as a master tailor and would now have had the means to earn a modest livelihood there. But it was quite clear that he could only live there now as Count.

Because of the evident preference and liking of which he was the object on the part of Nettchen, whenever there was an opportunity, there were already many rumours in circulation and he had even noticed that the young lady was called Countess now and then. How could he prepare such a denouement for this charming girl? How could he give the lie so wickedly to Fate, which had so wilfully raised him in station, and bring shame on himself?

He had received from his lottery agent, the one who called himself a banker, a bill of exchange which he cashed at a Goldach bank. This fact strengthened still more the favourable opinions about his person and his connections, since there was nothing further from the thoughts of the local businessmen than a lottery win. On the same day Strapinski betook himself to a splendid ball to which he had been invited. He appeared dressed in deep simple black and announced at once to those who came to greet him that he was compelled to leave on a journey.

In ten minutes the news was known by the whole assembly and Nettchen, whose gaze Strapinski sought, seemed to avoid his glance as though stunned, now going red, now pale. Then she danced several times in succession with other young men, sat down distractedly breathing fast and then without looking at him and with a curt bow she refused an invitation to dance with Strapinski who had at last approached her. Strangely excited and concerned, he went away, put his precious cloak around him and strode up and down a garden path, his locks blowing in the wind. It was clear to him now that he had stayed on in Goldach really only on account of this one person, that the vague hope of coming again into her presence had unconsciously animated him, but that the whole business was an absolute impossibility of the most hopeless kind.

As he was thus striding up and down, he heard footsteps behind him, quick and light but agitated steps. Nettchen went past him and judging by a few words she called out, she seemed to be looking for her carriage, although it stood on the other side of the house and here only winter cabbages and a few well-protected rose trees dreamed away the sleep of the just. Then she came back again and when he now stepped in front of her, his heart beating fast, and imploringly stretched out his hands to her, without further ado she fell into his arms and began to weep pitifully. He covered her glowing cheeks with his dark finely-scented locks and his cloak enveloped the slim proud snow-white figure of the girl as with black eagles wings. It was a truly beautiful picture which seemed to need no other justification.

But Strapinski lost all reason in this episode and won instead that good fortune which so often smiles on the foolish. That very same evening Nettchen revealed to her father on the drive home that none other than the Count would be hers, and the following morning bright and early Strapinski called on her father, charming, shy and melancholy as usual, in order to ask for her hand in marriage. The father replied, "Well, at last Fate and my foolish child's dearest wish has been fulfilled! Even as a child at school she always maintained that she would marry an Italian, or a Pole or a great pianist or a bandit chief with beautiful hair, and now it has all come true. She has refused all well-meaning offers from local people and only recently I had to send away that clever and able Melchior Bohni, who will be very successful in business one day and she made fun of him really terribly merely because he has ginger sideboards and takes snuff from a silver snuff box. Now, thank God, a Polish Count has turned up from some remote region. Take the silly goose, Count, and send her back home again if she shivers in your far-off land or if she gets unhappy and sobs. Oh! How delighted her dear mother would be if she had lived, to see her spoiled child become a Countess!"

Now there was great activity; in a few days the engagement would have to be celebrated in some haste, for the Alderman maintained that his future son-in-law should not be hindered in his business nor put off his planned journey through marriage arrangements, but that rather his business trip should be concluded as quickly as possible so that the marriage could take place the sooner.

On the occasion of the official engagement Strapinski bought his fiancée presents which cost him half his worldly wealth. The other half he spent on a celebration party which he wanted to hold for her. It was just approaching the festival of Mardi Gras and with clear skies they were enjoying the most magnificent late Winter weather. The country roads offered the most splendid sleighing, as happens only rarely and then hardly ever lasts, so Count Strapinski arranged a sleighing party and a ball at the inn which was usually favoured for such festivities and which stood on a plateau with the most beautiful view, about two good hours journey away and centrally situated between Goldach and Seldwyla.

At about this time it just so happened that Melchior Bohni had to attend to some business in this latter town and therefore, a few days before the festival, drove over there in a light sleigh, smoking his best cigar; and it just so happened too that the inhabitants of Seldwyla on the same day as those from Goldach also planned a sleighing party to the very same place, and in fact a costumed or masked party.

And so the procession of sleighs from Goldach set off at about midday with the tinkling of sleigh-bells, the sounding of coach horns and the cracking of whips, and it drove through the town so that the emblems on the old houses looked down in astonishment and drove out through the Town Gate. In the first sleigh sat Strapinski beside his fiancée; he was wearing a Polish overcoat of green velvet trimmed with cord and heavily lined with fur. Nettchen was well wrapped up in white furs; blue veils protected her face from the cool air and the glare of the sun. The Alderman had been hindered from driving with them by some sudden emergency, yet it was his team and his sleigh in which they drove, a gilded figurehead as decoration on the front representing the Roman Goddess

Fortuna, for the Alderman's town-house was called Fortuna.

There followed fifteen or sixteen other sleighs each with a gentleman and a lady, all finely dressed and in good spirits, but none of the couples so handsome and splendid as the engaged pair. Like ocean-going ships with their figureheads, each sleigh bore on the front the emblem of the house to which it belonged, so that the people watching cried out, "Look! Here comes Courage! What a beautiful sleigh Excellence is! Refinement looks as if it has just been newly varnished and Thrift seems to have been re-gilded! Oh, look at Jacobs Well and The Pool of Bethesda!"

In The Pool of Bethesda, which being only a modest one-horse sleigh brought up the rear, drove Melchior Bohni, quiet and content. As figurehead on his sleigh he had the emblem of that young Jew who waited at the pool for thirty years before being cured. So the squadron sailed along in the sunshine and soon appeared on the heights glittering far and wide and approached their goal. At the very same moment merry music rang out from the opposite direction.

From out of a heavily frosted wood there emerged a confusion of bright colours and forms which revealed itself as a procession of sleighs of strange appearance, standing out against the blue sky beside the white edges of the fields and likewise gliding along towards the centre of the scene. They seemed to be mainly the large heavy sledges used by peasants, fastened together in twos to serve as a base for odd structures and tableaux. On the foremost sledge towered an enormous figure representing the Goddess Fortuna, who seemed to be flying aloft in the air. It was a gigantic figure of straw full of shimmering tinsel, whose gauze robes fluttered in the breeze. On the second pair of sledges however rode an equally gigantic Billy goat, black and gloomy by contrast and with lowered horns apparently pursuing Fortuna. Hereupon followed a strange tableau which represented a tailor's iron fifteen feet high, then an enormous pair of snipping scissors which were opened and closed by means of a cord and which seemed to treat the sky above as a piece of blue silk. Other such current allusions to tailoring followed and at the foot of all these tableaux on the roomy sleighs, each pulled by four horses, sat the Seldwyla party wearing the most colourful costumes and with loud laughter and song.

Since both processions drove up simultaneously on the square before the inn, there was a noisy scene and a great throng of people and horses. The ladies and gentlemen of Goldach were surprised and astonished at this strange encounter. The Seldwylans on the other hand appeared at first nice and friendly. Their foremost sleigh with Fortuna bore the inscription "Man makes the Clothes" and so it turned out that the whole company represented nothing but tailors of all nations and ages. It was to some extent an historical-geographical pageant of the tailor's trade which concluded with the inverted and supplementary inscription "Clothes make the Man". In the last sleigh with this superscription, to represent the work of former heathen and Christian tailors of all lands, there sat venerable emperors and kings, councillors, military officers, prelates and nuns in the greatest solemnity.

This assemblage of tailors cleverly disengaged itself from the confusion and left the ladies and gentlemen of Goldach, the engaged couple at their head, to walk modestly into the house to occupy the lower rooms which were reserved for them, while the Seldwylans rushed noisily up the wide staircase to the large parlour. The Count's party found this behaviour quite normal and their surprise soon changed to merriment and approving smiles at the imperturbable good humour of the Seldwylans. Only the Count himself cherished dark gloomy thoughts, although in his present preoccupation of mind he felt no definite suspicions and had not even noticed where the people had come from. Melchior Bohni, who had carefully put away the Pool of Bethesda and stood watchfully near Strapinski, said out loud so that the latter could hear that the procession had originated from quite a different town.

Soon both parties sat down at the covered tables, each in their own storey of the building, and devoted themselves to merry conversation and pleasantries in the expectation of more enjoyment to come. This was heralded for the Goldach party when they strode across to the ballroom in pairs to where the musicians were already tuning their fiddles. As they were now all standing round in a circle and were about to sort themselves out ready to dance, a delegation appeared from the Seldwylans to put forward a neighbourly proposal that they be allowed to pay a visit to the ladies and gentlemen of Goldach and perform for their entertainment an exhibition dance. This offer could not easily be refused and anyway they expected excellent fun from the merry Seldwylans, so they sat down according to the directions of the delegation in a large half-circle, in whose midst Strapinski and Nettchen shone like princely stars.

Now one after the other the groups of tailors trouped in. Each illustrated in elegant pantomime the sentence "Man makes the Clothes" and its reverse, as they pretended to be making industriously some elegant piece of clothing, a princely cloak, priest's robes etc and then dressed some needy person with it, who then suddenly changed, straightened himself up haughtily and walked round pompously in time to the music. Even fables were portrayed with this meaning, since an enormous crow appeared which decked itself in peacock's feathers and hopped round cawing, then a wolf who was fitting a sheep's pelt for himself and finally a donkey who wore a terrifying lion-skin made of hemp and draped himself heroically with it as with a wide sleeveless cloak.

All who thus appeared stepped back after they had completed their performance and thus gradually turned the semi-circle of the Goldachans into a wide ring of spectators whose inner space at last became empty. At this moment the music changed to a melancholy serious tune and at the same time a final apparition entered the circle and all eyes were directed to him. It was a slim young man in a dark cloak, with fine dark hair and a Polish cap.; it was none other than Count Strapinski as he had walked along the road that November day and had climbed into the fateful coach.

The whole assembly gazed at this figure in breathless suspense as he walked round for a few paces at a melancholy gait in time to the music, then made his way to the centre of the circle, spread out his cloak on the ground, sat down on it tailor's-fashion and began to unpack a bundle. He pulled out a Count's coat, nearly completed and just like the one Strapinski was wearing at this moment, skilfully and quickly sewed onto it tassels and cords and ironed it out in exemplary fashion, testing the apparently hot iron with wet fingers. Then he pulled himself slowly up, took off his own threadbare coat, took a mirror, combed his hair and completed his toilet, so that finally he bore the exact likeness of the Count. Unexpectedly the music changed to a quick cheerful tune; the man wrapped up his belongings in the old coat and threw the package away over the heads of the audience into the back of the hall, as if he wanted to separate himself for ever from his past. Hereupon he walked round the circle in stately dance-steps as a proud nobleman bowing graciously here and there to those present until he reached the engaged pair. Suddenly he fixed his eyes steadily on Strapinski who was sitting there thunderstruck, stood still in front of him like a statue, while at the same time as though by agreement the music stopped and a frightful stillness fell like silent lightning.

"Well, Well, Well!" he cried with a voice that could be heard far and wide and he stretched out his arm straight at the unhappy Pole. "Look at my fellow-countryman there, that mongrel Pole from Silesia, who ran away from working for me when he thought I was finished on account of a little fluctuation in business. I'm delighted you are enjoying yourself so much and celebrating Shrove Tuesday so merrily! Have you found work in Goldach?" At the same moment he held out his hand to the young Count who sat there wanly smiling, and he grasped it involuntarily like a red-hot iron, while his double cried, "Come on friends, look at our meek little journeyman tailor, pretty as a picture, who was so well liked by our servant girls, and even by the parson's daughter, although she wasn't quite all there, it's true!"

Now the Seldwylans came crowding round Strapinski and his former master and shook him heartily by the hand so that he swayed on his chair and trembled. At the same time the music struck up again with a lively march. The Seldwylans, as soon as they had gone past the engaged couple, formed up to march out of the room, singing a carefully rehearsed diabolic laughing chorus, while the Goldachans, among whom Bohni had cleverly spread the explanation of the miraculous event like lightning, ran in confusion, getting mixed up with the Seldwylans so that there was one almighty tumult.

When this at last died down the room was almost empty; a few people stood against the walls and whispered to each other in embarrassment; a few young ladies hovered around Nettchen, uncertain whether to go up to her or not.

The pair sat there motionless on their chairs like a mummified Egyptian King and Queen, quite still and alone; you could almost feel the endless burning desert sand.

Nettchen, white as marble, turned her face slowly to her fiancé and looked at him strangely from the side. He stood slowly up and walked away with heavy steps, his eyes cast down, while large tears fell from them.

He went through the crowds from Goldach and Seldwyla, who covered the stairs, like a dead man stealing like a ghost from the fair, and strangely they allowed him to pass through as such, quietly moving out of his way without laughing or shouting hard words. He walked also between the sleighs and horses of the Goldachans already harnessed up for departure, while the Seldwylans now really made merry in their quarters, and he wandered half unconsciously along the same road towards Seldwyla which he had come along a few months before, his only thought now being never to return to Goldach. Soon he disappeared into the darkness of the forest through which the road wound. He was bare-headed, for his Polish cap was left lying on the window-sill of the ballroom along with his gloves; and so he strode along, his head sunk, concealing his freezing hands under his folded arms, while he gradually collected his thoughts and came to an understanding of the situation. The first clear feeling he was aware of was that of monstrous shame, as if he had really been a man of rank and stature who had now become disgraced through some fateful misfortune. Then this feeling resolved itself into a kind of consciousness of having been badly treated. Until his glorious entry into the accursed town he had never done any wrong. As far as his thoughts could reach back into the past he did not remember that he had ever been punished or scolded because of any lie or dishonesty, and now he had become an impostor for the very reason that the folly of the world had surprised him at an unguarded defenceless moment and had turned him into its plaything. To himself he seemed like a child who has been persuaded by another malicious child to steal the chalice from an altar. He hated and despised himself now, but he wept at himself too and his unfortunate aberration.

When a Prince takes another country and its people by force; when a Priest proclaims the teachings of his church without conviction but consumes the fruits of his living with dignity; when a conceited teacher enjoys the honours and advantages of an important teaching post without having the slightest idea of the importance of his knowledge and without advancing it in the slightest; when a dishonourable artist with frivolous work and empty illusion gets himself into vogue and steals the bread and reputation that are the fruits of honest work; or when a swindler who has inherited or obtained deceitfully an honest businessman's name and then by his folly and unscrupulousness defrauds thousands of their savings; all these people do not weep at themselves but rather rejoice in their well-being and do not remain for a single evening without merry company and good friends.

But our tailor wept bitterly at himself; that is to say he suddenly began to weep when his thoughts, continuing the depressing line they had taken, came back unexpectedly to the fiancée he had left behind and he grovelled on his knees to his unseen beloved in his shame. Misery and humiliation showed him in one vivid flash the happiness he had lost and changed this confused but loving wanderer from the straight and narrow into a rejected lover. He

stretched out his arms to the cold gleaming stars and
stumbled rather than walked along the road, stood still
again and shook his head, when suddenly a red glow
reached the snow around him and at the same time the
sound of bells and laughter rang out. It was the
Seldwylans driving home with torches. Already the noses
of the first horses had nearly reached him; he pulled
himself together, took a mighty leap over the edge of the
road and ducked beneath the first trees of the forest. The
wild procession drove past and died away finally in the
darkness and the distance without the fugitive having been
noticed. He however, after he had listened for a good
while motionless, overcome by the cold as well as by the
fiery wine he had drunk and his horrifying stupidity,
stretched out his limbs unnoticed and fell asleep on the
crisp snow, while an ice-cold breeze from the East began
to blow.

Meanwhile, Nettchen rose from her lonely seat. She had
watched fairly closely the departure of her beloved, had
then sat on motionless for more than an hour and then
stood up, beginning to weep bitterly and went in confusion
towards the door. Two of her friends now came to her with
words of doubtful consolation. She asked them to get her
cloak, wraps, hat and the like, in which things she at once
silently wrapped herself, drying her eyes vigorously with
the veil. Since however, when one weeps one must nearly
always also blow one's nose, she found herself obliged to
take out her handkerchief and give a mighty blow,
whereupon she looked round her proud and angry. This
glance took in Melchior Bohni, who was coming up to her
humbly, smiling and friendly, to point out to her the

necessity of having a driver and companion to take her back home. He said that he would leave the Pool of Bethesda behind at the inn and instead would accompany the Fortuna safely back to Goldach with the unfortunate girl he admired so much.

Without answering, she walked on with a firm step to the yard where the sleigh stood ready with the impatient well-fed horses, one of the last that remained. She quickly took her seat in it, gripped the reins and the whip, and while Bohni unsuspectingly bustled round contentedly getting out a tip for the stable-boy who had held the horses, she unexpectedly whipped up the horses and drove out along the main road with mighty bounds which soon changed to a steady cheerful gallop; but she did not go towards her home but along the road to Seldwyla. Not until the light-winged sleigh had disappeared from view did Herr Bohni fully realise what had happened and he ran off in the direction of Goldach, shouting "Hey, stop, come back!" Then he rushed back and pursued the beautiful fugitive in his own sleigh, or in his version of the story the girl who had been carried off by the horses, until he reached the gates of the excited town in which the scandal was already on everyone's lips.

 Why Nettchen had chosen that particular direction, whether in confusion or deliberately, is not certain; but two circumstances can here shed a little light, In the first place Strapinski's fur cap and gloves, which had been lying on the window-sill behind their seat, now oddly enough lay in the sleigh Fortuna next to Nettchen. When and how she had picked up these objects nobody had noticed and she herself did not know; it had been as though she were sleep-walking. She did not even know now that the cap and gloves lay beside her. Secondly she said to herself out loud more than once, "I must have two more words with him, just two words!"

These two facts seem to prove that it was not mere chance which guided the fiery horses. Also it was strange that Fortuna set out along the road through the woods on which the bright full moon now shone, as Nettchen moderated the pace of the horses and gripped the reins tighter, so that the horses almost pranced along in step while the driver kept her sad but nonetheless sharp eyes glued to the way ahead without missing the slightest unusual object to right or left.

And yet at the same time her mind was sunk in deep wretched oblivion. What are life and happiness? On what do they depend? What are we that our happiness or unhappiness depends on some ridiculous carnival lie? What wrong have we done that we should reap disgrace and despair through some happy trusting affectionate attachment? Who sends us such foolish phantom figures who interfere disastrously in our fate while they themselves dissolve like soft soap bubbles?

Such questions, more dreamed than thought, were flying around in Nettchen's mind when her eyes suddenly lit on a longish dark object which stood out from the moonlit snow by the side of the road. It was Wenzel stretched out there, his dark hair merging with the shadows of the trees while his slim body lay clearly in the light.

Nettchen instinctively pulled up the horses, whereupon a deep stillness lay over the woods. She stared fixedly at the dark body until it appeared almost unmistakeable to her clear-seeing eye and she gently fastened the reins, got out, stroked the horses calmingly for a few moments and then silently and carefully went up to the figure.

Yes, it was him! The dark-green velvet of his coat looked beautiful and noble on the snow by night. The slim body and the supple limbs, well-formed and clothed, all said quite clearly, even though he lay there numb on the edge of ruin and death, "Clothes make the Man".

When the lovely lonely girl bent closer over him and recognised him quite definitely, she also saw at a glance the danger he was in and was afraid he might already have frozen to death. Therefore she took hold of one of his hands which seemed cold and insensible. Forgetting everything else, she shook the poor unfortunate and called his Christian name in his ear, "Wenzel! Wenzel!" In vain; he did not stir but only gave sad weak little breaths. Then she fell down on her knees beside him, ran her hand over his face and in her anxiety banged him on the pale tip of his nose. Then, getting a good idea from this, she picked up handfuls of snow and rubbed them vigorously into his nose, face and fingers as much as she could until the lucky unfortunate revived, awoke and slowly raised himself up.

He looked round him and saw his guardian angel standing before him. She had thrown back her veil. Wenzel recognised every feature in the white face which was looking down at him wide-eyed.

He fell down before her, kissed the hem of her cloak and cried, "Forgive me! Forgive me!"

"Come, strange man!" she said in a suppressed trembling voice, "I want to speak to you and get you away from here." She signed for him to get into the sleigh, which he obediently did. She gave him his cap and gloves just as instinctively as she had picked them up, got hold of the reins and the whip and drove on.

On the other side of the woods not far from the road lay a farm where lived a farmer's wife whose husband had died not long before. Nettchen was the Godmother of one of her children and her father, the Alderman, was the woman's landlord. Only recently the woman had been at their house to wish Nettchen all happiness and to ask all sorts of advice, but at this hour she could not yet know anything of the course of events.

To this farm Nettchen now drove, turning off from the road and stopping in front of the house with a mighty crack of the whip. There was still a light behind the small windows for the farmer's wife was awake and busy, while the children and domestics had long been asleep. She opened the window and looked out in amazement. "It's only me, it's only us!" called Nettchen. "We've lost our way because of the new highroad which I've never driven along before. Make us a cup of coffee, Aunty, and let us come in for a moment before we drive on." Highly delighted, the farmer's wife hurried down, for she recognised Nettchen at once, and appeared pleased and astonished at the same time to see this great man, the foreign Count. In her eyes the good fortune and glamour of this world had stepped across her threshold in these two persons. Vague hopes of winning some small share in it, some modest advantage for herself or her children enlivened the good woman and gave her the stimulus to serve the young people. Quickly she woke a stable-boy to hold the horses, and soon she had prepared some hot coffee which she now brought in to where Wenzel and Nettchen sat opposite each other in the half-dark parlour, a softly flickering lamp between them on the table.

Wenzel sat, his head resting on his hands, and dared not look up. Nettchen leaned back in her chair and kept her eyes tightly closed as well as her beautiful but bitter mouth, from which one could tell that she was not asleep.

When her godchild's mother had set down the drink on the table, Nettchen got up quickly and whispered to her, "Leave us alone for a while, my dear. Go back to bed, we've had a bit of a quarrel and must talk it out this very day, now that we have a good opportunity." "I understand. That's a good idea." said the woman, who soon left the two of them alone.

"Drink this!" said Nettchen, who had sat down again, "it will do you good!" She herself touched nothing. Wenzel Strapinski, who trembled slightly, pulled himself up, took a cup and drank it, more because she had told him to than in order to refresh himself. He now looked at her and when their eyes met and Nettchen looked searchingly into his, she shook her head and said, "Who are you? What did you want with me?"

"I am not quite what I seem", he answered sadly. "I am a poor fool, but I will make up for it all and give you satisfaction and not stay in this life much longer!" He spoke these words so convincingly and without any affectation that Nettchen's eyes flashed imperceptibly. Nevertheless she repeated, "I wish to know who you really are, where you come from and where you intend to go!"

"It has all come about as I will now truthfully tell you", he answered and told her who he was and what had happened on his entry into Goldach. He especially emphasized how he had several times wanted to flee but finally had been prevented by her appearing as if in a bewitched dream.

Nettchen was several times overcome by an attack of laughter, but the seriousness of the situation too much predominated for it to have burst out. She continued rather by asking," And where did you intend to go with me and what did you intend to do?" "I scarcely know", he answered. "I hoped for more strange or lucky happenings. Sometimes I thought of dying in the way I intend, after I-" Here Wenzel stopped short and his pale face went bright red. "Well, go on!" said Nettchen, on her side turning pale, while her heart thumped strangely.

Then Wenzel's large eyes flashed sweetly and he cried, "Yes, now it's clear to me how it would have been. I would have gone with you out into the wide world and after living a few short happy days with you, I would have confessed the deception and at the same time killed myself. You would have returned to your father where you would have been well received and would have quietly forgotten me. Nobody needed to know of it. I would have disappeared without trace. Instead of making myself sick with longing all my life for a worthy existence, for a kind heart, for love", he continued dejectedly, "I would for one moment have been great and happy and far above all those who are neither happy nor unhappy and yet never want to die. Oh! If only you had left me lying in the cold snow! I would have fallen asleep so peacefully!" He had become still again and stared before him thinking gloomy thoughts.

After a while Nettchen, who was looking quietly at him, said after the violent beating of her heart caused by Wenzel's words had somewhat subsided, "Have you ever done this or any similar foolish thing before and deceived people unknown to you, who had done you no harm?"

"During this bitter night I've been asking myself the same question and do not remember ever having been a liar. Such an adventure I have never before undertaken nor experienced. Yes, in those days when the inclination first arose in me to be or appear to be someone of consequence, still half in childhood, I conquered my urge and renounced a happiness which seemed to have been granted me."

"What was that?" asked Nettchen. "Before she married, my mother was in the service of the wife of a neighbouring landowner and had been with her on journeys and to large towns. From this she had acquired a more refined manner than the other women in our village and was, it is true, rather vain; for she dressed herself and me, her only child, always a bit more elegantly and more carefully than was the custom round us. Father, a poor schoolmaster, died early however and so in the greatest poverty there was no prospect of the happy events my mother so liked to dream of. Rather she had to devote herself to hard work just to feed us and in so doing to sacrifice the dearest possession she had, better manners and a better appearance. Unexpectedly, when I was about sixteen, the newly-widowed lady said that she was moving with her household to the capital city for ever and my mother ought to give me to her. It would be a shame for me to become a day-labourer or farmer's boy in the village. She would have me taught something refined – whatever I liked – while I could live in her house and could do this or that light service for her. This seemed to be the most splendid thing that could happen to us at that time. So accordingly everything was agreed and prepared when mother became pensive and sad and one day suddenly begged me with many tears not to leave her, but to stay poor with her. She would not live long, she said, and I would certainly still achieve something worthwhile, even if she were dead. The lady, whom I sadly acquainted with this, came and remonstrated with her, but mother now got quite excited and cried repeatedly that she would not be robbed of her child; anyone who knew the child could---" Here Wenzel stopped again and did not know how to continue. Nettchen asked, "What did your mother mean by 'anyone who knew the child'? Why don't you go on?"

Wenzel blushed and answered, "She said something very strange, that I didn't really understand and that I have never in any case felt since; she said that anyone who knew the child could never part from it again and she meant by that that I was a good-natured lad – or words to that effect. In fact she was so worked up that I refused the lady despite all persuasion and stayed with my mother, for which she loved me twice as much as before, begging my forgiveness a thousand times for standing in the way of my good fortune. But when I was of an age to learn to earn some money, it turned out that there was not much else to do but be apprenticed to our village tailor. I did not want to, but mother wept so much that I gave in. This is the story."

To Nettchen's question, why then had he left his mother, Wenzel replied, "Military service called me away. I was sent to the Hussars and became a handsome red Hussar, although perhaps the most stupid one in the regiment, the quietest at least. After a year I was at last allowed a few weeks leave and hurried home to see my mother, but she had just died. So, when my time was up, I travelled alone through the world and at last here came upon my misfortune."

Nettchen smiled as all this came pouring miserably out and she watched him closely as he told it. It was now all quiet for a while in the parlour. Suddenly a thought seemed to occur to her. "Since you were always so esteemed and loved", she said suddenly, but nevertheless in a sharp but hesitating manner, "you have no doubt always had your love-affairs or the like and have more than one poor girl on your conscience, not to mention me!"

"On my honour," answered Wenzel going quite red, "before I came to you I have never so much as touched the fingertips of a girl, except for----""Well?" said Nettchen. "Well", he continued, "it was that lady who wanted to take me with her and educate me; she had a child, a girl of seven or eight, a strange passionate child and yet as good as gold and as beautiful as an angel. Many times I had to be her servant and protector and she had grown used to me. Regularly I had to take her to the distant parsonage where she received instruction from an old parson, and fetch her back again. Otherwise I had to go with her sometimes out into the open air if nobody else could go just at that moment. When I was taking her home for the last time over the fields in the evening sunshine, the child now began to talk of their impending departure and told me that I must at all costs go with them and asked if I would do so. I said that it could not be, but she continued to beg most touchingly and urgently, while she hung on my arm and prevented me from walking on, as children are wont to do, so that I thoughtlessly disengaged myself rather brusquely. Then she lowered her head and sought sadly and beautifully to suppress her tears which now came trickling through, and she could scarcely control her sobs. Embarrassed I wanted to appease her but now she turned angrily away and dismissed me in disgrace. Since then this beautiful child has often been in my mind and I have always thought fondly of her, although I never heard of her again."

Suddenly the speaker, who had become somewhat agitated, paused as though shocked and, turning pale, stared at his companion. "Well," said Nettchen also going pale and in a strange tone, "why are you looking at me like that?" But Wenzel stretched out his arm, pointed at her with his finger as if he was seeing a ghost and cried,"This I have also seen before. When that child was angry, then just like you now the fine hair round her brows and temples rose slightly so that you could see it move and it was like that the last time on the fields in the evening sunshine."

In fact the curls of hair which lay next to Nettchen's temples and over her forehead had moved gently as if from a breath of air blown into her face. Mother Nature, always so coquettish, had here used one of her secrets to bring the difficult business to an end.

After a short silence while her breast began to heave, Nettchen stood up, went round the table towards him and fell into his arms with the words, "I will never leave you. You are mine and I will go with you, come what may!" Now for the first time she celebrated her real engagement out of a deep determined conviction, by taking upon herself in her sweet passion the fate of another and keeping her word.

Yet she was by no means so stupid as not to want to direct this fate a little herself; rather she quickly and boldly framed new resolutions. For she said to the good Wenzel who was sitting there in a dream, lost in this renewed upturn of Fortune, "Now we will just go to Seldwyla and show the people there who thought to destroy us that they have only really succeeded in uniting us and making us happy."

The valiant Wenzel could not see the matter in that light. He would prefer, he said, to move away to some unknown place afar off and live there romantically and in secret but in quiet happiness. But Nettchen insisted, "No more romantic delusions! As you are, a poor wandering tailor, I will acknowledge you and in my home town, in defiance of all those proud mocking people, I will be your wife. We will go to Seldwyla and there through hard work and skill make those who have made fun of us dependent on us!"

No sooner said than done! After the farmer's wife had been called in and had been rewarded by Wenzel, who now began to take on his new role, they drove on their way. Wenzel now held the reins. Nettchen leaned as contentedly against him as if he had been a pillar in the church. For man's greatest happiness is to have his own way, and Nettchen had three days before come of age and could now have hers.

In Seldwyla they stopped in front of The Rainbow Inn where a number of the sleighing party were still sitting over a glass. As the pair appeared in the hotel parlour, the rumour spread like wildfire, "Ha, we have an elopement here! We really have started something!" But Wenzel walked through them with his fiancée. Without once looking round, after she had disappeared into her room, he made his way to The Wild Man, another good inn, and strode proudly through the Seldwylans, who were likewise still sitting there, into a room which he booked and left them to their astonished deliberations, in the course of which they were forced to drink so much that they would have hangovers the next morning. In Goldach too, at the very same time, the rumour of an elopement flew round.

Very early next morning the Pool of Bethesda also drove to Seldwyla, carrying the excited Bohni and Nettchen's perplexed father. They had almost driven in their haste straight through the town without stopping, when just in time they saw the sleigh Fortuna standing safe and sound before the inn and were comforted to think that at least the fine horses would not be far away. So when they had confirmed their supposition and had heard of Nettchen's arrival and stay at the inn, they had their own horses unhitched and went straight away into The Rainbow.

A short time elapsed however before Nettchen sent a request that her father should visit her in her room and there speak with her alone. Also it was said that she had already sent for the best lawyer in town who would appear in the course of the morning. The Alderman went up to his daughter with a somewhat heavy heart, considering what was the best way to win his desperate child from her perversity and he was ready for any desperate course of action.

But Nettchen met him calmly and with gentle firmness. She thanked her father touchingly for all the love and kindness he had shown her and made it clear at once in determined phrases, firstly that she no longer wanted to live in Goldach after what had happened, at least not for the next few years, and secondly that she wished to have the considerable amount she had inherited from her mother, which her father had long kept ready for the occasion of her marriage. Thirdly she intended to marry Wenzel Strapinski, and on this in particular her mind was unalterable. Fourthly she wanted to live with him in Seldwyla and help him to found an excellent business there and fifthly and lastly everything would turn out all right for she had convinced herself that he was a good man and would make her happy.

The Alderman began his task by reminding Nettchen that she knew how much he had always wished to be able to hand over her fortune to serve as the basis for her true happiness. But then he described with all the sorrow which had filled him since the first news of the terrible catastrophe the impossibility of the relationship to which she wished to hold fast and finally he showed her the means by which the difficult conflict could alone be worthily resolved. Melchior Bohni was prepared to put an end to all the rumours by the immediate security of his own person and to protect and maintain her honour in the world with his irreproachable name.

But the word 'honour' caused his daughter to get even more agitated. She cried out that it was honour which compelled her not to marry Herr Bohni, because she could not care for him, and to remain true to the poor stranger to whom she had given her word and who in any case she did care for.

There was now a fruitless argument on both sides which in the end brought floods of tears from the valiant girl.

Almost at the same moment Wenzel and Bohni, who had met on the stairs, rushed in and there threatened to break out a great tumult when the lawyer too appeared, a man well-known to the Alderman, and for the present he advised quiet discretion. When he learnt in a few preliminary words what it was all about, he ordered that above all Wenzel should retire to the Wild Man and there keep himself quiet, that Herr Bohni should mind his own business and go away, that Nettchen on her side should preserve the forms of bourgeois good manners until the matter was settled and the father should refrain from any use of force since the freedom of his daughter was quite clear in law. So there ensued a truce and a general separation for a few hours.

In the town, where the lawyer let it be known that a large fortune might perhaps come to Seldwyla as a result of this affair, a great tumult now arose. The sentiments of the Seldwylans suddenly changed in favour of the tailor and his beloved, and they decided to protect the lovers with all their power and to defend justice and the freedom of the individual in their town. When therefore the rumour went round that the beautiful young lady from Goldach was to be forcibly taken back, they banded together, posted armed vigilantes before the Rainbow and the Wild Man and with enormous enjoyment entered upon one of their great adventures, the remarkable sequel to the one of the day before.

The frightened and enraged Alderman sent Bohni back to Goldach for help. He galloped there and next day a large number of men with a considerable police force rode over in order to support the Alderman, and things began to look as though Seldwyla would be a second Troy. The parties stood threateningly facing each other. The town drummer was already tightening his drum-screws and practising a few beats with his right drumstick. Then came high officials, ecclesiastical and lay, onto the square, and the negotiations which were engaged in on all sides produced the result, since Nettchen remained firm and Wenzel did not allow himself to be intimidated thanks to the encouragement of the Seldwylans, that the publication of the banns of their marriage, after collecting together the necessary documents, formally took place and it was agreed that they should wait and see whether any legal objections, and if so which, would be raised on account of this procedure and with what result.

Such objections could be raised, in view of Nettchen's majority, only on account of the doubtful personage of the false Count Wenzel Strapinski. But the lawyer, who now handled his and Nettchen's affairs, ascertained that not the shadow of evil repute had touched the unknown young man either in his home nor on his journeys up to now and from everywhere only good and favourable testimonials came in about him.

As far as the events in Goldach were concerned, the lawyer demonstrated that Wenzel had in fact never for a moment passed himself off as a Count, but that this rank was conferred on him against his will by others; that in writing he had signed all available documents with his real name Wenzel Strapinski without any title and consequently there was no other offence possible except that he had taken advantage of a foolish hospitality, which would not have been vouchsafed him if he had not arrived in that coach and if the coachman had not played that silly prank.

So the war ended with a marriage, at which the Seldwylans fired off their so-called cathead canons to the vexation of the Goldachans who could easily hear the thunder of the guns as a west wind was blowing. The Alderman handed over to Nettchen her whole fortune and she said Wenzel must now become a great merchant tailor and draper in Seldwyla.

This duly happened, but not quite in the way the Seldwylans had imagined. He was modest, economical and hard-working in his business which he managed to greatly expand. He made for them their violet or blue and white check velvet jackets, their dress-coats with gold buttons, their red-lined cloaks, and they all owed him money for them, but never for very long. For, in order to get new still finer things which he ordered or had made for them, they had first to pay their former debts, so that they complained to each other that he was a real blood-sucker.

With all this he became stout and imposing, and scarcely looked dreamy any longer. As the years passed he became more experienced in business and more skilful, and in partnership with his soon reconciled father-in-law, succeeded in making such good investments that his capital soon doubled and after ten or twelve years, with as many children, which in the meantime his wife had born to him, he moved with her to Goldach, settled there and became a highly respected citizen.

But in Seldwyla, whether from ingratitude or revenge, he did not leave a penny behind.

Aquis Submersus

By Theodor Storm

In the gardens which formerly belonged to our ducal palace but which have been completely neglected since time immemorial, the hawthorn hedges, originally laid out in traditional French style, had even in my childhood deteriorated into straggling vestiges of pathways; but since they nevertheless still bear a few leaves, local people, who have not been spoilt by the luxuriant foliage all around, still treasure them even in this state; and from time to time some person or another, deep in thought, can be met with there. The custom then is to wander in their scanty shade to the so-called "Height", a small slope in the northwest corner of the gardens above the dried up bed of a fishpond, from where nothing prevents the widest view.

Most people probably look out to the west in order to enjoy the light green of the marshes and beyond them the silvery waves of the sea, on which floats the shadowy shape of the extensive island of Nordstrand; but my eyes turn involuntarily to the north where scarcely a mile away the grey pointed tower of a church rises above the higher but barren coastline; for there lies one of the special places of my youth.

The pastor's son from that village went with me to the Grammar School in my home town and many's the time we walked out there together on Saturday afternoons and then returned to our Cicero or Nepos in the town on Sunday evening or Monday morning. In those days there was still about half way there a good stretch of unbroken heath, which once had stretched in one direction almost to the town and in the other to the village. Here the honey bees and the pale-grey bumblebees buzzed among the fragrant heather blooms and the gold and green ground-beetles darted beneath their spindly stalks; here amidst the clouds of fragrance from the heather and the bayberry plants hovered butterflies which were to be found nowhere else. My friend, impatient to get home, often had great trouble in bringing his dreamy companion with him through all these wonders; yet once we had reached the cultivated fields we got ahead all the more merrily, and before long, as we were just beginning to trudge up the long sandy path, we could begin to see above the dark green of an elder hedge the gable of the pastor's house, from which the pastor's study with its small shuttered windows looked down in greeting on familiar guests.

In the pastor's house, where my friend was the only child, we were always treated with great generosity, and cared for in the most wonderfully natural way. Only the white poplar, the sole tall enticing tree in the village, whose branches rustled high above the mossy thatch of the roof, was, like the apple tree in the Garden of Eden, forbidden us, and was therefore climbed by us only in secret; apart from that, as far as I can remember, everything was allowed and made best use of by us according to our stage of life.

The main scene of our activities was the large field belonging to the pastor. A little gate led to it out of the garden. Here with boys' natural instincts we knew where to find the nests of larks and corn buntings which we would then visit at regular intervals to see how far the eggs or the chicks had developed in the last two hours; here by a deep water-filled pit, which when I think of it now was no less dangerous than the poplar, whose edge was thickly surrounded with the stumps of old willow trees, we caught the nimble black beetles which we called "Water Frenchies", or another time launched our fleet of boats made out of walnut shells or lids of boxes, which we had built in our own self-made dockyard. In the late Summer it sometimes happened that we went on a raid from our field into the sexton's garden which lay opposite the pastor's house on the other side of the pit; for we had to gather in our tithe from two stunted apple trees, and for this we sometimes received a friendly warning from the kindly old man. So many youthful pleasures happened in this field of the pastor's, in whose barren sandy soil no other flowers would thrive; only the sharp scent of the golden buds of the tansies, heaps of which could be found here on all the walls, still lingers in my memory today, when I relive those times.

Yet all of this occupied us only in passing; my lasting interest on the other hand was aroused by something quite different, something with which we had nothing to compare in the town. I'm not talking about the tubular nests of mud made by the mason wasps, which jutted out from the wall joints of the stable, although it was pleasant enough at a leisurely midday hour to watch the going in and out of these busy little creatures; what I do mean is the much larger building of the old and unusually magnificent village church. Right up to the shingle roof of the tall tower it was built of square blocks of granite and commanded from its position at the highest point of the village the wide expanse of heath, shore and marshes. The most attractive thing for me, though, was the interior of the church; even the enormous key, which seemed to have come down from the Apostle Peter himself, excited my imagination. And in fact, when we had been lucky enough to extract it from the old sexton, it opened up the doors to many wonderful things, from which a time long past looks out at us who are alive today, sometimes grimly and sometimes with the pious eyes of childhood, but always in mysterious silence. In the middle of the church hung a fearful larger-than-life crucifix, on whose gaunt limbs and distorted face were trickles of blood. To one side of it, fastened to a pillar rather like a nest, was the brown carved pulpit on which all kinds of grotesque animals and devils seemed to peer out from garlands of flowers and leaves A special attraction, though, was the great carved Altarpiece in the choir of the church on which images of the Passion of Christ were painted; one never saw in real life such strange faces as that of Caiaphas or of the soldiers in their golden armour casting lots for the cloak of the crucified; the only one that contrasted comfortingly with them was the lovely countenance of Mary who had sunk to her knees by the cross; in fact she would have easily stricken my boyish heart with a vision of love, if another figure with the still greater appeal of the mysterious had not enticed me away from her again and again.

Among all these strange or even uncanny things there hung in the nave of the church the innocent portrait of a dead child, a handsome roughly five-year old boy resting on a cushion trimmed with lace and holding a white water lily in his pale little hand. His tender countenance expressed as well as the horror of death one last pure trace of life, as though in supplication; an overpowering pity came over me when I stood in front of this picture.

But it did not hang there by itself; close by it a grim dark bearded man in priest's collar and velvet clerical headgear looked out from a dark wooden frame. My friend told me he was the father of that handsome boy who, according to legend, was supposed to have met his death in the watery pit in our field. On the frame we read the date 1666; that was a long time ago. Again and again I was drawn to these two pictures. A fantastic desire took hold of me to find out some more details, however meagre, about the life and death of the boy; I even tried to deduce them from the bleak face of the father who despite his priest's collar reminded me of the soldiers on the Altarpiece.

After such studies in the half-light of the old church, the house of the pastor and his wife seemed all the more hospitable. Certainly it was also full of years and my friend's father had been hoping for as long as I could remember for a new building; but, since the sexton's house suffered from the same weakness of age, no building work was done either on the one or the other. And yet, despite this, how friendly were the rooms in the old house; in winter the small parlour on the right, in summer the larger one on the left of the hall, where the pictures cut out of a religious almanac hung in mahogany frames on the whitewashed wall, where from the western window one only had before one a distant windmill and apart from that the whole wide expanse of the sky which in the evenings lit up with a rosy glow and then radiated the whole room! The dear parents, the armchairs with the red plush cushions, the deep old sofa and on the table at supper- time the cosy singing of the tea-kettle – it was all the bright friendly present. But on one evening - we were by then already in the fifth form- it suddenly occurred to me what history was tied up in these rooms and I wondered whether that dead boy, whose likeness now filled the gloomy church with his charming sad story, had perhaps once in the flesh run around here with rosy cheeks.

The cause of such reflections was probably the fact that in the afternoon, when at my instigation we had once again visited the church, I had discovered down in one dark corner of the picture four letters written in red which I had never noticed before.

"They read C P A S", I said to my friend's father, "but we can't decipher them."

"Well", he replied, "the inscription is well known to me, and if we take notice of the rumours, the last two letters can be interpreted as Aquis Submersus, in other words 'drowned 'or 'sunk in the water'; but that still leaves us in some difficulty with the previous C P! The young assistant to our sexton, who once got as far as the third form, is of the opinion it might mean Casu Periculoso – 'through a dangerous accident' -; but the old gentlemen of that time thought more logically than that; if the boy drowned as a result, then the accident was not just dangerous".

I had been listening eagerly. "Casu", I said, "It could equally well be 'Culpa' couldn't it?"

"Culpa?" repeated the pastor, "'through the fault of?'- but whose fault?"

Then the gloomy picture of the old pastor appeared to my mind's eye and without much reflection I cried out, "Why not 'Culpa Patris'?"

The good pastor was almost shocked. "Now, now, my young friend", he said and raised his finger in warning to me. "'Through the fault of his father?' Despite his gloomy appearance we won't accuse my blessed predecessor like that. In any case he would hardly have written something like that about himself."

This latter point seemed plausible to my youthful understanding; and so the real meaning of the inscription remained as before, a secret of the past.

Besides it had already become clear to me that those two pictures were far superior in the quality of their painting to some old portraits of priests which hung next to them; but the fact that experts were willing to recognize the painter as a skilful pupil of old Dutch masters I only found out now from my friend's father. But how such a painter had wound up in this poor village or where he had come from or what his name was, he was unable to tell me. The pictures themselves contained neither a name nor a painter's mark.

The years passed. While we were at the University, the good pastor died and the mother of my school friend later followed her son to the parish he had been appointed to some distance away; I had no longer any reason to wander out to that village. But since I was myself still living in my home town, it happened that I had to find school lodgings with some good citizens for the son of a relative. Thinking of my own youth I was strolling in the afternoon sunshine through the streets, when I suddenly noticed at the corner of the market place above the door of an old high-gabled house an inscription in Low German, which roughly translated would read;

> Just as vanish smoke and dust,
> So every human creature must.

The words may well not be visible to youthful eyes, for I had never noticed them despite the fact that I had often when at school fetched bread rolls from the baker who lived there. Almost instinctively I entered the house and in fact lodgings for my young relative were available here. The room of their old aunt, the friendly baker told me, from whom they had inherited the house and business, had stood empty for years; for a long time they had been hoping for a young guest to occupy it.

I was taken up a staircase and we went into a fairly low-ceilinged room furnished in an antiquated style, whose two windows with their tiny panes looked out onto the spacious market place. Earlier, the baker said, two ancient lime trees had stood beside the door, but he had had them cut down because they had made the house much too dark and would have quite hidden the beautiful outlook from here.

We soon came to an agreement on the terms in every detail; while we were still talking about the suitable furnishing for the room, I caught sight of an oil painting hanging in the shadow of a cupboard and this suddenly took away my whole attention. It was still in good condition and represented an elderly man, serious yet with a gentle look and wearing a dark costume like those worn in the middle of the seventeenth century by members of the better classes, who dealt more with state matters or scholarly concerns than with warfare.

It was not the head of the old gentleman, however finely and attractively and strikingly painted, which had caused this excitement in me; but the painter had portrayed him with a pale boy lying in his arms, a boy in whose hand as it hung down limply was a white lily; and this boy I had long known. Here too his eyes had closed in death.

"Where did this picture come from?" I asked, when I suddenly realised that the baker who was standing in front of me had paused in his explanation.

He looked at me in surprise. "That old picture? It belonged to our aunt", he replied; "it came originally from our great great uncle who was a painter and lived here more than a hundred years ago. We still have some of his possessions."

With these words he pointed to a small chest made of oak on which were neatly carved all kinds of geometric figures.

When I lifted it down from the cupboard on which it stood, the lid fell open and revealed its contents, some badly faded sheets of paper with very old handwriting.

"May I read these?" I asked.

"If you like", replied the baker, "you can take the whole thing home with you; it's only old papers, they're not of any value."

But I requested and was given permission to read these worthless papers here on the spot and while I sat in a great winged armchair facing the old picture, the baker left the room, still astonished, but leaving behind him the friendly promise that his wife would soon serve me a cup of good coffee.

But I just read and in reading forgot everything around me.

*

So here I was home again at last in Holstein and it was the fourth Sunday after Easter in the year 1661. My painting gear and other luggage I had left behind in the town and was walking now happily through the beech woods in their early green foliage along the road which leads up from the sea into the countryside. In front of me a couple of woodland birds flew to and fro and slaked their thirst from the water which stood in the deep wheel ruts, for a gentle rain had fallen over night and again early in the morning so that the sun had not yet risen above the woodland shade.

The clear song of the thrush which resounded from the woodland glades found its echo in my heart. Thanks to the commissions put my way by my dear master Van der Helst during the last year of my stay in Amsterdam I was free of all cares. I had in my pocket money for my journey and a Bill of Exchange drawn on a Hamburg bank; in addition to that I was magnificently dressed and my long hair fell to my cloak of miniver and nor did I lack at my side a sword from Liege.

But my thoughts hurried on before me and I constantly saw in my mind's eye Herr Gerhard, my noble generous patron, as he would reach out his hand to me in the doorway of his room, with his kindly greeting. "God bless you for coming, Johannes!"

Once he had studied law at the University of Jena with my dear father, who had far too early departed this life. Afterwards he had devoted himself diligently to the arts and sciences and had been a wise and enthusiastic advisor to Duke Frederick in his noble but vain attempts, thanks to matters of war, to set up a university in Holstein. Although a nobleman, he had always remained devoted to my dear father, and after his death had taken a more than was to be expected interest in my orphaned youth and had not only increased my frugal means but, through his distinguished acquaintances among the Dutch nobility, had persuaded my dear master Van der Helst to take me as his pupil.

I wanted to know whether the man I revered was still living safe and well in his manor house for which the Almighty could not be sufficiently thanked. For while I had been abroad devoting myself to art, at home the horrors of war had come upon my homeland, so much so that the troops who had been stationed there to support the king against the warlike Swedes had ravaged far worse than the enemies themselves, and had even caused the wretched death of several of God's servants. Because of the sudden death of Charles of Sweden peace had now been restored, but the fearful footprints of war were to be seen all round; many a farmhouse or cottage, where as a child I had been given a drink of sweet milk, I had seen during my morning walk burnt down at the roadside and many a field where normally at this time the rye would be putting forth its green shoots now lay desolate with weeds.

But none of this troubled me too much that day; my only desire was to prove to my noble patron through my art that he had not expended his gifts and his favour on someone unworthy. I didn't give a thought to the blackguards and stray ruffians who were said to be still hanging out in the woods from the war. But something else did worry me and that was the thought of the young squire Junker Wulf. He had never liked me, had even considered what his noble father had done for me as a kind of theft from himself; and many a time when, as often happened after my dear father's death, I spent the summer holidays on the estate, he had spoiled and marred the days. Whether he was now in his father's house I did not know, but had merely heard that even before peace had been declared he had been gambling and drinking with the Swedish officers, which did not chime with loyalty to Holstein.

As I was thinking this over I had emerged from the beech woods onto the rising path through the pine copse which lies near the manor. Like warm memories the spicy scent of the pines wafted round me; but soon I stepped out of the shadows into the full sunshine. On both sides lay meadows hedged with hazel bushes and in no time I was walking between the two rows of mighty oaks which led up to the manor house.

A strange feeling of dread suddenly came over me, for no apparent reason as I thought then; for there was nothing around but sunshine and from high in the sky the singing of the larks was cheerful and encouraging. And in the paddock where the beekeeper has his hives there still stood the old wild pear tree, its young leaves whispering in the clear air.

"Hello, old friend!" I said softly, but was not so much thinking of the tree as of the lovely divine creature, in whom as it so happened afterwards, all the happiness and suffering and also all the agonizing repentance of my life was to be bound up, for now and for ever. I mean of course Herr Gerhard's daughter, the only sibling of Junker Wulf.

Item; it was soon after the death of my dear father when I was spending the whole vacation here for the first time; she was at that time a small nine year old girl, her brown plaits swinging merrily; I was about a couple of years older. One morning I was coming out of the gatehouse; Dietrich, the old retainer who lived above the gateway and with whom, being a trusted man, I had been given a place to sleep, had made for me a bow of ash wood and also cast the bolts for it from lead and I wanted to try it out now on the birds of prey of which there were many screeching round the house. At that moment she came running out of the courtyard to me.

"Wait, Johannes", she said, "I'll show you a bird's nest there in the hollow pear tree; but they're redstarts, you mustn't shoot them!"

And with that she had raced ahead, but before she had come within twenty paces of the tree I saw her suddenly stop. "The bogey-man, the bogey-man!" she cried and shook her two hands in the air in rage.

It was a large screech owl which was perched above the hole in the hollow tree and looking down to see if it could catch a little bird flying out. "The bogey-man, the bogey-man!" shouted the little girl again. "Shoot, Johannes, shoot!" The owl, made deaf by its desire for food, still sat there staring into the hollow. So I bent my bow and shot, with the result that that the robber bird fell fluttering to the ground. From the tree a tiny bird soared twittering into the air.

From that time on Katharina and I were close friends; in the woods and in the garden, wherever she was, I was there too. But all too soon an enemy had to appear; it was Kurt von der Risch, whose father lived an hour away on his wealthy estate. Accompanied by his private tutor, with whom Herr Gerhard used to enjoy conversing, he often came to visit; and since he was younger than Junker Wulf he was assigned to me and Katharina; he seemed to particularly like the brown little daughter of the house. Yet that was completely in vain, for she only laughed at his crooked beaked nose which, as with most of his family, was set between two noticeably round eyes beneath a bushy head of hair. In fact when she caught sight of him from a distance she craned her head forwards and cried, "Johannes, the bogey-man, the bogey-man!" Then we would hide behind the barns or run at full pelt into the woods which stretched in an arc around the fields and then close by the wall of the garden.

In consequence, when Von der Risch became aware of this, it often came to a scuffle between us, but since he was more hot-headed than strong, I usually had the advantage.

When, in order to take my leave of Herr Gerhard, I stayed here for the last time, just for a few days, before travelling abroad, Katharina was already almost a young woman. Her brown hair was now worn in a golden net; in her eyes when she raised her eyelashes, there was often a playful gleam which made me very uneasy. Also a frail old spinster had been put in charge of her who was called by everyone in the house Aunty Ursel. She did not allow the child out of her sight and went everywhere with her carrying a piece of knitting.

As I was walking up and down with the two of them one October afternoon in the shade of the garden hedge, a tall lanky fellow dressed fashionably in a lace-trimmed jacket and feather hat came up the path towards us; and to my surprise it was my old adversary the young squire Junker Kurt. I noticed straight away that he was still paying court to my beautiful companion, also that this seemed to specially please the old spinster. It was 'Yes, Herr Baron' to everything he said or asked, while she laughed obsequiously with an affected voice and stuck her nose excessively in the air. But whenever I tried to get in a word she always talked down to me or called me simply 'Johannes' whereat Kurt screwed up his round eyes and acted as if he was looking down on me although I was half a head taller.

I looked at Katharina; she, though, took no heed of me but walked demurely beside the young nobleman, speaking to him and answering him politely. But her small red mouth was creased from time to time by a proud scornful smile, so that I thought, "Take comfort, Johannes. That young man's behaviour is causing the scales to tip in your favour!" Sulkily I stayed back and allowed the other three to go on ahead. But when they had entered the house and I still stood by the flower beds brooding on how, as in the past, I could provoke a good scuffle with von der Risch, Katharina came suddenly running back out, snatched an aster from the bed next to me and whispered, "Do you know what, Johannes? The bogey-man looks just like a young eagle, that's what Aunty Ursel just told me!" And she was off again before I was aware. But all my spite and anger was suddenly as if blown away. What did the Herr Baron matter to me now? I laughed merrily out loud in the clear golden light of day; for there had been with these high-spirited words once again that sweet twinkle of the eyes. But this time it had shone straight into my heart.

Soon afterwards Herr Gerhard sent for me to his room; he showed me once again the distant journey I must take to Amsterdam, handed me letters to his friends there and then spoke to me a long time as the friend of my dear departed father. For that very same evening I had to go to town from where a citizen would take me with him on his cart to Hamburg.

As the day was now drawing to its close I took my leave. In the room below, Katharina sat at an embroidery frame; she reminded me of Helen of Troy as I had seen her recently in a copperplate engraving, with her youthful neck just bending over her work. But she was not alone; facing her sat Aunty Ursel reading aloud from a French history book. As I drew near, she raised her nose towards me and said, "Well, Johannes, so you're here to say goodbye to me? You can also take your leave of this young lady!" Katharina had already stood up from her work, but just as she was holding out her hand to me, her brother Wulf with Kurt came rushing noisily into the room, and she only said, "Farewell, Johannes!" And so I left.

In the gatehouse I shook hands with old Dietrich who had my stick and knapsack ready for me. Then I walked off between the oaks towards the forest path. But as I did so I felt as if I could not just go, as if I was still owed a farewell, and kept stopping and looking behind me. I had also not taken the direct route through the pines but instinctively the much longer highway. But already the dusk was beginning to fall over the woods and I had to hurry before night should overtake me. "Farewell, Katharina, farewell!" I said softly and putting my best foot forward strode vigorously on.

Then, just at the place where the footpath merges with the road, my heart stood still, overcome with joy, for suddenly out of the darkness of the pines she was there. With glowing cheeks she came running towards me, leaping over the dried-up ditches so that her streaming silky brown hair escaped from its golden net; and so I caught her in my arms. With glowing eyes, still breathing hard, she looked at me. "I –I've run after you!" she stammered finally; and then, pressing a packet into my hand, she added quietly,"From me, Johannes! And you are not to despise it!" Suddenly her face grew sad, her tiny mouth seemed to be about to say something more, but a flood of tears broke from her eyes and, shaking her head miserably, she broke hastily away. I saw her dress disappearing in the darkness of the pines, then I could hear in the distance the branches snapping and then I was alone. It was so still, one could hear the leaves falling. When I unwrapped the packet there was the gold coin her godfather had given her and which she had often showed me; there was a note with it which I read by the light of the sunset. "So that you never get into difficulty!" was written on it. Then I raised my arms into the empty air; "Farewell, Katharina, farewell, farewell!" – I must have shouted it a hundred times to the silent woods; - and only as night fell did I reach the town.

Since then almost five years had passed. How would I find everything today?

And already I had reached the gatehouse and saw the old lime trees in the yard, behind whose light green foliage the two pointed gables of the manor house now lay hidden. But as I was about to go through the gateway, two dark grey bulldogs with spiked collars tore wildly from the yard towards me. They raised a fearful howling. One of them sprang at me baring its white teeth close to my face. Such a welcome I had never received here before. Then luckily for me a rough but familiar voice called down from the rooms above the gate. "Hello!" it cried, "Tartar, Turk!" The dogs drew back from me. I heard someone coming down the stairs and out of the door beneath the entrance stepped old Dietrich.

When I looked at him I saw just how long I had been abroad, for his hair had become snow-white and his eyes, formerly so bright and cheerful, now seemed dull and troubled as they looked at me. "Herr Johannes!" he said finally and held out both hands to me.

"God be with you, Dietrich!" I replied. "But since when do you keep bloodhounds in the courtyard which attack visitors like wolves?" "Well, Herr Johannes", said the old man, "they were brought here by Junker Wulf." "Is he home then?" The old man nodded.

"Well", I said," the dogs may well be necessary; there are still a lot of odd people hanging around after the war." "Oh, Herr Johannes!" And the old man still stood as if he didn't want to let me into the courtyard. "You've come at a bad time!"

I looked at him, but merely said," Of course, Dietrich; there's many a window where now the wolf looks out instead of the farmer. I've seen it myself; but peace is here now and Herr Gerhard will help, his hand is ever open."

And with that, I went to enter the courtyard although the dogs snarled at me again; but the old man stepped in front of me. "Herr Johannes", he said, "before you go on, listen to me! Your letter arrived by royal mail from Hamburg all right, but it didn't reach the person it was intended for."

"Dietrich!" I cried, "Dietrich!"

"Yes, yes, Herr Johannes! The good times are over here, for our dear Herr Gerhard is laid out there in the chapel and the candles have been lighted by his coffin. It'll be different around here now, but I'm a bond servant and I should be silent." I wanted to ask, "Is the young lady, is Katharina still in the house?" But the words would not come from my mouth.

Over there in a wing of the house at the back was a small chapel which I knew had not been used for a long time.

There was where I should find Herr Gerhard. I asked the old servant, "Is the chapel open?" and when he said it was I asked him to hold back the dogs; then I went across the courtyard, where I met nobody; only the song of a warbler came from the tops of the lime trees above.

The door to the chapel was only propped open and quietly and very uneasily I entered. There stood the open coffin and the red flames of the candles threw a flickering light on the noble countenance of the beloved man; the strangeness of death that lay upon it told me that he was now the citizen of another land. As I was about to kneel down to pray next to the body, a young pale face rose above the edge of the coffin opposite me, a face which looked at me almost alarmed from out of its black veils. But only for the space of a breath, and then the brown eyes looked up at me affectionately and it was almost like a cry of joy, "O, Johannes, is it really you? Oh, you've come too late!" And our two hands had joined in greeting over the coffin; for it was Katharina, and she had become so beautiful, that here in the face of death a hot pulse of life ran through me. Certainly the playful light of the eyes lay now shrunk in the depths; but from the black hood she was wearing the brown locks spilled out and the full mouth was all the redder in the pale face.

And almost confused as I looked at the dead man I said, "I really came in the hope of thanking him by painting his living portrait, of sitting with him for many hours listening to his gentle voice and all he had to say. Let me at least try to capture his features before they vanish for ever."

And when she nodded to me speechlessly, the tears streaming down her cheeks, I sat down on a stool and began to sketch the face of the dead man on one of the sheets of paper I had brought with me. But my hand trembled; and I don't know whether it was just from the majesty of death.

Meanwhile, from the courtyard outside I heard a voice which I recognised as that of Junker Wulf; immediately afterwards a dog howled as if it had been kicked or whipped; and then there was a laugh and a curse from another voice, which similarly seemed familiar to me.

When I looked at Katharina I saw her staring at the window with terrified eyes, but the voices and the steps passed by. Then she got up, came to my side and watched me reproducing her father's face. Not long afterwards a single step came back outside; at the same moment Katharina laid her hand on my shoulder and I felt her young body trembling all over.

Immediately the chapel door was flung open and I recognised Junker Wulf although his formerly pale face now seemed red and puffy. "Why are you cowering over the coffin all the time?" he called to his sister. "Junker von der Risch has been here to give us his condolences; you could at least have offered him a drink."

At that same moment he became aware of me and his small eyes bored into me. "Wulf", said Katharina as she stepped with me towards him, "it's Johannes."

The Junker did not feel the necessity of shaking my hand; he merely cast his eye over my violet doublet and said, "You're wearing fine feathers, we'll have to call you 'Sir' now!"

"Call me what you like!" I said as we walked out into the courtyard. "Although where I have just come from I was always treated with respect. You know well that your father's son can lay great claim on me."

He looked at me somewhat surprised, but only said, "Well, you can show what you've learned for my father's money; and payment for your work shall not be stinted."

I said that as far as payment was concerned, I had received abundantly in advance; but then the Junker responded that he would stick to what he had promised as befitted a nobleman, so I asked what in the way of work he wished to commission from me.

"As you know", he said and then paused, looking sharply at his sister," when the daughter of a noble family leaves her home, her portrait must remain behind in it."

At these words I felt that Katharina who was walking beside me grasped my cloak like someone about to faint; but I replied calmly, "The custom is familiar to me, but what exactly do you mean, Junker Wulf?"

"I mean", he said harshly, as if expecting to be contradicted, "that you should paint the portrait of the daughter of this house!"

A feeling almost of dismay ran through me; I don't know whether more because of the tone or the import of these words; but I thought now was scarcely the right time for such an undertaking.

Since Katharina was silent, although sending me a pleading glance with her eyes, I merely answered, "If your noble sister will allow, I hope not to discredit your father's patronage and my master's instruction. Just let me use again my chamber above the gatehouse with old Dietrich and what you wish shall be done."

The Junker was content with that and told his sister she might prepare me a light meal.

I wanted to ask one further question about beginning my work, but I kept silent again, for suddenly an intense feeling of delight at the commission I'd been given came over me, so that I was afraid it would burst out if I dared speak a word. So I didn't notice the two savage curs who were sunning themselves on the hot stones by the fountain. But as we got nearer they sprang up and came at me with bared teeth so that Katharina uttered a cry. The Junker, though, gave a shrill whistle at which they grovelled at his feet howling. "Damn me, but they're fine fellows", he laughed," a pigtail or fine cloth, it's all the same to them!"

I couldn't stop myself from saying "Junker Wulf, if I'm to be once more a guest in your father's house you might at least teach your animals better manners!"

His little eyes flashed at me and he tugged his pointed beard a couple of times. "That's just their welcome for you, Sir Johannes!" he said as he bent down to stroke the beasts. "Just so that everyone knows, a new regime has begun here now – for anyone who gets in my way I'll hunt down and send to the devil!"

With these last words which he almost spat out, he had drawn himself up; then he whistled his dogs and strode off over the courtyard towards the gate.

For a while my eyes watched him go, then I followed Katharina who beneath the shade of the lime trees was walking up the steps to the manor house, silent and with her head drooping. Just as silently we went together up the broad staircase into the upper floor where we entered the room of the late Herr Gerhard. Here everything was as I remembered it; the leather carpets with their gold flowers, the maps on the wall, the neat parchment volumes on the shelves, the beautiful landscape by Ruisdael the Elder above the desk - and in front of it the empty chair. I couldn't take my eyes from it; just like the body of the deceased down in the chapel, so this room too seemed to me without life and, although from the woods outside the Spring shone in through the window in all its newness, the room was filled with the silence of death.

I had almost forgotten Katharina during these moments. When I turned round, she was standing absolutely motionless in the middle of the room and I saw how her breast was heaving beneath the little hands which she had pressed to it. "There's nobody here any more, is there; nobody but my brother and his savage dogs?"

"Katharina!" I cried, "What's the matter? What's going on here in your father's house?"

"What's going on, Johannes?" and she gripped both my hands almost fiercely and her eyes flashed as if in anger and pain. "No, no; let my father rest first in his grave! But then – you shall paint my portrait, you'll stay here for a while – then, Johannes, help me; for the sake of him who is dead, help me!"

Quite overcome by pity and love at these words, I fell to my knees before this beautiful sweet creature and swore that all I was and all my strength were hers. Then a flood of tears fell softly from her eyes and we sat beside each other and talked long of our memories of the deceased.

When we again went down into the lower floor I asked after the old spinster. "Oh", said Katharina, "Aunty Ursel! Do you want to say hello to her? Yes, she's still here; she has her chamber down here for the stairs have long been too difficult for her to manage."

We stepped into a small room which overlooked the garden where the tulips were just breaking through the earth in the beds by the green hedgerows. Aunty Ursel sat in a tall armchair, looking like a shrinking heap in her black costume and crepe cap. She was playing a game resembling solitaire which, she told me later, the young Baron von der Risch – for that was his title now that his father had passed away – had brought back for her from Lubeck as an expensive present.

"Well", she said when Katharina had given her my name and as she carefully moved the ivory pegs, "you're back then, Johannes? No it won't come out. O c'est un jeu tres complique!"

Then she threw the pegs in a heap and looked at me. "Yes", she said, "you're magnificently dressed; but don't you know that you've entered a house of mourning?"

"I know now, Madam", I replied, "but when I came in through the gate I didn't know."

"Well", she said and nodded appeasingly, "it's not as though you're one of the servants."

On Katharina's pale face appeared a fleeting smile which absolved me from making any answer. Rather I praised the old lady for the charm of her living room; for the ivy from the tower which climbed up the wall outside had woven itself round the window and was waving its green tendrils before the panes. But Aunty Ursel said it was all very fine if only it weren't for the nightingales which were already beginning their nightly disturbance; she could in any case not sleep; and then it was too secluded here and it was impossible to keep an eye on the servants; and in the garden outside nothing ever happened except when the gardener's lad pruned the hedges or tidied up the boxwood borders.

And with that the visit came to an end; for Katharina reminded us that it was now more than time to fortify my way-worn body.

I was now lodged in my chamber above the gatehouse, much to the delight of old Dietrich; for in the evening after his work was done we sat on a chest and I listened to him talk as we had done when I was a boy. He would often then smoke a pipe of tobacco, a custom which had been started here by the soldiery, and come out with all kinds of stories of the hardships they had had to suffer from the foreign troops both here on the estate and in the village below. Once, though, when I had brought the conversation round to Mistress Katharina, he hadn't been able to finish his story, but had suddenly broken off and looked at me. " You know, Herr Johannes", he said, "it's a fearful shame that you weren't born with a coat of arms like von der Risch there!"

And since such talk made me blush violently, he clapped me on the shoulder with his hard hand, saying, "Well, now, Herr Johannes; that was a stupid thing for me to have said. We all have to remain where God Almighty placed us."

I'm not sure whether I agreed with him at that moment, but merely asked what sort of man von der Risch had become. The old man looked at me knowingly and puffed mightily on his short pipe as if the expensive weed grew in every hedgerow. "If you really want to know, Herr Johannes", he began, "he's one of those high-spirited Junkers who enjoy shooting the doorknobs off the houses in the market in Kiel; take my word for it he has the very best pistols! He's not so good at playing the violin, but since he is very fond of a merry tune he recently forced the Town Musician, who lives above the Holsten gate, at sword point to get up at midnight, not giving him time to put on his doublet and hose. Instead of the sun it was the moon in the sky, it was Epiphany-tide and was freezing hard; and he forced the musician, the Junker behind him with his sword, to play on the violin for him through the streets of the town in nothing but his shirt! Do you want to know more, Herr Johannes? The farmers at home rejoice when they are not blessed with girls; and yet --- but after his father's death he has money and our Junker, as you well know, has already consumed in advance all his inheritance." I really knew now all I needed to know; also old Dietrich had stopped speaking, saying as usual, "But I'm only a bond servant".

My clothes along with my painting gear had now arrived from the town, where I had left everything at the Golden Lion, so that I now went around as was fitting dressed in black. The daylight hours at first I turned to my own advantage. Upstairs in the manor house next to the late Herr Gerhard's chamber there was a large room, spacious and high, whose walls were almost completely hung with life-size pictures so that only near the fireplace was there room for two more. They were portraits of the ancestors of Herr Gerhard, mostly serious and confident men and women, with expressions which inspired trust. The two final ones were he himself in the prime of life and Katharina's mother who had died young. These latter two had been painted brilliantly in his own powerful style by our fellow countryman George Ovens from Eiderstedt. I now sought to capture with my brush the features of my noble patron, though only on a reduced scale and for my own pleasure; yet later it helped me to produce a larger portrait which is still the dearest companion of my old age here in my lonely room. The portrait of his daughter, though, lives inside me.

Often when I had laid aside my palette I stood for a long time before the beautiful paintings. I could see the likeness of Katharina's face in that of the two parents; the father's forehead, the mother's charm around the lips; but where was to be found the hard corners of the mouth and the small eyes of Junker Wulf? That must have come from much deeper in the past! Slowly I walked along the row of the older portraits, until far more than a hundred years back. And then I found a picture in a black worm-eaten frame, before which I had always stopped, even as a boy, as if it held me. It portrayed a noblewoman of about 40; the small grey eyes looked cold and piercing out of a hard face which was only half visible between the white neckerchief and the veiled cap. A slight shudder ran through me when looking at the already long departed soul and I said to myself, 'Here, this is the one! How strange are the ways of Nature! One characteristic which runs on secret and hidden in the blood of the generations; then long forgotten it suddenly pops up again to harm the living. I'll protect Katharina, not from the son of Herr Gerhard, but from this woman and her natural offspring.' And again I stood in front of the two most recent pictures which refreshed my soul. So I wiled away the time in the quiet room where around me only specks of sunshine played beneath the shadow of those departed.

I only saw Katharina at luncheon, sitting beside the old spinster and Junker Wulf, but, unless Aunty Ursel spoke in her high-pitched voice, it was always a silent depressing meal so that the food almost choked me. It wasn't the sadness at the recent death that was the cause, but it was something between brother and sister, as if the tablecloth had been cut in two between them. Katharina, after hardly touching her food, always went away soon, hardly even glancing at me. But the Junker when he was in the mood sought to detain me with drink, making sure I didn't overstep the bounds he had set, especially when defending myself against all kinds of taunts at my expense.

In the meanwhile, after the coffin had been closed several days, the burial of Herr Gerhard took place down in the village church where the family vault is and where now his bones rest with those of his forefathers and may the Lord grant them a happy resurrection!

But many people from the town and the surrounding estates had come to such a splendid funeral, although there were not many relatives, and even those were distant ones, since Junker Wulf was the last of the line and Herr Gerhard's wife had not been of local stock; and so it happened that in a very short time all had gone away again.

The Junker himself now urged that I should begin the work I had been commissioned to do and for which I had already chosen the place by a north-facing window in the picture gallery above. Aunty Ursel, who could not get up the stairs because of her gout, came to me and said it would be better in her sitting room or the chamber next door, in that way we would be able to converse; but I was only too pleased to dispense with such company and had a good painter's reason against it because of the light from the westerly sun there and all her talk was in vain. Rather on the very next morning I was busy covering the side windows in the room and setting up my easel, which I had prepared in the last few days with the help of Dietrich.

When I had just fixed the canvas to the blind frame, the door from Herr Gerhard's room opened and Katharina came in. –For what reason it was difficult to say; but I felt that this time she was almost startled to find herself face to face with me; her young face looked up at me in some sweet confusion from out of the black clothes she had continued to wear. "Katharina", I said, "you know I am to paint your portrait; are you happy for me to do it?" Then a veil fell across the brown pupils of her eyes and she said gently, "Why do you need to ask me that, Johannes?" These words sank into my heart like a surge of happiness. "No, No, Katharina! But you must tell me how I can serve you. Sit down so that we are not disturbed by some chance interruption and then speak! Or rather, I already know what it is. You don't need to tell me!"

But instead of sitting down, she came near to me. "Do you still remember, Johannes, how you once shot down the bogeyman with your bow? That's not necessary this time, although he's hovering over the nest again; for I am no nestling to be torn by his claws. But, Johannes – I have a blood relation - help me against him!" "You mean your brother, Katharina!" "I have no other. –He wants to give me in marriage to the man that I hate. While our father lay for so long on his sick bed I carried on the shameful struggle with him, and even by the coffin I had to force him to leave me in peace to mourn for my father; but I know that won't stop him."

I suddenly remembered Herr Gerhard's only sister, a canoness at Preetz, and wondered whether it might not be possible to approach her for protection and sanctuary. Katharina nodded. "Will you be my messenger, Johannes? I have already written to her but the reply fell into Wulf's hands and I never got to find out what it was thanks to his violent outburst of rage, which would have even come to the ears of the dying man if they had still been open to hear earthly sounds; but God in his mercy had already covered the beloved head with its final earthly slumber."

Katharina had now at my request sat down opposite me and I began to sketch the outlines of her features on the canvas. And so we came to discuss the matter calmly; and since, once the work had further advanced, I had to go to Hamburg to order a frame from the wood carver, we agreed that I would go via Preetz and carry out my mission. First, though, the work must be expedited urgently.

There is often a strange contradiction in the human heart. The Junker must have known that I would stand by his sister; despite that, whether it was his pride that caused him to despise me or whether he thought me sufficiently intimidated by his first warning, what I feared did not occur; Katharina and I were not disturbed by him on that first day nor on the other days. Once, indeed, he did enter and grumbled at Katharina about her mourning clothes, then slammed the door and we soon heard him in the courtyard whistling a riding song. Another time he had von der Risch with him. When Katharina gave a violent start, I asked her to stay in her place and painted calmly on. Since the day of the funeral when I had exchanged a distant greeting with him, Junker Kurt had not appeared at the house; now he came nearer and looked at the picture and said many nice things and also wondered why Katharina had so muffled herself and had not let her silky hair flow freely in curls down her back; as an English poet had so well expressed it, 'throwing light kisses backwards to the winds'. But Katharina who had kept silent till now, pointed to the portrait of Herr Gerhard and said, "You've obviously forgotten that that was my father!"

What Junker Kurt replied I no longer remember; as far as I was concerned he completely ignored my presence or treated me as a machine for painting a portrait on the canvas. He started to say this and that about the painting over my head; but when Katharina no longer bothered to reply, he quickly took his leave wishing the lady pleasant entertainment. But as he said it, I nevertheless saw a sharp glance like a knife point directed at me.

We didn't have to put up with any more disturbance after this and the work progressed with the season. Already the rye out in the woodland enclosures was in silver-grey bloom and down in the garden the roses were already in bud; we both, though, – I can write it down today – would gladly have let time stand still. Neither she nor I dared to touch on my errand of mercy to Preetz, not even with a single word. What we talked of I hardly know; only that I told her of my life abroad and how I had always thought of home; also that the gold coin she had given me had once when I was ill preserved me from distress as in her child's heart she had intended it should, and how later I had striven and worried until I had got the precious thing back from the pawnbrokers. Then she smiled happily and the lovely face bloomed ever sweeter from the dark ground of the picture; it seemed to me hardly my own work. Sometimes it seemed as if something passionate watched me in her eyes; yet if I tried to capture it, it drew shyly back and yet it flowed secretly through the brush onto the canvas, so that I was scarcely conscious that a ravishing picture arose, such as I never before or since have produced. –And finally it was determined that the time had come for me to start on my journey the next morning.

When Katharina handed me the letter to her Aunt, she was sitting once more opposite me. Today there was no playing with words; we spoke seriously and anxiously together. Yet as we did so I was still adding a few touches to the picture with my brush, occasionally glancing at the silent company on the walls, which was something I had rarely done when Katharina was present.

Then, during the painting, my gaze suddenly fell upon the portrait of that old woman which hung beside me and whose piercing grey eyes stared at me from out of the white veils. I shivered and almost fell off my chair. But Katharina's sweet voice sounded in my ear, "You've turned as white as chalk; what walked over your heart, Johannes?" I pointed with my brush at the picture. "Do you know her, Katharina? These eyes have been looking down on us every day."

"Her? I was scared of her as a child and even in daylight I often ran through here with my eyes shut. She's the wife of an earlier Gerhard and she lived here well over a hundred years ago." "She's not at all like your lovely mother", I replied, "this face was quite capable of saying no to any request." Katharina looked over at me in all seriousness. "She's rumoured to have cursed her only child", she said, "and the next morning the pale little girl was pulled out of a garden pond which was afterwards filled in. Behind the hedge near the woods it's supposed to have been." "I know, Katharina; today horse-tails and rushes still grow from the place."

"Did you know, too, Johannes, that a woman of our family is supposed to show herself whenever disaster threatens the house? She's seen here first gliding past the windows, then disappears in the garden pond outside."

Involuntarily my eyes turned again to the rigidity of the picture. "And why", I asked, "did she curse her child?" "Why?" – Katharina hesitated a moment and looked at me in some confusion but with all her charm. "I think she refused to marry her mother's cousin." "Was he such a loathsome man, then?" She threw me then almost a beseeching look and a deep blush covered her face. "I don't know", she said uneasily; and softly so that I could scarcely hear it, she added. "They say she loved someone else; someone not of her rank."

I had put down the brush, for she sat before me looking at the floor; if her little hand had not reached out from her lap and clasped her heart, she would have been herself like a lifeless picture. However lovely it was I broke the silence at last; "I can't paint like this; won't you look at me, Katharina?" And as she now raised her lashes from her brown eyes there was no more concealment; passionate and direct her gaze went straight to my heart. "Katharina!" I had jumped up. "Would that woman also have cursed you?" She took a deep breath. "Yes, me too, Johannes!" Then her head lay on my breast and we stood there clasped tightly together before the portrait of that ancestress who looked down on us cold and unfriendly.

But Katharina drew me gently away. "Let's not be defiant, my Johannes!", she said —At that moment I heard a noise on the staircase and it was as if something with three legs was labouring up the steps with great difficulty. When Katharina and I had consequently returned to our seats and I had picked up my brush and palette, the door opened and Aunty Ursel, whom we had long been expecting, came in coughing and hobbling on her stick. "I hear", she said, "that you're off to Hamburg to see about a frame; I must really see your work before you go!"

It is well-known by everyone that old spinsters have the sharpest senses where love affairs are concerned and very often bring trouble and misery to young people as a result.

No sooner had Aunty Ursel glanced at Katharina's picture, which she had never seen before, than she proudly screwed up her wrinkled face and asked me straight out, "Has this young lady been looking at you as she is doing there in the picture?"

I replied that it was in the nature of the art of fine painting to do more than just duplicate the face. But there must have been something unusual in our eyes or cheeks which attracted her attention, because her gaze went searchingly from the one to the other of us. "Is the work almost finished then?" she said in her highest voice. "Your eyes seem to have a sickly brightness, Katharina; these long sittings have not been good for you."

I replied that the portrait was nearly completed and there were just a few places on the gown that needed to be touched up. "Well then you don't need the young lady's presence any longer! Come, Katharina, your arm is better than this stupid stick here!"

And so I had to see the lovely jewel of my heart, just when I thought I had won it, taken away by the gaunt old woman. The brown eyes were scarcely able to send me one last silent farewell.

Next morning, on the Monday before Midsummer Day, I set out on my journey. On a farm horse which Dietrich had found for me I trotted out through the gatehouse early in the morning. As I was riding through the pine trees one of the Junker's hounds rushed out and went for the legs of my horse, even though it came from the Junker's own stable; but it seemed nevertheless suspicious of the person who sat in the saddle. For all that, both I and the horse escaped without injury and in the evening arrived in good time in Hamburg.

Next morning I got up and soon found a wood carver who had many picture frames ready prepared such that one only needed to fix them together and add the decorations in the corners. And so we quickly came to terms and the master carver promised to send it all after me well packed up.

Now there was a great deal to see in the famous city for a curious newcomer; like for example the silver beaker of the pirate Stortebeker in the Mariners Association, which is called the second symbol of the city and without having seen it, as it says in a book, no one can say he's been in Hamburg; and then also the wonder fish with the claws and wings of an eagle which had just been caught in the Elbe and which the citizens, as I afterwards heard, said was a portent of a sea victory against the Turkish pirates; yet although a proper traveller should not miss seeing such curiosities, my heart was all too heavy, both from anxiety and heart longing. And so after I had cashed my bill of exchange at a merchant's and found satisfactory lodgings for the night, I got on my horse again at noon next day and soon had left all the noises of the great city behind me.

That afternoon I arrived in Preetz, asked in the convent to see the reverend lady and was soon invited in. I recognized immediately in her stately person the sister of my dear late Herr Gerhard; except that, as often appears in unmarried women, the features of her face were more severe than those of her brother. After handing over Katharina's letter, I had to undergo a long and hard interrogation; but then she promised her support and sat at her desk to write, while the maid had to conduct me into another room where I was well entertained.

By the time I was able to ride away again it was already late in the afternoon, yet I reckoned to be back knocking on old Dietrich's door around midnight, despite the fact that my horse was already feeling the effects of the many miles we had come so far. The letter which the old lady had given me for Katharina I carried well wrapped up in a leather pouch under my doublet over my heart. So I rode onward as dusk increasingly fell, thinking only of her and again and again scaring my heart with loving thoughts.

It was a mild June night; from the dark fields rose the scent of the meadow flowers and the honeysuckle wafted its aroma from the dykes. In the air and among the leaves the tiny insects of the night hovered unseen or flew humming into the nostrils of my snorting horse; but up above in the blue black immensity of the firmament the constellation of Cygnus shone in the South East in all its untouched splendour.

When I had at last reached Herr Gerhard's lands I resolved to ride straight over to the village which lies to one side of the highroad behind the woods; for it occurred to me that the innkeeper Hans Ottsen might have a suitable handcart by which he could send the next morning a messenger into town to fetch the box from Hamburg for me; I only wanted to knock on his bedroom window to arrange this with him.

And so I rode along the edge of the woods, my eyes confused by the greenish glow-worms with their tantalising lights. And already there towered up before me, huge and sombre, the church within whose walls Herr Gerhard rested with his peers; I heard the hammer strike in the tower and the bell sounded midnight down into the village. 'But they're all asleep' I said to myself, 'the dead in the church or down here in the churchyard under the starry sky above, the living beneath the low roofs which lie there silent and dark before you'. So I rode on. Yet when I came to the pond from where one can see Hans Ottsens inn, I saw a hazy gleam of light from there shining on the path and the sound of fiddles and clarinets rang out towards me.

Since I wanted to speak with the landlord in any case, I rode there and quartered my horse in the stable. When after that I went into the barn, it was crowded with people, men and women, and there was a din and a wild milling around such as I had never in earlier years seen even at dances. The glow of the tallow candles which hung from a wooden crossbeam beneath the balcony lit up in the darkness many a bearded and weather-beaten face which one would not have liked to meet alone in the woods. But it was not just tramps and peasant-lads who seemed to enjoy the entertainment here; beside the musicians, who sat over on the other side on barrels, stood Junker von der Risch; he had his cloak over one arm, while on the other arm was draped some cheap trollop. But he did not seem to like the piece of music, for he snatched the fiddle from the fiddler's hands, threw a handful of coins on his barrel and demanded they played him the latest two-step. When the musicians hastened to obey him and the new tune rang out madly he shouted for space and swung into the closely packed throng; and the peasant lads stared goggle-eyed as the trollop lay in his arms like a dove in the claws of a vulture.

But I turned away and went into the parlour at the back in order to speak to the landlord. There sat Junker Wulf with a flagon of wine and he had old Ottsen beside him, tormenting him with all kinds of pranks; so for example he threatened to raise his rent and shook with laughter when the anxious man begged pitifully for mercy and leniency. When he caught sight of me, he did not stop until I sat down at his table thus making a third. He asked after my journey and whether I had enjoyed myself in Hamburg; but all I said was that I had just got back from there and the frame would shortly be arriving in the town, from where Hans Ottsen could easily fetch it in his handcart.

While I was organising this with the latter, Junker von der Risch came storming in and shouted to the landlord to bring him a cool drink. But Junker Wulf, whose tongue was already rolling around thickly in his mouth, grasped him by the arm and pulled him down on the empty chair. "Now, Kurt!" he cried. "haven't you had enough of those trollops yet! What would Katharina say about it? Come let's play cards together!" He pulled a pack of cards out from under his doublet. "Come on then! –10 and queen! – queen and knave!"

I stood and watched the game, which was so fashionable at the time, only wishing that the night would pass and the morning come. The drunkard however seemed on this occasion superior to the one who was sober; von der Risch played falsely one card after the other.

"Never mind, Kurt!" said Junker Wulf, grinning as he raked the coins he had won into a heap. "Lucky in love, unlucky at cards! Let the painter here tell you about your beautiful bride. He knows all about her; you'll get to know her from the artist's point of view." The other, as I well knew, did not know much about being lucky in love, for he struck the table with a curse and looked grimly at me.

"Well, fancy!, I do believe you're jealous, Kurt!" said Junker Wulf teasingly, as if he were tasting every word on his heavy tongue; " but don't worry, the frame's already finished for the picture; your friend the painter's just got back from Hamburg."

At these words I saw von der Risch prick up his ears like a bloodhound on the scent. "From Hamburg, today? Then he must have used Faust's cloak, for my groom saw him at noon today still in Preetz. He was in the convent visiting your cousin."

.

My hand moved involuntarily to my breast where I had put the pouch containing the letter for safe keeping, for the drunken eyes of Junker Wulf were upon me, and it was just as if my whole secret lay open before him. It was not long before the cards were slammed onto the table. "Oho!"

he shouted. "In the convent with my cousin! You've been doing two jobs, you rogue! Who sent you on the errand?"

"Not you, Junker Wulf!" I replied; "and that's all you need to know!" I reached for my sword but it was not there; I now remembered I had hung it on my saddle bow when I had put the horse into the stable.

And already the Junker was shouting again to his younger companion, "Tear open his doublet, Kurt! I bet you this pile of money you'll find a neat letter, one which you won't want delivered!" At the same moment I felt the hands of von der Risch get hold of me and a furious struggle began between us. I felt that I could no longer get the better of him so easily as when we were boys, but fortunately I then managed to grasp him by both wrists and he stood there in front of me as though fettered. Neither of us had said a word, but as we now looked each other directly in the eyes, each of us knew that he had his arch enemy before him.

Junker Wulf seemed to think the same; he struggled to get up out of his chair as if he wanted to come to the assistance of von der Risch, but must have drunk too much wine for he fell back again. Then he shouted as loud as his mumbling tongue could manage, "Hey Tartar! Turk! Where are you! Tartar, Turk!" And I knew now that the two savage hounds which I had seen hanging about by the bar in the hall would soon spring at my bare neck. I already heard them panting through the milling dancers, so with a jerk I threw my enemy suddenly to the ground, sprang out of the room through a side door which I slammed shut behind me and so reached the open.

And suddenly there lay around me again the peaceful night and the glow of the moon and stars. I did not dare to go first to the stable for my horse, but jumped swiftly over a wall and ran across the fields to the woods. As soon as I reached them I sought to keep to the direction of the manor house for the woods grow close beside the garden wall. The brightness of the stars and moon was here obscured by the leaves on the trees, but my eyes were soon used to the darkness and since I felt the pouch still safe beneath my doublet I groped my way briskly forward, for I intended to spend the rest of the night resting in my chamber and then to discuss with old Dietrich what was to be done, for I could obviously see that I could remain here no longer.

Now and again I stopped and listened, but I had managed to slam the lock on the door as I came out and so had given myself a head start. No sound of the dogs could be heard. But as I stepped from the shadows into a clearing lit by the moon, I heard a long way off the nightingales singing; and so I directed my steps in that direction for I well knew that around here they only had their nests in the hedges of the manor gardens. I soon recognised where I was and that I had not much further to go to the courtyard.

So I went towards the lovely sound which swelled ever clearer from the darkness before me. Then suddenly a different sound struck my ear and came suddenly nearer and froze my blood. I could doubt no longer, the dogs were breaking through the undergrowth; they were hard on my heels and I could already hear clearly behind me their hard breathing and their powerful bounds through the dry leaves on the forest floor. But God gave me his gracious protection, for I stumbled from the shadow of the trees against the garden wall and I swung myself over with the aid of the branch of an elder tree. The nightingales were still singing here in the garden and the beech hedges threw deep shadows. Once, before my journey abroad, on such a moonlit night I had walked here with Herr Gerhard. "Have a good look around you again, Johannes!" he had said then, "It might happen that when you return you will find that I am no longer here and then no welcome will be written on the gate; - but I wouldn't like you to forget this place."

This came to my mind at this moment and I had to laugh bitterly, for now I was here as a hunted man and I could already hear the hounds of Junker Wulf racing savagely outside by the garden wall. This was, as I had seen days before, not everywhere so high that the vicious animals could not get over it and there was no tree around in the garden, nothing but the thick hedges and over by the house the flower beds planted by the late Herr Gerhard. Then, just as the barking of the dogs rang out within the garden wall like a howl of triumph, I caught sight in my desperation of the old ivy bush which with its immensely strong stems climbed high up the tower. And so when the hounds came rushing from the hedges into the moonlit square I was already so high that they could not reach me as they leapt up; only my cloak which had slipped from my shoulder they managed to rip from me with their teeth.

So, clinging on and fearful that the branches higher up would not bear my weight for long, I looked around me to see if I could find some better support, but there was nothing to be seen but the dark ivy leaves around me. Then in my desperation I heard a window open above me and a voice called down to me --O God, if only I could hear it once again, before you call me from this vale of tears! -"Johannes", it called; softly but clearly I heard my name and I clambered higher on the ever more fragile branches while the sleeping birds flew up in alarm round me and the hounds sent up a howling from below. "Katharina! Is that really you, Katharina?" But already a trembling hand reached down to me and pulled me towards the open window; and I saw into her eyes which stared down full of terror.

"Come!" she said. "They'll tear you to pieces." Then I swung myself into her room. Yet when I was inside, the little hand left mine and Katharina sank onto a chair by the window and closed her eyes tight. The thick braids of her hair fell over her nightdress down to her lap; the moon which had risen above the garden hedge outside shone full into the room and showed me everything. I stood before her as if enchanted, so delightfully other and yet so completely my own did she seem. My eyes drank in the fullness of her beauty. Only when a sigh escaped her did I speak. "Katharina, dearest Katharina, are you dreaming?"

Then a painful smile appeared on her face. "I almost think I am, Johannes! Life is so hard and the dream so sweet!" But when the howling from the garden below rose up again, she started up in horror. "The hounds, Johannes!"

she cried. "What's the matter with the hounds?" "Katharina", I said, "if I am to help you, I believe it must be soon; for it would take much for me to come through the door into this house ever again." And I drew the letter from out of my pouch and told her how I had got into a dispute with the Junkers down in the inn.

She held the letter in the bright moonshine and read, then she looked me full and sincerely in the face and we discussed how we would meet the next day in the pine woods; and Katharina would find out beforehand on which day Junker Wulf had arranged to set off for the midsummer market in Kiel. "And now, Katharina" I said, "have you got anything that I could use for a weapon, an iron yardstick or something like that, so that I can defend myself against those two hounds below?" But she started up suddenly as if from a dream. "What are you saying, Johannes!" she cried and her hands which had rested till now in her lap, grasped mine. "No, don't go, don't go! There's only death down there and if you go, then there's death here too!"

Then I knelt down before her and laid my head on her youthful breast and we embraced in great anguish of mind and heart. "Oh, Katie", I said, "what trouble our poor love causes! Even if it weren't for your brother Wulf, I would still not be a nobleman and could not ask for your hand."

Very sweetly and solicitously she looked at me, but then she said almost teasingly, "Not a nobleman, Johannes? I rather thought you were! But – o no! Your father was only my father's friend and that means nothing in the eyes of the world!" "No, Katie, it doesn't and certainly not here", I replied and embraced her even more tightly, "but over there in Holland a skilled painter is the equal of any German nobleman. Even the highest in the land cross the threshold of Mynheeer van Dyck's palace in Amsterdam with the greatest respect. They wanted me to stay there, my master van der Helst and others! If I went back for another year or two, then we could get away from here; just stand firm against your dissolute Junker!"

Katharina's white hands stroked my hair; she hugged me and said softly, "Since I have let you into my bedroom, I shall have to be your wife." You have no idea what a firestorm these words caused in my heart, which was in any case already racing. A man haunted by three fearful demons, by anger and mortal fear and love, my head now lay in the lap of the girl I loved so much.

Then a shrill whistle sounded, the hounds below were suddenly silent and when the whistle came again I heard them run off as if wild and enraged. Steps were heard loudly in the yard. We listened so closely that we stopped breathing. But soon a door was first opened then shut and the bolt shot home. "That's Wulf", said Katharina softly, "he's shut the hounds in the stable." Soon we also heard the door in the hall below us open, the key turn and then steps in the lower corridor which died away where Junker Wulf had his bedroom. Then all was still.

At last it was safe, quite safe, but our chatter suddenly ceased. Katharina had leaned her head back; all I could hear was the beating of our two hearts. "Shall I go now,

Katharina?" I finally said. But her two arms drew me without a word to her lips and I didn't go.

There was no sound except the song of the nightingales from the depths of the garden and far off the rushing of the stream which flows behind the hedge.---

It was one of those nights when in songs the beautiful goddess Venus rises and goes around to confuse men's poor hearts. The light of the moon had died away in the sky, a sultry scent from the flowers wafted through the window, and above the woods the night sky lit up with silent flashes of lightning.—O Great Guardian, why were you not there for us?!

All I know is that suddenly from the yard the cocks cried shrilly and I held in my arms a pale weeping woman who would not leave me, ignoring the fact that the morning was dawning over the garden and casting its red glow into our room. But then when she did become aware of it, she drove me away as if possessed with deadly fear.

One more kiss, a hundred more; a hasty word to say that we would meet in the pine woods when the bell was rung for the servants midday meal; and then – I hardly knew how it happened –I was standing in the garden below in the cool morning air.

Once more, as I picked up my cloak which the dogs had ripped, I looked up and saw a pale little hand waving goodbye. But I was almost frightened out of my wits when looking back from the garden path my gaze happened to light on what seemed to be the lower windows near the tower; for I seemed to see a hand behind one of them too, but this one threatened me with raised finger and seemed colourless and bony like the hand of Death. But it was only for a second that I saw it. I thought at first of the story of the ancestor who was supposed to wander around, but then convinced myself it was only my disturbed imagination that had conjured up this apparition.

So, taking no further notice of it, I strode hastily through the gardens and soon saw that in my haste I had got into the reed marsh, and one foot sank in it over the ankle just as if something wanted to pull it down. 'Look out' I thought, 'it's the family ghost getting hold of you!' But I quickly pulled myself up and jumped over the wall into the woods.

The darkness of the dense trees suited my dreamy mood; here all round me still lay the blissful night and my senses allowed me to feel nothing else. Only after some time when I stepped out from the edge of the trees into the open fields did I become fully awake. A small group of deer stood not far off in the silver grey dew and above me the larks sang their morning song high in the sky. Then I shook off all idle dreams; at the same moment there rose in my mind, like desperation, the question, 'What now, Johannes? You've won the love of a dear heart; now you must know that your life is worth nothing compared to hers!'

So thinking it over, it seemed to me best if Katharina found safe refuge in the convent, that I then went back to

Holland, made sure of the help of friends there and came back as soon as possible to fetch her. Perhaps she might even soften the heart of her elderly cousin but if the worst came to the worst, it must happen without that!

Already I saw us on a cheerful barge sailing across the Zuider Zee, heard the chimes from the tower of the Rathaus in Amsterdam and at the harbour saw my friends push forward from the crowds to greet me and my beautiful wife with shouts of welcome and accompany us in triumph to our small but beloved home. My heart was full of courage and hope and I strode out more quickly and more vigorously as if in that way I could achieve happiness the sooner.

Alas! It didn't happen like that!

Absorbed in my thoughts I had gradually reached the village and I entered Hans Ottsen's inn from which I had so precipitately had to flee in the night. "Hey, Master Johannes" called the old man from the barn, "What did you do to upset our vindictive Junkers last night? I was just out there at the bar but when I came back in again they were cursing you ferociously and the hounds too were raging at the door, which you'd slammed shut behind you."

Since I gathered from such words that the old man had not really understood what had gone on I merely replied, "You know, even as boys von der Risch and I sometimes used to ruffle each others feathers, so yesterday there had to be a repeat performance."

"I know, I know!" said the old man, "but the Junker's now the master of his father's manor; you should take care, Herr Johannes, with such gentlemen you have to go warily." I had no reason to contradict him but ordered bread and drink for breakfast and then went into the stable where I fetched my sword and also got a pencil and my sketch book from my knapsack.

But there was still a very long time before the bell would ring for midday, so I asked Hans Ottsen to get his lad to take my horse to the manor; and when he had promised to do this I strode off into the woods again. But this time I went to the spot on the burial mounds from where the two gables of the manor house could be seen above the garden hedges, and which I had chosen for the background for Katharina's portrait. My thought was that when in the hoped for future she would be living abroad and would no longer set foot in her home, she would at least not be deprived completely of the sight of it. So I took out my pencil and began to sketch, careful to capture every little corner on which her eye might once have lighted. In Amsterdam it would then be finished, coloured and hung so that it would greet her straight away when I should take her into our room there.

After a couple of hours the sketch was finished. I added a twittering bird flying over it as if in greeting; then I went to find the clearing where we had arranged to meet and stretched out on the edge of it in the shade of a thick beech, longing for the time to pass.

I must nevertheless have quickly nodded off, for I was woken by a distant bell ringing and realised that it was the midday bell from the manor. The sun was already burning hotly down and diffusing the scent of the raspberries with which the clearing was covered. It reminded me how Katharina and I on our walks through the woods had gathered sweet refreshment here; and now my imagination began to have full play; now I saw her tender child's face over there among the bushes and now she stood before me looking at me with her lovely woman's eyes as I had recently seen her, as indeed I would now in the next few moments hold her in the flesh against my beating heart.

Then suddenly a feeling of fear came over me. Where was she then? It was already a long time since the bell had rung. I jumped up, walked around, stood and peered intently in every direction through the trees. Fear crept into my heart, but Katharina did not come, no footstep rustled in the undergrowth; only the summer wind sighed on and off in the tree tops.

Full of misgivings I at last went away and took a detour towards the manor house. When I was not far from the gatehouse and was coming through the oak trees, Dietrich met me. "Herr Johannes", he said and came hastily up to me, "you were in Hans Ottsen's inn last night; his lad brought me your horse back; what were you doing with our Junker?"

"Why do you ask, Dietrich?" "Why, Herr Johannes? Because I want to prevent mischief between you". "What does that mean, Dietrich?" I asked again; but I felt anxious as if the words stuck in my throat. "You well know yourself, Herr Johannes!" replied the old man. "I only had wind of it, it must have been about an hour ago. I was going to call the lad who's trimming the hedges in the garden. When I came by the tower below where our young lady has her room I saw Aunty Ursel with our Junker standing close together there. He had his arms crossed and did not say a word, but the old woman was talking all the more for that and was complaining strongly with her high-pitched voice, pointing now down on the ground and now up in the ivy which grows up the tower. Now I didn't understand any of this, Herr Johannes, but then, and note this well, she held out something in her bony hand, as if accusing, for the Junker to see; and when I looked closer it was a scrap of grey material, just like you have on your cloak there."

"Go on, Dietrich!" I said, for the old man was looking closely at my torn cloak which was over my arm. "There's not much else to say", he replied, "for the Junker turned suddenly to me and asked where you were to be found. You can believe me, if he had really been a wolf his eyes could not have flashed more bloodthirstily." Then I asked, "Is the Junker in the house, Dietrich?" "In the house? I think so, but what are you thinking of, Herr Johannes?" "I'm thinking, Dietrich, that I have to speak with him at once." But Dietrich grasped me with both hands. "Don't go, Johannes", he said urgently; "tell me at least what has happened; I've always been able to give you good advice before!" "Later, Dietrich, later!" I replied and with these words I tore my hands from his. The old man shook his head, "Later, Johannes", he said; "only God can tell!"

But I now strode across the courtyard towards the house. The Junker was in his room, said a maid who I asked in the hall. I had only once before entered this room which lay on the ground floor. Instead of the books and maps which had been there in his late father's time there were now many weapons of all kinds hanging on the walls, flintlocks and muzzle-loaders, also all kinds of hunting equipment; apart from that the room was unadorned and showed by that alone that nobody ever spent any length of time here and never in full possession of his senses.

I almost shrank back at the threshold, when I opened the door at the Junker's "Come in", for as he turned from the window towards me, I saw a horse pistol in his hand and he was fidgeting with the trigger. He looked at me as if I were mad. "Well" he said up-tight; "it's Master Johannes, if not his ghost!"

"You no doubt thought, Junker Wulf", I replied as I stepped closer to him, "that I would have gone anywhere other than here into your room!"

"That's what I did think, Master Johannes! How clever of you to guess! Yet nevertheless you've done me a favour in coming; I've sent people out to look for you!"

His voice trembled slightly like a lurking beast of prey about to spring, so that quite involuntarily my hand reached for my sword. Nevertheless I said, "Hear me out and allow me a word in peace, Herr Junker!"

But he interrupted "You will do me the favour of hearing me out first, Master Johannes!" and his words which were slow at first became gradually like a roar,-"a couple of hours ago when I woke with a heavy head, I remembered and like a fool regretted that when I was drunk I had set the savage hounds on your heels; but since Aunty Ursel showed me the scraps of cloth which they tore from your fine feathers – by God my only regret now is that the beasts failed to finish their work!"

Once more I strove to have my say and since the Junker was silent I thought that he would listen. "Junker Wulf", I said, "it is quite true that I am not a nobleman, but nor am I a man of no importance in my art and I hope one day to emulate those still greater; so I ask you politely, give me your sister Katharina's hand in marriage...."

My words dried up in my mouth. From his pale face the eyes of the ancient picture stared out at me; a shrill laugh rang in my ears, a shot----then I collapsed and only heard my sword, which involuntarily I had almost drawn, fall with a clatter on the floor from my hand.

*

It was many weeks later that I sat in the already much weaker sunshine on a bench outside the last house in the village, looking with dull eyes at the woods on whose farther edge the manor house lay. My eyes in their madness constantly sought anew the point where I imagined Katharina's chamber looked down on the already autumnal tree tops; for of her I had no news.

They had brought me with my wound to this house which was inhabited by the Junker's forest-keeper; and apart from this man and his wife and a surgeon unknown to me, nobody had come to see me during my long recuperation. Whence I had received the shot in the chest nobody had asked me; and it could never enter my head to invoke the Duke's justice against Herr Gerhard's son and Katharina's brother. He might well feel confident about that, but it was still more credible that he defied all these things.

Only once had my good Dietrich called to see me. Charged with this task by the Junker he had brought me two rolls of Hungarian ducats as payment for Katharina's portrait and I had taken the money thinking it was part of her inheritance, of which as my wife she would later not receive very much. But I did not succeed in having a confidential conversation with Dietrich, which I so longed to do, thanks to the yellow fox face of my host who looked into my room every moment; yet this much was made known to me, that the Junker had not travelled to Kiel and Katharina had not been seen since in the courtyard nor the garden. I hardly managed to ask the old man to give my greetings to the young lady if he should happen to meet her and tell her that I intended soon to travel to Holland but as soon as possible to return, all of which he promised to carry out in good faith.

After that, though, the greatest impatience seized me, so that against the advice of the surgeon and before the last leaves fell from the trees, I set off on my journey, arriving safe and sound after a short interval in the Dutch capital where I was received everywhere with great affection by my friends. I took it as a sign of good fortune that two pictures which I had left behind there had both been sold for considerable amounts through the good offices of my dear master van der Helst. Yes, and if that was not enough, a merchant, who had been well-disposed to me before, now told me he had been waiting for me to paint his portrait for his daughter who had married and moved to the Haag, and promised immediately to pay me a good price for it. So I thought that when I had completed that I would have in my hands enough precious metal in order to install Katharina in a well-appointed home without any further help.

And so I set to work with all speed, since my friendly patron was of the same mind, so that I soon saw the day of my departure happily coming nearer and nearer, without giving a thought to what dire difficulties I would have to contend with there.

But the human eye does not see the darkness which lies before it. So when the portrait was finished and I had received rich praise as well as gold for it, I was unable to leave. During the work I had taken no account of my weakness and my wound, which had not properly healed, now laid me low again. It was just when the waffle stalls had been set up on all the city squares for the Christmas festival that it happened and held me in its grip longer than the first time. Of course there was no lack of the best medical treatment and the affectionate care of friends, but day after day passed with me so anxious, for no news could come from her and no news reach her.

Finally after a hard winter when once again green waves rolled across the Zuider Zee, my friends accompanied me to the harbour; but instead of going on board in a happy frame of mind I was now filled with the deepest anxiety. Yet the journey went smoothly and took little time. From Hamburg I travelled with the Royal Mail service; then like almost a year before I walked on foot through the woods where the first shoots were scarcely turning green. The finches and the buntings, though, were already trying out their spring song, but what did they care about me today! I did not go direct to Herr Gerhard's estate, but although my heart was beating fast, I turned aside and walked along the edge of the woods to the village. I soon stood in Hans Ottsen's Inn and in front of the man himself.

The old man looked at me strangely, then said I seemed lively enough, "Only", he added, "you don't want to go playing around with guns again; they make worse marks than a paint brush." I was happy to leave him with that opinion which I soon noticed was widespread here and asked him first about old Dietrich. Then I had to hear that before the first snow of winter, as often happens with strong men, he had suffered a sudden but painless death. "He was pleased", said Hans Ottsen, "to go to his old master up above; and it was better for him like that." "Amen to that!" I said" dear old Dietrich!"

But in the meantime my heart was longing only, and ever more fearfully, for news of Katharina and my anxious tongue approached the matter in a roundabout way. I asked uneasily, "And what is the news of your neighbour, von der Risch?" "Oho", laughed the old man, "he's taken a wife and she'll soon set him to rights." Just for the first moment I was dismayed but then I quickly said to myself that he would not speak of Katharina like that; and when he gave her name, she turned out to be an elderly but very rich spinster from the neighbourhood. And so I probed further and asked how things were over there in Herr Gerhard's house and how the young lady and the Junker were getting on together in the same house.

Then the old man once again threw me a strange look. "You seem to think old towers and walls can talk!" he said. "Well, what are people saying?" I cried, but my heart was as heavy as lead.

"Well now, Herr Johannes", and the old man looked me confidently in the eye, "you'll know best where the young lady's got to! You were here in the Autumn and that wasn't the last time; I'm only surprised that you've come back, for Junker Wulf, I think, won't have been best pleased at the bad business."

I looked at the old man as if it was I who had taken leave of his senses; but then a thought suddenly hit me. "You miserable wretch!" I shouted, "you don't really believe that Katharina has become my wife?"

"Let me go!" replied the old man, for I was shaking him by the shoulders. "What business is it of mine? That's what people are saying! At all events the young lady has not been seen in the manor since New Year." I swore to him that at that time I had lain ill in Holland; I knew nothing about it. I don't know whether he believed me, but he told me that an unknown clergyman had come at about that time to the manor house at night and in great secrecy. Aunty Ursel had forced the servants to go to their rooms early; but one of the maids who had been eavesdropping through a crack in the door was supposed to have seen me walking across the hall to the stairs; then later they had clearly heard a wagon drive through the gateway and since that night only Aunty Ursel and the Junker had been in residence.

What I undertook from now on (and always in vain) to find Katharina or even just a trace of her can not here be recorded. In the village there was only the silly tittle-tattle which Hans Ottsen had given me a taste of; so I made my way to the convent where Herr Gerhard's sister was, but the lady would not allow me to see her; in any case I was told that no young lady had been seen with her. Then I travelled back again and so demeaned myself as to go to the house of von der Risch and appear before my old antagonist as a petitioner. He said scornfully that it may well have been the bogeyman who had taken the little bird, he had not taken any interest and he no longer had any influence with those from Herr Gerhard's manor.

Junker Wulf, who must have heard something of this, sent word to the inn that I should be in no doubt that he would set the dogs on me again if I thought to go there to see him. Then I went into the woods and lay in wait for him by the path like a footpad. Swords were drawn; we fought until I cut him on the hand and his sword flew in the bushes. But he just looked at me with his evil eyes and said not a word. In the end I came to Hamburg for a long stay, and from there I intended to carry on my searches without hindrance but with more circumspection.

But it was all in vain.

But now I will let my pen rest for the time being. Before me lies your letter, my dear Josias; I am to stand godfather to your little daughter, my great-niece. On my journey I will travel past the woods which lie behind Herr Gerhard's house. But all that belongs in the past.

*

Here ends the first part of the manuscript. Let's hope the writer enjoyed the baptism and refreshed his spirits amidst his friends.

My eyes rested on the old picture facing me; I had no doubt the handsome serious man was Herr Gerhard. But who was that dead child whom Master Johannes had portrayed so gently lying in his arms? Pondering this, I took up the second and last part of the manuscript, the handwriting of which seemed much less confident. It ran as follows;

> Just as vanish smoke and dust,
> So every human creature must.

The stone on which these words were carved was set above the mantel of the door of an old house. Whenever I went past it I had to turn to look at it, and on my lonely rambles the same saying often went along with me. When last autumn they demolished the old house I purchased this stone from the debris and today it is similarly embedded above the door of my house where it reminds me as well as many of those who pass by of the vanity of all things earthly. But to me it should also be a warning to get on with the recording of my life before the hand on my clock comes to a stop. So you, my dear nephew, who will soon now be my heir, may also along with my earthly possessions inherit my earthly sorrows, which in my life time I have not wanted to trust to anyone, even you, despite all affection.

Item; In the year 1666 I came for the first time to this town by the North Sea; it was thanks to a commission from a wealthy brandy distiller's widow to paint The Raising of Lazarus, a painting which she intended to give as an adornment to the church here in respectful and affectionate remembrance of her dear departed and which today can still be seen above the font with the four apostles. At the same time the mayor, Herr Titus Axen, who previously had been a canon in Hamburg and was known to me from there, wished to have his portrait painted by me, so that I had work to keep me here for a long time. I had my lodgings with my only brother who was older than me and who for a long time had held the office of Town Clerk; the house in which he lived as a bachelor, was tall and spacious, and was the same house with the two lime trees at the corner of the market place and Kramerstrasse which I inherited on the death of my brother and where as an old man I still live humbly yet eagerly awaiting reunion with my past love.

I had set up my studio in the large parlour of the widow's house; there was good overhead light there to work by and everything was arranged and ordered as I would wish. Just that the good woman herself was present far too much, for every few moments she would come trotting over to me from her bar with her pewter measuring vessels in her hand, would crowd round my maulstick with her plump body and have a good nose round my picture. One morning when I had just begun to paint the head of Lazarus she even demanded with many unnecessary words that the newly resurrected man should exhibit the features of her dear departed husband, despite the fact that I had never seen this gentleman and in fact had heard from my brother that he, like most distillers, carried round in his face the symbol of his profession in the shape of a purple nose. As you may imagine I had to put a tight rein on this importunate woman. So when new customers called to her from the outside vestibule and banged on the bar with their mugs and she finally had to leave me, my hand with the brush sank into my lap and I suddenly remembered the day when I had sketched with my pencil the features of a quite different recently departed man and remembered who had then stood so quietly beside me in the little chapel. And so thinking of the past I picked up my brush again; but when it had moved back and forth for a while I had to confess to my own amazement that I had given the face of Lazarus Herr Gerhard's features. From his shroud the eyes of the dead man looked up at me as if in silent reproach, and I thought; that's how he will confront you in Eternity!

I could not paint any more that day but went away and crept up to my room above the front door where I sat by the window and looked down through the gap between the lime trees at the market place. But there was a large milling crowd there, and everywhere as far as the weigh house and even as far as the church was full of wagons and people, for it was a Thursday and still the time when non-residents could trade with each other, so that the town constable along with the market watchman sat at their ease in the porch of the neighbouring house, since there were no fines to be imposed for the time being. The women from Osterfeld with their red jackets, the girls from the islands with their kerchiefs and fine silver jewellery, and amongst them the grain wagons piled high with the farmers on top in their yellow lederhosen –all this might well provide a picture for the eye of a painter just as when I had been learning in Holland; but the heaviness of my spirits dulled this brightly coloured scene for me. Yet it was not remorse, such as I had experienced earlier, but a grievous yearning that came over me more and more strongly; it lacerated me with its savage claws and yet at the same time looked lovingly at me. Down there it was bright day at noon on the swarming market place; but here before my eyes silver moonlight gleamed; like shadows two tiled gables rose, a window rattled and as if in dreams the nightingales sang softly and far off. O my God and Saviour, who is all compassion. Where were you at this hour, where was my soul to find it?--

Then I heard outside beneath my window a harsh voice speaking my name and when I looked out I caught sight of a tall gaunt man in the usual dress of a preacher, although his haughty dark expression with his black hair and the deep cleft above his nose would have better suited a soldier. He was just pointing out our house door with his walking stick to another stocky man of peasant appearance, but like him in black woollen hose and buckled shoes, while he himself strode away through the market throng.

Immediately afterwards I heard the doorbell ring, went down and invited the stranger into the living room where, perched on the chair I had urged him to sit on, he observed me minutely and carefully.

He turned out to be the sexton from the village north of the town and I soon learned that they needed a painter since they wished to endow the church with the portrait of the pastor. I made a few enquiries about what he had done for the parish to deserve such an honour since, judging by his age, he could not have been in his post very long. The sexton said that the pastor had certainly once instituted legal proceedings against the parish on account of a piece of arable land but otherwise he didn't know that anything special had occurred. However the portraits of his three predecessors already hung in the church, and since they had heard that I knew well how to do these things, it seemed a good opportunity to add the fourth pastor to the others. The latter, though, was not very keen on it.

I listened to all that and since I wanted to have a break for a time from my Lazarus and I could not start the portrait of Titus Axen because he had become chronically ill, I began to look at the commission more closely.

What they were offering me as a fee for such work was certainly very little, so that I thought at first they took me for some cheap-skate painter, one of the sort who go along in the baggage train in time of war to paint the soldiers for the girls they had left at home. But suddenly I took it into my head to spend my mornings for a time walking out over the heath in the golden autumn sunshine to the village which lay only an hour's walk from our town. I therefore agreed to the commission with the sole condition that the painting should be done out there in the village since there was no suitable opportunity here in my brother's house.

The sexton seemed quite content with that, saying that it had all been already provided for; the pastor had himself stipulated certain things; firstly the schoolroom at the sexton's house had been chosen for it; this was the second house in the village and was next to the pastor's, only separated from it at the back by the pastor's field, so that the pastor too could easily walk across from there. The children, who in any case learned nothing during the summer, would then be sent home.

So we shook hands on it and since the sexton had carefully brought the measurements for the picture, all the painting gear I needed could be taken over by the pastor's wagon.

When my brother came home late in the afternoon –for the town council had a lot of trouble at that time over the corpse of a knacker, which respectable people were refusing to bury – he said that I was getting a head to paint such as was not often to be seen in a dog collar and I should take plenty of black and reddish-brown paint; he told me too that the pastor had come to this area as a field chaplain with the Brandenburg troops, when he was said to have behaved even more wildly than the officers, but yet now was a fierce champion of The Lord who could hold his parishioners spellbound in a masterly way. My brother added that when he took up his priestly office in our district it was due to the intercession of some nobleman from over there in Holstein; the archdeacon had let fall a word to that effect at the audit of the monastery. More than that my brother had not learned.

So the morning sunshine next day saw me walking vigorously across the heath and I was only sorry that this had already lost its red mantle and its fragrant scent and so had lost all its summer finery. For there were no green trees to be seen far and wide, only the pointed tower of the village church which I was making for – which as I could already see was completely built of granite blocks-- rose higher and higher in front of me in the dark blue October sky. Between the black thatched roofs which lay at its foot were only low bushes and stunted trees for the northwest wind which blows straight from the sea demands free passage.

When I reached the village and had found my way directly to the sexton's, the whole school immediately rushed out to meet me with merry cries. The sexton bade me welcome at his front door. "You see how pleased they are to get out of their lessons!" he said. "One of the little rascals saw you coming through the window."

In the pastor, who entered the house immediately afterwards, I recognised the same man I had already seen days before. But today his gloomy appearance was as if lit up, for there was a pale handsome lad with him who he was leading by the hand; the child must have been about four years old and looked almost minute against the man's tall gaunt figure.

Since I wished to see the portraits of the former pastors, we went together into the church, which is built at such a height that in one direction one can see down over the heath and the marshes, and to the west down to the seashore which is not far distant. It must have been a flood tide for the sand flats were inundated and the sea was a shining silver. When I remarked how the highpoints of the mainland stretched out above the flooded sandbanks towards those of the island on the other side, the sexton pointed to the stretch of water which lies between. "There", he said, "once stood my parent's house; but in the year 1634 in the great flood it, like hundreds of others, disappeared in the raging waters; on one half of the roof I was thrown up onto the beach, on the other half my father and brother were swallowed up into eternity."

I thought to myself, 'then the church stands in the right spot; even without the pastor, God's word will be preached here.'

The boy, whom the pastor had taken into his arms, clasped both arms tightly round his neck and pressed his tender cheek against the man's darkly bearded face, as if he would find like this protection from the frightening infinity which lay spread out before our eyes.

When we went into the nave of the church I examined the old portraits and also saw a head among them which was perhaps worthy of a good painter, yet all were really just examples of cheap poor quality painting and so the pupil of van der Helst would be in very strange company here.

As I, in my vanity, was thinking this, the harsh voice of the pastor spoke beside me; "It is not my belief that the appearance of the body should last when the breath of God has left it, but I did not wish to oppose the wish of the parish; only, master, make it brief; I have better uses for my time."

After I had promised this gloomy man, in whose expression I nevertheless found appreciation for my art, my best efforts, I asked after a carving of the Virgin Mary which had been much praised by my brother.

An almost scornful smile crossed the pastor's face. "You're too late" he said, "it fell to pieces when I had it removed from the church." I looked at him almost shocked. "Why? Couldn't you bear to have the Saviour's mother in your church?" "The features of the Saviour's mother have not been passed down to us", he replied. "But do you then, in all piety, grudge Art for trying?" I asked.

He looked down at me grimly for a while, for, although I don't consider myself a small person, he towered above me by a good half a head. Then he spoke vehemently;

159

"Didn't the king summon the Dutch papists to come to the remnants of the island over there in order to defy God's punishment by working on the dykes? Have not the church authorities in the town recently had two of the saints carved in their pews? Watch and pray! For even here Satan prowls from house to house! These pictures of the Virgin are nothing but encouragers of sensuality and papism; art has always been hand in glove with the world!"

A dark fire gleamed in his eyes but his hand lay caressingly on the head of the pale lad who snuggled against his knee.

Because of that, I didn't bother to contradict the pastor's words; but suggested that we go back into the sexton's where I then began to try out my noble art on its opponent.

And so almost every morning I walked out across the heath to the village, where I always found the pastor waiting for me. Not much was said between us, but the portrait made all the faster progress as a result. Usually the sexton sat beside us and carved all kinds of objects out of oak, a craft much practised around here. I was given the little box he was working on then and put the first pages of this manuscript in it years ago, just as, God willing, these final ones will be kept in it too.

I was not invited into the pastor's house and never set foot in it. The boy was always with him at the sexton's; he stood at his knee or he played with pebbles in the corner of the room. When I once asked him what his name was, he answered "Johannes!" "Johannes?" I replied, "that's my name too!" He looked at me wide-eyed but said nothing further.

Why did those eyes move my very soul? Once indeed I caught the dark look of the pastor in them, when I rested my brush idly on the canvas. There was something in this child's face that could not have come from his own short life; but it was not a happy feature. That's how a child looks, I thought, who is brought up by a mother who is full of sorrow. I would have often liked to hold out my arms to him, but I was shy of the harsh man who seemed to protect him like a jewel. I often thought to myself; 'what sort of a woman could be the mother of this boy?'

I once asked the sexton's old maid about the pastor's wife, but she only told me briefly "Nobody really knows her; she hardly ever goes into the parishioners' houses, even when there's a christening or wedding." The pastor himself never spoke of her. From the sexton's garden, which peters out in a thick group of elder bushes, I saw her once walking slowly across the pastor's field to her house, but she had her back turned towards me so that I could only make out her slim youthful figure and in addition to that some curly locks in a style more normally worn by people of a higher class and which the wind wafted from her temples. The picture of her gloomy husband appeared to my mind and it seemed to me these two did not suit each other.

On the days when I was not out in the village, I had picked up again my work on Lazarus so that after some time these two pictures were nearly finished together.

So one evening after my day's work was done I sat with my brother in our living room. On the table by the stove the candle had almost burned down and the Dutch chiming clock had already struck eleven; we still sat by the window and had forgotten the present, for we were remembering the short time we had lived together in our parent's house; we also thought of our little sister who had died at the birth of her first child and for a long time now lay with her father and mother awaiting the joyful resurrection. We had not closed the shutters, for we enjoyed looking out beyond the darkness outside, which lay upon the earthly dwellings of the town, into the starlight of the eternal sky.

In the end we both fell silent within ourselves and as if on a dark stream my thoughts drifted towards her who was the source of all my rest and unrest. –Then it was as if a star from unseen heights suddenly fell like a stone in my heart; the eyes of that pale handsome boy, they were her eyes! Why had I not sensed it?—But what if it was her, what if I had already seen her! – what terrible thoughts stormed through my mind!

Meanwhile my brother placed one hand on my shoulder, pointing with the other out to the dark market place from where bright lights now came towards us swaying from side to side. "Look!" he said. "It's a good job we stopped up the cracks in the pavement with sand and heather! They're coming from the bell founders wedding; but by their lanterns you can see them stumbling back and forth."

My brother was right. The dancing lanterns bore clear witness to the excellence of the wedding feast. They came so near us that the deep colours in two painted window panes which my brother had recently purchased from a master glazier glowed as if with fire. But when the company right by our house turned into Kramerstrasse, all talking loudly, I heard one among them say, "Yes, you're right, the Devil's spoiled it for us! I'd been looking forward all my life to hearing a real witch singing in the flames!"

The lights and the merry people went on their way and, outside, the town lay quiet and dark again. "Alas!" said my brother, "that spoils what would otherwise have cheered me."

Only then did I remember that next morning the town was in for a gruesome spectacle. In fact the young woman who was to have been burned to ashes on account of her confessed league with Satan, had been found by the gaoler that very morning dead in her cell; but justice must still be meticulously done to the dead body.

For many people that was now like a dish served cold. Even the bookseller's widow, Frau Liebernickel, who keeps the green bookstall below the tower of the church, complained to me most vehemently at midday when I went in for a newspaper, that the song which she had had prepared and printed in advance about it, would now be no more suitable than a punch in the eye. But I, and with me my beloved brother, had our own thoughts on witchcraft and was glad that our Lord God – for it must have been

Him – had seen fit to take the poor young creature mercifully into his bosom.

My brother who was soft hearted began now to complain about the duties of his office for he had to read the sentence of the court from the steps of the Town Hall, as soon as the knacker had driven up before it with the corpse, and afterwards he had to assist with the carrying out of the sentence. "It cuts me to the quick", he said, "to hear the gruesome howling of the mob when they follow the cart down the street; for the schools will let out their pupils and the guild masters their apprentices. If I were free as a bird like you", he added, "I would get out to the village and carry on with the painting of the portrait of the dark pastor!"

Now in fact it had been arranged that I would not go out there again till the following day; but my brother tried to persuade me, not knowing how he was fanning the impatience in my heart. And so it happened that everything was fulfilled which I will faithfully set down in these pages.

Next morning, when the weathercock on the church opposite my bedroom window had scarcely blinked in the red early morning light, I had already sprung from my bed; and soon I was striding over the market place where the bakers, expecting many customers, had already opened their bread stalls. Also I saw by the town hall the constable and some servants were already busy about the place and one of them had already hung a black carpet over the banisters of the grand staircase. But I hurried out of the town through the archway below the town hall.

When I was on the path behind the palace gardens, I saw over by the lime pit where they had erected the new gallows a mighty stack of wood piled up. A few people were bustling around it, probably the gaoler and his men, putting easily combustible material between the logs. Already the first lads were coming running across the fields from the town. I paid no further heed to it but went vigorously on my way, and when I came out from the trees I saw on my left the sea inflamed by the first rays of the sun as it rose above the heath in the East. Then I just had to fold my hands and pray;

O Lord my God, his son who gave,
All human souls from sin to save,
Be gracious now to those who fall,
And grant your heavenly love to all.

When I was out where the broad highway runs across the heath, I met many groups of peasants coming towards me; they were dragging their little boys and girls with them by the hand.

"Where are you in such a rush to get to?" I asked one group, "it's not market day in town today." In fact, as I well knew, they wanted to see the burning of the witch, that young limb of Satan. "But the witch is dead!" I said. "Yes, that's annoying", they said, "but it's the niece of our midwife, old mother Siebenzig, so we couldn't stay away and had to go along with the rest."

More and more parties came along, and now even carts appeared out of the morning mist, not laden with grain but full of people. Then I turned aside into the heath although the night dew still dripped from the plants, for my soul demanded solitude and I saw from a long way off that it looked as if the whole village was on the way to the town. When I stood on the burial mound which lies here in the middle of the heath, it came to me that I must go back to the town or turn off to the left down to the sea or to the little village that lies below right by the beach, but before me in the air there hovered happiness, an insane hope, and it shook me to the core and my teeth ground together. 'What if it was really her I so recently saw with my own eyes, and what if today –' I felt my heart beating like a hammer in my ribs; I went a long way round through the heath; I did not want to see if the pastor was on one of the carts travelling to town. - But in the end I still went to his village.

When I reached it I strode hurriedly to the door of the sexton's house. It was locked. I stood for a while indecisive then I began to knock on the door with my fist. Within all remained quiet, but when I knocked louder the sexton's half-blind old servant Trienke came out of a neighbouring house. "Where's the sexton?" I asked. "The sexton? He's gone into town with the pastor." I stared at the old woman; it was if a bolt of lightning flashed through me. "Is there anything you need, Sir?" she asked. I shook my head and merely said, "So there's no school today then, Trienke?" "Heaven forbid! The witch is being burned!"

I got the old woman to open the house, fetched my painting gear and the almost completed portrait from the sexton's bedroom and, as usual, set up my easel in the empty schoolroom. I made a few brush strokes on the clothing but I was only trying to deceive myself. I had no desire to paint, and in fact had not come here with that in mind.

The old woman came in, grumbled about the evil times and talked about farm and village matters which I did not understand. But I felt driven to ask her once again about the pastor's wife, whether she was old or young, and also where she had come from, but I couldn't get the words out of my mouth. On the other hand the old woman began a long complicated tale about the witch and her family here in the village, and about Mother Siebenzig who was afflicted with second sight; also she told me how one night when the gout wouldn't give her any rest Mother Siebenzig had seen three shrouds flying above the pastor's roof; but such visions always fade and pride comes before a fall; for the pastor's wife, despite all her refinement, was only a pale weakly creature.

I didn't want to listen to any more of such gossip so I went out of the house and round the path to the front of the pastor's house which lies on the village street. With fearful longing I turned my eyes to the white windows but could make out nothing behind the blank panes but a couple of flower vases such as can be seen anywhere; but I walked on, nevertheless. When I came to the churchyard the wind carried to my ears from the town the sound of bells ringing, but I turned and looked down to the west where the sea was again rolling along like liquid silver at the edge of the sky and yet there had been a raging disaster there in which the hand of the Almighty had in a single night taken many thousands of human lives. Why then was I twisting and turning like a worm? We don't see where His ways lead us!

I no longer know where else my feet took me then, I only know that I went round in a circle, for when the sun had almost reached its noontime zenith, I arrived back again at the sexton's. I did not however go into the schoolroom to my easel, but through the back gate to the house again.

I have never forgotten the small shabby garden although I have never set eyes on it again from that day to this. Like that of the pastor's house on the other side, it formed a broad strip in the field; in the middle, though, between the two was a group of willow bushes which served as a frame for a water-filled pit, for I had once seen a maid climbing up from it with a full bucket as if from an abyss.

With not much in my mind, which was totally filled with an uncontrollable restlessness, I was just passing the sexton's crop of home-grown beans, when I heard from out in the field the sweet-sounding voice of a woman talking lovingly to a child.

 Involuntarily I walked towards the sound, drawn to it just as once the Greek God Hermes had enticed the dead. Already I was on the far side of the elder bushes which, for lack of a fence, here petered out into the field. Then I saw little Johannes, with his arms full of the moss which grows here among the thin grass, walking behind the willows on the other side; he was probably using it to lay out a little garden in his childish way. And again the sweet voice came to my ear, "Pick a bit more; now you have a good heap! Yes, yes, I still want some more; over there by the elders there's enough!"

And then she herself stepped out from behind the willows; I had long since had no more doubts. Looking down on the ground in her search, she walked straight towards me so that I was able to observe her undisturbed. It seemed to me that she once again in a strange way resembled the child she had once been, for whom I had once shot the bogeyman from the tree. But this childhood face today was pale and neither happiness nor courage was to be seen in it.

So she gradually came nearer without being aware of me. Then she knelt down by a patch of moss which ran on under the bushes, yet her hands did not pluck any of it; she dropped her head on her breast and it was as if, unseen by the child, she wanted to rest from her sorrows.

Then I called softly, "Katharina!"

She looked up, but I grasped her hand and pulled her to me, like one without a will of her own, into the shade of the bushes. But now I had at last found her again and stood before her quite unable to say a word, she looked away from me and said, in an almost strange voice; "Well, Johannes, it's like this. I knew of course that you were the foreign painter; only I didn't think that you would come today."

I heard that and then I blurted out, "Katharina, --so you're the pastor's wife?" She didn't nod, she just looked at me stiffly and painfully. "He took on that burden and gave your child an honest name."

"**My** child, Katharina?"

"Didn't you feel that? He sat on your lap after all; he told me so once himself."

Oh, may such sorrow never afflict another man's heart again!—"And you, you and my child, you are to be lost to me?"

She looked at me, she did not weep, she was just deathly pale.

"I won't have it!" I cried, "I want---"And a succession of wild thoughts chased through my brain.

But her little hand was laid on my brow like a cool leaf and the pupils of her brown eyes in the pale face looked at me beseechingly. "Johannes", she said, "you won't want to be the one to make my life even more wretched."

"And can you live like this, Katharina?"

"Live? –There's one blessing; he loves the child –what more can I ask?"

"And about us, does he know what happened?"

"No, No!" she cried vehemently. "He took the sinful woman to wife –nothing more. O God, isn't it enough that each new day belongs to him!"

At this moment a gentle song came to our ears. "The child" she said, "I must go to the child; some harm may come to him!"

But all my senses were directed towards the woman they desired. "Stay a bit", I said, "he's happy playing there with his moss."

She stepped to the edge of the bushes and listened out. The golden autumn sun shone down so warmly and only a slight breath of air came up from the sea. Then we heard from the other side of the willows the voice of our child singing;

Two Angels by my bed
Two Angels when I'm dead
And two to show my soul the way
To Heaven above where I will stay.

Katharina had stepped back and her eyes looked at me all large and ghostlike. "And now farewell, Johannes", she said softly, "we shall never see each other again here on earth!"

I wanted to clasp her to me; I stretched my arms out to her, but she fended me off and said gently, "I am another man's wife; don't forget that."

But at these words an almost savage anger seized me. "And whose, Katharina", I said harshly," whose were you, long before you were his?"

A painful cry of distress shook her breast; she clapped her hands to her face and cried, "What have I done! Oh my poor dishonoured body!"

Then I almost lost control of myself; I clasped her abruptly to me, I held her as though with iron bands and she was mine again at last! And her eyes looked deep into mine and her red lips accepted mine; we embraced passionately; I could have killed her if we could have died together. And as I blissfully feasted my eyes on her face, she said, almost suffocated by my kisses, "It's a long fearful life! Oh Jesus Christ, forgive me this moment!"

An answer came, but it was the harsh voice of that man who I now heard for the first time speaking her name. The voice came from over in the pastor's garden and once again and still harsher it called, "Katharina!"

Then all happiness was gone. With one despairing glance at me she was off as silent as a shadow.

When I went back into the sexton's, I found that he too had returned. He began at once to talk insistently about the sentence carried out on the poor witch. "You don't think much of it", he said, "else you wouldn't have come out to the village today when the pastor had driven the farmers and their wives into town."

I didn't have time to answer; a piercing scream rent the air; all my life it will ring in my ears!

"What was that, Sexton?" I cried

The man tore open the window and listened, but nothing further occurred. "As God is my witness", he said, "it was a woman who screamed; and it came from over there in the pastor's field."

In the meantime old Trienke, the maid, had come through the door. "Well, Sir!" she called to me. "The shrouds have come down on the pastor's roof!"

"What's that supposed to mean, Trienke?"

"It means that they've just pulled the pastor's little Johannes out of the water."

I rushed precipitately from the room and through the garden to the field; but below the willows I found only the dark water and traces of damp mud beside it on the grass. I did not stop to think, it was quite natural that I went through the white gate into the pastor's garden. As I was about to enter the house, the pastor himself came towards me.

The tall gaunt man looked totally devastated; his eyes were red and his black hair hung tangled in his face. "What do you want?" he said.

I stared at him, for words failed me. Yes, what did I want really?

"I know who you are!", he continued. "She's told me everything at last."

That loosened my tongue. "Where's my child?" I cried.

He said, "His two parents have let him drown."

"Then let me go to my dead child!"

But when I tried to go past him into the hall, he pushed me back. "His mother", he said, "is lying by the corpse and crying to God for her sins. You shall not go to her, for the sake of her soul's salvation!"

What I myself said at the time I have completely forgotten; but the pastor's words sank deep into my memory. "Listen!" he said, "Much as I hate you with all my heart, for which God in his mercy will pardon me some day, and much as you hate me also I expect, yet we have one thing in common. Go home now and prepare a panel or a canvas! Come back with it tomorrow early and paint on it the poor dead child's face. You may donate this likeness not to me or my house, but to the church here where he lived out his short innocent life, so that it may remind men that before the bony hand of Death all is dust!"

I looked at the man who shortly before had taken to task the noble art of painting for being hand in glove with the world; but I promised that it should be done.

At home meanwhile some news was waiting for me which suddenly like a flash of lightning conjured up from the darkness all my guilt and remorse so that I saw the whole chain of it shining before me link by link.

My brother, whose weak constitution had been hard hit by the dreadful spectacle at which he had had to assist that day, had taken to his bed. When I went in to see him, he sat up. "I must just rest a while longer" he said putting in my hand a sheet from the weekly paper, "but read this! You'll see that Herr Gerhard's estate has passed into other hands, for Junker Wulf has died a wretched death caused by the bite of a rabid dog."

I reached for the paper my brother was holding out to me; but it wouldn't have taken much for me to collapse in a heap. This dreadful news made me feel as if the gates of paradise had sprung open before me but standing at the entrance was the angel with the fiery sword; and from my heart there came again the cry, Oh, Great Guardian why were you not there for us! This death could have meant new life for us; now it was just one more horror to add to the other.

I sat upstairs in my room. Dusk fell; it was night; I gazed at the eternal stars and finally I too sought my bed. But refreshing sleep was not to be my lot. In my agitated mind I felt strangely as if the church tower had moved close to my window; I felt the striking of the clock vibrating through the wooden bedstead, and I counted every chime the whole night long. But in the end the morning dawned. The beams on the ceiling still hung like shadows above me when I jumped out of bed and even before the first larks rose from the stubble fields I had already left the town behind me.

But early though I had started, I met the pastor already standing on the threshold of his house. He accompanied me into the hall and said that the wooden panel had duly arrived, and also my easel and the rest of my painting equipment had been brought over from the sexton's. Then he laid his hand on the handle of the parlour door.

But I held him back and said, "If it's in this room, please be kind enough to let me carry out my heavy task alone!"

"Nobody will disturb you", he replied and drew back his hand. "Anything you need to refresh yourself you will find in that room there." He pointed to a door on the other side of the hall; then he left me.

My hand now, instead of the pastor's, lay on the door handle. It was deathly still in the house; for a while I had to compose myself before I opened it.

It was a large almost empty room, probably intended for confirmation classes, with bare whitewashed walls; the windows looked out over barren fields towards the seashore. But in the middle of the room stood a white bed on a bier. On the pillow lay a child's ashen face, the eyes closed, the small teeth shining like pearls from the pallid lips.

I knelt down by my child's body and said a fervent prayer. Then I prepared everything needed for my work; and then I painted –quickly, as one must paint the dead who will not have the same expression again. From time to time I was startled by the all-pervading silence, but when I paused and listened, I soon realised that there was nothing there. Once it even seemed as if I heard gentle breathing. I stepped over to the deathbed but when I bent down to the pale little mouth, only deathly cold struck my cheeks.

I looked round me; there was another door into the room, which might lead to a bedroom, perhaps it had come from there! But however hard I listened I heard nothing more; my own senses must have been playing tricks with me.

So I sat down again, looked at the tiny body and painted on; and when I saw his empty hands lying on the linen, I thought, 'You must give a small present to your child!' And I painted him in his portrait with a white water lily in his hand, as if he had fallen asleep playing with it. Such flowers were rarely seen in these parts even as a wished-for gift.

In the end hunger drove me from my work; my exhausted body required refreshment. So I laid down my brush and palette and went across the hall to the room which the pastor had pointed out to me. As I entered, though, I almost shrank back with surprise, for Katharina stood there in front of me, dressed in black mourning clothes and yet with all the magic glow which happiness and love can produce in a woman's face.

Alas, I realised only too soon that what I was seeing here was only her portrait which I myself had once painted. Even for this there had been no more room in her father's house.—But where was she then in reality? Had she been taken away, or kept shut away here? For a long, long time I gazed at the picture; the old times came back and tortured my heart. In the end, since I must, I had a mouthful of bread and swallowed a couple of glasses of wine; then I went back to our dead child.

When I went back into the room and was about to sit down to work again, it looked as if the eyelids in the little face had risen a little. So I quickly bent down, deluding myself that I could once again get a glance from my child's eyes; but when I found the pupils still motionless, I was filled with horror. I felt as if I saw the eyes of that ancestor of the family and that they wanted through the face of our dead child to say to me; "My curse has overtaken you both!" - But at the same time – I could not for all the world have failed to do it – I clasped the small pale body in both my arms and raised him close to my heart and with bitter tears hugged my beloved child for the first time. "No, No, my poor boy, it's not your soul looking out of those eyes and which won the love of even that dark man; it's just death looking out. That look did not come from the depths of some horrific past, it's nothing else but your father's guilt; that's what has dragged us all down into the black flood".

Carefully I laid my child back down on his pillow and gently closed his eyes. Then I dipped my brush in dark red and wrote in the shadows at the bottom of the picture the letters CPAS. They stood for Culpa Patris Aquis Submersus, drowned through the guilt of his father. And with the sound of these words, which cut through my soul like a sharp sword, I finished painting the picture.

While I had been working, the silence of the house had again prevailed, but in the last hour a slight noise had intruded now and again through the door behind which I had supposed was a bedroom. – Was Katharina there, unseen, in order to be near me in my heavy task? – I could not make it out.

It was already late. My picture was finished and I wanted to prepare to leave, but I felt as if I had to take one last farewell and without it I could not go. So I stood hesitating and looked out through the window onto the barren fields where dusk was already beginning to fall; then the door from the hall opened and the pastor came in.

He greeted me silently, then with folded hands he stood and contemplated alternately the face in the picture and that of the small body before him as if he was making a careful comparison. But when his eyes fell on the lily in the painted hand of the child, he raised both his hands as if in pain and I saw a real flood of tears suddenly fall from his eyes.

Then I stretched out my arms to the poor body and cried aloud, "Farewell, my child! My Johannes, farewell!"

At that same moment I heard soft footsteps in the neighbouring room; it was as if small hands were groping at the door; I clearly heard my name called --or was it that of the dead child? Then there was the sound of women's clothes rustling behind the door, and the sound of a body falling was audible.

"Katharina!" I cried. And already I had sprung to the door and rattled the handle, but the door was locked. Then the pastor's hand lay on my arm; "That is my duty!" he said. "Go now! But go in peace; and may God be merciful to us all!"

I really did go then; before I realised, I was already walking out on the heath on the path to the town. Once again I turned round and looked back at the village which now only rose like shadows from the evening dusk. There lay my dead child -- Katharina -- everything, everything! My old wound began to ache in my chest; and strangely I was suddenly conscious of something I had never heard here before, the dull roar of the surf from the distant shore. I met nobody, I heard the cry of no birds, but from the dull surging of the sea there sounded again and again, like a grim lullaby; Aquis submersus – aquis submersus!

Here ended the manuscript.

What Herr Johannes had once had the temerity to hope for in the fullness of his craft, that he would one day equal the great masters of his art, was destined to remain words spoken in the empty air. His name does not belong among those whose names are well-known; it would be difficult to find him in any lexicon of artists. Even in his limited local area nobody has heard of a painter of his name. The chronicles of our town certainly still mention the great painting of Lazarus, but the picture itself was thrown out at the beginning of this century after the destruction of our old church along with the other art treasures and it has disappeared.

Aquis submersus.

The Confirmed Bachelor

By Adalbert Stifter

A fig-tree which bears no fruit is dug up and thrown in the fire. But if the gardener is kind and indulgent he watches for its green foliage each spring and lets it grow till the leaves become fewer and fewer and there comes a time when only the bare branches stand out against the sky. Then the tree is removed and its place in the garden is lost. The thousands of other branches in the garden and the millions of leaves continue to turn green and rejoice, without ever one of them saying, "I sprang from its seeds and will bear its sweet fruit." The sun continues to shine obligingly, the blue sky smiles from one millennium to the next, the earth clothes itself in the self-same green and the generations descend on their long chain down to the most recent: but it is only this unfruitful tree which is really obliterated and lost for all time; for its existence has stamped no image of itself and no trace of it goes down into the stream of time-----.

In front of a house on an island sat an old, old man and trembled with fear of dying. He could have been seen sitting there for many years already if he had been willing for eyes to see him. There was never a wife to sit beside him, never a child to step into the shadow which he threw on the sand from the bench; in the house all was silent and when he went in he himself closed the door and when he went out he opened it himself.

Far away from the old man's solitude, many days' journey away, is another place where trees blossom, nightingales sing and more than five young lads, brimming over with life, are walking along. All round them is a glittering landscape, cloud shadows fly past and below in the valley the towers and houses of a great city can be seen.

One of them called out, "I've decided once and for all that I will never marry." It was a slim lad who had said this; the others laughed, snapped twigs, threw them at each other and strode on.

"Who would ever want to marry", said another, "and have a wife like a chain round his neck, be like a slave, or sit in a cage like a bird on a perch?"

"Yes, you idiot, but what about dancing, being in love, fooling around then?" answered a third and there was another burst of laughter.

"Nobody would have you, anyway."

"Nor you."

"What do I care?"

The next words could no longer be heard. Another merry shout came back and then nothing more; for the boys were now climbing the steep slope which leads up from the level ground, and their hair tossed as they moved. But far off to the left, on the other side of the blue mountains shining out there on the horizon lies the island where the lonely old man sits.

They stride on vigorously in the sparkling sunshine, all round are greening twigs and on their cheeks and in their eyes shines that imperturbable confidence in the world. All around them lies the Spring and it is just as inexperienced and confident as they are.

And merry chatter and talk dances on their glib tongues. At first they talk of everything and everyone at once, then they speak of the highest things, then of the lowest and have soon exhausted both. Then total freedom is the topic, as well as justice and infinite tolerance and any who don't agree are shouted down and discomfited. Their country's enemies are crushed and on the heads of the heroes will shine the light of fame. Meanwhile it is only the bushes that flourish around them, only the brooding earth that germinates and begins to sparkle with its first tiny Spring creatures as if with jewels.

Then they sing a song, chase each other, try to push each other into the ditch or the bushes, cut switches and sticks, and all the time are climbing higher and higher up the mountain and above the dwellings of men.

Oh, what a mysterious, secretive and enticing thing is the future; and how clear and stale it seems when it becomes the past! All these young men are already charging full pelt into it as if they can not wait. One boasts of things and pleasures well above his years, another assumes boredom as if he was tired of everything already and a third speaks words which he has heard old men say at home to his father. Then they snatch at a butterfly fluttering by and find a brightly coloured stone on the path. But the old man on the island just sits, looks at nothing and the empty air and the futile sunshine play around him.

And they push ever higher upwards. Above at the edge of the woods they look back on the town and make bets with each other about whether they can make out such and such a house or building or not, and then they go in beneath the shade of the beech trees.

The wood continues almost on a level. But on the other side gleaming meadows with isolated fruit trees descend into a valley which, silent and hidden, follows the contours of the mountains, from which gush two sparkling rushing streams. The water babbles merrily over the smooth pebbles, past dense orchards, garden fences and houses. It is all so quiet that one can hear the distant cock crowing in the clear afternoon air or the single stroke of the bell as the clock chimes the quarter hour. Hardly ever does a townsman visit the valley and none has made his summer home here.

But our friends run more than they walk across the meadows down into the softly rounded valley bottom. Noisily they come down to the gardens, stride across the first footbridge, cross the second and walk along beside the streams and finally enter a garden which is thick with elders, walnut trees and lime trees. Here they sat round one of the tables firmly planted deep in the grass, its top displaying all kinds of carved names and hearts, and ordered a meal - today for once like real responsible men. Each ate what he wished, then they quarrelled with the waiter, threw sticks for a poodle to fetch and finally, after they had departed and had walked through the wider mouth of the valley, they rowed across the river, frightening to death some women who happened to be passing. They had crossed at a dangerous spot, although they did not realise it. On the other side they paid a man to row the boat back and tie it up at the place where they had taken it from.

Then they pushed on through reed beds and meadows till they came to the railway embankment, from where, perched high a goods train, they travelled back to the town. In the light that remained of the day they flew along merrily on their iron road, flew across plains, between embankments and past houses, gardens and parks till they reached their destination, and the sun which had accompanied them so cheerfully all day, now lay far off like a golden ball, expiring low down between green garden bushes – and when it grew more and more pale and had finally set, the friends could see the mountains on which they had enjoyed the morning hours like distant blue silhouettes which stood out against the golden evening sky.

Then they went into the town and in its hot dusty alleys the dusk already held sway. And when they came to the place where they had to separate, they took leave of each other cheerfully. "Goodbye" cried one. "Goodbye" said another. "Good night, say hello to Rosina for me." "Good night, say hello to August for me if you see him and Theobald and Gregor." "And the same to Karl and Lothar." "And Edward and Theodor---"

And more and more names were called out and ever more. They wished to be remembered to this one and that one; for young people have numerous friends and are always recruiting new ones. And even after they had gone their separate ways there still could be heard from the narrow streets, "Good night – Good night."

Then all was still and each rolled on home to seek rest and sleep for his tired limbs.

The old man on the island, though, lay in his bed which stood in a strong well-protected room and closed his eyes in order to sleep.

Two of the young men had gone the same way after they had all separated, and one said to the other, "Is it really true, Victor, that you have no intention of ever marrying?" "Yes it's true", replied the other, "and I'm really unhappy."

But his eyes were so clear when he said this and his lips so fresh as the breath passed over them.

His companion was silent and they walked on along the same road. Finally they went into the same house and went up the stairs past rooms full of lights and people.

"Look, Victor," said one, "I've had a bed set up for you next to mine so that you get a comfortable night. Rosina will send us up some food and tomorrow, if you want, you can go back home through the woods. It's been a heavenly day. I don't want to spoil the end of it among other people – wouldn't you rather eat up here with me than down at the table? I told mother so."

"Of course I'd rather" replied Victor, "for it's very boring when your father takes so much time between courses and talks so much all the time. But tomorrow at daybreak, Ferdinand, I must go back home."

"You can go as soon as you like", said the other. "The door key's always in the niche by the door." During this conversation they began to undress and divest themselves of their heavy dusty boots. One article of clothing was laid here, another there. A servant brought lamps and a maid a tray provided with large quantities of food. They ate quickly without picking and choosing. Then they looked first out of one window and then out of another, went round the room, looked at the presents which Ferdinand had only recently received, counted the red evening clouds and finally lay down on their beds. Even in bed they continued to talk, but before a few minutes had passed neither of them was capable any more of starting a conversation, let alone carrying one on; for they were both asleep, in that deep healthy refreshing sleep of youth.

And not them alone; all their companions of that day and thousands and thousands of others sank slowly into the daily grave of sleep. The night with its mantle of stars moved on by, stepping slowly, oblivious of whether youthful hearts had enjoyed the previous day or elderly ones had moved one day nearer death – it just passed by and moved softly star after star to the west till in the morning it finally lifted that light grey veil at its edge which heralds the day, a day already rife with the misty images of thousand upon thousand of pleasures which it has in store for mankind and the thousand upon thousand of sufferings with which it is destined to afflict them.

Who will be the first to be visited by one of these, accompanying him as a loving friend or tormenting his every step?

It was one of the young men who had so light-heartedly and enthusiastically enjoyed the previous day; it was Victor who was already walking along the street when the first of that pale, milky light from the veil of sky had still scarcely shone over the sleeping town. As if driven by a surge of emotion he strode along the deserted streets so that his footsteps echoed from the masses of stonework.

We will go with him and see what happiness or sorrow the day will bring him.

Yesterday he spoke a fateful word, but he doesn't know it; in the old man on the island his future is foreshadowed, but he does not suspect it. Cheerfully he goes to meet his fate whether it turns out in reality like that of the old man or differently.

At first he was the only one walking along the streets, the only person to be seen; then he met morose sleepy figures who had to be at work early and he heard distant rattling as the wagons began to bring foodstuffs into the town – but he pushed on. Once outside the town gate he was finally surrounded by the damp cool green of the fields. The sun was just rising and the tips of the wet grasses sparkled red, blue and green. The larks warbled all the

more joyfully since the nearby town, usually so noisy, was
still so silent.

As soon as he felt himself beyond the walls, Victor
immediately left the straight road and struck off to one
side along a path across the fields which led up towards
the mountains, and specifically to that group of trees
beneath which the nightingales had sung the day before.
He continued on along the path, which gradually rose
higher and higher, arrived beneath the trees, heard the
nightingales singing today as they had yesterday, and went
on past, as he had done yesterday. He climbed the same
slope which rises from the trees to the edge of the woods;
he didn't look back at the town, but pushed on onto the
woods, hurried on and then descended across the meadow
to the same valley, which we said was so silent and had
two sparkling streams running through it. He went across
the first footbridge, only today he stood still for a while
and looked down at the shining pebbles – he crossed the
second – he wandered along the stream but before he
reached the garden where they had had lunch the day
before he came to an elder bush, such a large elder bush
that it leaned almost over the whole stream and disturbed
its flow with roots and twigs which hung down broken and
decayed. From the bush away from the stream ran an ash-
grey garden fence on which more than seventy spring
rains had already fallen, and in the fence close by the bush
was an unusual little wooden gate, as grey as the rest of
the wood, but so innocent and harmless that it closed
nothing, having neither lock nor bolt, but only set up so
that the lower hinge was further away from the gatepost
than the upper one which meant that the gate had to swing

back again when one opened it. Victor pushed lightly against it and went in through, went round the elder bush so that the branches brushed his cheeks, and on the other side glimpsed the snow white wall of a house, which stood out against the lilacs and fruit trees revealing its gleaming windows, behind which hung white unruffled curtains.

Victor went up to the house. In front of it there was an open space on which stood the well and an ancient apple tree against which leaned numerous stakes and all manner of other things. An old Pommeranian dog wagged its tail to greet the new arrival, and the hens, the friendly neighbours of the house, scratched more furiously beneath the stakes of the apple tree as if they wanted to demonstrate their joy that he had walked past them. He stepped through the open door, went past the kitchen, his feet crunching the sand which lay on the stone slabs, and then strode into the downstairs parlour, which revealed a shiny polished floor when he entered.

There was nobody in the parlour except one old woman who had opened a window and was busy dusting the white tables, chairs and cupboards and setting to rights the things which had been moved the evening before. Distracted by the noise of his entrance she turned her face towards him. It was one of those beautiful old women's faces, which are so rarely to be seen, with its soft placid colours and the myriad small lines, each expressing kindness and friendliness. Here theses lines were endlessly contrasted with those of a creased snow white cap. On each cheek lay a small fine fleck of red.

"Wait", she said, "I've forgotten the milk again. I should have kept it warm—look, it's by the fire but that's gone out. Just be patient, Victor, I'll fan it up again."

"I'm not hungry, Mother" said Victor. "Before I left town I ate a couple of slices of cold meat left over from last night's meal."

"But you must be hungry" answered the woman. "You've been walking over two hours in the morning air and coming through the damp woods. You did come through the woods, didn't you?"
"Yes, it's so much nearer."
"You see, I put the things by the fire over an hour ago in case you should happen to be early – only I forgot about them."
"But I really don't want to eat."
"Eat anyway, Victor, do eat", she said and without waiting for an answer she went out into the kitchen where she quickly fanned the fire by the two pots which stood on the black coal and then came back in.

"Are you tired? she said, seeing the lad sitting now on a chair.
"No" he replied, "I'm not tired. How far is it over the high meadow?"
"Oh, you always go so fast because you think your feet will go on for ever, and while you're walking you don't notice them, but when you sit down on a chair you find they're tired."

Victor didn't answer but bent down low to the dog,

stroking its long soft hair with his hand as it raised itself caressingly to him, and looked steadily into its eyes –he always stroked the same place and always looked in the same way.

The woman, meanwhile, carried on with her task. Rising on the tips of her toes she tried to reach the dust on chests and shelves which defied her and chairs and stools had to help increase her height and get rid of the hated intruder. On one chest lay a child's toy, a little pipe with a hollow bowl in which were things that rattled – it had probably not been used for years and would probably never be again; but the woman wiped it neat and clean on all sides and put it back in its place. She did exactly the same with other things that stood around on the boxes as ornaments.

"But why don't you say anything about yesterday, then?" she said suddenly, seeming to notice the silence reigning.
"Because nothing gives me any pleasure any more", replied Victor.

The woman said no word, not a single word to this statement, but she carried on with her dusting and her regular shaking of the cloth out of the open window. After a short time, though, she began again and said, "Look here, Victor, what you just said is completely wrong and you just don't understand yet. Look at me, I'm almost seventy years old and even I don't say that nothing gives me any pleasure, because one must enjoy everything; it's all so beautiful and will only get more and more beautiful the longer one lives. When I was eighteen I also kept on saying nothing gives me any pleasure any more – I said it when those pleasures I had set my mind on were denied me. Everything God sends is beautiful even if one doesn't know it – and when one really thinks about it and really gets to know things, it turns out in the end that there's nothing but sheer pleasure in the world. Did you not see when you came in that the lettuces by the fence, which there was no trace of yesterday, are today all out? Up in the mountains they were hard hit by the heavy frosts."

"I didn't notice" answered Victor.

"Look", continued the woman, "I've something else to say to you now. I've got everything ready for you. I had to send the small trunk back to the carpenter for it was too rough. If you put your books in it, they might have got damaged on the way. When you were out yesterday I worked the whole day. Everything you need to pack I've laid out already next to the case. I bought you a fine soft leather one, like you once said you liked. We've mended all your linen so there's not a single thread broken. As far as clothes are concerned you're decent and have three changes of clothing not counting what you're wearing. Be careful with the packing and don't squash things – do you hear? I've already sorted out what goes in your knapsack and put it with it. – But where are you going, Victor?"

"To pack."

"But, my boy, you haven't eaten. It'll be nice and warm by now."

She hurried out immediately and brought in two bowls, a cup and saucer and a bread roll on a round shiny-clean tray with a raised brass edge. She put everything down, poured out and tasted it to see if it was all right and warm enough and then pushed it all in front of him, trusting to the aroma to overcome his refusal. And in fact her experience didn't let her down for the lad who at first just began to have a little sip, finally sat down and ate with all the healthy pleasure which is so typical of youth.

In the meantime she had gradually finished her work, and, putting away her dusters, slyly watched him affectionately from time to time. When he had finally finished up all that she had brought in she let the dog lick up the last vestiges from the saucer, then carried the crockery back into the kitchen so that the maid could wash it up when she came home, for she had gone to the market to buy the day's provisions.

Having come back from the kitchen, the woman sat down in front of Victor and said, "Now you've had something to eat, you can listen to me. If I were really your mother, as you always call me, I would be really cross with you for saying nothing gives you any pleasure any more. Even if there was something sad in store for you, at your age you should be able to bear it cheerfully. Nobody will ever be able to say of me, however old I am, that he ever saw me shed a single tear because I was in trouble or pain. And you should be the same – and even more. You should thank God that your limbs are still young so that you can go out to find those pleasures which don't come to us here – Look, Victor, you don't have any fortune – Your father incurred many debts in this life thanks to the misfortune that struck him down; perhaps on the other side he will have eternal bliss, for he was a good man and always had a soft heart. Just imagine how overcome I was, overcome with joy I mean, when they read out his will and learned that you were to live with me and were to learn here in the village everything that you will ever need to know when you're in town. –I thought, 'The poor man! When all's said and done he was really a good man deep down. I forgave him and always thought he was so very good.' And when it comes down to it, I have to tell you, Victor, that you're not all that poor, for the money they gave me every year for your keep I put by and have always added the interest to it. Don't say anything about that to your guardian; he doesn't need to know. You must have something when people turn up so that you can give them the best and don't have to be ashamed or take a back seat. If your uncle contests the small estate you inherited, don't worry; it's so cumbered with debt that not a single roof tile belongs to it any more. I know that, I had them look it up for you in the land register. I'll always make sure you've got money in your pocket in case of need and the money saved up for you will never get any less as a result. And I'll look after other things too. You'll never need to buy a stitch of underwear. Hanna's bleaching things outside, half of which are intended for you. In future it'll all have to be finer as befits your new status, and the knitting, sewing, darning I'll do myself and Hanna must help. A man taking up his first official post should be equipped like a bridegroom and, Victor, he should be in a state of Grace! Say your prayers to God who has given you this post so many others were after, and be humble that he gave you the gifts to achieve it.—So you see, taking all in all, I would be cross at what you said if I were your mother, because you don't recognize that the Lord is looking after you; but because I'm not your mother, I don't know if I've done you enough good and given you enough love to give me the right to be angry with you and to say; " My lad, you were wrong and it was bad of you. ---But don't get too offended by my saying this, Victor, and go in God's name to your uncle's because that's what he wants. Your guardian also thinks it's a good idea. Did you see Rosina yesterday?"

"No, I didn't see her."

"Once you're established in your job, she could be your wife one day; think how powerful her father is, - he's conducted the onerous task of being your guardian honestly and diligently, and he's not ill-disposed to you for he always expressed his pleasure when you did well in your exams. But all that's still a long way off and it might easily turn out quite differently. Your father could have been equally important – he had a brain which they didn't realise – even your mother, your real mother ---well, she was also really good and pious but she died much too soon. Well, don't be sad, go up and sort everything out. You mustn't pull your clothes apart, I've put them together so that they fit in the case, just put them in, and listen, Victor, one more request; couldn't you say something nice to Hanna this evening or tomorrow morning before you go off; it wasn't right that you two were forever quarrelling."

Victor didn't say anything in reply to all this, but he got up quickly and went out of the door, banging his arm and shoulder against the doorpost. Once outside he went hurriedly up the stairs to his room. The dog followed him.

The windows on the upper floor look out at the various things around the house. Victor's room overlooks the elder bush, fruit trees and the rippling stream, others look out onto the front garden and the well, others still onto the vegetable garden; but through each one could be seen one of the mountains which, silent and bathed in sunshine, surround the valley and protect it and also the orchards which wrap it in rich profusion, basking in the warm air which is trapped between the mountains.

As Victor came up, a girl was standing at one of the landing windows looking out. When she heard his steps she turned round and said, "It's you, Victor, I didn't know you were here yet. Why didn't you look up at our windows when you went by yesterday?"

"Because we were celebrating Ferdinand's birthday", said the person thus addressed, "and because we'd agreed that for the whole day we had no father or mother or anyone else to order us about, so that the day would belong to us and we would belong only to it. So our valley was merely the place where we intended to have lunch, not where our house happens to be, and that's why I didn't look up. Do you see now, Hanna?"

"No, I don't", said the girl, "I would certainly have looked up a bit."

"Because you're nosy and get things muddled", replied Victor.

"That may well be", she said and ran down the stairs, so that you could hear the rustle of her clothes till she had got to the bottom.

Victor now opened his door and went in his room. The windows were open; the reflection of the stream below threw a trembling light on the white ceiling, on the floor were peaceful silhouettes of the tree branches outside and the continuous rippling and repeated splashing of the stream filled the silence; but everything in the room was different from usual. Nothing was in its usual familiar place. The cupboards had been thrown open and the drawers in the chests had been pulled out and were empty, while their contents lay around on top of them; the pure white linen sorted into piles and tied together in bundles with red, blue or green silk ribbons, then the clothes, neatly folded and arranged in suitable heaps-- on a chair was a knapsack with its contents beside it – the suitcase waited open on the floor, its straps loosened – the flute was packed in its case, the case wrapped in paper and sealed – on the desk lay a dressing case, in the corner of the room was a trunk and on the floor was scattered torn-up paper; only his pocket watch hung in its usual place and ticked as usual and only the books stood in the bookcase and waited to be used.

But Victor did nothing with all these things and, instead of packing, sat on a chair and hugged the dog to his heart.

The chimes of the church clock as it struck the hour penetrated into the silence of the room, but Victor didn't know what hour it was – the maid, who had now returned, could be heard singing in the garden – in the distant mountains there was a glitter from time to time as if a piece of polished silver or a sheet of glass lay there – the pattern of shadows on the floor moved forward – the trembling light on the ceiling had stopped because the sun had by now risen too high – the horn of the herdsman could be heard as he drove his animals – the clock struck again; but the young man still sat on his chair and the dog sat in front of him and looked up at him without moving.

Finally, when he heard the footsteps of his mother coming up the stairs, he jumped up and threw himself into his task. He tore open the doors of the bookcase and began to quickly lay out the contents in piles on the floor. His mother merely stuck her head a little way in at the open door and when she saw him so occupied, she turned round and tiptoed out again. But he, once he had started to be active, stuck to his task and went at it more and more feverishly. All the books were pulled out of the two bookcases which were stuffed full and when he had done this and the empty shelves stared out at him through the open doors, he began to put the books together in small piles according to their sizes, then he tied each pile tightly with string and stuck on a written label on which no doubt was written the designation of the books. Most of them he put in the trunk and the others he put for the time being on the table. Then he set about the papers. All the drawers in the desk and in the two other tables were pulled out, and all the papers which were inside were examined one after the other. Some were merely glanced at and put back in their places, others were read, many ripped up and thrown on the ground and many more put away in coat pocket or wallet. Finally when all these drawers too were empty and had nothing to show inside except the sad dust which had over long years trickled between the papers and into the cracks which had formed or widened during this time, he tied these papers too into bundles and put part of them in the trunk, and part with the books on the table. Then he packed his case and many mementoes of former days, such as a tiny silver candlestick, a locket with a gold chain, a telescope, two small pistols and the like were tucked in between the soft protective linen. When everything was stowed, the lid was closed, the straps buckled and an address label stuck on. The knapsack still stood open on its chair. Hastily all the manifold things which his mother had laid out next to it and which she considered necessities for his journey were stuffed into its many compartments, and when he had finished, had strapped it all up and given it a pat with the flat of his hand, the carpenter also came in the door and brought a small trunk, assuring him that it was now so smooth inside that even meerschaum could be packed in it without danger. Victor was satisfied, dismissed the man and put in all the books and papers which he had previously selected on the table. Then he screwed down the lid and stuck an address label on it.

Now he had finished and once more looked round the room and the walls to see if anything had been left lying or hanging which must still be packed; but there was nothing else there and only the devastated room met his gaze.

Among the contents of the room which had now become so strange there was only the bed which still stood as it had always stood, but even it was covered in dust and dirt. For a while he stood there motionless. The dog, which up to now had watched all the activity with suspicious eyes without missing a single movement and had had to dodge right or left when he got in the young man's way, now stood calmly in front of him and looked up as if asking 'what now?'

Victor wiped the sweat from his brow with the flat of his hand and with the towel, took a brush lying there and brushed the dust from his clothes and then went back down the stairs.

A great deal of time had passed in the meanwhile. When he came down into the downstairs parlour nobody was there. The morning sun which had shone in so warmly and had made the curtains so shiny white when he had arrived early that morning from town, had now become a noon-day sun and stood directly above the roof, pouring down its blinding light and warm rays directly onto its grey wood. The fruit trees were quite still, their leaves, which that morning had been so damp and sparkling, have become dry, and more dull and motionless; the birds slip silently into the branches and peck at their food. The curtains are drawn back, the windows are open to the landscape shimmering in the heat, in the kitchen burns a glowing smokeless fire, the maid doing the cooking stands by – everything is in that state of deep stillness which somebody once described as 'Pan sleeping'.

Victor went into the kitchen and asked where his mother was. "In the garden somewhere", answered the maid. He went out into the garden to look for her. He walked between the neat flower beds in which the various plants were coming into bud and starting to put forth green leaves. The gardener was putting in plants and his lad was pumping water into a channel so that it would run into the water butt some way off. And the blackcurrants and gooseberries were bursting with green fruit, and the plum trees, the apple, cherry and pear trees stood amidst tall grass, flowers were in bloom here and there and already all the cloches had been taken from the spring borders and lay in heaps nearby. Victor walked past it all. It had always been like this in the past and would be when he was miles away. His mother was not in the garden. But behind it there was a beautiful green meadow with short velvety grass on which the washing was spread out to whiten in the sun. There she stood looking at the snowy whiteness at her feet, which seemed to lie in long drawn out strips in the sunshine beaming down. From time to time she checked items to see if they were dry yet, or fastened a loop to the peg with which they were held to the ground or held the flat of her hand like a shield before her eyes and looked around the district.

Victor went up to her. "Have you finished", she said, "or have you left some for this afternoon? There's a lot, isn't there, however little it seems. You've been a long way today already and it's all right to leave the rest till later. I wanted to pack it all myself yesterday but I thought you should do it so that you learn how."

"No, mother" he replied, "I haven't left anything for this afternoon. I've finished it all already." "Let me see", said the woman as she reached out to feel his brow. He leaned forward towards her a little and she brushed a lock of hair which had fallen across his brow out of his eyes. "Hm!" she said, "you've got yourself over-heated." "It's such a warm day ", he replied. "No, no, it's also from working and if you've already done everything, what will you do with yourself this afternoon?"

"I'm going to go up the stream and past the rock walls and the beech wood – but I came out here, mother, about something else and have something I'd like to say to you, although it'll make you angry."

"Don't frighten me, child, just come right out with it. Is there something else you want? Has anything gone wrong?"

"No, nothing's gone wrong, it's rather the opposite. You said something today, mother, which I didn't understand and which I can't get out of my mind."

"What did I say, Victor?"

"You said that in my father's will some money was set aside which was to be paid to you each year for my maintenance and you also said that you had received the money and invested it for me, that you had even added the interest to it so that it should all remain intact."

"That's right. That's what I said and that's what I did."

"Well, look mother, my conscience tells me it's not right for me to take the money from you, because it doesn't belong to me – and I preferred to say it to you amicably in advance rather than just refuse the money and annoy you. – Are you cross?"

"No, I'm not cross", she said as she looked at him beaming with joy, "but don't be foolish, Victor, you must know that I didn't take you into my home to make a profit –I would never take a child for the sake of a profit – So whatever is left of the money each year is rightfully yours. Your guardian provided all your clothes, you didn't cause any expense for food, you ate scarcely as much as a bird and the vegetables and fruit and other things you enjoyed we had ourselves – do you see now? –And the fact that I grew to love you, that wasn't something your father told me to do and you can do nothing about that. Now do you understand?"

"No I don't understand – and you're so good to me again that you fill my heart with even more shame. If there had really been just a little left over and you had only saved that up for me, that would have been loving and generous, and now you say that all of it was left over and that's almost painful to hear. You've nevertheless done more than can possibly be accounted for. You gave me a room of my own and furnished it as I liked, you gave me food and drink and yourself only extra work; and again you bought me everything I needed for my journey, and I was always provided with the produce of the fields and garden, your linen was in my cupboard - and when I had everything and nothing more was wanting, you still gave me more and when I had that you secretly gave me what you thought I would like -You loved me more than you did Hanna!"

"No, Victor, there you do me an injustice. Hanna is my child, I carried her in my womb; this happiness was my lot only late in life when I could already have been her grandmother. I gave birth to her with great joy amidst the sorrow at the death of your father – and I think I love her more. But it often seems to me that I really carried you too –and I really should have done! –I love you both equally and when you both come of age you can share the money with each other. It's not right, anyway, to stop someone doing what they consider right. Leave the money, Victor, and I won't speak of it again; let it lie and some day we shall see what to do with it. And whatever kindnesses I did for you, I did for Hanna too. That's what mothers do – and if I saved up for you, I did for her too, and remember you've brought a lot of happiness into the house, for since you've been here I could save much more each year than ever before. When you look after two you're more skilful and more experienced, and where God provides blessings for two he often provides enough for three – Oh Victor, my son, when I think back – Oh God, when I think back, it's as if – where have all the years gone and how have I come to be so old? Everything is still as beautiful as it was yesterday – the mountains still stand, the sun still beams down on them and the years seem just like one day. Up there in the woods, you see, is a place where the mountain slopes lean towards each other and the light trickles down so peacefully on the beeches like a golden ray – there's a special place there – a wide flat stone, an old beech tree beside it and a little stream running by – don't forget that place, Victor, don't forget it your whole life long."

"But, mother, I don't know the place and you've never shown it me."

"Yes, I've never shown it you and now I hardly ever get into the woods. You'll find other places which seem more beautiful to you or perhaps you'll find it today when you go up there, or some other time. It's easy to recognize. The beech tree stretches out a long flat branch low over the stone so that you can lay pieces of material on it and hang up a lady's hat – it's really quiet all round. – But forget all that, Victor, just be calm, don't think any more about the money and above all don't be sad - I know you're suffering and you take everything more seriously than it is. But have you also noticed that not a single twig in the garden is stirring and the tree tops are motionless in the air; there could be a storm, you mustn't go too far."

"I won't go too far and I know the signs of a storm in the sky – if one comes near I'll head straight home."
"Yes, you'll come home, I know you will. Will you go with me into the parlour now, it's almost time for lunch, or will you stay around here till it's time to eat?"
"I'll stay in the garden for a while."
"Yes, stay in the garden; I'll just fasten the loops here and see whether the birds have made the washing dirty."

He stayed and watched her for a few minutes. Then he went into the garden and she watched him go. And then she fastened one loop and then another till they were all done and she wiped away the dirt made by a goose's foot or some other bird on the washing – and she lifted one item here and another there so that they didn't stick too closely to the grass ---and whenever she looked up she saw him standing before one or other of the bushes in the garden, until suddenly the clear sound of the midday bell rang out in the still air, a sign to call the parishioners to prayer and by long established custom the sign in this house to gather together for the midday meal. She saw how he turned round and strode towards the house. Then she followed him.

Guests had come. His guardian with all his family was there. They'd wanted to give Victor a surprise and at the same time spend a day in the country.

"You see how good we are", said his guardian. "We will see you once more and have a farewell meal with you today and then tomorrow, without having to go into town again, you can set straight off on your journey as befits a worthy student who has a few weeks vacation before he has to settle down to a boring job."

"God go with you, my son", said the wife of his guardian and kissed Victor on the forehead. "Didn't I do that nicely?" said Ferdinand, the son, as he shook his friend's hand. But Rosina, their wondrously beautiful daughter, a girl of twelve, stood to one side and said nothing.

Victor's mother must have known about the visit for the table was laid for exactly the number of people who were there. The guardian and his wife sat at the head, Hanna, Victor's foster sister, sat next to Rosina, while Victor sat next to Ferdinand and his mother sat at the foot, since she had to frequently go in and out to see to things and often cast a glance backward and forward between Rosina and Victor.

Everyone was merry. The guardian told tales of his adventures when he was travelling as a student, he laid down some rules and gave some advice of a practical cheerful nature; his wife made hints about a future bride and Ferdinand said that he would very soon visit his friend. Victor, though, didn't have much to say and, scarcely had all the people left and the farewell formalities been said and the final words of his guardian "Good bye Frau Ludmilla!" still hung in the air, he was already on his way alone up by the stream and walked off in the direction of the rock walls and the beech woods.

"Let him go, let him go", murmured the old woman, "his heart will be very heavy."

"Where's Victor, then?" asked Hanna as it drew on to evening.

"He's gone to say goodbye", she answered, "he's gone to say goodbye to the countryside – God knows he has very little else."

Hanna made no reply to this and went into the garden between the bushes and in among the little plum trees. And the rest of the afternoon was spent, as time in this house was usually spent; people carried on with whatever jobs they had to do, the birds twittered away in the trees, the hens walked about in the yard, the grass and plants grew a bit more and the mountains were adorned with the golden glow of evening.

And when the sun had already left the sky and only the pale empty disk still stood above the valley, Victor came back from the walk which he had set out on so hastily after lunch. He came along the back fence of the garden in order to reach the gate which leads in through the meadow where the washing is dried. The white strips of washing were no longer there, only the greener and damper patches of grass indicated where it had been during the day – even the cloches had been put back over most of the flower beds because the clear sky promised a cold night – and from the house rose a thin column of smoke, because his mother was perhaps already seeing to the evening meal. Victor as he went along by the hedge had turned his face towards the west and the glow from there lit up his face softly, the cooler air flowed through his hair and the sky was reflected in his grieving eyes.

Hanna had seen him walk quite close past her as she stood on the inner side of the hedge but she hadn't spoken to him. The girl was busy collecting from a roughly pruned bush some pieces of a silk material which had been laid there during the day to dry. She took down piece after piece and laid them together in a pile. When she looked round after a while, she saw Victor standing in the garden by the great rose hedge. Later she saw him again by the lilac bush, but the lilac was much closer to her than the rose hedge. Then he went a little further away again and finally he came up to her suddenly from the opposite side and said, "I'll help you carry some of it in, Hanna."

"No it's all right, Victor" she replied, "it's only a few light pieces of cloth which I dyed and left here to dry."

"Hasn't the sun faded them?"

"No, this violet has to be laid in the sun, preferably the spring sun, and then it gets even more beautiful."

"Well, has it become beautiful?"

"Just look."

"Oh, I don't understand these things."

"It's not as beautiful as the ribbons last year, but it's good enough."

"It's very fine silk."

"Very fine."

"Is there any finer?"

"Yes, you can get finer."

"And would you like to have a lot of beautiful silk clothes?"

"No, I don't really care, other clothes are also beautiful and silk is a proud thing to wear and isn't suitable for every day."

"The silkworm is a poor old creature, isn't it?"

"Why, Victor?"

"Because you have to kill it to take its web."

"Is that what they do?"

"Yes, they drench its web in steam or smoke it with sulphur so that the creature inside dies, for otherwise it eats through the threads and comes out as a butterfly."

"The poor thing!"

"Yes, and then it's taken away from its homeland, Hanna, where it can creep around on sunny mulberry bushes, and it's fed in our parlours on leaves which grow outside and are not so bright as in their homeland. –And the swallows and the storks and the other migrating birds go away from us in the autumn, perhaps a long way away, into other countries; but they come back again in the spring –the world must be really, really big."

"Poor old Victor, don't say such things."

"I want to ask you something, Hanna"

"Well ask away, Victor."

"I must thank you again, Hanna, for the very beautiful purse you made me, the fabric is so fine and soft and the colours are really beautiful. I've put it up and won't put any money in it."

"Oh, Victor, it was a long time ago when I gave you that, it's not worth thanking me – just put your money in it; I can always make you another so that you're never short of one. I've made you something else that's nicer than the purse but mother didn't want me to give it to you till this afternoon or tomorrow morning."

"I shall like that, Hanna, I'll like it very much."

"Where were you then the whole afternoon, Victor?"

"I went up the stream as I had such a long time to spare; I looked in the water and watched it rushing so busily towards the village, how dark and light it is, how it tries so hard to get round the stones and the sand bars and then doesn't stop there – I looked at the rock walls which always stand and look down on the ripples – I finally went up into the beech woods where the trunks will be really high in a couple of years or ten –really high. Then I just walked around. Mother told me of a place where there's a broad flat stone beside a tall beech which stretches out a long branch low down and where a stream runs. I wanted to find the place, but I couldn't."

"Oh, that's the beech spring in Hirschbuhl, I know it well and I'll show you tomorrow, if you like."

"But I shall no longer be here tomorrow, Hanna."

"Oh no, tomorrow you won't be here. I keep thinking you'll always be here."

"No—dear Hanna, divide up these pieces of silk, I'll help you carry them in."

"I don't know what's got into you today, Victor; they're so light a child could carry ten times as many."

"It's not the weight, I just wanted to carry something for you."

"All right, well carry some of them. If you want to go straight into the house, we'll quickly gather up what's there and go."

"No, no, I don't want to go in yet, it's not that late, I want to stay in the garden a bit longer – what I said about the purse isn't the only thing I have to say to you."

"Go on, then, what is it?"

"The four doves which I've been looking after –they're not really all that beautiful but I feel sorry for them if they have nobody to look after them."

"I'll look after them, Victor, I'll take good care of them. I'll open the cote for them and close it again in the evening, feed them, scatter sand and talk to them about you."

"And then, one more thing, I must thank you for all the linen."

"For goodness sake, it wasn't me that gave it you but mother, and we've got plenty of it in our cupboards so that we shan't miss it."

"The little silver box which looks like a tiny chest, you know the one, with the filigree work and the tiny lock, which you always really liked – I haven't packed that because I'm leaving it for you as a present."

"No, it's much too nice, I can't take that."

"I beg you, please take it Hanna. You'll please me very much if you take it."

"Well, if it pleases you I'll keep it for you till you return and I'll look after it very carefully."

"And see to the carnations, the poor things by the fence – and don't forget the dog; he's already old but he's a loyal friend."

"No, Victor, I won't forget him."

"But that's not everything I wanted to ask you – I must ask you something else. "

"Ask away, Victor."

"Are you angry with me?"

"What a silly thing to say, I've never been angry with you in my whole life".

"Mother thought – because I've often quarrelled with you – that things weren't right between us, and they weren't."

"No, no, Victor –you're the best person in the world and there can never be a better."

"Oh yes there can, you're better, Hanna. You've always been the one who's been teased and yet stayed patient, I know."

"Victor, don't upset me, that's only something you've thought up today."

"No, I always knew you were too good to me, I just didn't think about it –please listen; I want to pour out my heart to you, Hanna; I'm really unhappy!"

"Good gracious, Victor, my dear Victor, whatever is the matter, then?"

"You see, mother told me today that she never wants ever again to see a man weeping for sorrow or pain – and the whole day my eyes have been full of heavy tears; I've had to hold them back to stop them falling- and when after lunch I went up along the sad little stream and past the rock walls, it wasn't because I was bored but because I really couldn't look at anyone – and then I thought; I've nobody in the whole wide world, no father, no mother, no sister. My uncle robs me of my few possessions and the only people who are good to me I have to leave."

"Oh Victor, dear Victor, don't get so upset. Of course, your father and mother are dead, but that was such a long time ago that you can hardly have known them; instead you have found another mother who loves you as much as any real one, and since then you've never complained about those who died. It's very sad that we now have to part, but don't sin against God, Victor, who's set us this test. Bear it without grumbling. I've born it all day and didn't grumble; I would have gone on bearing it too if you'd never come to speak to me."

"Oh Hanna, Hanna, Hanna!"

"And when you're away, we'll worry about what to send you and I'll go into the garden every day and look at the mountains over which you've gone."

"No, don't do that, it would be too pitiful."

"Why?"

"Because none of that helps – and it's not because I must leave and we must part."

"What is it then?"

"Because everything's over and because I must remain the loneliest, most forlorn man on earth."

"But Victor, Victor."

"I just want to tell you that for some days now I've known for certain that I will never, never marry – it can't happen, it will not be possible ---You see I'll have no home, I belong to no one; the others will forget me—and that's good. –Do you see? –I never knew before, but now it's clear, quite clear that it's all in vain –don't you see?--- Why are you suddenly so quiet, Hanna?"

"Victor!"
"What, Hanna?"
"Were you thinking about----?"
"Yes, I was."
"And then?"
"And then---then---oh, it's all in vain, all in vain!"
"You must remain true to her, Victor!"
"Of course, always, always, but it's no use."
"Why?"
"I told you; my uncle's taken my estate; she's well-to-do, I'm poor and for a long, long time will be unable to support a wife; and someone will come courting who can support her, give her beautiful clothes and presents and she'll accept him."
"No, no, no, Victor, I'm sure she won't – and I'm sure she'll always love you, more than anyone else."
"And when I come back, Hanna, I'll never, never upset you again and we'll always, always love each other."
"Always, always" she said quickly and, turning towards him hastily, grasped his hands which he held out towards her. And so they stood and burst into bitter tears.

They still held in their hands the pieces of silk which Hanna had gathered up at the beginning of the conversation and divided between them, but they paid no attention to them but kept still and went on weeping.

Then came the gardener's boy and said," Mother sent me to tell you to come in and eat."

At once they went hand in hand down the path to the house and into the downstairs parlour. Mother saw they both had eyes red from weeping and was pleased that they had made things up.

They sat down at table, the dishes were brought in and mother served each with what she thought they liked the best, and so all three ate their meal as was usual every midday and evening.

Hanna had very large brown eyes and her mother often looked over at them surreptitiously. When they had finished, and before they all separated to go to bed, the present had to be fetched. It was a wallet with a pure white silk lining and mother had already put money for his journey in it. "I'll take out the money, "said Victor, "and keep the wallet safe."

"No, Victor", said Hanna, "you must leave the money in it. It looks so pretty to see the fine printed paper resting on the silk –You must leave it in and use the wallet."
"Well, all right, I'll use it but I'll take very good care of it."
"And I'll soon make you another one."
Mother locked the compartment with the money in with a tiny key and then urged them to their beds. "Leave that till

tomorrow", she said, when Victor wanted to say his thanks, "and go to bed. By five o'clock you must be up on the mountains, Victor. Sleep well and I've already arranged for the boy to wake us if I oversleep- Good night, children." And each of them took a light and went with it to their rooms.

Among the many shadows made by the things lying untidily around, Victor no longer felt at home. He set his light on one of the boxes and looked out of the window at the old familiar lilac and the trickling stream, but the lilac had already become a dark clump and the stream was no longer visible and in the place where it was supposed to flow was a patch of shadow, and only one star which shone out from it showed that it was there, and only a soft, soft rustling and rippling which penetrated into the room showed it too, when all the voices in the house and the village had finally stilled. Myriads of tiny sparks of light glimmered in the sky but not the smallest outline of the crescent moon.

Victor lay down to sleep his last night here and to await the most remarkable morning which he had ever experienced yet.

And the fateful morning was here. When Victor scarcely believed he had taken the first refreshing breaths of sleep, it was already here. There was a soft knocking at his door and the voice of his mother, who had needed no lad to wake her, was heard. "It's four o'clock, Victor, get dressed, don't forget anything and come down. Do you hear?"

"I hear you, mother."

And he jumped up – beset by two anxieties, his sadness and the excitement of his journey, he got dressed and went into the parlour downstairs. Breakfast was already on the table in the grey morning light – never had it been so early- and it was eaten in silence – mother and Hanna watched him steadfastly. He laid his knife down now here, now there, he picked up something and put it away again – then he buckled on his knapsack and took his hat-- he felt to see if he had his wallet and then looked again as if there was something else there ---"Mother, I must thank you...."he finally said but could get no further. The old woman went to the holy water by the door, sprinkled a few drops on him, made the sign of the cross on his brow, his mouth and breast and said, "Be good, my child, as you always were and keep your good gentle heart –God will bless everything you do. Write often and don't fail to say when you need something. You have a really good heart, my Victor, my dear Victor, fare well!" And with these words she broke into tears and could only move her lips without a sound coming out.

After a while, when she had pulled herself together, she went on, "Don't be sad, cheer up; what's wrong with going off on your travels? If our mountains weren't there and the apple tree, and if our stream didn't run past, - I'd go off with you myself into foreign parts. There are many thousands of good people and they will love you. Take good care of your money and the letters of recommendation which your guardian left for you yesterday. The boxes and trunks will reach you at your destination, and don't get overheated and don't drink water too cold - and so – so Victor go and don't forget us."

Silently, his lips trembling uncontrollably, he held out his hand to Hanna who was dissolving in tears and rushed out. Outside stood the servants and menials and the gardener. Silently he shook hands with them right and left, went down the narrow garden path and out through the gate.

"How handsome he is", said his mother almost crying out loud as they all watched him go, "how handsome, with his brown hair, his manly gait, his lovely vulnerable youth. Oh God!"

And the tears ran out from between her fingers as she held both hands over her eyes. And the others silently melted away and went to their work. "Mother, you're weeping now for sorrow", said Hanna after a while, when everyone had already gone and Victor had long been out of sight. "No, child, I'm weeping for joy", answered her mother, forcing a smile to her lips and looking in the direction in which Victor had gone. "You don't recognize them, child, they're tears of joy." "Well, mine aren't" said Hanna pressing her handkerchief harder to her eyes.

In the meantime Victor had gone round the lilac tree, across the footbridge and out of the orchard, the rising meadows and fields receiving him, and as he heard amidst the faint indistinct sounds of the village at this height also the angry howling of his dog which had had to be caught and tied up so that it didn't follow him – so suddenly the hot tears flowed and he almost cried aloud, "Where will I find another mother like her and people who love me so much? --- Yesterday I hurried out of town to spend a few hours in the valley and today I'm going away to be somewhere else for ever."

When he had at last almost reached the top of the mountain, he looked back once, the last time. He could still make out the house, the garden and its fence. Amidst all the green he saw something that was red like Hanna's silk material – but it was only the roof of a chimney.

And then he walked up the last slope, the glowing air shimmered above the valley—a few last steps over the summit and everything had disappeared behind him and a new valley and a new air was before his eyes. The sun had meanwhile also risen quite high, dried the grass as well as his tears and dropped its warming rays on the land. He went steeply up the slope and when after a while he took out his watch it showed half past seven. "Now my bed will stand there empty, the last thing that was true to me; the sheets will have been taken off and only the inhospitable wooden frame will remain", he said to himself and walked on.

And he climbed higher and higher; some distance now lay between him and the house he had left and some time lay between his present thoughts and the last words he had spoken. His way led him up slopes over which he had never gone, now upwards and now down, but in the main higher and higher –he was really glad now that he had not had to go into the town to say good bye as he had planned because he saw no one; the small farms and dwellings he came across lay to the right and the left of his path – here and there a person walked past and took no notice of him. Noon approached and he walked on and on.

The world grew larger and larger, ever more radiant and wide – and all around were thousands and thousands of joyful beings.

2

And the world grew larger and larger, ever more radiant and wide, and thousands of joyful beings were all around as Victor strode from mountain to mountain, from valley to valley, bearing the great sorrow of his childhood in his heart and fresh eyes full of wonder in his head. Each day he spent far from his home made him more of a man. The immense dryness of the air brushed against his brown hair; the white clouds, gleaming like snow, piled up above him here as they did over his valley at home, his cheeks had already become darker, he carried his knapsack on his back and his stout walking stick in his hand. The only creature which bound him to his home was his old dog Spitz who ran along beside him in a terribly emaciated state. On the third day after his departure the dog had completely unexpectedly and unaccountably come after him. Victor was just going up a cool damp forest path early in the morning when, looking back as he often used to do and delighting in the sparkle of the wet pine trees, he became aware of something hastening towards him; but how astonished he was when the dark ball came nearer, jumped up at him and revealed himself as his foster mother's loyal old dog Spitz. But in what a terrible condition he was; his fine coat had become matted with mud and was full of white road dust down to the skin. When he wanted to give quick barks of joy, he couldn't; for his voice had become hoarse, his eyes, striving to look upwards, had grown dim and were red with tiredness and when he tried to jump for joy he fell with his back leg in the ditch.

"Dear poor old Spitz", said Victor bending down to him, "look what you've taken on, you foolish old animal!" But the dog wagged his tail at these words as if he'd received the greatest praise.

The first thing Victor did was to wipe him down a bit with a cloth so that he looked better, then he took out a couple of slices of bread which he had put aside that morning in case he should meet a beggar, sat on a rock and began to feed them piece by piece to Spitz who swallowed them down ravenously and hurriedly and still looked at Victor's hands for more when they were long since empty. "I haven't any more", said Victor, "but when we come to the first farmhouse we'll buy a bowl of milk and you can have it all for yourself."

A few steps further on, where a very thin trickle of water ran from a mossy cliff, Victor filled with water the leather travelling cup his mother had given him and wanted to give it to Spitz to drink, but he only tasted a bit and looked at the giver unconcernedly, for he had probably drunk from all the hundreds of ditches and streams he had crossed. Then they went on together and at the first inn they came to Victor wrote a letter to his mother to say that Spitz was with him and that she shouldn't be upset.

As far as the milk was concerned, Victor kept his word and in other ways too Spitz got as much as he could eat; and, if he now ate more in one day than in three at home, he nevertheless wasted away so much through the effects of the unaccustomed exertion which, God knows, must have been fearful, that he trotted along beside the young man as if only hanging loosely inside his own skin. "It'll soon get better", thought Victor, and so they strode on.

Victor couldn't understand why the animal had this once decided to follow him, when usually, even when he was away for days, he had at a simple word of command stayed at home and waited for him. But then he concluded, not without justice, that Spitz, whose whole existence was the study of all the doings of his superior friend, his young master, must have known that this time he was going away for ever and had therefore done his utmost to follow him.

And so they went on their way from now on together; over hill after hill, over field after field – and often the young man could be seen washing the dog at a stream and drying him with grass and leaves, and often the dog could be seen standing by his master and looking up at him when he stopped on a slope to look far and wide across the meadows, across the strips of fields, the dark patches of woodland and the white church towers of the villages; then the waves of corn, which obviously belonged to someone, undulated like the sea near the path; hedges surrounded it which must have been planted by someone; birds flew in this and that direction as if to different homelands. For days he had spoken to no one, unless it were a carter or traveller who had asked him, "Which way are you going, friend?" or a landlord who had raised his hat to him when he departed and said, "Have a good journey! Goodbye!"

On the eighth day after he had left his mother and his valley he came to a district which lay neat and prosperous amidst gently rolling hills alternating with orchards as in his valley at home, adorned with well-to-do houses and where there was not even the tiniest patch of ground which was not used and on which nothing grew. The stream was like a splash of silver amidst the green, and the blue mountains, which he had so long seen, now swung in a curve nearer to his road and showed already the matt colours and fissures in their walls.

"How much further is it to Attmaning?" he asked a man sitting beneath the trees in a village inn drinking fruit-wine.
"If you do another good stretch today you could reach it in good time tomorrow" he replied, "but you must take the footpath and strike out via the river Afel towards the mountains."
"I really want to get to Hul."
"You won't find anywhere good to stay there, but if you climb up over Mt Grisel, to the right of the lake, you come

to a place where a genial blacksmith lives and there you'll find a very different welcome."

"But I have to get to Hul."

"Well it'll take you another three hours hard going from Attmaning."

Victor sat down by the man and refreshed himself and the dog. After talking over this and that with his neighbour, he got up again and, to use the man's expression, did another good stretch that day, till he came to the Afel, a clear blue stretch of flowing water. Next day in the clear light of dawn he could be seen going along the footpath which led from the main road towards the mountains. The immensely high massifs came closer and closer to him during the course of the morning and revealed many varied charming, colourful sights. He came to roaring torrents; men delivering coal drove past; sometimes a man with a pointed hat and goatee beard went by; and before it was even twelve o'clock Victor was sitting in the inn at Attmaning, which he found when he had reached the main road again, and he was looking at the mountain pass where everything sparkled in the blue light and a narrow strip of water flashed like the blade of a scythe.

Attmaning is the last point of the hill country where it comes up against the high mountains and its bright green trees, close mountains, its pointed church spire and sunny position make it the loveliest spot to be found on earth.

Victor stayed till nearly four o'clock sitting in the shade of the inn roof and enjoying the sight of these high mountains, their beautiful blue colours and their filmy ever-changing light. He had never in his life before seen anything like it. What was the highest, mightiest mountain in his valley compared to them? When it struck four and the blue shadows gradually sank along the mountain walls and distorted their earlier shapes so strangely, he asked where Hul was to be found.

"Up there by the lake", said the landlord pointing to the gap in the mountains which Victor had so long been looking at during the afternoon. "Do you really want to get up to Hul today?" he asked after a while.
"Yes" said Victor, "and it'll be easier now the cool of the evening has set in."
"Then you mustn't waste any time, and if you have nobody else I'll lend you my lad to go with you through the wood and he can then show you the way from there."
Victor didn't think he needed any guide, for the pass seemed quite close and unthreatening, but he went along with the offer nevertheless and wasted no time in gathering his things together.

It seemed strange to him that people when they spoke of Hul always said 'up' while the mountains there, he felt, seemed to come so close in the haze that he judged the gleam of the water to lie far below, although he also saw that the river Afel sprang from that region and flowed foaming down to Attmaning.

"Rudi, take the gentleman up onto the saddle and then show him the way down into Hul" shouted the landlord indoors and straight away a blond-haired red-cheeked lad with friendly blue goggle-eyes came out and said, "Come on, then, sir!"

Victor had paid for his midday meal and was ready to set out. Straight out of the inn yard they left the main road which led into the broader valley and the lad led him to one side into a stony path between dense gigantic oaks and maples. The path soon went steeply upwards and Victor could from time to time see, through the tops of the trees below, the massifs which marched ever closer and became all the darker the lower the sun sank and the more it cast glowing and shimmering colours on the green foliage of the trees. Eventually the wood became quite dense, the deciduous trees disappeared and they were walking amidst rough impenetrable firs which were only interrupted here and there by frozen rock slides which Victor had not seen when he had looked up at the mountains from Attmaning. He kept thinking that surely now they would start going downhill, but the path wound on along a slope which seemed to keep on renewing itself, as if the forest must be endless and as if the lake moved on before them. The lad told him all sorts of things and walked barefoot beside him on the sharp stones. Finally after a good hour and a half he stopped and said, "This is the saddle; if you go down that path, not the other, past the shrine to the carrier killed in an accident, round the corner of the lake where a lot of rocks have fallen, you'll see houses and that's Hul. Keep looking out through the branches so you can see the water, because another path goes down to the Afel gorge and that would be the wrong way."

Having said this and received his reward from Victor, he went back along the same path up which he had brought him. The place from which the lad had so unconcernedly turned back, as if it were nothing, had the most unexpected effect on Victor. Mountain people often call a 'saddle' a massive ridge which runs between higher peaks and joins them together; and since it usually also separates two valleys, it often happens that when one slowly climbs up from one, suddenly and totally unexpectedly one gets the most amazing panoramic view into the other. And so it was here; the forest had torn itself in two, the lake lay at his feet and all the mountains which he had already seen from the flat land and from Attmaning now stood all round him, so silent, clear and close that he thought he could reach out and touch them. Their walls were not grey but their gullies and fissures were veiled in a misty blue and the trees stood like matchsticks on them but were not even visible on others which brushed smoothly against the blue sky. And round them all, hemming them in, lay the lake, a flat motionless vision, which seemed to remove all the heights to a distance, so that the eye had enough space to gaze at them through the sweet cloud of scent given out by the dark green of the surrounding pine needles.

Not a house, not a human being, not a single animal was to be seen. The lake which Victor had seen from Attmaning as a white line, was here broad and dark, with not even a spark of light but only took its tone from the hazy mountain walls surrounding it, and on its banks lay things which he didn't recognize and which were merely reflected in the still water.

Victor stood and contemplated all this for some while. It was so quiet that one could almost sense the scent of the pines but not the usual swaying of the trees. Nothing moved except the late evening light which gradually passed across the surface of the mountain walls and the cool shadows which followed it.

Almost fearfully he then went down the path the lad had showed him. The mountains sank gradually into the forest, the trees swallowed him up again, except that now, as the lad had predicted, he always saw the river gleaming darkly between the lower branches on his left. Just as he had thought on the way up that the mountain was never coming to an end, so it now went interminably and gradually downwards. He had the lake on his left the whole time as if he could dip his hand into it, and the whole time he couldn't reach it. Finally the last tree fell away behind him and he stood down by the Afel again, just where it left the lake and hurried on its way between vertical cliffs, not leaving even a hands breadth along its edge for a path for people to walk along. It was so isolated here that Victor felt as though he was a hundred miles from Attmaning. There was nothing there except him and the shallow stream which continually empted itself noisily into the Afel. Behind him was the green and silent forest, in front the gently moving expanse of water, closed off by a blue mountain wall which seemed to go down into the depths. The only work of human hands he saw was the footbridge over the Afel and a metal grating through which it had to flow. Slowly he walked across the footbridge followed by the dog who was quiet as a mouse and trembling. On the other side they walked on turf alongside the cliffs. Soon the place the lad had spoken of was to be seen; a heap of rocks lay scattered around and into the lake so that it was easy to see that a landslide might have occurred here. Victor rounded a sharp corner and suddenly Hul lay before him; five or six grey cottages which stood not far away on the shore surrounded by tall green trees. The lake too, which before had been hidden by the projecting angle of the mountain, here opened out and all the mountain walls and heights which he had seen from the saddle surrounded it. For Victor it was a strange and above all a new world which he had first to grow accustomed to.

When he came to the houses he saw that each had a roof which projected out into the lake with small boats tied up beneath it. He didn't see a church but on one of the cottages was a turret made out of four red painted poles and between them hung a bell.

"Is there a place here called The Hermitage?" he asked an old man whom he found sitting in the doorway of the very first house.

"Yes", replied the old man, "The Hermitage is on the island."

"Could you tell me who would ferry me over there?"

"Anyone in Hul could take you over."

"So, could you do it then?"

"Why not, have you got business there?"

"I've been sent for and am expected."

"That's different. Are you coming straight back again?"

"No."

"Well, wait here a minute."

Saying this, the old man went into the cottage from which he soon returned accompanied by a strong young red-cheeked girl who with her arms bare set about pushing a boat out into the water while the old man put on his coat and carried out two oars. A wooden seat was fastened in the boat for Victor and he sat down on it with his knapsack beside him and holding Spitz's head as he snuggled up to him. The old man took his place at the prow sitting facing backwards, and the girl stood in the stern, oar in hand. At the same moment the two oars struck the water together, the boat jumped forward and slid out smoothly into the water, with every stroke of the oars jumping forward further into the darkening rippling surface. Victor had never been on such a large expanse of water. The village receded behind him and the mountain walls around the lake began to move past. A wooded spit of land stretched out, finally split off and proved to be an island. The two rowers directed their course straight for it. The nearer they got the clearer it rose and the wider became the distance between it and the mainland which had formerly been concealed by a mountain. Gigantic trees could be seen on it, at first as if rising straight out of the water, but then standing proudly on high cliffs which ran down vertically with many sharp rocks into the lake. Behind the green of their foliage gradually rose a mountain peak which, lit by the red glow of the evening, sank deeper and deeper into the dark green and moved slowly along the island the nearer they approached it at an angle.

"That's Mt Grisel on the opposite shore of the lake", said the old man, "a fine mountain but not all that difficult. A path goes over it to Blumau and Gescheid where the smiths are based."

They had now come into the shadows which fell deep into the water from the masses of leafy trees on the island and they rowed along in them. Then there came over the water from Hul the sound of the bell which hung on the four poles and called the people to evening prayers. The two rowers immediately drew in their oars and quietly made their evening orisons, while the boat as if impelled by itself drifted along the grey cliffs which overlooked the lake from the island. On the mountains all round an occasional light was to be seen The lake itself had strange patches; some of them gleamed and even sparks shot up and over all came the continual busy tolling of the bell as if rung by invisible hands; for Hul was out of sight and all round the lake there was not a single place that even remotely looked like a human habitation.

"There must be a bell in the monastery, too. I believe it's a fine prayer bell", said the old man after he had put his cap back on and taken up his oar again, "but it's never rung, at least I've never heard it, in fact I've never even heard a clock strike. My grandfather said how beautiful it was when the sound of the bells lay on the lake – for the monks were here then – and when it drifted solemnly around through the mist without one knowing where it came from. For you will have seen that we rowed round the mountain and that the island can't be seen from Hul. It's Mt Orla, this mountain, and two monks once climbed it through deep snow when the lake was frozen but would not bear their weight and when they had run out of food.

They cut a path in the ice for the boat as far as the mountain and then climbed over the summit down into Hul. For you must realise that no footpath is possible between Mt Orla and the lake. Since then in more than a hundred years the lake has never frozen over again. In ancient times the monks first came here, when there was no house anywhere on the lake and no living thing to see his reflection in it except the stag when he came to drink. The monks went across to the island on pine branches and first of all built the Hermitage, from which gradually the monastery arose and in later years also Hul itself where christian people fished and travelled to the Hermitage to hear mass. For in those days the rulers of these parts were still pure pagans and their men killed all those who came over from Scotland with the cross to convert them. But on the island they were protected, for, as you'll see, it's like a fortress. There's only one place where one can land, where these rocks leave an opening and the lake runs onto good sand. Everywhere else there are sheer walls and as soon as even the lightest wind blows up, the lake is full of white horses so that even the best boat is afraid. Fishing is not done often in the year here and the old man wouldn't like it either."

Meanwhile they had gradually approached a long stretch of the shore of the island and had almost reached the place where the cliffs were lower leaving a lovely sandy bay between them which led into a sloping area of woodland. As soon as the rowers reached this spot they turned the boat in and allowed it to run up onto the sand. The old man got out and pulled the boat still higher by the chain in the prow so that Victor could get out without getting his feet wet. He climbed over the prow and Spitz jumped after him.

"If you follow this path", said the old man, "it'll bring you to the Hermitage. May God be with you, and if you don't stay long and he doesn't give you a boat to cross with, send me a message via old Christoph and I'll pick you up at the same place at any time you like."

Victor in the meantime had fished out of his purse the fare that had been agreed and handed it to the man. "Goodbye", he said, "goodbye, good friend, and if you'll allow, I'll call in your house on my way back for a while and perhaps you'll tell me some more of your old stories."

To the girl who had stayed motionless in the stern of the boat he didn't dare to say anything, but he looked at her in friendly fashion. "Oh, how could my stories interest a young educated man like you?", said the old man. "Perhaps more than you think and more than those I read in books", said Victor.

The old man smiled because this answer obviously pleased him, but he said nothing more but bent down, rolled up the short chain in the prow and made preparations to leave. "God be with you, young sir" he said after a while, gave the boat a push, quickly jumped in and the boat rocked back into the water. In a few minutes Victor saw the two oars rising and falling in rhythm as the boat's prow slowly turned out into the bay.

He walked the few steps to the shore till he reached the upper edge of the beach where one could see far out over the lake. From there he watched them leaving and said to his companion, as if he were rational and could understand the words, "Thank God we've reached the end of our journey. The Lord has led us this far safe and sound, whatever else may happen."

He gave one last glance back over the beautiful wide surface of the lake, now growing dark as evening came on, then he turned and went along the path which lay before him into the bushes. The path had quite clearly once been a roadway, which had now all but disappeared and was hemmed in on all sides by rampant stunted shrubs. At first he continued slightly uphill between bushes and tall leafy trees but then the path went on level, the undergrowth disappeared and only unusually strong maple trees stood around on a dark meadow almost as if set in a regular order. Victor walked through this strange garden, again came to bushes then to a strange place where stone fountains and stone dwarfs stood in the grass. A stone flight of steps in the middle of the lawn led down into a moat, in which the path continued a while then again climbed a similar flight of steps on the opposite wall of the moat and ended at a tall barred gate made of iron in a thick windowless wall. It was locked and not far on the other side of it through the bars Victor could see the beginnings of a house which merged into the bushes, with a covered staircase leading down towards a level courtyard on which were flowers and fruit trees. On the far side of the courtyard must be the lake again, for Victor saw through the iron bars the fine haze which gathers over water in the mountains in the evenings and he saw the walls of Mt Grisel shimmering with a violet light.

There was no bell and no knocker on the gate but the face of an old man looked out at him as he made all sorts of attempts to open it. The man had stepped out of the bushes and stretched his head out to see Victor.

"Have the kindness", said Victor, "to open the gate and take me to the master of the house, if this really is The Hermitage."

The man said nothing but stretched out his face even more towards Victor and looked at him for a while and then asked, "Did you come on foot?"
"I came on foot as far as Hul," replied Victor.
"Is that really true?"
Victor blushed, for he never lied. "If it weren't true I wouldn't have said it. If you're my uncle as it almost seems, I have here a letter from my guardian which will tell you who I am and that I've come here because you requested it." Saying this he drew out of his breast pocket a neatly folded letter and handed it through the bars.

The old man took the letter, put it away without reading it and said, "Your guardian's a fool and feeble-minded. What's he to me? I already know all about it. You don't look any different from your father when he started his stupid tricks. I saw you coming over the lake."

Victor, who had never in his life been spoken to like that, was silent and merely waited for the other to open the gate. But the old man said, "Take a piece of rope with a stone and drown this dog in the lake, then come back here and in the meanwhile I'll open the gate for you."

"Who am I to drown?"

"Why that dog you've brought with you."

"And if I don't do it, you won't open the gate?"

"No, then I won't open it."

"Come, Spitz", said Victor, and he turned round, ran with all the strength he was capable of down the stone steps through the moat, across the meadow with the stone dwarfs, through the maples, through the bushes and reached the bay, shouting out "Boatman! Old boatman!" – but it was impossible that he would hear him, the rattle of a machine gun could not have been heard at this distance. The boat looked no bigger than a black fly against the dark summit of Mt Orla which projected far out into the evening glow of the lake. Victor took out his handkerchief, tied it to his stick and waved it about in the air so that he would be seen; but he wasn't seen and finally, while he was still waving, even the black fly disappeared round the corner of the mountain. The lake was quite empty and Victor only saw the lightly foaming surf breaking along the cliffs of the island.

"Never mind, Spitz, never mind." he said. "Come on, we'll sit in the bushes by the shore and spend the night there. Tomorrow a boat will turn up and we'll attract their attention." No sooner said than done. He found a place where the grass was short and dry and where the bushes arched thickly over without hindering the view of the lake. "You see what a good idea it is", he said," to put something aside each morning". So saying he took out two rolls of bread which he had brought early that morning from the inn by the Afel and began to feed himself and the dog with it. The mountains, the beautiful mountains which had so delighted him all day as he came closer to them, were now becoming ever darker and formed scattered mysterious patches, dark and threatening, on the lake, because here and there the evening sky still cast a light pale yellow radiance which flashed and disappeared. Because of the extreme tiredness of their limbs, sitting seemed really pleasant; the bread was eaten with great satisfaction and so the two strange companions sat by the shore, protected by the bushes as with greater and greater speed the darkness began to gather over the lake, the mountains and the sky. Victor had done up all the buttons on his coat and tied his scarf round his neck again – the longing for sleep overcame all his tired young limbs and so he laid his head on his knapsack as the darkness already surrounded him like a wall. The bushes whispered because a light wind rose and the surf echoed clearly from cliff to cliff.

Accompanied by these impressions which became ever weaker, his senses grew dull so that his consciousness of his position became confused and was about to be extinguished totally when he was suddenly awoken again by an angry growling of his dog. He started up – a few steps from him, right by the landing place, stood a human figure, standing out darkly against the iridescent water of the lake which gleamed unsteadily while the bushes were only black inextricable clumps. Victor strained his eyes to the utmost to see more of the figure, but only made out the outline of a man- whether young or old could not be determined, nor why it was there standing so still and apparently looking out eagerly at the water. Victor sat up and stayed equally quiet. At a new louder growling by the dog, the figure suddenly turned round and cried, "Is that you, young gentleman?"

"So, and what do you want?"

"I want you to come in to dinner, the time is almost past."

"To dinner? What dinner? And who are you looking for?"

"Well. You're the young gentleman with the skinny dog and the master's been waiting for a quarter of an hour already."

"Are you his servant?"

"Yes, I'm Christoph."

"The servant of the master of the house called The Hermitage?"

"That's right."

"Well tell him I shall stay here all night and that I would rather hang a stone round my own neck and throw myself in the lake than drown the dog with me."

"I'll tell him all that."

With these words the man turned round and was about to leave, but Victor called after him, "Christoph, Christoph!"

"What is it, young gentleman?"

"Is there no other house or cottage or anything apart from the Hermitage on the island?"

"The old monastery is locked up, so is the church, the granaries are full of debris and likewise shut."

"It's no matter, no matter. I shall never visit my uncle's house again and expect no shelter there. –But tell me, do you often travel over to Hul? I think the old fisherman told me you did."

"I fetch everything over from there."

"Well, listen, Christoph; I'll pay you as much as you like if you make it possible for me to get over to Hul tonight."

"Even if you paid much more, it's still impossible – for three reasons; all the boats are in the boathouse with the heavy wooden door locked and each is fastened to a post. It's a mad idea; even if there was a boat, there is no boatman to take you. –Do you see those geese? They're sitting snow-white and close together on the rocks over on the Orla shore in long, long rows –but now it's getting dark here; when the evening breeze stops, the mist covers the whole lake in an hour and then it's impossible to say which direction a boat is going in. If you spring a leak on a stony shallows you could get out and stay up to your chest in water till you starve to death. Nobody will see you for days on end and nobody rows intentionally over the reefs that run beneath the water. Do you understand?"

Victor didn't altogether understand, but he made no reply to this. "And thirdly", said the man, "I can't ferry you over because that would make me an unfaithful servant."

"Am I a prisoner here, then?"

"No, but the master has not given me any order to take you to Hul and unless he does I won't take you over."

"Then I'll stay sitting here till a boat comes near enough for me to attract its attention."

"In eight days, three weeks even, one will come."

"What do you people want with me then?"

"The master is waiting for you to come to dinner."

"How can he be waiting? He saw me go away and didn't even once call me back."

"I know nothing about that, but he was expecting your arrival, you're here and so a place has been laid for you. Call him, Christoph, he said, he doesn't know the times of our meals – and then I thought you would have run to this place in order to get back across the water – yes, for a moment I really thought when I didn't see you that you had called back the boatman; but no, that isn't possible, he must be round the other side of Mt Orla by now – so come and eat!"

"No, I'm not coming; he wanted to kill my dog."
"The master gave you good advice; if you don't follow it, it's no matter to him. Put the dog on a lead and keep him with you, the dog's no concern of ours."
 "But he's so good; he would never harm anyone, not even a child" cried Victor, pouring out his feelings.
"We won't harm him either if he means so much to you. – Who could have known that? –so come to dinner! You've travelled to see your uncle and it's your duty to be here so that he can speak to you as is necessary."

"Mother wanted me to and my guardian urged me to travel here and come on foot as my uncle specified –I've now come on foot, the poor animal found me and accompanied me at risk of his own life – I'll go in and speak to the man – but before I'll let the slightest harm come to the animal, I'll suffer injury and death myself- and my dear mother and my guardian whom he called a fool know where I am and won't just accept it if something happens to me."

"Nothing's going to happen to you, you're our guest", said the old servant with more warmth than one would have expected of him, "but come on now, I'm afraid the master will have started the meal and not waited."

"He can carry on eating, we're not bothered. We've had our evening meal already." And with trembling hands Victor picked out of his knapsack a piece of cord, such as he always carried in reserve, and fastened it to the ring on the collar which Spitz wore. "Come on, you poor old friend", he said, "nothing's going to happen to you, just stay by me."

Then he picked up his knapsack which had served as a pillow and likewise his stick and followed old Christoph who went on in front, along the same path which he had gone along before as it was getting dark, through the maples, past the dwarfs, through the moat till they reached again the same barred gate. Christoph took something small out of his pocket and made a short piercing whistle with it. Immediately the gate was opened by invisible hands –Victor didn't understand it at all- and closed again behind them with a crash. From the courtyard inside the gate one could in fact see the lake, but Mt Grisel Victor could not see, for on the water lay a thick white wafting mist. In the house which now revealed itself as extensive and angular only three windows were lit up, two on the first floor and one on the ground floor, all the rest was in deep blackness. Christoph led the young man up the covered staircase which led directly down from the first floor into the garden, then along a dark passageway in which they had to feel their way and finally into the room to which the two lighted windows belonged. There he left him and went away. The same old man, whom Victor had seen earlier that evening inside the barred gate, was sitting at a table and eating, the only difference being that, instead of the strange grey clothes he had worn during the day, he was now resplendent in a wide flowery dressing gown and had on a red gold-edged cap.

"I've got to the lobster already", he said to the young man as he entered. "You were too long coming. I have my regular time which is necessary for my health. You'll be served directly. Sit down."

"My mother and guardian send you their best greetings", Victor began, remaining standing with his knapsack on his back; the old man did not allow him to finish, but broke in, "What do I care about them? I wanted you here, and you've come and I recognize you and so start as if you'd been in the house ten days already and go on from there. Tomorrow you'll see the portrait of your father when he was as young as you. It looks exactly like you except for the clothes. Here are plates and here is the chair."

Victor laid his knapsack on a chair, put his walking stick in a corner – the high spirits with which he had come onto the island were now stifled and so he went straight to the chair indicated, pulling Spitz by the cord after him. There he ate the soup which had been served to him in the meantime, holding Spitz with his left hand close by his feet. The old man was eating the lobster which he rapidly ripped apart and sucked out. But the three fat dogs which lay at his feet scowled at poor old Spitz.

"Have you dragged back that old skeleton?" said the old man. "Anyone who has an animal should feed it. It would be better for him if you threw him in the lake. I could never stand students' dogs. I can still picture them like mournful ghosts from my time at university. And such people always want to have dogs. Where did you get it and why did you bring it to me and give it nothing to eat on the way?"

"It's my foster mother's dog, Uncle," said Victor. "I didn't get it anywhere nor buy it, nor swap for it; but on the third day after my departure he came after me. He must have run around much more than he had ever done before in his whole life; he must have overcome great fear and that's why he became so thin the following days although I gave him what he asked for; allow me therefore to keep him with me till I can hand him back and don't do anything to harm him; for if you do then I must ask you to have me taken back to Hul tomorrow so that I can return to mother and my guardian."

"And you've had him with you day and night?"
"Of course."
"But he could tear out your throat."
"He'd never do that- why would he think to do that? He has lain at my feet, laid his head on them and would rather starve than leave me or harm me."
"Well give him some food then and don't forget some water so that he doesn't become rabid."

After these words they carried on eating in silence and his uncle kept his gaunt face down on his plate and as he ate, it turned as red as the lobster, and his piercing eyes concentrated on the nearest vicinity of his plate. From time to time he handed down to one or other of the dogs a chosen titbit. An old woman had gradually brought in for Victor so many dishes that he was lost in astonishment. He ate them till he was full and handed Spitz down his share. Also a strangely large number of wines stood on the table and each one had its own special glass. The old man must already have drunk from them all, for the glasses were already pushed to one side, each with some dregs in the bottom, and only one small green stem glass was still in use. Victor had drunk water as was his custom and his uncle had not offered him any wine. Victor thought the water fresher, stronger and more elastic than any he had ever tasted. When the lobster had finally been served to him, while his uncle was eating a piece of cheese, then fruit, and then all kinds of sweetmeats which stood around on the table, the meal was over. The old man stood up and carried the various dishes with their glass covers and put them in the cupboards which were fitted into the walls, added the wine bottles and closed the brown stained doors with his own hands. The old woman carried away the remains of Victor's meal and when at that moment Christoph came in, his uncle said, "Make sure you shut them in so they can't get out, but let them run around for a while on the sand first." And at these words the three dogs got up as if on command; two followed Christoph out and the third he grasped by the skin and dragged out.

"I'll show you your bedroom myself", said his uncle, and from the back of the room, where Victor could indistinctly see all sorts of strange things, he took a candlestick from a stand and lit the candles in it. Victor picked up his knapsack by one of the straps, did the same with his stick, and followed his uncle, leading Spitz behind him by the cord. They went along one passageway in which stood ancient chests, turned into a second which went at right angles to the first, then into a third which was barred by an iron grille and, Victor thought, led back to the front of the house. At the end of this his uncle unlocked a door and led Victor into two rooms, one of which was remarkably large and the other was very small. "You can shut the dog in the next room", said his uncle, "so that he can't harm you. And close the window against the night air."

With these words he lit a large candle standing on the table and without further ado left. Victor heard him shutting the iron grille, then the dragging steps in their slippers died away and the silence of the dead reigned in the house. In order to make sure he had heard correctly Victor went out into the passage to investigate. It was true; the iron grille was locked. "You poor man", said Victor, "are you really so afraid of me?"

He put the light back on the table by the battered tin wash basin and walked to the large pair of barred windows which stood side by side. A pale night sky beset with few stars looked in through the iron bars. A small disk of the waxing moon must have been behind the clouds, for a weak milky light flowed from them, but the moon itself could not be seen. Mt Grisel stood out black, like a flat silhouette against the matt silver of the sky, and there was a star to one side of one of the shoulders of the mountain which sparkled like a medal hanging from it.

"I wonder in which direction the little white house lies", he thought to himself, for because of the various windings of the path along the Afel and the diverging of the passages in the house he had lost all sense of direction.

"There the stars will be shining down, the elder will be still and the stream will ripple but no one will be looking down to see the sparks of light in the water and how the sleeping mountains bend over it in greeting and the dark treetops stand. The windows will be shut and the things in the parlour will remain untouched and unmoved for weeks."

In front of his present windows, too, there was a stretch of water, wide and majestic, but he couldn't see it, for a motionless white mist lay on it, whose upper surface no longer ended in soft flocks and misty threads as before but was cut off by a firm straight line.

A very damp cold night wind came in through the windows. He closed them and now inspected the second chamber. It was like the first, a table, a chest, some chairs – except that it had no bed like the larger room. In a niche hung a Russian picture on which was painted a monk. In this room, too, Victor shut the narrow barred window and went back to his sleeping place. All the time he had automatically taken Spitz with him on his lead, but now he loosed the knot on the ring, took off his collar and said, "Lie down wherever you like, poor old friend; we won't shut ourselves off from each other. "

The dog looked at him as if to say quite plainly that it was all strange to him and that he didn't know where he was.

Victor now for his part locked the door of his room, undressed and lay down in bed. For a while he left the light burning on his bedside table but when his eyelids became too heavy and his evening prayers were finished, he blew out the candle and turned to the wall. Even in his dreams came the thought that in this large house he had seen only three people, all of them old. Spitz lay down as usual at the foot of his bed, did nothing to harm him, and for the two exhausted creatures the night went by in a flash.

When Victor woke next morning, he was startled by the splendour that was revealed; Mt Grisel stood opposite, sparkling and gleaming from all its fissures, and although in the night it had seemed the highest, he now saw that even higher mountains stood beside it which he had not seen in the night and which now shone with a soft blue and revealed in several places flecks of snow which settled low in the fissures like white swans. Everything sparkled and shimmered in confusion, tall trees stood before the house so wet that he had never seen the like before, the grass dripped and everywhere broad shadows fell – and it all was seen again in the lake which, swept clean of every flock of mist, lay there like the finest mirror. Victor threw open his window and stuck his healthy face out through the iron bars. His astonishment was extraordinary. In sharpest contrast to all the confusion of light and colour all round was the deathly silence in which these enormous masses stood. Nobody was to be seen, not even in front of the house; only a few birds twittered now and again in the maple trees. What a morning chorus there must be on all these mountains which were covered with extensive forests, but they were too far off for him to hear it. Victor stretched his head out as far as he could to look around; he saw one portion of the lake. Everywhere there were high cliffs and he couldn't make out where he had come in. The sun too had risen in a quite different place from what he had expected, namely behind the house and his windows were still in shade which only emphasized the light of the opposite mountainsides. With the moon too, which yesterday, judging by its light, he had taken to be a narrow sickle, he was equally in error, for it stood now in the sky as a crescent, low down towards the jagged summits of the mountains. Victor had not yet discovered the effect of the light on the mountains. How the light must have flooded these distant cliff faces for they were as if lit up like the tower of the church in his village which, in the moonlight rose so shimmering white in the blue night air! Although the sun was already fairly high in the sky, the air which streamed in through his windows was still as cold and damp as ever he had been used to at home; but it did not trouble him for it was so strong and sharp that it completely invigorated him.

He finally stepped back from the window and began to unpack his knapsack in order to change his clothes from those he had worn on the journey; for today, he thought, his uncle would want to speak with him and explain why he had insisted on him coming to see him on this lonely island. He chose some clean linen, brushed the dust from his second suit which he had brought with him as well as his travel clothes; he made full use of the mirror-like water in the large jug to wash off the travel dust from his body and dressed himself as stylishly and smartly as he had learnt to do in the over-clean house of his foster mother. He even combed and brushed Spitz who was such an unwelcome guest in this house. Then he put his collar on and tied his cord to the ring. When they were both ready, he opened the door and went out to see if he could find some sort of breakfast or drawing room. He had in mind the room where they had eaten yesterday evening, because he suspected that it might prove to be a kind of room where people gathered. When he was out in the passage it occurred to him that today for the first time while he was standing at the window he had forgotten to say his morning prayers; so he went back into the room, stood again by the window and said the simple words which he had thought up in his mind for this purpose. Then for the second time he set out to find his uncle.

The iron grille in the passageway was no longer locked, he passed through it and easily found his way out into the second larger passage, but beyond this he could not find the brown door of yesterday's dining room which he had noticed was provided with a brass ring which also served as a knocker. Everywhere he turned there was another passage which looked similar to the one which he had come along or perhaps was the same; for everywhere he thought he recognized the old cupboards he had seen the day before. Today he could not see them so clearly for the windows in the passage were boarded up and only through the cracks and through the small patches of window which had been left here and there could a little light enter.

Finally when he had convinced himself that he was going round in circles and in fact kept coming back to the same cupboards, a door suddenly opened in one of them and the old woman who had waited on him the evening before at dinner, came out carrying cups and dishes. When she vanished again at a place near him where he had seen no door, and disappeared as if into the earth and since she had left the cupboard door open, Victor looked inside and noticed to his astonishment that it was only a false door and on the back wall was the brown door with the brass ring. He knocked and went in. He had now really arrived in yesterday's dining room and saw his uncle already in the broad grey coat he had been wearing yesterday when Victor had arrived at the barred gate. He had a stuffed bird in his hand and was clearing the dust off it with a brush.

"Today I'll tell you the timetable we go by in my house", said his uncle; "I've had to take my breakfast already because it was the time for it. Pour some water for the dog into that wooden trough." And with these words he climbed up onto a three-legged stool and put the bird up into one compartment of a glass case, took another out and began to brush that in the same way.

Victor could now see in daylight how unusually haggard and wasted the man was. His features expressed no benevolence and no sympathy but were turned in on themselves, like in someone who is on the defensive and who has loved none but himself for countless years. His coat hung loosely at the sleeves and at the collar a baggy piece of shirt stuck out by the badly tied cravat which was dirtier than any Victor had seen as he grew up. In the room there was a large number of stands, shelves, nails, antlers and the like, on all of which something stood or hung. But it had all been guarded so doggedly that dust lay everywhere and many had evidently not been moved from their place for years. On the inside of the dogs' collars, of which a whole bundle hung there, the dust lay thick; the folds of the tobacco pouches were stiff and had not been changed for uncountable ages; the pipes fitted loosely in the rack and the papers beneath the countless paper weights were yellow; the room, which instead of a ceiling had an enormous pointed dome, had originally been painted, but the colours in their light and shade had become a uniform old-fashioned grey. On the floor lay a faded carpet and only where the old man was accustomed to sit at his meals was a smaller rug with bright colours laid on it. At the moment the three dogs were rolling all over it.

Victor stood still and watched his uncle. He continued with his work as if no one else was present. He must have not done this for a very long time and had set about it today at daybreak, for already a large number of birds had been cleaned while the others still all stood grey with dust behind their glass doors. The old woman, who had earlier passed Victor without speaking, now brought in a tray with his breakfast and set it equally silently on the table. Victor concluded that it was for him since she had brought it when he appeared and he set to and ate as much as he was accustomed to eat in the mornings; for everything customary on these occasions in England was there, from the tea and coffee down to the eggs, cheese, ham and cold roast beef. Spitz had it best for Victor gave him more than he had perhaps ever in his life had for breakfast before.

"Have you poured some water in the trough?" asked his uncle.

"No", replied Victor, "but I'll do it straight away." He took the glass jug which stood on the table filled with the same magnificent spring water as yesterday and poured some of it, really just to satisfy his uncle, into a small wooden well-polished trough which stood by the wall near the door. After Spitz had drunk, his uncle came away from his work and called his dogs to the water, but since none evinced any desire for any because they had probably already drunk their fill, his uncle pressed down the handle which stuck up from the side of the trough and a round panel in the bottom of it opened and let the water flow out through a hidden pipe. Victor almost smiled at this arrangement, for at home all that was done in a simpler and friendlier way; Spitz was in the open air, he drank from streams and ate his food under the apple trees.

"Lunch is at exactly 2 o'clock", said his uncle who was again continuing to dust the birds. Victor was astonished and asked, "Won't you want any more to eat before then?"

"No", answered his uncle.

"Then I'll go out and have a look at the lake, the mountains and the island."

"Yes, do that, or anything else you like", said his uncle. Victor hurried out but he found the doors which led to the staircase locked and so had to go back into the room to ask his uncle to have them opened. "I'll open them for you myself", he said, put his bird down, opened the doors with a key which he carried in his pocket and let Victor go down.

Victor quickly put the stairs behind him and when he was in the open and the flood of light beat down on him, he turned round and observed the house he had just left. It was a strong dark building with the one upper storey in which he had spent the night. He recognized his room by the open windows, for the others were all shut and sparkling with the manifold colours produced by the effect of age. All stood behind strong iron bars. The main door was blocked up and the covered stairway seemed to be the only entrance. How different it was from at home where window after window stood open, soft white curtains wafted and from out in the garden one could see the cheerful fire in the kitchen flickering! Tall trees stood round this dismal house and in front neat flower beds ran down towards the lake. In many places benches had been set up.

From the house a double avenue of ancient lime trees, so impenetrable that they kept the ground beneath them always damp, led to another building whose tall great door was locked and rusty. Above the arch of the door were the stone symbols of high spiritual rank, the staff and mitre along with other heraldic devices of the place, but at their feet there was grass of a beautiful dark green from the shade of the lime trees. A not very large quadrangle with ash-grey walls and a black tiled roof ran back into the overgrown trees, the windows were barred and behind most of them were grey boards eroded by rain. Victor tried to find a way along the side of the building in order to find another entrance but he found none and everywhere he came up against a wall which seemed to enclose the whole, together with his uncle's house, and probably had no other exit but the barred iron gate. He found a large orchard which had grown wild and which extended back in a wide angle jutting out from the circular wall and from which he could catch sight of the two solid but unusually low towers of the church. But since he could not get there and it was all in vain, he turned away from these ruins from the past and his eye was gently delighted by the life blossoming and eternally young all round him in the present. All the mountain walls with their clear early morning light looked down onto this green island bedecked with plant life, and so great and so overwhelming was their calm that the ruins, those vestiges of past human life, were merely the one grey point totally ignored by the life bursting forth far and wide. Dark treetops threw their shade over them, the climbing plants crept up the walls and into the crevices – down below the lake shone and the sun's rays played on all the heights in a feast of gold and silver.

Victor now decided to walk round the whole island; he felt good about it now for the first time; but he found no way out of the spell in which these ruins and the dark house were held; everywhere he ran into the same wall, even when it was hidden behind the thickest and most flourishing bushes. For a considerable while he stood at the barred gate, looked at the bars, tried the lock – but to go back to his uncle and beg him to have it opened he was reluctant to do – and anyway who could have opened it? In the whole house he saw no servants and no people at all, as if, apart from the old man and the two old creatures who served him, all had died out, and he did not want to bother his uncle. Therefore he left the gate alone again and wandered along the open flower-bordered courtyard towards the lake in order to look down from the cliff edge, if there was one, into the water. There was a cliff and when he stood at the extreme edge, it was as high as a house. Below, the water gently fringed the beach; opposite towered Mt Grisel whose friendly rock faces and white stones were reflected in the water; all around the hazy mountain walls closed off the dark smooth motionless water and when Victor looked back at the green island with its walls and deathly silence he felt extraordinarily anxious for this place. He tried to see if there was a way to climb down to the water, but the cliff, lashed by rain and storms, was as smooth as iron, and it even went inwards down towards the water and formed an overhang. How enormous must be the mountain walls of Mt Grisel, he thought, which seen from here rose like palaces while the cliffs of this island seen from Mt Orla appeared only like a white strip of sand!

The young man now walked along the shore as if it were easier for him to walk the bounds of what seemed like his prison. He came to the wall which here fell steeply and smoothly to the lake. He had to turn back again and he walked back along the same boundary only to get to the other end where the wall again descended. But before he reached it he came upon an opening which was hewn into the masonry like a cellar door and revealed steps going down. Victor thought this could be a stairway leading down to the lake, perhaps to fetch up water. He straight away went down. It was like a vaulted cellar stairs which led downwards with many steps. But how astonished was Victor when the darkness of the stairs gradually got lighter and he arrived down at a real water hall. Two side walls of large smooth square stone ran out into the lake with stone ledges running beside them so that one could walk along beside the surface of the water which formed the floor of the hall. Above was a solid roof, the walls had no windows and all the light there was came in through the side open to the lake but barred by a grating made of very strong oak slats. The fourth wall at the back was formed from the rocks of the island. Many wooden pegs were driven into the ground and many of them had a rowing boat attached by means of an iron lock. The room was very large and must once have housed many such boats, which was shown by the worn appearance of the iron rings, but now there were only four which were fairly new, very well built and attached with chains and locks to the rings. The slatted grating had several doors to allow boats out into the lake but they were all locked and the timbers went far down into the water.

Victor stood still and looked into the green sparkling light of the lake which shone in between the black oak slats. He sat on the edge of one of the boats and tested the water with his hand; it was not as cold as, to judge by its transparent clarity, he had expected. He gradually took off his clothes one after the other. Since his childhood, swimming had been one of his favourite enjoyments and since he had heard that his uncle's house lay on an island in a lake he had brought with him in his knapsack all his swimming kit – but here it was of no use; for as soon as he got into the water between the boats, he found that it was too shallow and where it began to get deeper was where the wooden grating began and so close were the slats to each other that not even the slimmest body could have got through – so there was nothing for it but to bathe his body in the refreshing swell on this side of the grille. When he had done this and put his clothes back on he climbed back up the steps he had come down and continued his walk along the edge of the shore. What he had foreseen turned out to be right; after much clambering up and down he came to the wall again which here too sank vertically and smoothly into the water, not even leaving enough space for a rabbit to slip past it. Victor stood idly in this place for a while, then went back to the courtyard with the flowerbeds and sat there on a bench. The house was still as it had been in the morning; only the windows of his room stood open, all the rest were shut. No one came out and no one went in, the shadows moved along the dark walls and to Victor it seemed as if he was already a year away from his home. He remained sitting on the bench till his watch showed the time to be two o'clock.

Lunch differed from dinner the day before only in that this time both uncle and nephew ate together, otherwise it was the same as yesterday; his uncle said little, or next to nothing; the dishes were many and very good. Several wines stood on the table, his uncle offered them to him, but Victor said that he had always drunk water and declined them. Even now his uncle said nothing about whether or when he wished to speak to Victor as he was the whole time expecting; but when the meal was over he stood up and busied himself with all kinds of things lying round in the room in which he rummaged around. In the afternoon, since the heat in this valley bottom was as great as was the cold in the morning, and Victor again roamed around his restricted space, he saw him sitting on a bench in the full sun, but he didn't call to him and Victor did not go to him.

So passed the first day. The evening meal, which he was informed was at nine o'clock, ended for Victor the same way as yesterday; his uncle led him to his room and locked the iron grille in the corridor. One thing occurred to the young man, that he had not seen old Christoph the whole day and that only the old woman had waited at table, if one could call it 'waited' when she merely brought in the dishes and set them down. Everything else was done by his uncle himself; even the bottles of wine and the cheese he locked away again afterwards.

Next morning after breakfast he said to Victor, "I promised you yesterday to show you the portrait of your father, so come." With these words he unlocked a side door of the breakfast room and led Victor into an adjoining room which was sparsely furnished but had more than a hundred firearms of all types and all ages displayed in glass cases. Hunting horns, game bags, powder pouches, hunting sticks and thousands of these sorts of things lay around. They went through this room, then through the one adjacent which again was quite empty. In the third hung a single picture. It was round like the shields on which coats of arms are often painted and surrounded by a wide scorched pierced frame of great age.

"That is your father", said his uncle.

A handsome young man in the rudest health, hardly more than a boy, was depicted on the round shield, wearing baggy brown clothes decorated with gold lace. The quality of the painting was nothing special, but done with that depth and accuracy as is often to be seen on family portraits of last century. The gold frame sparkles, the white hair is carefully tended and the face beneath it bursting with health.

"It was the foolish custom in the academy in which we were educated", said his uncle, "that all the pupils should have their portraits painted and hung up in such shields in the corridors and halls. Only sons of the nobility were educated there. Your father had a high opinion of himself and had his portrait painted. I was much more handsome than him but I attached no value to it and didn't sit because I didn't want to. Now the academy has closed down and the portraits dispersed. His came here."

Victor, who no longer had any memory of his father or his mother, since both had died in his earliest childhood, his mother first and shortly afterwards his father, now stood with the deepest feelings before the portrait of him to whom he owed his life, and the picture took him back to a long past time when the original of the portrait had been happy, young and hopeful, just as Victor was now as he looked at the picture. Victor, when he thought of him, had never been able to imagine his father like this; - this was not the picture of the man in the dark coat whom he had seen standing by his cot and whom until now he had had merely a blurred image of in his head. He had to think that this father, if he had still been alive, would also now be old, but when he thought this he could not imagine that he was like his uncle. He made up his mind to ask his uncle for the painting before he left the island. He couldn't be very attached to it since he had hung it quite alone on the wall in this untidy room.

His uncle in the meantime stood beside the young man without participating in any way, and when Victor made the first signs of moving away from the picture, he went on in front at once to show him out of the rooms without saying another word either about the picture or the boy's father except "It's a remarkable likeness." He left the young man standing in the dining room and went through a hidden door which Victor had not noticed before into a room or some sort of cubby-hole and did not come out again.

Victor stood and looked at this door, sizing it up from top to bottom. Then he turned round and went quickly out. When he again found the doors to the covered stairway locked, he didn't go back in to his uncle to ask for them to be opened, but tried to find the passage where he had seen the old woman with the cups disappear the day before. He found it too and made his way through it down into the kitchen where he in fact found no one except the same old woman busy with the preparation of the various things necessary for the midday meal. Only one other much younger and foolish-seeming girl helped her with this. Victor asked whether she could let him out into the gardens? "Oh, certainly", she said, led him up the same stairs which he had come down and fetched his uncle who calmly opened the doors and let him out.

The day passed just as had yesterday. They ate at midday. His uncle didn't want him for anything and Victor again strolled around among the bushes. Towards evening old Christoph came rowing to the island in a boat and was let in through a door in the wooden grille. He had fetched groceries and other necessities and Victor who had stood by as he landed, did not understand how the old man had obtained this great quantity of things which he had rowed across the lake. Also he was sorry that he had not known of his departure because he could have given him a letter to his mother.

And the third day and the fourth went by like their predecessors. Over on the other side stood Mt Grisel, to the right were the blue mountain walls, below the lake shimmered and reflected the greenery of the mass of trees on the island and through the branches blue patches of Mt Orla could be glimpsed. And right in the middle, like a grey weathered lump of rock lay the monastery with the house. Victor had already visited every part of the walls, had sat on all the benches and stood on all the promontories.

On the fifth day he dressed more carefully, went to his uncle and asked him to say why he had wanted him to come; for next day he wanted to begin his journey home. "It's still three weeks before you take over your new position", said his uncle.
"But I want to go away tomorrow".

"I'm not going to let you go till the day when you have to set off for your vocation."

"You must let me go or I'll go out and throw myself from the cliffs into the lake and be dashed to pieces."

"Throw yourself off then, if you're that weak", said his uncle looking in front of him with his usual expression.

Victor cast a glance of utmost scorn at the man – he was ashamed to show weakness and determined to defy him by being patient. "And when that day comes, you'll have me rowed over to Hul?"

"Then I'll have you rowed over to Hul."

"Fine." And with these words he stuck his beret on his head and went away.

Now he was free. By the covered stairway hung a little bell. If he wanted to go out or come in he rang it and each time his uncle appeared and calmly unlocked the gate for him. For many hours he wrote in his room. At meal times he said nothing and when the meal was over he went out. Unabashed he searched the house upstairs and down but he could find out nothing. He got to know every part of the space surrounded by the walls; he had studied the coming and going of the light on the mountains and the shower of different colours which passed over them as the hours of the day changed or when clouds covered the sky. Through the still air, when the sun stood high in the sky at noon or when it had gone down at the edge of the mountains, he listened out for the little bell in Hul ringing for prayer – for on the island no striking of a clock nor clang of a bell was to be heard – but he heard nothing; for the green wall of trees was between his ear and the sound

– and when evening had come he took his bathing suit and went swimming in the lake. He noticed, though, when his uncle had opened the wooden grating for Christoph on his return, that one of the slats which went deep down into the water was shorter than the others and so left a gap through which one could perhaps by diving down get out into the lake. The attempt succeeded; and so every day he made his way into the boat house when the worst of the heat was past, and swam around in large circles outside the wooden grating. At night, when the full moon which now adorned the sky had passed over the house, he opened his windows and saw the magic glittering and twinkling and the fading of the light and saw the black stone masses not touched by the light standing like strangers in this bare twilight world. He spoke not a word to Christoph or the old maid if he met them, because he did not think it dignified to speak to servants when he did not speak to their master.

So some time passed.

One day when he was walking across the courtyard at around 5 o'clock towards the boathouse in order to bathe, as usual dragging poor old Spitz on his lead behind him, his uncle spoke to him. He was sitting as was his custom on a bench in the sunshine and he said "You don't need to take the dog on a lead like that, you can let him go free with you, if you like."

Victor glanced at the man and saw at least no sign of dishonesty in his face, even if there was no other expression. Next day Spitz went free and nothing happened to him and he remained free all the following days.

Another time, while Victor was swimming and happened to look up, he saw his uncle standing in a doorway which opened out of the roof of the boathouse and looking down at him. The old man's expression seemed to indicate pleasure at the way the young man breasted the waves so powerfully and with a friendly eye he watched the dog swimming beside him. The very handsomeness of the young man, too, spoke in his favour as he dressed again, displaying a body, which in its innocence and purity was yet to suffer the powerful effects of age and of the unknown future which Fate had in store for him. Whether some love also stirred in him for this lonely young man, who was closer to him than any one else in the world, who can say? Also it was not clear whether this was the first time he had watched or he had done it often, but the next day when Victor walked across the courtyard at five o'clock and saw his uncle working on the flowers, the only occupation he had ever seen him do, and had passed him without saying a word, he found to his great astonishment when he entered the boathouse that one of the doors in the wooden grating stood open and every day at the same time it was open, even though it was locked at all other times.

There were also other signs that his uncle watched him. When he once again stood wistfully by the barred gate, something he had never done before, and pressed his face between two of the bars, there was above him the sudden rattle of a chain which he had often noticed going up one of the bars and disappearing into the wall, - and after this rattling he felt by the gentle pressure of the bars against his body that the gate was open and he could get out. He used the opportunity and explored all parts of the island.

His uncle had touched Victor's heart the most when he allowed him to let Spitz off his lead. Now on his part too the young man began to observe his uncle more closely and to wonder whether he was really so hard and not perhaps just an unhappy old man.

And so they went on living side by side, two shoots from the same stock, who should have been closer than other people and who were further apart than any – two shoots from the same stock but so very different; Victor the free, cheerful work still in progress, with the gentle longing in his wide eyes--the other the image of decline, with an intimidating expression and sin reflected in his every feature. The wretched man had once taken this sin upon himself, thinking it was something pleasurable, something to profit him.

Only four people lived in the whole house; his uncle, old Christoph, Rosalie, for that was the name of the old housekeeper and cook, and finally the foolish Agnes, already an old maid, who was Rosalie's assistant. Victor walked around among these old people and beside the old decayed walls like someone who did not belong here – even the dogs were all old, the fruit trees in the garden were old, the stone dwarves, the wooden slats in the boathouse too! Victor found only one thing which was still in the prime of life like himself, namely the mass of foliage which with its luxuriant shoots grew rampantly over all signs of the past and out from within them.

The young man had already tried to find his uncle's bedroom several times but could not find it; and now he kept remembering two things which he had by chance heard the old woman say; "He trusts no one; so how could anyone persuade him to engage someone from Hul as a servant? He won't do that. -- He'd rather shave himself so that no one cuts his throat, and every night he shuts in the dogs so that they don't devour him." Victor could not help but constantly think of the extreme helplessness these statements implied, and he did this all the more since there were now signs of a more lenient attitude towards him. The iron grille in the passageway to his room was no longer locked, the wooden grating in the boathouse was always open at the time he swam, and, in order to get in and out through the main barred gate which shut off the whole area, Victor had received from his uncle a small whistle, at the sound of which the gate would open; for it was locked by no ordinary key, but from one of the old man's rooms –though he didn't know which – a connecting chain ran through the wall and by means of this he could open and close the gate from the room.

The first words which these two relatives said when they spoke to each other again were occasioned by a strange cause, one might almost say out of envy. For when one evening Victor was coming back from an expedition across the island accompanied by all four dogs – for the three belonging to his uncle had attached themselves to him and had become much happier and more active –his uncle, who happened to be still in the garden, saw this and said; "Your Spitz is far better behaved than my three brutes who are not to be trusted; I don't know how they come to be so attached to you."

"Just love them as I do Spitz and they'll behave as well as he does", replied Victor.

The man looked at him with strange searching eyes and made no reply. But from now on they spoke to each other again at table and on one occasion in particular Victor became very animated when the old man, either by chance or intention, asked him about his future and his plans. He would take up his official post, said Victor, would work at it to the best of his ability, would put right every fault he met with, would frankly lay before his superiors everything which needed to be changed, would tolerate no backsliding or fraud, in his free time would undertake to study Europe and its languages in order to prepare himself for future literary work, then he would also study the nature of war in order some day to be able to oversee the whole process in the highest service of the state or in times of danger to serve as a general. If he had any talent at all, he would not like to completely neglect the muses, in the hope that he could rouse and inspire his countrymen.

During this speech his uncle had crumpled up little balls of bread and had kept his thin red lips tightly clamped together as he normally did. "You swim really well", he said, "I watched you again for a while yesterday; but the sweep of your right hand is a bit too short and you thrash around with your feet too much. Wouldn't you like to try and go hunting some time? I'll give you one of my guns and you can go round the island shooting."

"I don't want to shoot the beautiful song birds I see here" answered Victor "for I like them too much and in the whole of the rest of the island I've only seen old fruit trees with new forest trees growing among them so there is very little likelihood of a fox or any other game worth shooting."

His uncle went on drinking his wine and eating his confectionary and then they went to bed. Victor was now no longer escorted by his uncle to his bedroom as in the first days, but after the evening meal he lit his candle himself and made his way with Spitz to the two rooms.

So the time passed and the day approached on which according to his uncle's promise he should be rowed over to Hul. He had intentionally made not the slightest mention of it up to now. On the evening before, his uncle rummaged through all kinds of papers and, as is the way with old people with clumsy hands, mixed them all up. Then he pushed them into a corner and went to his meal for which Victor had been waiting by the table for a long while. The evening passed as usual and the morning appeared which was the very last date for him to leave. The young man's heart was beating fast as the day dawned and he was curious to see where it would all lead and what his uncle would say. They came to breakfast together and it was eaten with the same leisureliness as every day. Then the old man in his loose-fitting grey clothes went several times in and out of the doors and finally said, "You'll want to be off then, today or tomorrow?"

"I must leave today, Uncle, if I'm not to be late", answered Victor.

"You'll be able to find a conveyance out there in Attmaning."

"I've already reckoned on that. I must be off today if I'm to get anywhere."

"You must go today? –You must –well if you must, Christoph will row you over as I promised. Have you already packed up all your things?"

"I've everything packed and in order."

"You've packed everything?- right, I see –You've already packed and are very glad – There's something else I wanted to say to you – now what was it? Listen Victor."

"What is it, Uncle?"

"I've been thinking and wondering whether you would try ---, whether you would be willing to stay for a while with a man who has nobody else?"

"How can I?"

"I had a leave of absence for you –wait a minute, I think I put it in the pipe drawer." And he opened and closed several drawers in the table and in the chests in which were the pipes and tobacco pouches till he pulled out a paper and handed it to Victor. "There, you see?" Victor was astonished and confused to the highest degree, for the paper was in fact a leave of absence for an indefinite time. "You can keep it now if you like", said his uncle. "Whenever you want I'll arrange for you to be taken over.

In the meantime you can go out as often as you like and wherever you like."

Victor didn't know what to think. He had been waiting for this day for a long time; now he saw this strange old man, whom he really hated, standing before him begging. The old shrunken face seemed immensely forlorn, indeed it appeared that even some deep feeling trembled within it. The young man's good heart was moved – only for a moment he did not move then he said with the frankness which was so characteristic of him, "I'll be glad to stay a bit longer, Uncle, if you wish it and have good reasons for thinking it right."

"I have no other reason than the wish to have you here for a while" said the old man. Then he picked up from the table the paper containing the leave of absence and after vainly searching through three drawers for a place finally laid it in a fourth which contained specimens of minerals.

Victor, who this morning had left his room not suspecting that things would turn out like this, now made his way back to it and slowly unpacked his knapsack again. He was now doubly uncertain and doubly anxious to know where all this was leading and why it was that his uncle had gone to all the trouble to procure a leave of absence for him before he had even taken up his post. For one moment it flashed through his mind; what if it was affection, if the man preferred a living human presence to the abundance of dead lifeless things and odds and ends with which he surrounded himself? But then he remembered the indifference with which the old man had picked up the paper from the table and found a drawer in which he could hide it. Victor had long since noticed that he never put a thing back in the same place but always in a new place. And while he was searching around he had completely forgotten the young man and let him go out without saying a word to him.

So he was still here. In the house his uncle had a book room but he had not read anything for a long time, so that dust and moths had attacked the books. Victor, who had only recently discovered the collection and received the key to the room, set up the ladder to each shelf, dusted everything and read and absorbed whatever appealed to him. Also it gave him great satisfaction when he could go up into the loft of the boathouse and could jump into the lake from the door through which his uncle had watched him. The monks had put in the door in order to haul up quickly things from the boats which could only with great difficulty have been brought up the steps. From his uncle's gun cabinet he had taken out a fine old German rifle and enjoyed cleaning it and firing it. He had been to see the monastery after Christoph had shown him a passage to it from the house; he had seen the silent dust-covered bells hanging there; he had wandered along the passageways where the old abbots looked down from blackened pictures with their names and dates in bright red beneath; he had stood by the altars stripped of their gold and silver and had stepped across many a stone doorstep, worn down by endless feet, into the cells which now echoed and were filled with stale air. But it was not only on the island he was allowed to see everything, his uncle also offered to row him in a boat to every part of the lake, but up to now he had not taken him up on this. Despite all this, after a few days he bitterly regretted that he had agreed to stay, for the man disgusted him because he ate and drank so much and said nothing further.

"I'll soon let you leave now" said his uncle one day after lunch, when a tremendous storm was passing over Mt Grisel, sending the pouring rain into the lake like diamond cannon shots so that it boiled and seethed, which was why they had remained sitting at table a bit longer than usual. Victor made no reply to this but his heart beat faster.

After a while his uncle began again, speaking slowly and said," It's all a waste of time - it's all over now; youth and age don't go together. Look, you're good enough. You're well-built and upright, you're more than your father ever was – I've been observing you and one could perhaps build ones hopes on you; you have a fine youthful physique with which you breast the waves, walk through the woods, where the green branches are now shooting so luxuriantly and overrunning the fruit trees; it carries you along the cliffs and through the old walls and through the wind – but what is it?-- It's a possession that goes far, far beyond all measure-- a possession that cries out to me; 'you've lost your chance, you'll never get him to look upon you lovingly, for that's a thing you've never sowed and never planted – and the years have passed and gone down on the other side of the mountains and no power can bring them back to this side where already the cold shadows lie. Go now to the old woman. It's no good expecting any letter from her. Go and be happy and joyful there."

Victor was shocked to the highest degree. The old man sat so that the lightning flashed in his face and at times in the darkening room it seemed as if fire rippled through the man's grey hair and light flickered across his disagreeable features. If the empty silence and the dull indifference had seemed bleak to him before, this strange agitation now appeared to Victor all the more appalling. The old man had raised his long body in the armchair and showed something like deep emotion. Victor did not reply immediately to what his uncle had said, whose meaning he sensed rather than understood-- but then he said, "I frankly confess that it has been making me very uneasy that I still haven't received any answer to the many letters I sent home, despite the fact that Christoph has been four times to Hul and Attmaning since I've been here. That's why I kept on asking if there were letters."

"You won't get any answer."

"Why ever not?"

"Because I prevented it; because I wrote and told her not to send you any. They are all healthy and well in any case. But let's leave that."

"No, Uncle, we won't leave that! –I don't know why I'm here; I don't know why I stayed; but now I want to leave immediately; you promised and I want to be rowed across at once."

"You see how much you love that old woman?!- I always thought so –oh I thought so!"

"If you loved someone, someone would love you in return."

"I loved you!" cried the old man out loud, so that Victor almost trembled – and there was a momentary silence.—

"Well – I see you have nothing to say. Where's the love in return? –Well? Have you loved me in return?" asked the old man warily. Victor could not say yes to this and he remained silent. "You see?" said the old man, "I knew it – but calm yourself, it's all right, everything's all right. You'll get away and I'll give you a boat so you can get across. –Won't you wait until the rain has passed?"
"As long as that and even longer if you have something serious to say to me, but you must realise that merely being bitterly inflexible and wilful cannot bind a person to you!"

"Am I to learn your ways, or you mine?"

"I don't know, I think neither. But you must confess that it's at least strange that at the beginning you kept me prisoner on the island although I'd come because you yourself demanded it, or rather because my mother and my guardian persuaded me to do it -- and then you must admit that it's strange that you cut me off from letters from my mother and that it's even stranger what you did to me even before we knew each other. But look, Uncle, it's better if we just leave all that; in fact I beg you to drop it. Just give me a boat and I'll go."

"No, my young falcon, we won't leave it. You'll speak in another tone yet. Listen to me. There's nothing strange in what I did. It's quite clear that I wanted to see you. I wanted to see you over a period, because one day you will inherit my wealth. No one has provided me with a child. I've always moved on when one of my acquaintances died till I came to this beautiful island. There was once a monastery here which was abolished. I bought the site and the land and this house which was at first a hermitage, then the refectory of the monks. All the trees and all the grass are allowed to grow at will and I like to walk among it. –I wanted to see you, Victor! I wanted to look in your eyes, look at your hair, your limbs, see what you're like – just as a man looks at his son.—If they'd kept on writing to you they'd have kept you in the same hateful dependency as before. I wanted to drag you out into the sun, into the world, otherwise you'll be a weak thing like your father and so ineffective that you'll betray what you mean to love. You're harder edged than him and are not afraid to use your elbows –that's good, I praise you for that; but you should not give your heart to women who are prone to waver, but to people who are as firm as a rock – and I am one of those. –You couldn't bring yourself to love me, though; but you were afraid of me, weren't you? It's all right. A person who is incapable of hardness and violence on occasion, is also unable to love with deep vital force. It would have been fine –you've shown your teeth and that you have a good heart – you'd have been my son –you'd have been driven, compelled from within, to love and respect me- but if you'd done this, then the others would have seemed small and despicable to you, those weaklings who could never get to me, to where the gold lay and the streams gushed forth – but before you got that far a hundred years would have had to pass and it's all in vain. That was what was troubling me. But it doesn't have to be like that, it could all be different –How often have I desired to see you before they sent you. Your father should have given you to me – but he thought I was a vulture who would tear you to pieces, whereas I would have made you into an eagle who could carry the world in his talons and if necessary cast it down into the abyss without a qualm. But because he loved that woman and left her and was not strong enough to escape her completely, he put you, when he died, under her wing so that you would be a trusty little hen to bring in the chickens and to cry out when a horse's hoof trod on you. Even in these few weeks you've grown since you've had to fight against power and pressure. –But go away now; it doesn't have to happen, everything can be different.—I had you come to me - on foot, I said, so that you would get to know fresh air and tiredness –I had you come to me so that I could give you a piece of good advice, which neither that quill pusher, your guardian, nor that woman could give you. What I could do after the death of Hippolit your father I did, as you'll hear in a moment. Now listen to my advice; you have in mind to take up a position which they've obtained for you so that you can, as they put it, earn your bread and be provided for?"

"Yes, Uncle."

"And I've already obtained a leave of absence for you. You see how much they need you and how important the position is that's awaiting you! A leave of absence for an indefinite time. I can have you released any time and there'll be someone else waiting who needs the position. What can you do that amounts to anything, you who's scarcely more than a child and has hardly held a grain of sand in his hand. Why spend your whole life doing something that profits no one and which would devour the life from your body? I have a very different plan. The greatest and most important thing you have to do now--- you must marry."

Victor stared at him wide-eyed and asked, "What?"
"You must marry. Not immediately but you must marry young. Each person exists for himself, and other people know that too, who devote themselves to a career and the career is for them a fertile field which will bear fruit –yes, each person exists for himself but not everyone manages to play his cards right and survive, and many throw away their lives for a pittance, The man appointed to be your guardian thought he was looking after you well when he reined in your youthful spirits, so that you had enough to eat and to drink; the woman with her limited kindness scraped together a small sum, I don't know exactly how much, a small sum with which you can keep yourself in hose for a time- she meant it for the best, it's true – but I have cared more than both of them. You'll soon learn how, but I must first tell you why I advised you to marry. Each person exists for himself, but he only really exists when he brings into play all his magnificent strengths, when the tides of his life reach their high point and he drains the cup of life to the dregs. And if he is wise enough to win enough space to allow free play to all these strengths, the great as well as the small, then he can best be there for others, as much as is possible. Indeed the most passionate devotion to others, even to death, is in the end nothing but the highest, most joyful blossoming of the flower that is one's own life. But whoever in his poverty brings into play a life force which is only just enough to satisfy a basic need, like hunger, he is trapped in total and

pitiful folly and he harms those around him. Victor, do you know what life is? Do you know that thing they call age?"

"How can I, Uncle since I'm still so young?"

"No, you have no idea, you can't know. Oh it's a vast field, two spans long, which brings forth different fruit from those one sowed. Life is a dazzling thing with untold depths into which one falls – and even at the bottom it is still beautiful –and age is a butterfly in the dusk which flutters mysteriously around our ears and then is gone before one can recognise its colours. So we stretch out our arms and refuse to go with it because we've left it too late. And when a really old man stands at the summit of his achievements, what use is it to him if he has not created some existence to last after him? If he has sons, grandsons, great-grandsons to stand round him then he's a thousand years old; he lies down tired but happy and his other life continues over part of the earth and no one notices when he moves aside and is no longer there.—That's why you must marry and that's why you must have air and space so that you can flex your limbs. And that's what I've seen to, because I knew they couldn't do it. After your father's death they took away my authority, but I've seen to things better than both of them. I made it my task to save your estate which otherwise was lost. Don't be surprised, just listen. What was the good of the small sum your mother saved or the limited provision from your guardian? That you would be broken and stunted? I have been miserly but more sensibly so, than they were generous in throwing away their money and then not being able to help themselves or anyone else. I lent your father in his lifetime small sums of money, the sort of thing brothers usually give each other. He gave me receipts for them which I registered with his estate. When he died and the other creditors who had enticed him into debt came to plunder the nest I was already there and wrested it from them and from your guardian who also wanted to snatch what pitifully small amount was left for you. They were short sighted! I gradually gave the creditors what they were owed, together with interest, but not what they had wanted to fleece from you. Now the estate is debt-free and the fifteen-year income has been deposited in the bank for you. Tomorrow before you leave I'll give you the papers. Now leave tomorrow early; I've sent Christoph out to tell the old fisherman who brought you to come and pick you up; for Christoph has no time tomorrow to take you. It's good if you now go quickly. Look after the land as the old Romans did. Enjoy it now as you like. If you're wise everything will be fine; if you're a fool you will rue it in old age as I do. They called me a miser but if I was a miser, I nevertheless enjoyed life as passionately as ever I thought it could be enjoyed, but it all went wrong. You are, it seems, my heir and I would like you to do better than I did. Therefore my advice, but this is not a condition, is that you travel for two or three years, come back, marry and at first keep on the steward I put in charge of the estate for you; for he will teach you with due respect. That's my advice and now do as you like."

The storm had passed over in the meantime and the room was gradually filled with soft sunshine. Victor sat there looking grave, did not say thank you nor make any reply.

The old man as he was speaking had become quite red and his eyelashes twitched as if from some violent agitation of his nerves.

There was a pause for some time.

After a while the old man began again speaking slowly and said, "If you already have feelings for a girl, that's neither here nor there in marriage, but take her for your wife; if you have no such feelings it doesn't matter; for they come and go –I myself once had such feelings - since I'm telling you this, I'll tell you about that too –wait, perhaps I can find the picture."

Saying this, he got up and rummaged around in cupboards first in one room then in another, but he couldn't find the picture. Finally he pulled it out of a drawer by its dusty gold chain, wiped the glass with the sleeve of his grey coat and said, "Look – she was beautiful."

Victor's face went bright red and he cried, "That's Hanna, my sister."

"No", said the old man, "that's Ludmilla, her mother. Has she never spoken of me and your father?"
"Never."
"She thinks me the most awful villain."
"She's never said anything bad about you; I never knew more than merely that you were my uncle."

"Hm –so that's how she is –I thought so. If only she'd been a bit stronger, everything would have been different.

Things are how they are. She was beautiful. I had her portrait painted and I courted her. But then I found her once in the forest – her hat and scarf hung on the lower protruding branch of a beech tree. She was sitting on a wide flat stone, my brother Hippolit sat beside her and had his arms around her – it had long been the place for their rendezvous and she had always hated me – at first I wanted to murder him, but then I tore down the material which hid me and shouted, "Why don't you do everything openly and get married." I wanted then to put his property in order and advance him in his career so that he could take her to wife – but when he was away for a time, and the unlucky event occurred that he married your mother, I confronted Ludmilla and mocked her. – I'm surprised you didn't know anything about it."

"Not a word."

"A lot of years have gone by since then – he had an incredible power of persuasion and was very handsome – but all that happened in the past." Saying this he picked up the picture again from the table, wrapped the chain round it and put it in a small drawer next to his collection of pipes.

"The sand is dry again already; you see, as I told you recently, the ground here is loose shale on a rocky base and sucks up the rain when there's a cloudburst like a sieve. For the flowers I have to add enormous quantities of humus. That's why the fruit trees of the monks are dying off and the forest trees grow so thickly, as they do on our mountains all round." Since he had now got up from the table, Victor knew that he wouldn't sit down again now but would soon turn to something else. And so it turned out. For a while he tidied up his things then he went down into the garden and tied up the dahlias.

Victor, though, did not leave the house but sat in his room and stared out of the window. The storm had passed; warm sunshine appeared between the breaks in the clouds and since evening had fallen some of the mountains were embraced by dark banks of cloud while others towered from the cloud wrack like glowing coals, until gradually it all died out and was extinguished and there was nothing but dense darkness.

When it was time, Christoph fetched Victor to the dining room; the evening passed like every other and the two relatives spoke hardly a word to each other. Then Victor could be heard till midnight walking up and down in his room.

In the morning breakfast was earlier than normal. Victor's knapsack and stick lay ready and Spitz was dancing for joy. "I'll accompany you as far as the barred gate", said his uncle and pressed a spring in the wall so that one could hear the gate rattling open.

Victor had buckled on his knapsack, had his stick in his hand and his hat on his head. His uncle went with him down the staircase and over the garden to the gate. Neither said a word en route. At the gate his uncle stopped, pulled a packet from his pocket and said, "Here are the papers for you."
But Victor answered; "Allow me, uncle, not to take them."
"What? Not take them? What's the matter with you now?"

"Allow me and don't force me –I can't take them; let me have my way this time, I beg you."

And when the old man had stuffed the packet back in his pocket, Victor looked at him for a while. From his clear eyes sprang shiny tears, signs of deep emotion – then suddenly he bent down and kissed impetuously the wrinkled hand. The old man made a muffled unearthly sound – it was like a sob – and pushed Victor out through the gate.

At the landing place the cheery old man from Hul was already waiting with his boat and also the friendly blue-eyed girl was standing in it. But Victor was monosyllabic and watched the green tongue of land recede slowly around Mt Orla as if it were swallowed up, until only the blue mountain walls remained standing round the lonely stretch of water and were reflected in it.

He went hurriedly from Hul, past the rock fall, across the footbridge over the outflow of the Afel and up along the long forest path. At the saddle he stopped and looked back at the lake. Mt Grisel was hardly to be seen but the bare dusky mountain walls which had so amazed him on his way here he now knew was Mt Orla. He looked at it now for a while and thought that behind it lay the island and there everything would now be as so often before when he came back from his explorations, from the waving maple trees, the roaring of the surf – that somewhere the two lonely old men would be sitting, one here, the other there and neither would be speaking to the other.

In two hours he was in Attmaning and as he stepped from the dark trees towards the place, he heard by chance the bells ringing and never had a sound seemed so sweet or sounded so charming in his ears. In the inn yard were cattle dealers with the beautiful brown mountain cattle which they were driving down to the flatland and the parlour was full of people, young and old, since it was market day. It seemed to Victor as if he had been asleep and had just come back to the world. Instead of the boy, the landlord this time provided him with a small carriage which would take him to the next transit post – and with this vehicle he came back to the fields of men, to their roads and their merry doings.

After a few days spent in carriages of all kinds, he again crossed the gleaming meadows down into the valley; he went over the first footbridge, over the second, past the lilac and in through the gate.—"Mother, I've brought you back Spitz", he cried when he caught sight of the little house. All the doors and windows were open and welcoming and the old woman stood by the apple tree in her usual clean dress.

Hanna ran out of the house at the sound of his voice and suddenly stopped and couldn't get out a word. "Welcome, my son. God be praised, you dear child", said his mother and enclosed him in her arms which trembled for joy. "We know everything", she said after a while when the embrace had loosened, "Your uncle has sent letters and papers to your guardian."

"Mother, he's a wonderful man", said Victor.

"Yes, he's an unusual man, she answered. "He's done good to all and yet no one has loved him. I was very anxious about letting you go to him – yes, he's good but with him I always think of that text in the Bible, where God is supposed to have appeared to the prophet; God was not in the rolling of the thunder, not in the roaring of the storm – but he was in the rustling of the wind through the bushes. This time everything was well, your guardian and everyone says you should follow what he says and a splendid life will be before you."

"Yes, but will Hanna be willing?" said Victor.
"Hanna? Who said anything about Hanna?" asked his mother with eyes shining for joy. Victor was covered with burning confusion and could not reply, while Hanna stood there with cheeks bright red as if they would burst. "She will be willing", said his mother again. "Just leave it be for the present, children. Now she must work on your equipment if you're to go off into foreign lands. They've already started on it all, the trunks are back and your uncle has already obtained your discharge and if the seamstresses can both come we'll be ready in a fortnight. In the meantime visit all your friends in town and in the country; visit them to say hello and goodbye --But you're really brown, Victor. Come in, come in."

And with these words she drew him into the parlour and asked him if he was hungry and what he would best like to eat. He scarcely dared to look at Hanna and when his mother went into the kitchen, the girl ran with her.
What else is there to tell?

At the approach of autumn there was another farewell but a quite different one from that in the spring. After three years Victor came back from his travels and shortly after that two people stood before the altar, whose features were the duplicates of two others who once would have wished to stand before the same altar, but who through guilt and misfortune were torn apart and then regretted it their lives long.

All the friends who had taken part in that hike on the occasion of Ferdinand's birthday were at the wedding. Rosina, already a young wife, was there, his guardian with his wife, and then Hanna's and Rosina's playmates.—

His uncle was not there; the old man sat alone and gloomy on his island.

Between Heaven and Earth

By

Otto Ludwig

The little garden lies between the house and the slate-roofed shed. You have to pass it as you walk from the one to the other. Going from the house to the shed you have it on your left, while on your right you see a part of the yard with the wood store and stable, separated from the house next door by a lattice fence. Every morning the house opens two sets of six green shutters onto one of the liveliest streets of the town, while the shed opens its large grey door to a side-road; the roses on the tall bushes in the garden look out onto an alley which serves to connect its two larger sisters. On the other side of the alley stands a tall house which in its refined isolation does not deign to look upon its narrow neighbour. It has eyes only for the bustle of the High Street; but if one looks more closely at its closed eyes at the back, one soon finds the reason for their everlasting sleep -- they are only artificial, merely painted onto the outside wall.

The house to which the garden belongs does not look so spruce on the other sides as it does on the side overlooking the High Street. Here a pale pink distemper does not stand out too glaringly against the green shutters and the blue slate roof. Towards the back, the weather-side of the house is shielded from head to foot in an armour of slates; the other gable wall joins straight onto the row of houses whose beginning, or end, it forms. At the rear, however, there is ample evidence that there's a bad side to everything. Built on to the house here is a covered gallery, not unlike half a crown of thorns. Supported by rough-hewn wooden posts, it runs along the length of the top storey and opens out on the left into a small room, to which there is no direct access from the top of the house. Anyone wanting to go from there to this "annexe", must go out of the back door, walk six steps along by the wall, past the dog kennel, to the wooden steps, rather like in a chicken roost, and when he has climbed them, he has to walk the whole length of the gallery back to the left. The last part of this journey, though, is relieved by the view into the garden – at least in summer, and provided that the line that goes from one end of the gallery to the other is not full of washing. For in winter the shutters go up and are not taken down again till spring. With a bar across they form an impenetrable wooden wall in which the openings for the light seem set far above the reach of anyone of normal height.

But if the attractiveness of the buildings is not everywhere the same, and if the covered gallery, the stable and the shed stand out in sharp contrast to the house, nevertheless there is everywhere in evidence something that attracts more than the mere beauty of form or shiny white plaster. The eye of the beholder is struck by the purest cleanliness that smiles out at him from even the remotest corner. In the garden it is almost too self-conscious to smile. The garden seems to have been tidied not with a hoe and broom but with a fine brush. The little flower beds that stand out so clearly against the yellow gravel of the path appear to have been drawn on the ground with ruler and compass rather than with a piece of rough twine and the box hedges around them look as if they have been trimmed every day by the most careful barber in town with comb and scissors. And yet the blue coat which, if you stand in the covered gallery, you can watch walking in the garden as regular as clockwork twice every day, is kept even cleaner than the garden. When the old gentleman leaves again after doing his many jobs – and this happens too at exactly the same minute every day, as punctually as he arrives,-- the white apron which he wears over his clothes shines so spotlessly that there seems no reason why he should have put it on at all. When he walks between the tall stems of the standard roses, which seem to have taken his upright bearing as their model, each step he takes is exactly like the other, no longer and no shorter, and never does he break his even pace. If you look at him more closely as he stands amidst his creation you see that he has only imitated on the outside the pattern that Nature herself has created within him. The regularity of the individual parts of his tall form seems to have been measured with the same anxious care as the flower beds. When Nature formed him her face must have borne the same conscientious expression as the old man's, and its very strength must have appeared wilful were there not mingled with it a dash of loving kindness, of enthusiasm even. And still Nature seems to watch over him with the same loving care as he lavishes on his little garden. His hair, cut short at the back and skilfully shaped into a curl over his forehead, is of the same spotless white as his neckerchief, waistcoat, collar and the apron he wears over his buttoned-up coat. Here in his garden he is the final touch which completes the picture; outside the house, though, his appearance and his manner must seem rather strange. People standing in the street instinctively stop talking, children stop playing, when old Herr Nettenmaier walks by, with his silver-knobbed cane in his right hand. His hat still has the pointed top, his blue overcoat the narrow collar and the padded shoulders of a style long past. In fact he has enough peculiarities to become a laughing-stock – but this never happens. It is as though there was something invisible about his imposing figure which suppressed any frivolous thought.

If the older inhabitants of the town should meet Herr Nettenmaier and pause in their conversation to greet him respectfully, it is not just because of this magical air about him. They know what they respect in the old gentleman. Once he has gone by they follow him with their eyes in silence until he disappears round the corner. Then a hand will be raised and a stiff index finger will speak more eloquently than a mouth ever could – of a long life adorned with every civic virtue and not disgraced by a single flaw. A respect which gains in force when one realises how much more severely a life shut off from the outside world is usually judged, such a life as that led by Herr Nettenmaier. He is never seen in a public place unless some contribution to general welfare is to be discussed or carried out. Any recreation he allows himself he finds in his garden. Otherwise he sits at his ledgers or supervises in the shed the loading and unloading of the slates which are mined in his own quarry and distributed throughout the region and far beyond its borders. A widowed sister-in-law runs his house for him and her sons do the same for the roofing business which is closely tied up with the slate trade and whose scope suffers hardly at all in comparison. It is the spirit of their uncle, the spirit of order and conscientiousness to a fault, which has fallen on the nephews, and won and kept for them, too, so much respect that they are sent for from far and wide whenever roofing for a new building is required or considerable repairs need to be done to an old one.

It is a peculiar kind of family life in the house with the green shutters. The sister-in-law, a still beautiful woman, not much younger than the master of the house, treats him with a kind of silent respect, even devotion. Likewise the sons. On the other hand, the old gentleman, for his part, treats his sister-in-law with a respectful consideration, a kind of chivalry, that in its earnestness and reserve has something quite touching about it. To his nephews he shows the affection of a father. Yet here, too, there is something between the two sides which introduces into the relationship a certain formal courtesy. No doubt this is partly due to the quiet reticence of the old gentleman which has communicated itself also to the other members of the family, just as his other peculiarities have, even down to unimportant details like posture and movements, judgement and taste. If in the family circle little talking is done, this is because an expression of the wishes or opinions of the one seems superfluous when the other with sure instinct already knows it. And how can that be difficult when they all really live one and the same life?

Yes, it is a peculiar kind of family life in the house with the green shutters!

The neighbours are surprised that Herr Nettenmaier hadn't married his sister-in-law. It's thirty years now since her husband, Herr Nettenmaier's elder brother, was accidentally killed while repairing the roof of St George's church. Then it was generally believed he would marry his brother's widow. His father, who was still alive at the time, had in fact wished this to happen and the son himself had not seemed disinclined. Nobody knows what stopped him. But it didn't happen, even though Herr Nettenmaier took over his brother's family and children in a fatherly fashion and showed no inclination to marry anyone else, though numerous opportunities for a good match presented themselves. It was then that their strange life together had begun.

It is natural that the good people of the town should be surprised; they don't know what had gone on at that time in the minds of the four people involved, and had they known, they would perhaps have wondered all the more.

Not always has peace reigned in the house with the garden, that Sunday peace which now spreads its wings over even the most strenuous activities of its inhabitants. There had been a time when bitter pain at lost happiness, when wild desires had divided its inmates, when even the threat of murder had spread its evil shadow through the house, when despair at self-created misery had crept in through the back door and up the stairs at still of night, wringing its hands, had passed along the covered gallery and down the path again between the garden and the stable to the shed, restlessly prowling back and forth. At that time, too, the garden was the favourite haunt of a tall figure, but the wilfulness of this old man's face was not toned down by gentleness. When he strode across the road, the boys stopped their merry play, but this figure did not look down at them so kindly. Perhaps, because his sight had almost failed. Certainly that older Herr

Nettenmaier was also a respected man and deserved the respect of his fellow citizens no less than his gentler double after him. He was a man of strict honour. In fact only too much so!

What had swelled the hearts of the inhabitants of the house to bursting point at that time, what had passed in the dark recesses of their minds and partly revealed itself in the self-forgetfulness of fear, or in deeds, desperate deeds; all that is perhaps now going through the mind of the man who has been the subject of this story up to now. It is Sunday and the bells of St George's announcing the start of the morning service ring out into the garden, where Herr Nettenmaier is sitting, as he usually does at this time, on a bench in his arbour. His gaze rests on the slate-covered roof of the spire of St George's which also seems to be looking back at him. Today it is 31 years since he returned to his native town after a longish period of absence spent learning his trade. Then as now the bells rang out as he caught a glimpse of the old spire for the first time down a forest path beside the road as he came home. Then his immediate future was closely tied up with the old slate roof; now he read his past there. For ---but I'm forgetting, the reader doesn't know what I'm talking about. That's exactly what I'm about to tell him.

2

So we will turn back through those 31 years and find a young man instead of the old one we have just left. He is tall like him, but not so strong. He has brown hair like the old man, cut short at the back and skilfully shaped into a curl over his high white forehead. The severity of the old man does not yet appear on his face, the scars of mental anguish have not yet left their mark on his good-natured expression. But he by no means has that air of frivolous unconcern so characteristic of people of his age, still less the easy-going casual manner which so easily becomes a habit with travelling journeymen. The steep path he is following still takes him through dense forest but the sound of the bells of St George's rises up from the town below to these woody heights, tenaciously flooding through the trees and bushes like a mother rushing to meet her home-coming child. Home! What emotions are contained in that one small word! What feelings arise in the human heart when the voice of home, the sound of the bells, calls out a welcome to the home-comer, the sound which has called the child to church, the boy to confirmation and first communion, bells which have spoken to him every quarter of an hour! All our good angels hug each other with love when we think of home.

Tears welled up in the serious yet kindly eyes of our young traveller. He would have wept aloud had he not been too ashamed to do so. It seemed to him that he had only dreamed the time he had spent away, and now that he had awoken he could hardly remember the dream; as if he had only dreamed that he had grown into a man while he had been away; as if again and again he had felt that he was only dreaming that he was away in order to be able to tell of it when he had woken from it back home. What would have struck an observer was that, even at this moment of emotional excitement, he did not overlook the threads of gossamer which the welcoming air from his home town wafted against his coat collar, and that he carefully dried his tears so that they should not fall onto his neckerchief, and with the most stubborn persistence removed the last vestiges of silvery thread before he gave himself up heart and soul to thoughts of home. But even his attachment to his home was merely one expression of his obsession with cleanliness, which regarded everything extraneous that brushed against him as some kind of defilement; and that need, too, arose from the warmth of feeling with which he embraced everything that was closely bound up with his person. The clothes he wore were to him a piece of home from which he had to remove everything that did not belong.

Now the path turned a bend; the mountain ridge, which before had hemmed his view, now lay to one side, and above the young saplings rose a church spire. It was the spire of St George's. The young man paused in his walk. However natural it was that the highest building in the town should be visible to him first before all the others, nevertheless he forgot this, thinking rather of the inner meaning contained in this circumstance. The slate roof of the church and its spire needed repairing. This work had been entrusted to his father, and it was the reason, or at least the pretext, why his father had sent for him to come home earlier than he had intended when his son had left. Perhaps tomorrow his part of the work would begin. There, vertically above the wide arch through which he could see the bells swinging, was the hatch through which one climbed outside onto the roof. There the two planks

would have to be pushed out to support the ladder which
he would climb up to the broach-post, where he would
fasten the rope of his cradle for the windy journey around
the roof. And, as it was his nature to weave strong
emotional bonds around the objects with which his work
brought him into contact, so he saw the sudden appearance
of the spire as a kind of greeting, and he involuntarily
stretched out his hand in the air towards it, as though to
shake a hand that had been extended to him. Then the
thought of work hastened his footsteps until a clearing in
the wood and his arrival on the highest slope of the
mountain showed him the whole of his native town lying
at his feet.

Again he stood still. There was the family house, behind it
the slate-roofed shed. In the same district, and not far from
it, the house where she had lived when he went away.
Now she lived in his father's house, was his father's
daughter, his brother's wife, and he was to live from now
on under the same roof and see her daily as his sister-in-
law. His heart beat faster at the thought of her. But none of
the hopes which had before bound him to her memory
now filled it. His feelings for her had become those of a
brother for a sister and what troubled him now was more
like anxiety. He knew she no longer thought kindly of
him. She was the only person in the whole house who did
not welcome his return. How had it all come about? Had
there not been a time when she seemed to be fond of him,
when she had been as eager to meet him as she was later
intent on avoiding him? Down there in the suburbs stood
the clubhouse of the local shooting club. How much taller
the trees around it had grown since he had waved a last

farewell to it from this hilltop! Down there under that acacia tree he had stood shortly before he had left, on the occasion of the Whitsun shooting match. It had been a beautiful spring evening, the most beautiful he had ever known, he thought. Indoors the other young people were dancing, while he walked blissfully round and round the building where he knew she was dancing. He still felt awkward in the presence of women and girls and did not know how to talk to them. At that time he had been even more like it than he was now. How much he would have liked to tell her – when he was alone how much he had to tell her and how well he knew how to say it if only he could chance to find her alone – and was it not strange how busily Fate worked to arrange such a meeting – but the very thought that the moment had now come drained all his courage and made the words on the tip of his tongue retreat to the depths of his soul. So it had been when she came out from the clubhouse alone, her cheeks glowing from the dance. She seemed to just want to cool off for she fanned herself with her white handkerchief, but her cheeks only became still redder. He felt she had seen him and was expecting him to draw nearer, and that she knew he could tell what she was thinking, and it was this that made her cheeks redder. Since he hesitated, however, she was forced to go back into the hall. Perhaps, too, she heard a third person approaching. His brother came out of another door of the hall. He had seen them standing facing each other in silence and perhaps, too, had seen the girl blushing. "Are you looking for Beatrice?" asked our hero, in order to hide his embarrassment. "No!" replied his brother "She isn't at the dance, thank goodness. Nothing can come of it anyway. I must find someone else, and until I can I'll have to make do with beer!"

There was something wild in his brother's speech. Our hero looked at him in amazement ad yet with some concern. "Why can nothing come of it?" he asked. "And what's up with you, anyway?"

"I suppose you think I should be like you, quiet and patient – as long as you haven't got any fluff on your coat, at least. I'm not made like that and if something frustrates me I have to let off steam. Why can nothing come of it? Because old blue coat says so, that's why!"

"Father did call you into the garden yesterday -------"

"Yes, and those ruler-straight white eyebrows of his must have gone up at least an inch and a half. But it's only what I expected. "You've been going out with Beatrice, the debt-collector's daughter. That is to stop immediately!""

"Is it possible? Whatever for?"

"Have you ever heard old blue coat give a reason? Have you ever asked him "Why, then, Father?" I'd like to see his face if one of us dared to question him. He didn't say, but I know why he put a stop to Beatrice and me. I've been waiting for it all week. When he raised his hand I knew he would point to the garden and I was ready to follow like some condemned criminal. That's the place where he issues his decrees. Things aren't going too well for the debt-collector, they say. The word is that he needs more than his salary will reach to and -----but you're a fussy devil yourself, just like old blue coat. But how can the girl help it? Or I? Well, he says it must stop, but I feel sorry for the girl and I don't know how I can forget her. I need to get drunk or find myself someone else."

Our hero was used to his brother's ways. He knew that what he said was not meant as wildly as it sounded and his brother in any case had proved his love and respect for his father by his obedience. Nevertheless our hero would have preferred it to be shown in his speech as well as his deeds. His brother had not been far off the mark with his banter, though. It seemed to Apollonius as if something unclean lay on his brother's soul and involuntarily he several times stroked his hand over his brother's collar as if it could be wiped away on the outside. Dust from the dancing had settled there and as this was removed he had the feeling that with it went all that was really troubling him.

The subject changed. They now came to talk of other things, of the girl who had come out to get some fresh air. Apollonius certainly didn't realise that he himself had brought the subject up, but since all his thinking was centred on the girl, his mind remained fixed on her once he had started. He forgot his brother, to such an extent that in the end he was really only talking to himself. His brother now seemed to become aware for the first time of all the beauty and goodness which our hero praised with such unconscious eloquence. He agreed with all that was said more and more enthusiastically until he broke into wild laughter, which aroused our hero from his self-forgetfulness and made him blush quite as much as the girl had done before.

"And so here you are prowling round the hall where she's dancing with others, and if she shows herself you haven't the nerve to strike up an acquaintance with her. But just wait; I'll be your envoy. From now on she won't dance with anyone but me, then no one else can queer your pitch. I know how to chat up girls. Let me do it for you."

They were standing about ten yards from the main door of the dance hall, Apollonius facing it and his brother half turned to one side. Our hero was horrified at the thought that the girl would find out that very day all that he felt for her. He felt ashamed, too, of his own self-conscious clumsy behaviour and what she must think of his need of an intermediary. He had already raised his hand to stop his brother, when the sudden appearance of the girl herself wiped everything else out of his mind. Alone as before, she came quietly out of the door. From behind the handkerchief, with which she fanned herself, she seemed to be looking furtively round. He saw her cheeks turn red again. Had she seen him? But she turned her face in the opposite direction. She seemed to be looking for something in the grass in front of her. He saw her pick a small flower, lay it on a wooden bench, and, after standing for a moment as if uncertain whether to pick it up again, turn back to the door with sudden decision. A half involuntary movement of her arm seemed to say "I hope he'll take it, it was picked for him." Again she blushed up to her dark-brown hair and the haste with which she disappeared through the door seemed intended to obviate any feeling of repentance she might have felt, or concern that her action might not be understood.

His brother, who seemed oblivious to all this, had continued to speak in his lively vehement way, but his words were lost on Apollonius; our hero would have had to have two lives to hear them, for the only life he did possess was concentrated in his eyes. Now he saw his brother hurrying towards the hall. Too late he thought of stopping him. He followed him to the door, but in vain. There the flower caught his attention again, the one the girl had left for someone, a lucky someone if it was found by the person for whom it was intended. And while he continued to call mechanically to his brother to keep silent, without being heard, he was asking himself; are you the one for whom she left the flower? Did she leave the flower for anyone, anyway? His heart answered happily "yes" to both questions, but his brother's plan still distressed him.

If it was a love token from her and for him, then it was the last.

Twice he looked furtively into the hall when the door opened; he saw her dancing with his brother, then sitting out a dance while his brother talked away earnestly to her in his hasty way. Now he's talking about me, he thought, his whole face aglow. He dived for the shade of the nearby bushes when she left the hall. His brother took her home. He followed them at as great a distance as he felt necessary in order not to be seen by her. When his brother returned from accompanying her, he stepped quickly away from the door. He felt almost naked with shame. His brother had seen him, though, and said, "She still won't have anything to do with you. I don't know whether it's just affectation or whether she really means it. I'll meet her again. Rome wasn't built in a day! But I must admit that you've got taste. I don't know why I haven't noticed before. She's quite different from Beatrice – and that's really saying something."

From then on his brother had danced constantly with Christiane Walther and spoken for his brother, and each time after he had taken her home, he had given our hero an account of his efforts on his behalf. For a long time he was still not certain whether she was giving herself airs or really was not attracted to our hero. He reported conscientiously what he had told her about his brother's qualities and what she had replied to his questions and assurances. He still had hope when our hero had long since given up any. And even if he had not gathered it from what she said to his brother, he would have had to recognize from her behaviour towards him, that his affection for her had no hope of being returned. She avoided him when she saw him just as assiduously as she seemed to have sought him out earlier. Had it really been him she had sought at the dance, assuming she had been seeking anyone at all?

His brother suggested a hundred times that he should seek her out and plead his cause to her himself. He employed his whole power of invention to create for our hero an opportunity to speak to her alone, but every suggestion and every offer was turned down. It was all useless. All that he ever managed to achieve was to irritate the girl still more.

"I can't stand watching you get more and more pale and thin any longer", said his brother one evening, after telling him how he had spoken for him again that day in vain. "You need to get away from here for a while; that'll do you good in two respects. When I tell her you've gone away because of her, perhaps she'll change her mind. Believe me, I know girls and know how to handle them. You must write her a touching letter of farewell. I'll see she gets it and I'll soften her heart for you. And if that doesn't do it, it'll be good for you to spend a year or two away from here, where everything reminds you of her. And anyway foreign parts will make a new man of you, make you someone who'll have more idea of how to get on with girls. You must learn to dance, that's half the battle. Anyway, old blue coat has been approached by his cousin in Cologne with a view to sending one of us over to him. I read it in a letter which fell out of his pocket the other day. Tell him you'd got an inkling of it from something he'd said and if that was what he wanted you'd go. Or better still, let me do it. You're too honest."

And that's what in fact he did. It's doubtful whether our hero would ever have really been able to make up his mind to leave home voluntarily; for he could never understand how people could live anywhere but in his home town; to him it had always seemed like something in a fairy-tale that other towns even existed with people living in them; and he had imagined the lives and activities of these people as something unreal, not like those of the locals, but as a kind of shadow-play, only existing for the spectators but not for the shadows themselves. His brother, who knew how to handle the old man, brought the conversation round, as if by chance, to the subject of the cousin in Cologne, was clever enough to interpret the intimations given by Herr Nettenmaier in his hypocritical way as hints of what was in store, gathered others that concerned our hero and wove the whole together. After several conversations of this sort he seemed to assume it to be the old man's express wish that Apollonius should go to the cousin's in Cologne. In this way the idea was planted in the old man's mind and, since it now ranked as his own idea, he proceeded to brood on it. There was little work in hand and little prospect in the immediate future of any considerable increase. Two hands could be dispensed with as, if they remained in the business, their strength would be condemned to idleness half the time. The old man hated nothing more than what he called "loafing". All that was necessary to make up his mind was some resistance on our hero's part. But **he** knew nothing of his brother's plans. His brother had wisely not let him into the secret, for he knew him too well to expect any assistance from him in an enterprise he would have rejected as both dishonest and disrespectful to his father.

"You want to send Apollonius to Cologne" said his brother one afternoon to the old man. "But will he want to go? I don't think so. You'll have to send me off to learn the trade instead. Apollonius won't go. At least not at the moment he won't."

That was enough. On the very same evening the old man beckoned our hero down into the garden. He stopped by the old pear tree and said, as he removed a small twig from the trunk, "Tomorrow you're to set off to our cousin's in Cologne."

Spinning round suddenly he confronted the person thus addressed and saw in amazement that Apollonius nodded his head obediently. He seemed to be sorry that he wouldn't have to break some stubborn defiance. Did he think the young man was thinking defiant thoughts even without saying them and did he want to break even the defiance of thought? Whatever it was, he bellowed at him, "This very day you're to pack your bags, do you hear?"

Apollonius said, "Yes, Father."

"Tomorrow at sunrise you're to be on your way". After seeming almost to want to force a defiant answer, he perhaps now regretted his anger. He made a slight movement. Apollonius went obediently. The old man followed him and came several times up to his room to remind him, in a tone no longer quite so grim, of many things he should not forget to pack.

And from the tower of St George's, the clock was just finishing striking 4 am when the door of the house with the green shutters opened and our young traveller, accompanied by his brother, stepped out. At the same spot from which he now looked down on the town below him, his brother had taken leave of him, while he had stood for a long time watching him go back. "Perhaps I'll win her for you yet", his brother had said, "and then I'll write and tell you at once. And if nothing comes of it, well, there are other fish in the sea. You're as handsome a fellow as anyone, and if only you'll get rid of your gauche behaviour, you can attract any girl you want. That's the way it is, girls can't make up to us and anyway I wouldn't fancy any girl who threw herself at me. And, anyway, what does a lively girl like her want with a dreamer like you? Our cousin in Cologne is sure to have a few beautiful daughters. Well, farewell now. I'll deliver your letter this very day."

And with that his brother had departed. "Yes", said Apollonius to himself as he watched him leave, "he's right. Not about our cousin's daughters, though, or any other girl, however pretty she might be. If I had been different, I perhaps wouldn't be having to leave home now. Was I the one she left the flower for at Whitsun? Was I the one she was trying to meet then –and even before? Who knows how difficult it must have been for her. And since it was all in vain, must she not have felt ashamed? No wonder she wants nothing more to do with me. I must learn to be different!"

And this decision had been no idle promise. His cousin's house in Cologne proved to be in no way conducive to dreaminess. Family life there was quite different from that he had known at home. The cousin was old, but was as full of joie de vivre as the youngest member of the family. No solitariness was possible there. A lively sense of humour allowed no kind of eccentricity to develop. Each one had to be on his guard- no one could take things easy.

Apollonius would have had to learn to be different even if he had not wanted to. In the business, too, things were done differently from back home. The old man in the blue coat had given his orders like the God of the Hebrews speaking from the cloud and with a voice of thunder. He would have thought it a loss of prestige to have to give his reasons, so there were no whys and wherefores and his sons did not dare ask. Even if the orders he gave were perverse, they had to be carried out once given. Things which did not concern the business he did not discuss with his sons at all. Here, on the other hand, his cousin's way was to ask his assistants for their opinion before giving his own views about some aspect of the business, and then an opinion alone was not enough, he wanted to know the reasons for it too. Then he would raise objections; if their opinion was the right one they had to fight it through to a successful conclusion; if they were wrong he obliged them to think out for themselves what was right. In this way he trained helpers to whom he could leave many things, and who did not have to bother him about every trifling detail. And he dealt with other matters in the same way. There were few circumstances of daily life which he did not discuss in this way with his family – and Apollonius was treated as a full member of that. While at first he seemed to be aiming at training the young people to judge for themselves, he also gave them a storehouse of maxims and principles, which promised to bear all the more fruit since the young people had been brought up to discover them for themselves. One thing, though, that he did not question, was his young relative's conscientiousness, his persistence in the work and his cleanliness of body and soul. But he did not fail to point out by hints and example that even these virtues could prove harmful if taken to extremes.

Apollonius recognized clearly that it was his good fortune that had led him to his cousin. He lost more and more his dreamy disposition. Soon his cousin could leave the most difficult tasks to the young man's capable hands, and he carried each out, without the help of any advice, to the complete satisfaction of his cousin, who had to admit that he himself could not have begun the task more circumspectly, carried it on more energetically, nor finished it more quickly or more successfully. Soon the young man was able to form a judgement about the way the business had been carried on back home. He had to admit that it had not been the most efficient way, in fact many things which the old man had decreed were rather perverse, but then he bitterly reproached himself for his lack of filial respect and made every effort to justify his father's actions to himself, and if that were impossible, compelled himself to think that the old man had had his good reasons which he was too dull to comprehend.

Letters came from his brother. In the first he wrote that he was now a little clearer about the girl's attitude and that in fact her coldness to Apollonius was due to her affection for someone else, whom, however, she could not be prevailed upon to name. In the next letter, which scarcely mentioned the girl, Apollonius read between the lines a feeling of pity for him for a reason which he could not discover. The third letter gave the reason for it only too clearly. It was his brother himself who had been the object of the girl's secret affection. She had given him many signs of it, after he himself had given up his first love in accordance with his father's wishes. He had not suspected it, and when he had tried to win her for his brother, the shame and the conviction that he did not love her had prevented her from speaking.

Now Apollonius came to the painful realisation that he had been wrong when he had thought that her silent love token had been intended for him. He was amazed that he hadn't seen his error straight away. Hadn't his brother been as near to her as he when she laid the flower on the seat, the flower which had been found by the wrong person? And when she had met him alone so apparently casually- indeed when he brought to mind these occasions which were the personal property of his dreams – it was his brother she had been seeking; that was why she was so dismayed to meet him; that was why she fled every time she caught sight of him, for he was the one she was not looking for. She didn't speak to him, but with his brother she could laugh and joke for fifteen minutes at a time.

These thoughts characterized hours, days, weeks of the deepest torment; but his cousin's confidence in him, which had to be repaid by solid worth, the healing effect of hard creative work well-done, and the manliness to which he had matured thanks to both of these, all these factors proved their worth in the struggle and emerged from it with their strength increased.

A later letter he received from his brother told him that old Walther, who had discovered where his daughter's affections lay, and the old gentleman in blue had come to an understanding that Fritz, his brother, should marry the girl. And when the old man said "should", he meant "must", Apollonius knew that as well as his brother. The girl's affection for him had really touched his brother's heart; she was beautiful and good; should he oppose the wishes of his father for Apollonius' sake, for the sake of a love that was hopeless? Assured in advance of Apollonius' assent, he had yielded to the dispensation of Heaven.

The whole of the first half of the following letter, in which he announced his marriage, echoed the same self-righteous tone. After many warm words of consolation, came the excuse, or rather the justification, for why he had not written for two years since the last letter. There followed a description of his domestic bliss; a girl and a boy had been born to him by his wife who was still devoted to him with all the ardour of her young love. His father, in the meantime, had been suffering from an eye disease and had become more and more incapable of running the business in his old masterful way. That had made him even more odd. At first for a short time he had left the reins entirely in the hands of his son, but it was not long before his old need to dominate, sharpened by the boredom of enforced idleness, had come to the fore again. Now, though, he did not know enough about the business in hand (which he had not been bothering about); but as soon as he did, he made a point of forcing through his own dominant will. And just for that reason he had thrown out the plan by which Fritz had been working. But by now work had been started and expenses incurred and this was all lost. And so he had had to fall back on his son's help again; but even when this arrangement was working at its best it did not make up to the old man for the loss of his own way of doing things. In the end he had had to realise that things couldn't be done his way any longer. Money, time and labour had been dissipated, and what hurt him still more was that he had laid himself open. After several such unsuccessful attempts to seize the reins again like some blind coachman, he had withdrawn completely from the running of the business. Merely to subordinate himself as adviser to someone else, and to his own son at that, who had until recently merely carried out his father's will unquestioningly and subserviently, that was too much for the old man. Only in the garden could he find something to occupy him. There he could think up new tasks if he was not satisfied with those that the care of a garden had always demanded. He could remove the old, put in new plants and make room for others, and this is what he did. The absolute ruler of this small green kingdom, in which from now on no question was tolerated, where apart from the laws of nature only one law reigned, his will, here he forgot or seemed to forget that once he had wielded a mightier sceptre.

In his following letters, though, his brother wrote less about the business and the eccentric old man and more about the festivities of the shooting club, and a civic society that had been formed to make it possible for the more middle-class citizens to enjoy their pleasures separate from the lower classes of the community. From all the descriptions of bird shoots and trap shoots, concerts and balls, all of which revolved around him and his new wife, from all this shone out the smug self-satisfaction of the writer. Only in a postscript to the last letter was slight mention made of more serious matters, that the town wished to have the roof of the spire of St George's church repaired and had entrusted him with the task. Old blue coat was urging him to ask Apollonius to return home to help with this work. His brother was of the opinion that Apollonius would not want to give up the situation he so obviously enjoyed in Cologne for such an insignificant reason. The repair could be speedily completed with the workforce they already had. The damaged places on the church roof were only few and in any case, even if he disregarded the aversion his wife felt for Apollonius, which he had up to now so vainly opposed, it would be an unnecessary torment to stir up again what he must be glad to have forgotten. He would easily find a pretext to avoid obeying such an eccentric whim. The conclusion of the letter made a teasing insinuation about a love-affair between our hero and his cousin's youngest daughter, which the whole town was supposed to be talking about. His brother sent her his kind regards as his future sister-in-law.

Even if such a relationship did not exist, Apollonius knew that it lay within his power to bring it about. His cousin had already dropped several hints to that end; and the girl herself would not have been averse. Our Apollonius had become a young man whom few could easily have refused when his heart and hand still stood at their disposal His custom of always acting according to his own judgement and of controlling the activity of a number of efficient workers with complete self-reliance, had made his way of speaking more self-assured and his manner more confident. And what remained of his former shyness with women and his inclination to sink dreamily into himself, only heightened the impression of masculine self-confidence, whose expression it merely toned down.

Yes, he knew that he could be his cousin's son-in-law if he so wished. The girl was pretty, good, and devoted to him like a sister. But he could only see her as such and had never felt any desire that she could be more to him than that. His attraction to Christiane he thought he had got over; he did not know that it was only she who stood between him and any other girl. When he learned that Christiane loved his brother, he had taken the little tin box, which contained the flower, from his breast pocket, where he had carried it since that evening when he had picked it up under the mistaken impression that it had been put there for him. When Christiane had become his brother's wife, he had packed up the box with the flower and sent it to his brother. He could not throw away what had once been dear to him, but he could no longer keep the flower. Only the one for whom it had been intended could keep it, only the one to whom the hand belonged, which had given it.

His father called him home; he must obey. But it was more than mere obedience that motivated him. He did not just return, he returned gladly. His father's word was more a permission than a command. When the spring sun shines into a room which has been shut up and unlived in for a whole winter, one sees that the life which lay like a dried up corpse on the floor was only sleeping. Now it stirs and stretches and becomes a whirling cloud that rushes joyfully into the golden rays. Not his father alone, but every house in his home town, every hill, every garden, every tree in it, called to him. His brother, his sister – for that was how he now thought of Christiane – both called to him. He felt sure that it was only the fact that she was now his sister that attracted him towards her. Yet she did not call him. She felt an aversion towards him, his brother had written, an aversion so strong that for six years his brother had fought against it in vain. It seemed to Apollonius that he must go home for that very reason, to show her he did not deserve her ill-will, that he was worthy to be her brother. He wrote this in the letter to his brother announcing his intention of obeying his father's call, and which informed his brother of the day on which he should expect him. He could assure him that the memory of former times would not torment him, that his brother's fears were unfounded.

So that was how it had come about that thoughts of her now aroused none of the old hopes. When he looked down from the hilltop, he asked himself, "Shall I succeed in being her brother, who is now my sister?"

For a while longer he stood there looking down. But his attitude had now changed and his look was different. In thought he had lived through the last six years again and had once more become a man, leaving the bashful dreamy boy behind. When his gaze now fell on the spire and church of St George's, his hand rose, but not involuntarily as before, as if to shake an invisible hand stretched out to him. He reproached himself for gawping like a child. He must as soon as possible get to examine the roof in detail in order to form a judgement of what needed to be done.

Love of home was still as strong in him as ever, but it was no longer the love of a boy for whom home is a mother enfolding him in her arms; it was the love of a man. Home was for him a wife, a child, for whom he felt the urge to work.

3

If you could look into the house with the green shutters today at about noon, you would notice that the thoughts of its inmates were not running along their usual everyday lines. You could see it by the way in which they stood up and sat down again, opened doors and closed them, picked things up and put them down again without doing anything with them and obviously not intending to. If you can imagine what state of mind you would probably be in if you kept taking your watch out of your pocket and, even before finishing putting it back again, had forgotten what time it was, and so took it out again and, not knowing why you had done so, held it to your ear and without having heard whether it was ticking or not, found the key and wound it up, perhaps for the third time in an hour; if you can imagine that, you will be able to guess, assuming you can still remember what you didn't even know to start with, what is driving all of them to this purposeless activity. Even the young man who is just trying to wind up his watch for the sixth time in an hour is so little conscious of what he is doing that he will try it again for the seventh time in the next few minutes. Then his well-nourished stocky frame sits on the chair by the window, but whether he is looking out into the street or is occupied with the thoughts which flutter past his consciousness like shadows of clouds, in the same purposeless turmoil as he appears to be in outwardly, one cannot tell. He sits there in his dark Sunday-best suit facing a young woman. He could have seen how beautiful she is, how charmingly this preoccupied air becomes her – far better than it does him. At times he does seem to notice, but then it seems no pleasure to him. At those times the thought shadows on his face seem to grow deeper and flutter past less quickly than before. He looks more closely at the young woman's regular features, almost as if he is spying on her, as if he is anxiously wondering whether the expression of antipathy they wear will last till ----but then, if by chance a firmer footstep sounds in his ear from the street outside, he starts up but avoids her beautiful wide-open eyes which turn towards him, aroused by the sound of the step.

In the garden old Valentine can do nothing right for an old gentleman in a blue coat who is equally as old as himself. He is too excited and stops to listen and look out through the fence to the street too often, with the result that he cuts now too little and now too much. And the old gentleman rebukes him; sometimes only to hide his own emotion, it seems. There is a visible tremble to the hands with which he examines whether the box hedge round the flower beds is cut as meticulously level as he would have done it himself had he still possessed the sharp eyes he once had. Old Valentine would have often had to wipe a tear from his hollow cheeks at the helplessness of the old man and at a thousand comparisons between then and now which the very sight of him conjures up; but his eyes and his thoughts are on the road on the other side of the fence.

At the back of the house, at the end of the passage near the shed door, a sullen-looking journeyman in shirt-sleeves is sitting on a pile of slates. The expression on his face alternates, for no obvious external cause, between unpleasant obsequiousness and malicious defiance. It seems as if he is rummaging through his stock of facial expressions like a girl in her jewellery. He keeps both types ready in order to have the right one ready to hand; he doesn't yet know which one he's going to need

At the front of the house the maid is listening through the crack in the front door which is rarely opened. But none of her acquaintances go by. Soon she will think of some pretext to stop the first person walking past, merely in order to break the news, as though casually, that they are expecting the younger son back from foreign parts that day. In the meantime she tells it to the dog who, in his efforts to keep the different groups in touch with each other by going to and fro between them, has just arrived by her. And at once he turns back to the yard as if to pass on what he has heard. The old dog is infected by the restlessness of the humans. On another day he would be sleeping outside in his kennel at this hour.

The old habit seems to strike him as he is about to walk past his kennel. He lies down beside it, but he doesn't shut his eyes; he seems sunk in deep thought. Is he thinking of the wide earth with its mountains, valleys and rivers, with its towns and villages? And roads running from place to place and on every road travellers, both those departing and those returning?

If you had an eye so sharp that you could see the heart strings of all these travellers spun out along the roads over hill and dale, dark threads or light according to whether hope or despair sat at the spinning-wheel, what a fantastic web they would weave! Many threads break, light ones grow dark, dark ones light; many remain stretched taught as long as there is life in the heart from which they are spun. Many retract with inexorable force. Then the mind of the traveller hurries on before him and is already knocking at his father's door and resting on warm hearts, on cheeks wet with tears of joy, in arms which enfold and embrace him and will not let him go, while his feet are still striding along far away on foreign soil. And when in reality he stands on the threshold of home, how different then his reception often is from that which he had dreamed. How different the people have become! Twice every minute he says to himself, "Yes, it's them", and twice again, "it's not really them". Then he seeks familiar places, the houses, the river, the mountains which surround the valley; they at least can't have changed. But they too have become different. Sometimes it is the things or the people themselves that have changed, but often it is just the eye that beholds them again. Time paints things differently from the way that memory does. Memory smoothes over the old wrinkles, time paints in new ones. And all that had been so familiar in memories must now be got used to again in reality.

Was Apollonius perhaps thinking along these lines as he still half-expected, but still doubted, that his brother would come to meet him? Did his brother, as he got up so quickly from his chair, feel that Apollonius would probably be looking out for him? He already had the door-handle in his hand. He let it go. Did it occur to him that he might miss him, so stayed where he was in order to spare his wife and his brother the painful moment when they would have to face each other alone? She with dislike and he with the knowledge of her dislike. Now the figure of his brother of old rose before him and it seemed as if it released him from anxiety on that score. This was the way he had usually dismissed him when he had been present, as if saying to himself, "He's just a dreamer!" and then he made a quick gesture as if to show how different he himself was, how much better he understood life and the ways of the fair sex. With a glance of reassurance he inspected himself in the mirror; his thickset frame, his full red face set deeper into his shoulders than he thought, but at least not more deeply than he considered handsome; he stuck his hands in his trouser pockets and rattled the money in them. He reminded himself that he had already said to the journeyman in the shed, "There's to be no change in the work. You are to take orders from no one but me. I am the master here." And the journeyman had laughed in such an ambiguous way as if to say "Yes" aloud to the speaker, but to himself, "I'll let you think so, but I'm the boss really." Fritz Nettenmaier thought, "He won't be staying long, I'll see to that!" And with that gesture which again seemed to say, "I'm a fellow who really understands life", there came into his mind the dance at which that very evening he would feel its truth even more satisfyingly because he would be able to read it in every eye without fear of a rival.

His young wife seems to be thinking along the same lines. She too looks into the mirror; their eyes meet there. Marriage is supposed to make husband and wife more like each other. Here this proved correct. Living together had made two faces look alike which in other circumstances would have probably looked just as unalike. But it had not really made both look like each other, but only one of them like the other. The features they had in common, as any sharp eye could see, were his alone; he had only given, but not received. And yet it would have been better for both if the opposite had been the case, even though he would not admit it and she did not feel it, at least not at this moment. Perhaps not tomorrow or the next day either. What a great deal of time is sometimes necessary, and how much pain will have to be suffered, if we are to wash away from a once beautiful face all that the habits of years have besmirched it with!

The door flew open and the blushing face of the maid appeared. "He's coming!" Anyone standing at a window along the road will look down with real pleasure on the fresh, slim, manly figure walking along with his rucksack on his back and his stick under his arm. For he has no hand free. In his right hand he is leading a little girl, while two smaller boys are hanging on tightly to his left, a circumstance which does not make his progress any easier. The neighbours who knew he was expected fill the windows and doorways. He has not only to answer the children who are bombarding him with questions, but other people too. He must reply to the old men's greetings and banter, wave to school friends, bow to girls whose faces are suffused with blushes. He can't take his hat off; the children won't let go of his hands. But those greeting him do not expect it; they can see how impossible it is for him. And when he has gone by, a wave of the hand behind him is as much as to say, "Well, he's still the same handsome modest lad", and a raised finger adds, "but he's not a lad any longer, he's become a man, and what a man!" If the window is shut, all are loud in praise of him, except for the girls who are mature enough to return his bow with an involuntary blush; they are more silent than usual and the sun, which today is shining so much more brightly than on other days, has the strangest effects on them. At first an impulsive movement of the feet towards the windows; then a just as strange and sudden reawakening of long dormant friendships whose subjects live in the neighbourhood of the Nettenmaier's house and whom one simply must visit; finally a strangely often returning rush of blood to the head which one might have taken for a blush had there been any cause for it.

But would the changes which had come over our traveller while he was away please his brother as much as they did the neighbours?

He has reached the door of the family home. In vain he has sought a familiar face at the windows. Now a stocky young man in a black tail-coat comes rushing out. So rapidly does he appear, so wildly does he embrace him, so firmly does he clasp him to his white waistcoat, so closely does he press his cheek against his and so long does he leave it resting there, that one could almost believe that he loves his brother inordinately, or -----that he doesn't want his brother to look him in the eye. But he has to release him eventually; he takes him by the right arm and pulls him indoors.

"It' so good that you've come! It's wonderful to see you! It was really not necessary –a whim of old blue coat, and he no longer gives the orders in the business. But it's really good of you. I'm only sorry that you've had to make your fiancée's eyes red for nothing." –'Your fiancée' was said so clearly and in such a loud voice that it could be heard and understood in the living-room.

The newcomer, his eyes moist, looked into his brother's face, examining every feature as if to see whether all was still there that had been so dear and precious to him. His brother did nothing to make this task any easier, anything to hinder him in fact; he only looked at what lay between Apollonius' chin and toes. He had perhaps intended to turn on his heels as in the old days and take the lead. But from the little he had seen, he no longer had 'a dreamer' to contend with, and so the turn was never made.

"It's what father wanted", said the new arrival ingenuously, "and as for a fiancée----"

His brother interrupted him; he laughed out loud in his old way, so that if Apollonius had continued speaking no one would have been able to understand him. "O.K.! O.K.! But once gain it's really great that you've come to visit us, and you must stay at least a fortnight, whether you like it or not. Don't mind her," he added quietly, pointing with his right hand through the door which he had just opened with his left.

The young woman stood with her back to the door by a cupboard in which she was rummaging. Embarrassed, and not exactly friendly, she turned round, and then only towards her husband. Still her brother-in-law could see nothing of her except for a part of her right cheek with a burning blush on it. The only other fault one could find with her behaviour showed itself in an unmistakeable candour, an inability to be other than she was. She stood there as if bracing herself to receive an insult. The new arrival went up to her and grasped her hand, which at first she seemed to want to snatch back, but then left lying limply in his. He was delighted to greet his sister-in-law. He apologized for any annoyance he might cause her by coming and hoped by honest endeavour to overcome the dislike she evidently felt for him.

But in however considerate and polite an expression he clothed these hopes and desires, he merely expressed them in his thoughts. The fact that everything was as he had expected it to be, and yet was quite different, robbed him of all courage and naturalness.

His brother brought the painful pause – for his wife answered not a word – to a welcome end. He pointed to the children. They still thronged round their new uncle, unperturbed by all that was distressing the grown-ups, which in any case they did not notice or understand; and he, for his part, was glad of the opportunity to bend down to them and have to answer a thousand questions.

"What a demanding brood they are!", said his brother. He indicated the children, but looked furtively at his wife. "For all that, I'm amazed how well you've got to know each other. And so quickly", he added. Perhaps his mind continued working on the idea expressed in that remark. "You obviously know how to get on with people and make yourself popular." A shadow as if of apprehension came over his florid face. But the fear was not on the children's account, or else he would have looked at them as he said it, and not at his wife.

Apollonius continued to speak animatedly to the children. He had not heard the question or perhaps did not want to betray to the woman scolding them just whose picture it was that he carried so vividly within him. The similarity with their mother had allowed him to recognize the little ones, who had chanced to meet him along the road, as his brother's children. But the question as to how they had so quickly got to know him would have had to be put to old Valentine. It had, after all, been he who had kept telling them about their uncle who would soon be coming to see them. Perhaps only in order to be able to talk to someone about a person he liked so much. His brother and sister-in-law avoided such conversations and the old gentleman had not become so familiar with his ex-journeyman as to discuss with him things which might offer him the pretext of falling into a kind of intimacy with him. Old Valentine could have said that the children had not met their uncle by chance. They had gone off to find him. Old Valentine remembered how so many home-comers were met by their loved ones on the road and he had felt sorry that it was only his favourite who would not be met and greeted in this way before reaching his father's door.

Apollonius suddenly fell silent. He was horrified to think that embarrassment had made him forget his father completely. His brother sensed his agitation and said, relieved, "He's out in the garden." Apollonius jumped up and hurried out.

There among his flower-beds squatted the figure of the old gentleman. On his knees, he was following old Valentine, who was shuffling along before him, and he was checking his work with his hands. He found many uneven places which must immediately be put right. It was no wonder. Every minute old Valentine was thinking at least twice, "Here he is now!" And every time he thought this his shears made a crooked cut in the box hedge. And the old gentleman would have grumbled still more had the same thoughts not made his own hands unsure, hands which had now become his eyes.

Apollonius stood before his father and could not speak for grief. He had long known his father had gone blind and had often in his grievous thoughts imagined him so. But always he had imagined him as usual except for a kind of shade over his eyes. He had thought of him sitting down or leaning on old Valentine, but never as he saw him now, the tall frame helpless like a child, the crouching posture, the hands trembling and groping uncertainly before him. Now he knew for the first time what it meant to be blind.

Valentine set down the shears and laughed or wept on his knees; one could not tell which. The old gentleman bent his head to one side at first, as if listening, then he took control of himself. Apollonius saw that his father thought of his blindness as something to be ashamed of. He saw how the old gentleman forced himself to avoid any movement which might draw attention to the fact that he was blind. He now knew for the first time what it meant for this old gentleman whom he loved so much to be blind. The old gentleman suspected that the new arrival was near him. But where? On which side? Apollonius sensed that his father felt ashamed of this uncertainty, and he forced his unwilling heart to cry out, "Father! Dear father!" He fell on his knees by the old gentleman and wanted to throw both arms round him. The old gentleman made a movement which seemed to be asking for forbearance, although it was only intended to keep the young man from him. So Apollonius threw the rejected arms around his own chest instead in order to hold back the grief which, if it had passed his lips, would have betrayed to his father how deeply he felt for his suffering. The same forbearance caused old Valentine, too, to change the involuntary movement he was about to make to help the old gentleman up, into a grab for the shears which lay between them. He, too, wanted to conceal from the new arrival what could not be concealed – how deeply he had come to feel for the old gentleman.

The old gentleman had now risen and held out his hand to his son, as if he had been away as many days as it was really years. "You must be tired and hungry. I'm having a bit of trouble with my eyes – but it's nothing to speak of. Anything you want to know about the business, ask Fritz. I've given up –I just want peace now. But that's not really it; young men have got to be independent some time. You get more pleasure from the business then."

He took one step nearer his son. There was something like a struggle inside him. He wanted to say something that nobody else should hear but his son. But he said nothing. The ghost of an idea of mistrust and the fear of losing his dignity appeared fleetingly on his stony face. He gestured to his son to go. But he himself remained standing motionless, until his sharp ear heard the living-room door open and shut. Then he went to the arbour, full of energy and apparent unconcern as usual. Inside it he stood for a long time, his face turned to the green wall at the back, and appeared to be earnestly inspecting the tendrils of box thorn which formed it. All kinds of thoughts passed across his brow. They were uneasy thoughts, more rarely illumined by hope than darkened by suspicion; and all concerned the business and the honour of the family, about which he gave the impression to all and sundry, even members of the family, of not bothering in the slightest.

Why had he suppressed what he wanted to say to his son? Was it about the business or the honour of the family? And did he know or suspect that the one, who now had to care for both in his place, stood leaning on the garden gate and could hear what he said, even if he spoke to his son in secret, at least could see that he did so? Was this the reason why he had sent for Apollonius to come home?

And did this questioning of his motives still seem to him incompatible with his position of authority?

They formed a strange company in the living-room at lunch. The old gentleman as usual ate alone in his room. Even the children had been sent away and only returned after the meal. The young wife stayed more in the kitchen or somewhere outside and when she did sit for a few moments at the table, she was as mute as when he had first arrived; the cloud of resentment did not once leave her brow. His brother was used to his father's condition, while Apollonius was still cut to the quick by its first sharp impact. His brother talked to Apollonius only about the old man's eccentricities; how old blue coat didn't really know what he wanted and soured his own life unnecessarily as well as that of all those in the house. If Apollonius tried to speak of the business and the repairs to the roof of St George's they were about to undertake, his brother would only talk about the social events which he hoped would make his brother's visit more pleasant and always referred to his stay as if it were a passing visit. If Apollonius said that he had not come just to enjoy himself but to work, his brother merely laughed as if this were some great witticism, implied that Apollonius was offering to help when there was really nothing to do and assured him that he appreciated a good joke, however dryly told. Then when his wife had gone out, he asked about Apollonius's relationship with his cousin's daughter and then laughed again that his brother should have turned into such a wag, in whom one could no longer recognize the old dreamer.

After the meal the children came in again and with them more life and cheerfulness. While Apollonius faced the old relationships as if they were new and strange, for the children the new relationship had already taken on the form of long familiarity. The whole afternoon his brother and, it seemed, his sister-in-law were completely taken up with the forthcoming dance. His brother forgot more and more any uneasiness he might once have felt about the impression he would make, as the most important person at the festivities, on the new arrival. He used the time before the dance was due to begin to give him a foretaste of it by relating stories and dropping hints of the honours and attention he had received on such occasions from the most prominent citizens. He became visibly more cheerful and strutted ever more proudly in and out of the room. Even before the guests at the ball had a chance to say so, the very creaking of his well-polished boots was as much as to say, "Here he is! Look! Here he is!" And when in the meantime he rattled the money in his pockets with both hands, it was as if there rang out from every corner of the room, "Now there'll be fun! Now things will go with a swing!" And on through the reception committee – already no longer walking but floating, swimming along to the music – every dance played in his honour – he felt no floor beneath him, no feet, no legs any more, and he scarcely felt young Frau Nettenmaier floating along at his side, hanging on to his right fin, the most beautiful among the beautiful, just as he was the most jovial amongst the jovial, the thumb on the hand of the dance.

And two hours later there really was heard on all sides, "Here he is!" and from all corners, "Now there'll be fun!"

Wherever they passed they were invited to sit down and join the party. No hand was so often shaken, nor held so long, as that of jovial Fritz Nettenmaier, and no member of the company had so much unfeigned praise poured in his ears. But how charming he was, too! How condescendingly he accepted all this homage which was so richly deserved. How witty he appeared; how agreeably he laughed – and not only at his own jokes either, for there was no particular virtue in that since they were so funny that he would have had to laugh at them anyway – but at the jokes of others, too, however little they deserved it compared to his. It is true there were also a few people there who paid little attention to him, but he didn't deign to notice them, and those who showed this tendency most obviously were "Philistines, common, unimportant people!" as he whispered to his brother with pitying scorn. It was strange really, how accurately one could measure their greater or lesser importance as people and as citizens by the degree of their veneration for Fritz Nettenmaier. There he stood, his red head sunk into his shoulders, which were themselves raised higher than usual by the unconcealed feeling of his own importance – and his own private opinion of himself was even more openly evinced than that expressed loudly by the most important people in the hall. His arms were now pressed against his body in graceful angularity, now stretched out to give one of the important people a hearty tap on the back with his stick, a gesture which was always answered with a grateful smile.

When the dancing began Fritz drew his brother into an ante-room. "You must dance" he said. "You would only meet with a snub if you asked my wife and I wouldn't want that. I'll introduce you to a girl who knows what she's doing and can keep you in step. Chin up, lad, keep trying even if it doesn't go right at first."

Flushed with vanity, Fritz Nettenmaier had forgotten the last six years. His brother to him was still the old dreamer whom he had sometimes for his own pleasure forced to dance. So when now he brought the girl over, Apollonius had to give way in order not to appear impolite.

Herr Fritz Nettenmaier was the most good-humoured man in the world as long as he knew himself to be the sole object of universal admiration. In such a mood he could perform acts of self-sacrifice for those whom his dazzling personality set in the shade. So too now. As he sat among the important people, whom he treated to Champagne, and saw in the eyes of his wife the satisfaction with which she saw him heaped with honour, a feeling came over him as if he had forgiven his brother some great wrong, and as if he were being extraordinarily noble about it and thus deserved all these tokens of respect, and nevertheless deigned to be moved by them with remarkable unpretentiousness. Apollonius was just then dancing past him. He saw that he was no longer the old dreamer, but he forgave him that, too. All eyes were directed at this beautiful dancer and his elegant deportment. Fritz asked his wife to dance, and in the certainty that he must outshine his brother, still had the pleasure of forgiving him innumerable wrongs that he had never done him.

But the ungrateful wretch! He did not allow himself to be outshone. Fritz Nettenmaier danced jovially, like a man who knew the world and the ways of the fair sex; his brother, on the other hand, seemed stiff and formal. He did not nod his head in time with the music, he did not jerk the top of his body to the right when his left foot stepped forward and vice versa; he did not move back and forth across the dance floor with panache, cutting out other couples on the way; he certainly did not dance jovially, nor like a man who knew the world and the ways of the fair sex; and yet all eyes remained on him and Fritz Nettenmaier excelled himself in vain.

It was the dullest dance Fritz Nettenmaier had ever attended; it could not have been more dull if he had stayed at home. Fritz asserted this opinion with great oaths, and the important people who were drinking his champagne agreed absolutely with his opinion as usual.

Some important ladies expressed to Frau Nettenmaier their righteous indignation at her brother-in-law. That he had not asked his sister-in-law to dance first was an unforgivable slight to her. Frau Nettenmaier, who felt the wrong done to her jovial husband as deeply as if it were done to herself, said her brother-in-law must have known that he would only have received a snub from her. But Apollonius was more and more admired and honoured and the dance, in consequence, became ever duller. So dull that Fritz Nettenmaier and his wife decided to leave at an hour when he was usually only just beginning to enjoy himself. Nevertheless he heaped coals of fire on his ungrateful brother's head. In his brother's name he asked the girl to allow his brother to escort her home. Then he left the ante-room and went back into the dance-hall to his wife, and left the building with her, to the most unfeigned disappointment of the important people, who still had a thirst for champagne.

Apollonius, when he had done his duty by escorting his lady home, found the door of his father's house open and all the inhabitants already asleep. At least no light was to be seen anywhere and all was quiet. His brother had allotted him the little room to the left of the gallery for his use. To Apollonius' delight, the six years he had been away had not changed the house, as it had its inhabitants. He went quietly through the back door, past Moldau the dog who gave a friendly growl and whose rough neck he stroked in gratitude for this sign of his faithfulness, climbed the stairs, walked along the gallery and found a bed in his room. But, before undressing, he sat for a long while on the chair by the window, comparing what he had found on his return with what he had left behind on his departure.

The thoughts and pictures conjured up by this comparison drifted on into his dreams. His father stood before him again and announced that he must leave next morning for Cologne, and as he spoke his strong frame broke down and he fumbled around helplessly on the ground with trembling hands and was ashamed of his blindness. His brother sat by him and drank champagne. His sister-in-law came out of the house, the lovely open face full of the trustfulness and sincerity she had seemed to have before; the flower which she intended to lay down before Apollonius fell out of her hand when she caught sight of his brother, and the new trait in her character that he had not known before, her vacuousness, her frivolous search for pleasure, her bitter resentment of Apollonius, this spread over her like a dirty spider's web. He wanted to lose himself in work, but his brother kept shaking the hoist until he almost fell from the giddy heights to the flagstones below and said that a visitor for a fortnight was not allowed to work. He wanted in any case to be back home again, and the strange thing was that it was now Cologne that appeared as home and his native town seemed so strange that his conscience reproached him most bitterly. Then he found himself again on the hoist high up on the roof of the tower. There everything was different from what it should have been, the slates laid in the wrong direction, and now he was stuck in the hatch leading to the roof, completely enveloped in dirty spiders webs; he had his Sunday best clothes on; they were covered in dirt; he wiped and brushed until he was bathed in sweat but they would not come clean.

And whenever he woke from these vain efforts he repeated aloud to himself the resolution he had made before getting into bed. Next morning he must find out what he was here for, must get clear his relationship with his parental home. If there was no work for him, the morrow would see him on his way back to Cologne.

He was up with the sun; but he had to wait a long time until his brother was pleased to rise from his bed. He used the time to walk as far as St George's; he wanted to satisfy himself as to what needed to be done there. When he returned, he met his brother just coming out of the living-room accompanied by another gentleman. Apollonius knew him from before as the architect responsible to the Town Council for public works. They greeted each other. They had spoken together the day before at the dance where the gentleman in question had not appeared to be one of the most important citizens, but rather one of the "Philistines, the common unimportant people". He seemed to be quite pleased to meet Apollonius at this particular moment. After a few conventional exchanges, he came to the purpose of his visit. That very morning, specialists were to hold a final consultation on what needed to be done to the roof of the church and the spire, so that the result could be reported to the Council meeting that afternoon and a final decision made. Fritz Nettenmaier and the architect were just on their way to St George's where the other specialists were already assembled.

Fritz did not want to spoil his brother's visit, as he put it, by burdening him with business that need not particularly concern him; but, although he did not say it, neither did he want to leave him at home. He tried to make an arrangement with Apollonius to meet him later at the hut in the woods from where they could go on a walk together. Apollonius assured him in all innocence that he would rather attend the discussions and when the architect explicitly invited him to go along with them in the role of an expert, no pretext could be found to prevent it. Perhaps Fritz Nettenmaier had an inkling that he would soon have much more to forgive the new arrival.

Waiting for them by the door of the tower they found the other members of the commission, two independent master slaters and three council workmen, the master carpenter, master mason and master tinsmith. Already several flying scaffolds had been erected for the purpose of examining the roof; in the church loft, next to the largest of these, the discussion took place. Apollonius stood modestly a few steps apart in order to listen, and also to speak if he was asked. He had earlier examined the roof carefully and formed an opinion of the matter.

The two independent slaters pointed out the necessity of a more extensive repair. Fritz Nettenmaier, on the other hand, was convinced that with a small amount of patching, which he specified, the roof would last for years to come. The three council workmen were in eager agreement with him; they were some of the jovial and important people from the dance the evening before, and concluded in all honesty that if they drank a man's champagne they must also share his opinions. The independent slaters knew quite well that the Council feared the costs of a more extensive repair and was putting off what was most necessary from year to year. Since in any case they themselves had no prospect of the repair work being assigned to them, they didn't make any undue effort to help Fritz Nettenmaier get the work and the profit which he didn't seem keen on getting for himself. So, during the course of the conversation, they came more and more to the opinion that, depending on how you looked at it, Fritz Nettenmaier was right too. Perhaps the architect, an honest man, comprehended their motives as well as those of the important people. He had been silent all this while, but with a dissatisfied expression, when he suddenly remembered Apollonius. He saw something in his expression which seemed to correspond to his own opinion. "And what do you say?" he asked, turning to him.

Apollonius stepped modestly one step nearer. "I wish you would take a look at the matter as closely as possible", said the architect. Apollonius replied that he had already done so. "I don't need to remind you", continued the architect, "how important this matter is."

Apollonius bowed. The architect kept back what he was about to add. In the young man's face, despite its apparent softness and gentleness, there could be seen such strict conscientiousness and stubborn honesty, that the architect was almost ashamed of the admonition he had been about to make.

Apollonius began with the results of the examination of the roof he had made that morning. He described the state of the parts he had been able to examine, and what conclusions could be drawn from these about the rest. For eighty years, as was known from the church accounts, the church roof had received no large-scale repairs. Even if the slates themselves could defy the elements a bit longer, and that was only providing they were made from good material, this was certainly not the case with the nails with which the pieces of slate were fixed to the laths and battens. And where he had been able to test them he had found the nails either completely destroyed or at least near to total destruction. The church roof was a very steep shed-roof; since the nails no longer served their purpose, many of the slates had slipped out of place and allowed moisture to seep in; there the laths and battens, even when they were made of oak, appeared quite rotten, and such places were to be found all over.

It appeared, therefore, unavoidably necessary to completely re-roof the church and the spire, and to replace the laths and battens wherever they proved to be rotten. One more winter could only make the situation much worse, and putting it off would in the end cost more than any money they might save in interest charges now; for the repair could not be postponed beyond at most the next year without the gravest consequences. He led the assembled company to places which could serve as proof. He himself did not draw the conclusions but made use of the skills he had learned from his cousin to overcome all opposition.

The trust and respect the architect felt for Apollonius grew visibly. In the conversation that followed he turned almost exclusively to him and shook him heartily by the hand when he left the meeting. He hoped Apollonius would take an active part in the work if, as he now no longer doubted, it was approved by the Council, and he charged him with drawing up a report as to how best to tackle the work. Apollonius thanked him modestly for this confidence which he would seek to deserve. As to his collaboration in the work itself, he replied, it was his father, as master, who would have to decide. "I'll go straight there with you now", said the architect, "and speak with him."

If up to now his brother had been in charge of the business and been recognized as master by the important people, he had not yet achieved this status in reality. The old man had been as reluctant to allow him to be master, as to formally hand over the business to him; he wanted to reserve himself the unrestricted right to intervene where he thought necessary.

The old gentleman heard them coming some way off and felt his way to the bench in his arbour. There he sat as they entered. When greetings had been exchanged, the architect asked Herr Nettenmaier how he was feeling now. "Thank you", replied the old gentleman, "I have a bit of trouble with my eyes, but it's nothing to speak of." He smiled and the architect exchanged a glance with Apollonius which won Apollonius over to him heart and soul. Then he told the old gentleman the result of the conference and caused Apollonius to blush with modesty and lose his usual composure for a time. The old gentleman moved the brim of his hat a little lower over his face so that nobody could read there the thoughts which struggled so strangely with one another.

If you could see under the brim you would have thought at first that the old gentleman is pleased; the shadow of suspicion with which he had received Apollonius the previous day is lifting. So he doesn't need to fear that Apollonius will make common cause with his brother against him! Yes, there appeared a certain something in his face which almost seemed like Schadenfreude at the humiliation of the older son. Perhaps he would have butted in and said in his usual laconic way, "You're to take my place from now on, Apollonius, do you hear?", had the architect not been so enthusiastic in his praise and had it not been so deserved.

"Yes" he said diplomatically, in order to conceal his thoughts which he only half expressed, "yes, that's youth for you! He's so young". "And yet already so able!", added the architect.

The old gentleman nodded his head. Anyone with an interest in it, like the architect, might have thought that he nodded in agreement. But he only said, "It's youth that counts in the world today." Yes, he felt proud that his son was so able, ashamed that he himself was blind, pleased that Fritz could no longer do just as he liked, that the honour of the family would now have one more guardian, afraid that his son's ability, of which he was so proud, would make him superfluous himself. And he could do nothing to stop it; he could do no more, he was nothing any longer. And as if it was Apollonius that had spoken this, he rose stiffly as if to show him that he should not feel triumphant too soon.

The architect begged the old gentleman to allow his son to stay for the duration of the work and to permit him to take an active part in it. The old gentleman was silent for a while as if waiting for Apollonius to refuse. Then he seemed to tacitly assume that he was refusing, for he gave the order with grim brevity, "You'll stay! Do you hear?"

Apollonius made his way up to his room to unpack his things. He was still at it when the news came that the Town Council had approved the repair.

So it was decided; he was to stay. He was to be allowed to
work for his beloved home town and put to good use what
he had learned while he was away.

Should anyone wish to get an overall impression of
Apollonius Nettenmaier, he must now look into his room.
The main goal of all his desires was reached. He was full
of joy. But he did not jump up and run round the room, he
did not drop things, nor misplace them, he did not look in
his case or on the chair for what he was already holding in
his hands. Happiness did not confuse him, it made his
mind clearer, indeed it made him more eccentrically
meticulous than ever. He did not miss the slightest piece
of fluff or speck of dust on the clothes he was unpacking;
he brushed his hand over them no whit the less than he
usually did; only by the way he did it could one see what
was going on inside him. It was as if he was caressing
them at the same time. The pleasure he felt in newly-
acquired possessions did not for one moment overshadow
that he felt in those he had owned a long time. It was as if
everything had been given him anew, and his relationship
to each of his possessions showed the mark of a loving
respect. When he thought of the way the architect had
praised him, his pleasure at it in the isolation of his room
was at one with the same modest blush of protest with
which he had accepted it in the presence of others. For him
there was no difference between his private and his public
behaviour.

When he had settled himself in, he immediately set about
the task of drawing up the report the architect required.
The decision on the repairs had been taken on his advice,

he had not merely participated as his father's journeyman, as a mere workman; he felt he had entered into a special moral obligation to his home town; he must do whatever lay in his power to carry it out. He would have needed no such prompting. He would in any case have done all that he could, but he knew himself too little to realise that.

In this heightened mood it seemed to him easy to overcome all that threatened to make his stay uncomfortable on the part of his brother and sister-in-law. Of course his brother only wished him to go because of his wife's dislike of him and that could be removed by persisting in the honest endeavours he was making to that end. He had never offended his brother; he was ready and willing to take second place to him in the business. He did not believe that one can give offence unwittingly, that in fact duty can sometimes compel us to give offence. He did not think it would be possible for his brother to offend him. He did not know that it is possible to hate the person we offend and not just the person who offends us.

Down by the shed the sullen journeyman stood grinning at Fritz Nettenmaier and said, "Oh yes, I can size a man up at first glance. Herr Apollonius too! But no matter, it won't last long!"

Fritz Nettenmaier chewed at his nails and decided to overlook the accompanying gesture which was supposed to provoke him to ask what the man meant by that. He went to the living-room and as he went, he flew into a rage against some imaginary person who was not there. "Integrity? Experience of the business, as that common architect fellow says? I know why you're pushing in and making yourself at home, you fussy devil! Play the innocent as much as you like, I ---"and here he made a gesture as much as to say, "I'm one of those people who knows all about life and the ways of women!" With that he turned to the door, but the movement this time was not as jovial as it usually was.

How many think they know the world when they really only know themselves!

The spirit of the house with the green shutters knew more than Apollonius Nettenmaier, more than all of them. He looked through the window at night, where Apollonius was still writing his report by the lamp, and his pale shadow fell on the paper in front of the young man. The writer heaved a deep sigh, he didn't know why. Then the spirit strode with anxious face along the path to the shed and the old dog on his chain howled in his sleep, and didn't know why. The young woman saw his hand move over her husband's brow; she was frightened, her husband was frightened too and did not know why. The old gentleman dreamed that a dead body was being carried into the house with shame, and the house creaked in all its timbers and did not know why. And the spirit wandered through the rooms for a long time when all were already in bed, up and down, to and fro, in the gallery, in the garden, in the shed, and in the corridor, and all the time it wrung its pale hands; it knew why.

4

The world of the slater lies high up in the air, between heaven and earth. Far below the noisy turmoil of the wanderers of the earth, high above the wanderers of the heavens, the clouds passing silently by. For months, years, decades even, this world had known no inhabitants except for the restlessly fluttering flocks of jackdaws, cawing loudly. But one day, halfway up the roof of the steeple, a narrow hatch opens; two scaffolding poles are pushed out by unseen hands. To the spectator below it looks as if they are trying to build a bridge of straw into Heaven. The jackdaws have fled to the pommel and weather-vane on top of the steeple and look down and ruffle their feathers with fear. The poles project only a few feet and the invisible hands stop pushing. Instead a hammering begins in the very heart of the roof-frame. The sleeping owls wake with a start and stagger smartly out from their niches into the open eye of day. The jackdaws are horrified at the noise, the child of man far below on terra firma does not hear it; the clouds in the heavens above pass indifferently by. For a long time the banging continues, then it stops. And out onto the poles and at right angles to them are pushed two, then three short planks. Behind them appears a head and a pair of strong arms. One hand holds the nail, the other hits it with a swing of the hammer until the planks are nailed firmly on. The flying scaffold is finished. That is what its builder calls it, and for him it can really be a bridge into Heaven in more ways than one. On the scaffold a ladder is now set up, and if the roof of the steeple is very high, ladder upon ladder. Nothing holds them together but the iron clamps; nothing holds it in place but four human hands on the scaffold and the broach-post of the steeple against which it rests at the top. Once it is firmly fastened above the hatch and to the broach-post with strong ropes, the bold slater will no longer see any danger in climbing it, however distressing it is for the child of man below on terra firma as he looks up to the dizzying heights above and thinks the ladder is made out of matchsticks like a Christmas toy for children. But before the ladder has been fastened on – and in order to do that he must first have climbed it – he may well wish to commend his poor soul to God. For then he is really between heaven and earth. He knows the slightest slip of the ladder – and a single false step can cause it –will send him plummeting down helplessly to a certain death. Stop the clock striking beneath him, it might startle him!

Involuntarily those watching far below clasp their hands together and hold their breaths; the jackdaws, frightened away from their last refuge by the climber, caw loudly as they flutter wildly round his head; only the clouds in the sky pursue their course above him unmoved. Only the clouds? No. The daring man on the ladder is just as unmoved as they. He is no vain daredevil seeking to cause a sensation; he pursues his dangerous path in a purely professional way. He knows the ladder is secure; he himself has built the flying scaffold and knows it is secure; he knows his heart is strong and his step sure. He does not look down where the ground stretches out green arms towards him, he does not lookup where the passing of the clouds across the sky can cause a fatal dizziness to film his steady eye. The middle of the rungs is where his eye is fixed and it is not long before he is standing at the top. There is no heaven and no earth for him except the broach-post and the ladder which he fastens securely together with his rope. The knot is tied; the spectators breathe again and in every street redounds the praise of this brave man and the account of his doings up there between heaven and earth. The children in the town play at being slaters for a whole week.

But only now does the brave man begin his work. He fetches another rope, brings it up and fixes it so that it rotates round the broach-post below the pommel. To it he fastens the pulley with three blocks, and to the pulley the rings of his cradle. This consists of a plank to sit on with two holes cut out for his legs to hang down, at the back a low handrail, on both sides boxes of slates, nails and tools; between the leg-holes at the front stands the prod, a small anvil on which to cut the slates to shape with his slate-hammer; this contraption, held by four strong ropes which meet at the top in two rings attached to the hook of the pulley, is the cradle, as he calls it, the light craft in which he sails round the steeple roof high in the air. By means of the pulley he pulls himself up and lets himself down with little effort, as high or as low as he likes; the ring above turns with the pulley and cradle in whichever direction he chooses round the steeple. A slight kick with his foot against the roof sets it in motion and it can be stopped wherever he likes. Soon there are no longer any spectators standing below looking up; the slater and his vehicle are no longer a novelty. The children go back again to their old games. The jackdaws get used to him; they look on him as a bird like them only bigger, but peaceable like themselves; and the clouds high up in the heavens have never concerned themselves with him anyway. The ladies envy him the view. Who else could look out so freely over the green plains and see the mountains, range after range into the distance, first green then more and more blue until the sky, bluer still, leans down to meet them. But he is just as little concerned about the mountains as the clouds are about him. Day after day he works with his slater's-iron and claw-hammer, day after day he hammers slates into place and knocks in nails, until he has finished hammering and knocking. One day man, cradle, ladder and scaffold have disappeared. Removing the ladder is just as dangerous as fastening it on, but this time no one below clasps his hands together anxiously, no mouth speaks of this man's deeds high up between heaven and earth. The crows are rather bemused for a whole week, then it is as if they had merely dreamed years ago of some strange bird. Far below, the noisy turmoil of the wanderers of the earth continues, high above the wanderers of the heavens, the silent clouds, still pass on their way, but no one flies around the steep roof except for the flocks of cawing jackdaws.

For the purpose of his report to the architect, Apollonius had undertaken further extensive surveys of the roof. The steeple itself was roofed with metal, which had already been in place nigh on two hundred years. As he moved round on his cradle, he found the metal plates close to complete disintegration. They had been afraid of this. Lead roofing on tall buildings works out incomparably more expensive than slates provided one has these in the near locality. The slater can take what slates he needs up with him in his cradle, but he can't do that with the much heavier sheets of lead. The slater can cover the whole roof with slates from his cradle; lead roofing makes strong scaffolding necessary. Apollonius proposed that the steeple should also be roofed with slates. The master smith, a man of some eminence, argued of course that people had known just as much about these things in the past as people from Cologne did – that was supposed to be a dig at Apollonius. His brother agreed with this; if they had thought in the past that slates did the job as well as lead, they would have used slates in the first place. On the other hand, of course, there were in those days no slate mines in the vicinity. The slates would have had to have been brought from far away and thus the slate roof for the steeple would have worked out more expensive than lead. The church roof at that time was covered with tiles and only later, when the slate quarries nearby were opened, with slates. The smith and Fritz Nettenmaier did not know that, or preferred not to know it. The growing prestige of his brother annoyed Fritz. But Apollonius knew it and with this new information was able to refute his brother's objections.

His proposal had been accepted. The suggestion was made that they should leave the whole direction of the work in Apollonius's hands. But, in order not to offend his brother, he asked to be allowed to decline this offer. So little did he want to offend his brother that he didn't give any reason for his request. From his time in Cologne he was accustomed to acting independently. From the attitude of his brother, now that they had met up again, he foresaw many restraints. He knew that he was taking on himself a heavy burden when he promised the architect that the work would not suffer as a result of this 'ménage a deux'. The worthy architect, who guessed at Apollonius's motives and respected him all the more for them, obtained the Council's approval for this arrangement and whenever it was necessary went out of his way behind the scenes to represent his protégé and support his policies against those of his brother.

It was a difficult task Apollonius had set himself; it was much more difficult than he knew. His presence here had not pleased his brother from the very beginning; Apollonius attributed that to the influence of his sister-in-law; and since then he had become even more alienated from him – and no wonder! Apollonius had already got to know his brother's vanity and ambition; and Fritz felt himself disadvantaged in comparison by all that had happened since. Apollonius thought to reconcile his sister-in-law's hostility by time and honest endeavour, and his brother's injured pride by outward subordination. If no further obstacle appeared, he dared to hope that he could carry out this task however hard it seemed. But what really stood between him and his brother was something else, something quite different from what he thought. And the fact that he did not know it made it all the more dangerous. It was suspicion born of the consciousness of guilt. Whatever Apollonius did to remove the supposed obstacles could only make the real obstacle grow.

If only he had not come back! If only he had not obeyed his father! If only he had remained away in foreign parts!

From the steeple hangs the cradle, and now the church roof itself is a hive of activity too. Strong hands hammer the cleats into the planking and with strong ropes drag along the cripple-box. This consists of two triangular sections constructed of strong planks. The angle of inclination of the roof determines the ratio of its two sides, for its bottom, padded with straw, rests its full width on the surface of the roof, while at the top the planks are fixed horizontally to form a level surface. On it stands or kneels the slater as he hammers; ready to hand beside him hangs the box for nails and slates, driven into the planking with his pointed hook.

Apollonius left the distribution of the work to his brother. Fritz Nettenmaier at first acted strangely in that he gave one to understand that he thought Apollonius had come to play the master here, not the servant. It was part of the suspicious direction his thinking had now taken, to assume that beneath everything his brother might do lay some hidden intention, some planned calculation. He suspected therefore that Apollonius wished to take over the work on the church roof too. Anyone working there could at any time see whether the cradle up around the steeple was occupied or hung empty from the flying scaffold. He played the innocent, saying he assumed Apollonius would rather be employed on the roof of the steeple, on the work which he himself had proposed should be done. Apollonius did not refuse. Fritz thought he was agreeing, although it was not really what he wanted to do, but he did not want to show it; Fritz felt like a man who has successfully outwitted an opponent, a feeling which was renewed whenever he looked up from his work on the cripple-box to the cradle and the flying scaffold on the steeple, certain that his brother could not leave the cradle and go home without his seeing it and being able to steal a march on him. Then Apollonius seemed once more the old 'dreamer', while he himself was the one who knew the ways of the world. Next moment perhaps he would again see the cunning in his brother and he found it very satisfying to feel sorry for himself as the one without guile for whom traps were constantly being set, to be able to hate the brother who hated him. He lacked Apollonius's need for clarity, which would have shown him the contradiction in this and would have compelled him to remove it once recognized. Perhaps he sensed this contradiction and suppressed it deliberately. So the consciousness of his own guilt presupposed as real the hatred which it had to reproach itself with having merited.

It was not long before Apollonius noticed that the orderliness, that quick and precise cooperation to which he had become accustomed in Cologne, did not exist here, but only the way his father had always handled things in the past. The slater had to wait a quarter of an hour or more for the batch of slates; the labourers lazed around and had a good excuse in the confusion and idleness of the trimmers and sorters. His brother laughed half pityingly at Apollonius's complaint about this. Such orderliness as he demanded did not exist anywhere and was not, in any case, possible. Privately he had one more reason to scoff at the 'dreamer' who was so impractical. And even if orderliness had been possible, the work was contracted on a daily basis. They would be paid just the same for the time lost as for that used. And as Apollonius personally did all he could to eradicate this slipshod routine, he again seemed to his brother to be the toady of the architect and the Council, while he himself in his own estimation was the plain man who spurned such artifices. His brother only wanted to get him out of the saddle and had still worse things in mind, but with all his cunning he wouldn't succeed; it was for this very reason Apollonius had come home. And yet he still thought the dreamer would get his wings clipped if he tried to introduce new ideas when he, Fritz, who knew the ways of the world, had not succeeded. He who knew his stuff better than even old blue coat himself did in his day.

Fritz Nettenmaier thought to outdo the old man by whistling more shrilly through his fingers, coughing more grimly and spitting with more intensity. The qualities which really compelled respect for the old gentleman, the consistency which, even where it had degenerated into eccentricity, still created respect, the calm self-assured dignity of an upright character, those qualities he failed to see. As he didn't possess them himself he also failed to see them in others. If there was any way in which his demeanour contrasted with that of the old gentleman, which he sought to impose on his own, then it was his restlessness and inner instability that was constantly at variance with it. The hypocritical way of speaking, for example, he seemed only to have borrowed from the old gentleman in order to mock his own superficiality and emptiness. From the stiff blue-coat manner, he sometimes descended suddenly into his own condescending joviality, and to a degree where a joke wiped away all distinction between master and man with its dirty fingers, as if it had never existed. Then, when just as suddenly he pulled himself up and became all masterful again, that did not bring back the lost respect, but merely gave offence. In the end he had to put up with the fact that many of the workmen took no notice of him and did whatever they liked.

Apollonius, on the other hand, possessed by nature and from his training with his cousin all that his brother lacked; he had the dignity, the consistency almost to the point of eccentricity. His inner confidence made all the difference; he did not have to make his presence felt – he did not need to make that visible effort to achieve respect which so seldom achieves its aim. And so he succeeded in doing what he set out to do. Soon there was the most exemplary orderliness in the work, and all seemed to appreciate it; except for Fritz Nettenmaier. The quick cooperation of the men, which took place as smoothly as if by some unseen law, made the blue-coat manner in which he felt so important completely superfluous. One more reason for his uneasiness was that this new orderliness emanated from his brother; from that same brother whom he had already so much to forgive and whom he was less and less willing to forgive. He did not know, or did not want to know, how great a spell can be cast on others by a self-reliant personality, although he had reluctantly to recognize the fact; and still less did he know that he lacked this quality while his brother had it. He was convinced in his own mind that his brother had used means which he felt to his own satisfaction that he himself was too noble to use. By these means his brother had alienated the men from him. Apollonius had no inkling of what was passing in Fritz's mind; he, in fact, was on his guard against Apollonius as one must be on guard against those who use cunning; for such enemies can only be defeated with their own weapons. The brotherly friendliness and respect with which Apollonius treated him was a mask beneath which Apollonius thought to hide his evil plans more securely; he repaid him and rendered him harmless more easily if he hid his own watchfulness under the same mask. Apollonius's good-humoured willingness to subordinate himself to him on the surface appeared to his brother like mockery in which the workmen, won over by cunning, knowingly participated. In his sensitivity he himself grasped at the methods which he imputed to his brother. He was prevented from openly opposing him by the circumstance that Apollonius made such a good impression, even on him, although he wouldn't have allowed this reason to count. So he laid aside the thunderous 'blue-coat' manner and descended to the lowest rung of his joviality. He began by nods and winks, then gradually with words, to express his sympathy for the workmen who were sighing under the tyranny of this fawning intruder, as he tried to prove him to be; since he did not have the courage to rouse them to open rebellion, he sought to entice them to take small individual liberties. He began daily to buy them rounds of drinks. They ate and drank, but stayed as before in the groove which Apollonius had marked out for them.

The working man has the sharp eye of a child for the strengths and weaknesses of his superiors. They easily saw through Fritz's behaviour and by it he lost the last remnants of any respect; they learned from this, even if they hadn't already known, with whom they could afford to fall out and whom not. And if they hadn't been sure, then the differing attitude of the architect to the two brothers would have shown it them. And since they were not so subtle and did not have the reasons that Fritz Nettenmaier had, they showed their opinion openly. They took liberties with him which showed him that the result of his condescension was quite the opposite of that he had intended. Now once more he angrily drew the thundercloud of the blue coat around him, whistled more shrilly than ever, so that it echoed in the great bell up in the tower; walked on extra tall stilts, again raised his shoulders level with the dark hair on his head; the grimness and intensity of his earlier coughing was child's play compared with the way he did it now. But the workmen soon knew that such things only happened in Apollonius's absence and if he should chance to approach, it would stir up, like the rising full moon, the most terrible storm.

Fritz Nettenmaier soon despaired of ever restoring his lost prestige on the work site. Naturally he put down the results of his own foolishness to Apollonius's ever-growing account. The feeling that he was superfluous gripped him as it had the old gentleman, but did not provoke quite the same effects. What the garden did for the old gentleman the slate-shed now did for the older son – at least as long as he saw Apollonius up on his cradle or on the church roof. But now he brought the blue coat manner with him into the living room as well. His children too – and this was easy for he did not bother with them himself – had early been won over by his brother – naturally by evil means. These 'evil means' were the very ones which he himself never used; unaffected goodness and the wise discipline of love. But even in his wife he saw more and more something like a natural ally of his brother against him. He saw it long before he had the slightest cause for it and that was the shadow which his guilt threw over the future in his imagination. By its very nature his guilt will compel him through the perversity of his defensive reactions to turn this shadow into a living reality which will fill his life with the desire for retribution.

Fears, heightened by foreboding, seemed to flicker past his consciousness in bright flashes and to tell him that his changed attitude to his wife must only hasten the inevitable. Then he was suddenly twice as friendly and jovial to her, but even this joviality bore within it something of the nature of the foetid ground from which it grew.

One remedy in particular is generally recommended for this sort of sickness; its name is distraction, forgetfulness of self. As if the steersman on sighting the threatening reef, where caution is doubly necessary, chooses that moment to lose his head. Fritz Nettenmaier took this remedy.

From now on he missed no dance and was absent from no public entertainment. He felt for ever free of danger if only he was away for an hour or two from the place where he saw it threatening. He was more out of the house than in it. But he did not go alone. He considered the remedy more necessary for his wife than for himself. His guilty conscience, out for revenge, anticipated what was only a remote possibility in the future as if it were happening now. And his wife was still so much on his side that she was now angry with the brother whose influence she recognized in the changed behaviour of her husband towards her, although she did not recognise what that influence really was. She had, in fact, expected only insults from her brother-in-law. So far this expectation had already turned one cheek to the newcomer and had coloured that red as if it were already fulfilled. Did she not know that he had come merely to insult her?

Apollonius, on whom all this weighed like a heavy cloud, like some incomprehensible foreboding, only understood one thing; his brother and sister-in-law were avoiding him. He kept away from the places they visited. He would have done so anyway, for the deepest needs of his nature tended more towards concentration than distraction. For him, being on his own was a better remedy than distraction was for both of them. He saw how different his sister-in-law was from what she had seemed before. He could not help but congratulate himself that his sweetest hopes had not been fulfilled. Work gave him enough self-awareness; what it left over was absorbed by the children. It was natural that at their age they should need to model themselves on some mature person, who by giving and accepting love could become their pattern and the standard by which to measure people and events, and so they pressed round their uncle who cared for them as lovingly as their parents neglected them cruelly. How could

Apollonius know that in this way he only increased the guilt in his account with his brother.

And the old gentleman in the blue coat? Had he in his blindness some inkling of the clouds which were building up round his house? Or was it this which oppressed him sometimes when, meeting Apollonius, he only exchanged a few superficial words with him? Then too forces were in conflict on his brow, but they were not seen by his son behind the eye-shade. There is something he wants to ask, but he doesn't ask. The old gentleman is so deeply enveloped in the clouds that nothing passes from him into the world outside and nothing passes in. He acts as if he knows about everything. If he doesn't he shows the world his helplessness and himself invites the world to take advantage of it. And if he asks a question, will he be told the truth? No! He considers the world as stubbornly against him as he is against it. He does not ask. He listens when he knows no one can see him listening, feverishly intent on every sound. Into each one he reads something that is not there; his overstretched imagination builds from it giant rocks that weigh him down; but he doesn't ask. He dreams of nothing but things which bring shame on him and his house; he empties the whole armoury of dishonours and plumbs the depths of every disgrace known to mankind. Everything that is not a disgrace is exaggerated into one by his abnormally heightened sense of honour, which no salutary inner calm can take the edge off, but he would rather bear the deepest shame than he would ask. He makes prodigious mental efforts to ward off what is impending, but he won't ask. How often does the mind's eye show the mother her unborn child! Will there come a time when the old gentleman's thoughts become reality?

The nature of guilt is that it does not entangle only its author in new guilt. It has a magic power to draw all those with whom it comes in contact into its turbulent net and there to ripen all that is malignant into new guilt. He is a lucky man who can resist this power with a pure heart. Even if he is not able to save the one who is guilty, at least he can be an angel to the rest. These four people are bound together with all their differences into one living knot, a knot severed by one man's guilt! What joint fate will they weave for themselves, these people in the house with the green shutters?

5

Now weeks had passed since Apollonius's return, and still he had not lived up to his sister-in-law's worst fears. In the first few days Fritz Nettenmaier thought he could see in her a desperate effort to keep a hold on herself, a fitful attempt to maintain her composure; now this was giving way to something like astonishment. He saw, and only he, how she began more and more bravely to watch Apollonius when he was not aware that she was looking at him. She seemed to be comparing his behaviour, his

actions, with her expectations of them. Fritz felt how little
the two matched up in her mind. He made every effort to
whip up his wife's antagonism to its old pitch. He did it,
feeling all the while how vain it was; for a single glance at
his brother's mild honest countenance must tear down
what he painfully built up over the course of days. He
realised how subtly he needed go to work and yet how
clumsily he did so in reality; for the same power which
sharpened his sense of proportion forced him to go over
the top when it came to action. He knew that what he had
begun must run its course to his ruin. He sought oblivion
and plunged his wife with him deeper and deeper into the
whirl of social activities.

Medicines used in too great quantities are said to produce
the opposite effect from that intended. That was what
happened with Fritz's remedy; at least as far as his wife
was concerned. Previously she had longed for any
opportunity for amusement, anything to get away from
everyday drudgery; but now that this in turn had become
the everyday, she once more sighed for the quiet life at
home. Surfeited with the honours heaped upon them by
the 'important people', she now noticed for the first time
that there were also others, people who judged her
husband by a different standard. She began to make
comparisons and the 'important people' lost out more and
more to the common herd. She thought back to that
tedious ball on the evening of Apollonius' arrival. Then
she had avoided Apollonius; she had expected to be
insulted by him. Now she watched out for him across the
dance floor; no one noticed except Fritz Nettenmaier, who
appeared to notice it least of all. For he laughed and drank

more wildly and more jovially than ever. She felt only boredom, a boredom constantly seeking diversion; she did not know that she was looking for anyone. Fritz knew it though and almost choked on his laughter. He knew more than she; he knew who she was looking for. Jovial towards everyone else, he began to play 'the blue coat' with her.

It will not be long before he brings her to the point of comparing the man she once feared with him.

She sat in the garden while the old gentleman dreamed his heavy midday dreams. Fritz Nettenmaier lay on the sofa in the sitting room suffering from the after-effects of a night spent in wild revelry. Just before this he had looked up at the roof of the steeple. She felt so particularly happy at home. And why shouldn't she? Were not her children playing round her? She did not think how often she had longed to get away from these same children into the mad social whirl which now no longer attracted her. She sewed. The boys played at her feet as quietly as if the old gentleman himself were present. But not so; if the old gentleman had been in the garden they would not have dared to enter it. The little girl had put her arms around her mother, who in her natural freshness still seemed a girl herself. Little of the similarity to her husband now remained in her face. That similarity had only been an external one and her features seemed only to have been touched on the surface; no deep experience had left its mark on them.

The little girl had been speaking to that bigger girl, her mother, about dolls, flowers, other children, and in her own particular way had said many things twice over and half-said others. Now she raised her head with a seriousness beyond her years, looked at her mother thoughtfully, and said," I wonder what it can be?" "What?" asked her mother "Well, when you've been here and go away again he watches you so sadly." "Who?" asked her mother. "Uncle Apollonius of course. Who else? Have you grumbled at him or smacked him like you do me sometimes when I take sugar without asking? You must have done something to him or he wouldn't be so sad."

The girl chattered on and soon forgot her uncle over a butterfly. But her mother did not forget. She no longer heard what the girl was saying. What a strange feeling she was experiencing, pleasant and painful at the same time. She had dropped her needle and hadn't noticed it. Was it dismay? It seemed like that, rather as one is dismayed when one talks to a person and suddenly realises it's not the person one thought it was. She had thought that Apollonius wanted to offend her and here was her daughter saying she had offended him. She looked up and saw Apollonius coming from the shed towards the house. At the same moment another man suddenly appeared between her and the man walking past, as if he had materialised out of the ground. It was Fritz Nettenmaier. She had not heard his approach.

With strange haste he moved on from some unimportant question to speak of that tedious ball. He told her what people had thought of it, how everyone had felt incensed by the insult Apollonius had given her on that occasion in not asking her to dance, not even the first dance. It was strange that now she was reminded of it she felt it more strongly than ever; but not in anger, but with a kind of melancholy sorrow. She did not say this. It wasn't necessary. Fritz Nettenmaier was like a man in a trance. He didn't need to look at her; with closed eyes he could sense what his wife felt from a leaf on a tree or a slat in a fence, from a white wall even. "We'll soon be rid of him now, I think", he continued, as if he had not been studying the stable wall. "There's no place here for two households. And Anne is used to plenty of room.

Anne was the name of the girl with whom Apollonius had had to dance at that notorious ball and had had to take home. She had often been to the house since then under various pretexts which her bright red cheeks belied. Her father too, a distinguished citizen, had taken pains to make Apollonius' acquaintance, and Fritz had helped things along as much as he could.

"Anne?" cried the young woman as if suddenly alarmed.

'It's a good job she's incapable of lying', thought Fritz, relieved. But then it occurred to him that her inability to dissemble could well benefit his brother's malicious plans. He had used jealousy as a last resort. That had been stupid of him again and he regretted it already. She can't hide her feelings and even if he were still the dreamer of old, her agitation must betray to him what was going on in her mind; indeed her agitation must betray this to her too. But she still did not know it herself as yet. And then – he stood again at the point to which every likely outcome led him, namely the two of them coming to an understanding –

'and then', he forced the words out between his teeth so that every syllable almost brought blood – 'and then she'll really find out!"

His brother was expecting him in the living room. "He'll have to think up some pretext to explain why he came by here expecting her to be alone, for he knows I've seen him", he thought to himself and followed his brother.

Apollonius was really waiting for him in the living room. His brother made his presence felt by turning on his heels as soon as he saw him. Apollonius was looking for his brother to warn him about the surly journeyman. He had heard a lot of disquieting things about this man and knew his brother trusted him absolutely. "So you're telling me to get rid of him, are you?" asked Fritz and could not prevent his ill-will from shining through his dissimulation. From the tone in which he spoke to him, Apollonius could not help but read his true opinion, which was, "So now you want to poke your nose into the shed and drive me out of there too. Try it if you dare!"

Apollonius looked his brother in the eye with unconcealed pain. He brushed his hand over his brother's lapel as if to wipe away all that was troubling their relationship and said, "Have I done something to offend you?"

"Me?" laughed his brother. His laughter was supposed to say "I can't possibly think how", but in reality came out as "Do you ever do anything else? Do you ever have any intention of doing anything except what you know will offend me?"

"I've been wanting to say something to you for a long time", continued Apollonius, "but I'll leave it till tomorrow; you're not in the mood today. That about the journeyman was something you had to know and it wasn't intended the way you took it!"

"All right, all right!", laughed Fritz, "you've convinced me. It wasn't meant that way!"

Apollonius left and Fritz went on and finished what he had really been saying. "It wasn't meant the way you want to make me believe it was, you fussy devil. And not meant the way I took it? Do you think I've -------. Anyway that journeyman is a bad lot, but you wouldn't have bothered to warn me if you hadn't needed a pretext." He made a deliberate turn on his heels; even in his sorry state this happy use of the old gentleman's art of diplomacy, of saying nothing by only half-saying it, had pleased him.

His pleasure was short-lived; the old worries soon screwed him back on their rack. And now a more recent worry had been added to their number. He had been neglecting the business; the journeyman, master of the slate shed in his absence, had had plenty of opportunity to steal from him and had certainly made use of this opportunity. As far as the repairs to St George's were concerned, he had long since ceased to be active; Apollonius had had to take on an extra journeyman to replace his brother. For a long time now he had brought in no new business and earned nothing, yet he missed no public entertainment. The respect of the 'important people' showed an increasing tendency to decline and was only maintained by increasing amounts of champagne. He had enmeshed himself in debts which were increasing every day and the moment must soon come when the appearance of affluence so painfully preserved must vanish. He knew that he was respected only so long as he counted as the most jovial among the jovial. He was clever enough to recognize the worthlessness of such respect and the efforts to attain it, but not strong enough to be able to do without it. All this was no small increase to the old mental torment, and both the old and the new stemmed from his brother, from him alone!

Anne Wohlig had frequently been to the house since Apollonius' return and Christiane, with the naivety that was the result of her own natural truthfulness, had found no fault with her most contrived pretexts. But now it was different. She had suddenly become so clear-sighted that the obvious pretexts assumed the proportions of unforgivable crimes. A girl who could be so false was repugnant to her and she herself was too honest to conceal it. Anne tried to put this reaction down to Christiane's dislike of her brother-in-law. It was well known that Christiane begrudged the poor man his brother's love. She had been heard to say that she would snub him if he dared to ask her to dance. And you only had to look at him to see that she did not let the poor man enjoy his stay in his father's house. Irritation made Anne, too, candid; she expressed those of her thoughts which could be expressed without revealing the soft spot he held in her affections. Christiane now had to hear from yet another mouth the reproaches her own child had already made to her.

The girl went. Apollonius came past again, returning from speaking to his brother. \He could still see Anne as she left the house. But nothing showed in his face which might have justified her only half-understood fears. And so Fritz Nettenmaier also, watching his brother in secret from behind the back door, did not see so much in her expression as he feared to see.

The child says: you have done something to upset him; Anne says: you hate him, you won't let him be happy. And his melancholy way of watching her about the house – for she soon caught him at it herself unnoticed – says the same. Like a flash of lightning, but one that brought joy, it suddenly struck her that he did not look at Anne with a melancholy expression, nor with joy, no! but with indifference as at any other girl. They've all been telling her: you hate him; you've upset him and want to hurt his feelings; and she's been thinking he hates her and wants to offend her. And hasn't he offended her in fact? She looks back into the past, to the time when he offended her. She has long since ceased to be angry with him about that, she has only feared new insults. Can she still be angry with him now that he is so different; when she herself knows that he doesn't offend her; when people say, and his sad look confirms, that she is hurting him so deeply? And so she thinks back eagerly, so eagerly that the music rings out round her once more and she is sitting among her friends again on the bench by the window of the clubhouse, wearing the white dress with the pink bow. Once more she stands up, driven by the dark press of people, and walks dreamily through the dancing throng to the door—and outside; isn't that the same face that watches her now about the house, so honest, so gentle in its melancholy? And isn't that the same feeling of compassion she had then that she has now, that accompanies her wherever she goes and never leaves her? Then she avoided him and no longer looked at him for he was false. False! Is he that again now? Is he that still?

A nightingale bursts into song in the old pear tree above her, so wonderful and somehow so powerfully heartfelt and deep. From the tower of St George's four trumpets sounded the evening chorale. Above them, as if borne by their swelling tones, Apollonius swung past on his light cradle. The glow of sunset gilded the ropes on which it hung. Wherever she looked there shone out those sad true eyes of his, the eyes with which he watched her as she went about. The little girl looked up at her with them and talked about her uncle, how kind and good he was. Or was she talking of things in the past? Time did not exist any more, past and present were one. The last similarity with Fritz Nettenmaier had disappeared from her face. Her mind swayed restlessly to and fro between Heaven and Earth. What she was contemplating was a puzzle, a puzzle with a sweet meaning, but she did not know it. She was a puzzle to herself. But not to her husband!

Fritz Nettenmaier wondered all day what it might be that Apollonius wanted to say to him next morning. "Tomorrow, because I'm not in the right mood today. In the right mood? I've shown that fussy devil my hand too soon. If I hadn't he would have just gone on his way; now I've warned him and put him on his guard. I'm too honest with shysters like him; I'm bound to lose. Right, tomorrow I'll be in the mood all right, I'll act as if I'm blind and deaf. As if I can't see what he's after even if he makes it crystal clear. I'll make sure I have a spider's web on my lapel so that he has something to brush off. I can't bear to be looked in the eye by someone like that, by such a hypocrite!"

Thus prepared, and resolved to outsmart the deceiver even if it meant the severest test of his self-control, Apollonius found his brother waiting for him the following morning. Apollonius too had come to a decision. He intended in future not to allow himself to be diverted by any mood of his brother's; it was simply a question of removing the source of these moods. Fritz wished him the heartiest, sincerest 'good morning' he could muster.

"If you will only listen to me in a calm and brotherly way", said Apollonius, "this morning will be, I hope, the best morning you or I and all of us have ever had."

"And all of us", repeated Fritz and put none of his interpretation of these words into his tone of voice, as he said, "I know that you always think of all of us; so go on, get it off your chest, and I'll do the same!"

Apollonius left out what he had intended to say by way of introduction. He had learnt to be canny and cautious, but to be canny and cautious towards his own brother would have seemed to him false. Even if he had known of his brother's guile, he would not have considered using the same weapons himself. He would have tried to convince himself that he had misunderstood the signs.

"I think, Fritz, "he began warmly, "that we ought to have behaved better to each other than we have up to now." Good-naturedly he took half the blame on himself. His brother, in his thoughts, put it all down to Apollonius, but jovially tried to assure him of the opposite, as Apollonius continued, "Things have not been the same between us as they once were, or as they should be. As far as I can see the only cause of this is your wife's dislike of me. Or do you know of some other reason, perhaps?"

"I know of none", said his brother, shrugging his shoulders regretfully; but he was thinking privately of Apollonius' returning home against his advice, of the infamous ball, of the consultation in the church loft, of his exclusion from the repairs, of his brother's whole plan, of that part of it that had already been carried out, and of that part that was still to come. He was thinking that at that very moment Apollonius was working on this last part and how much depended on his guessing the next move and frustrating it.

Meanwhile, with no inkling of what his brother was thinking, Apollonius continued, "I don't know what your wife's dislike of me stems from. I only know that it can't come from anything that I have done intentionally. Can you tell me what it is? I don't want to accuse her of anything; it's possible that it's just something about me that she dislikes. Whatever it is, I'm sure it's not something I should feel proud of, or allow to continue. And I shall be the last to allow it to continue once I know what it is, you can be sure of that. If you know what it is, I beg you to tell me. And you mustn't just put up with anything bad about me either, however much it may hurt you to tell me what it is. If you know and don't tell me it can only be for that reason. But you won't offend me by doing so, Fritz, I assure you."

Fritz Nettenmaier did what Apollonius had just done; he judged his brother according to his own standards. The result could only turn out to Apollonius' disadvantage. Apollonius took his pensive silence for an answer.

"If you don't know", he continued, "then let's go together and ask her. I must know what I should do. Life must not go on like this any longer. What would father say if he knew? It's a reproach to me day and night that he doesn't know. It's better for all of us, Fritz, so come on, let's not waste any more time."

Fritz Nettenmaier only heard his brother's unreasonable demand. He was to take him to her! He was to take him to her now! Did Apollonius already know of her state of mind and want to take advantage of it? The question was superfluous; if they saw each other now, they must surely come to an understanding. Then all would have come about that for weeks he had not rested a single hour from trying to prevent. It would have come about, as he knew it must, despite all his desperate efforts. They must on no account come face to face now; they must not see each other now, not until he had built a new dividing wall between them. But what was he to build it from? There was no time to think of that now. He must think of some pretext to prevent going to her. And so in order to gain time to think of one, he laughed, "Of course, go ahead and ask. If you ask, you'll be told. But why have you suddenly thought of all this? Why now?" A thought had suddenly struck him with the force of a bolt of lightning, and had impelled him involuntarily to ask this question.

Apollonius was already at the door. He turned back to his brother and answered him with a joy that seemed to the latter, who wasn't looking him in the face, almost satanic. On the other hand Apollonius would have caught in his brother's expression a kind of diabolical fear, had the latter turned his face towards him. And yet perhaps not. He would have probably considered his brother merely sick, without suspecting in the slightest what was really causing his brother so much anxiety. Indeed what pleased him must surely also please his brother.

"In the past", replied Apollonius, "I was always afraid that I would make her still more angry. And you would surely have liked that even less than I would."

His brother laughed and agreed, nodding his head and shoulders in his jovial way, merely in order to have something to do. And his "And now?" seemed half-choked with laughter, not with something quite different.

"Your wife has changed recently", continued Apollonius confidingly. "She's different now".

"She is", answered Fritz Nettenmaier with an involuntary start and was about to add what he thought she really was. It was a coarse word. But would Apollonius, who had brought her to that, have said it to him? No, his fears have not yet been realised. And if it is inevitable that they will be, he can at least still delay things for a while. He forces himself to keep down the agitation in his voice. He would have liked to ask, "And how do you know she's --- different?", were he not sure that his voice would tremble and betray him. He must find out who has given the game away to his brother. Has he already spoken to her? Has he sensed it in her eyes, from afar? Or is there a third person in the game, an enemy whom he already hates even before he knows of his existence?

Something of his brother's unfortunate habit of interpreting other people's thoughts seems to have rubbed off onto Apollonius. His brother does not ask him; his face is turned away; he is plumbing the deepest recesses of his mind, desperately searching but not finding; he does not ask and yet Apollonius answers him.

"It was your little Annette who told me", he said, laughing as he thought of the child. " 'Uncle' said the silly girl, 'mother isn't so cross with you any more. Go and tell her you won't do it again, then she'll be kind and give you a sugar lump'. That's how she put the idea into my head. It's wonderful how sometimes it seems as if an angel is speaking to you out of the mouth of a child. Your little Annette might well turn out to have been an angel to us all."

Fritz Nettenmaier laughed so heartily at the child that Apollonius' laughter burst out anew. But Fritz knew it was a devil that had spoken out of the child's mouth; the child had been like a devil to him and could be so again. And yet he still had to laugh at her, at the merry child with her 'damned' brain wave. He had to laugh so much that it went unnoticed how disjointed and agitated his reply sounded. "Tomorrow, if you like, or even this afternoon; I really haven't got time now. I'll walk along to St George's with you. I have pressing business to attend to. Tomorrow. Devil take that confounded child!"

Although laughingly said, Apollonius had no idea how seriously that curse had been meant. Laughing at the child himself, he said, "Good! We'll ask her tomorrow and then everything'll be different. I can't tell you how pleased I am, like Annette and you too Fritz, I'm sure. Life's going to be quite different from now on!" With his innate good-nature, Apollonius was delighted at his brother's positive reaction! He was still feeling the same as he passed to and fro across the roof of the church in his cradle.

Just as restlessly, his brother's fear fluttered round that deep darkness that hung over him, threatening to bury him; his heart hammered ever more frenziedly at his crumbling plans to stop his fall, but the cradle of his thoughts did not hang between Heaven and Earth, watched over by the light of Heaven; it fell lower and lower, down between Earth and Hell, and Hell marked it ever more darkly with its glow.

7

Annette had once more put her arms around her mother, who was sitting in the arbour. She looked up at her again with Apollonius' eyes and talked to her about him. And if, as is the way with children, she wandered off the subject, her mother brought the conversation back to him again with unconscious skill. Then, for a moment, there was a rustling sound among the leaves of the arbour behind her. She may have thought it was the wind, or didn't hear it at all; perhaps because it did not speak to her of Apollonius. Had she been able to see, she would have jumped up from her seat in terror. What made the leaves rustle was the violent shaking of a clenched fist. Behind it was a red face, distorted by the effort to hold back the raised fist, else it would have struck the child's smiling face. A go-between and so young! That smiling parricidal face! The little girl is wearing a blue dress; blue is Apollonius' favourite colour. His own child in the enemy's colours! And the mother – oh, Fritz Nettenmaier can still remember the time when she went around every day dressed like that. And has she no fear? Does she think that what happened then gives her the right not to be afraid of him? The right to live in shame, because it is his shame? It is all this that makes his raised fist itch to strike.

Now her mother says, s if to herself, for she has forgotten the child; "Poor Apollonius!" –What holds his fist back now? – "I must tell Fritz how sorry I feel for him. He's so good, isn't he Annette?" But Annette is singing and doesn't hear the question. And no answer is really required. "Fritz is angry with him because he insulted me once. I forgot all that long ago. He's different now and Fritz is wrong to think he's still the same. And perhaps he was never really like that and people have lied to Fritz. We'll be good to him to make him happy. I can't bear to see him look so sad any longer. I'll tell Fritz." Thus she brings her monologue to an end. The whole of her sweet trusting nature has been aroused once more and Fritz Nettenmaier realises that any action to which his anger may provoke him will inevitably bring about what has not yet happened, must only hasten what is to come. He has become poor, terribly poor. The future is no longer his; he cannot calculate days ahead; he can only live from minute to minute; he must hang on to what lies between the present and what is to come. And between them there is nothing but torment and struggle.

Up to now he has loved his wife, as he did everything, as was his nature, superficially and jovially. Now conscience has deepened his feelings. Fear of losing her has taught him a different kind of love and love has taught him in return another kind of fear. If he had loved her originally as he did now, her deepest feelings would perhaps have opened to him; she would have loved him, too. They have lived together now for years, have walked side by side, but their deepest feelings have remained hidden from each other. Physically a wife and mother, she has nevertheless remained inviolate in her deepest feelings. He has not aroused her deeper emotional needs, he did not know what they were; he could not have satisfied them anyway. He only recognizes them for the first time when they are turned towards someone else. He feels for the first time what he had, without his ever really possessing it, now that it belongs to another. What are his feelings when he sees her face come alive, like a bud unfolding, when he had thought it already in full bloom. What an unsuspected vision of Heaven is revealed where he had before been satisfied to find his own reflection. And however much he saw, his eye, although abnormally wide open, was far too narrow to see all the wealth of loyalty, devotion, admiration and humility which was lit up in the dawning of this pure countenance. His pain for a moment overcame his hatred. He had to creep away, to avoid having to confess his guilt to her whose glance, although soft and gentle, he now feared as if he were a criminal.

Towards evening the young woman was suddenly aroused from her day-dreaming by two men's voices. She was sitting on the grass not far from the door of the shed which was closed. Fritz had just entered the shed with his brother from the back alley. She heard him teasing his brother about Anne Wohlig. Anne was the best catch in town and his brother was a rogue who knew the ways of the world and all about how to handle the fair sex. Anne was already preparing her trousseau and her cousins were going from house to house gossiping about her marriage to Apollonius. Christiane heard him ask when the wedding was to be. She had been itching to get away; she forgot this; she forgot to breathe. And she could have shouted aloud for joy a moment later when Apollonius said he was not getting married, not to Anne, nor to anyone else.

His brother laughed. "I suppose that's why you spent the whole evening of your return dancing only with her and then took her home?"

"I would have danced with your wife", replied Apollonius. "You warned me she would snub me because she was so resentful of me. I didn't want to dance at all. You brought Anne to me, and as you left, you asked her if I might see her home. I couldn't do otherwise. I've never thought that Anne ----."

"------might be your wife?" laughed his brother. "Well, she's pretty enough for --- well, for a bit of fun, and worth the effort to get her to fall for you."

"Fritz!" cried Apollonius angrily. "But you can't be serious", he said quickly recovering his composure. "I'm sure you know me better than that; but even as a joke you shouldn't insult a nice girl like that."

"Pah!" said his brother, "she brings it on herself. Why does she keep coming to our house and throwing her cap at you?"

"She's never done that", replied Apollonius warmly. "She's a nice girl and means nothing wrong by it!"

"Yes, else you'd have taken her to task over it", laughed Fritz, and there was scorn in his voice.

"Did I know what she was thinking?" asked Apollonius. "You're the one who keeps teasing her about me and me about her. I've done nothing to arouse any such thoughts in her. I'd have considered it a sin!"

The men went back the way they had come. It did not occur to Christiane that they might have come along the path where she was standing. All the candour and honesty within her was enraged against her husband. No one had lied to him; he was the one who was false. He had lied to her and to Apollonius and she had insulted Apollonius in error. Apollonius, who was so kind that he could not bear to hear jokes made at Anne's expense, had also not made fun of her. It had all been a lie from the very beginning. Her husband was persecuting Apollonius because he was false while Apollonius was honest. Her innermost heart turned away from the persecutor to the persecuted. From the turmoil of all her feelings there rose triumphant a new feeling, a virtuous feeling and she gave herself over to it with all the impartiality of her innocence. She did not recognize it. May she never do so! For as soon as she recognizes it, it becomes a sin. And already the feet that will bring that fatal recognition ever nearer are swishing through the grass.

Fritz Nettenmaier had to build up his new dividing wall before taking his brother to see his wife. That was why he had come. His gait was erratic; he was still trying to decide what to do and could not make up his mind. He was even more unsure when he stood before her. He sensed what she was feeling from the expression on her face; it was far too honest a face to conceal anything. It understood too little of the feelings it expressed to think it necessary to conceal them. He felt he would not get anywhere with her now with the old calumnies. He could enlighten her about her own feelings, then get at her through her sense of honour, her feminine pride. He could force her ----to what? To pretend it wasn't true? To deny it? To conceal the truth once she knew what it was she wanted? Would she not say to herself, 'to deceive a deceiver, to take back secretly what has been stolen from one, that is no deception, that is no theft? That was it! The consciousness of his own guilt gave him a false impression of things and of people. He knew his wife's strong sense of honour as well as his brother's exceptionally strict honesty, and he would have trusted both of them in everything; only in one thing he did not trust them, and that was when he had the feeling that he deserved to be deceived by them.

So he decided to stick with the old path he had been following up to now. He made ma small digr5esssion in what he was saying to talk about 'the absurd ways of that old fusspot'. He knew that small follies are more likely than large faults to kill off a growing attraction. He mimicked the way Apollonius walked back along a path he had taken with his light to make sure he had not dropped any sparks. He made fun of the way he could not sleep at night if he thought his usual meticulous standards had slipped on some piece of work, or if a workman had not deserved the sharp words he had said to him in the heat of business. He ridiculed the way he jumped out of bed to straighten a ruler which he had left protruding over the edge of the table. All the time Fritz brushed and blew imaginary bits of fluff from his sleeve. He saw quite clearly that his efforts were having the opposite effect. Nettled by this he tried still stronger methods. He said how sorry he felt for poor Anne, whose head Apollonius had turned by his hypocritical ways; told her how coarsely Apollonius made fun of her in public.

On the cheeks of his young wife a dark red flush had appeared. Those whose nature is open and pure have a deep-seated abhorrence of all falsehood, perhaps because they feel instinctively how vulnerable they are to this enemy. She trembled with agitation as she stood up and said," You're capable of that, I know; but he's not."

Fritz Nettenmaier was taken aback. In the appearance of the person, who stood before him so full of scorn, there was something that took the wind out of his sails. It was the power of truth, the majesty of innocence when confronted with the sinner. He pulled himself together with a great effort. "Did he tell you that? Have you got that far with him already?" he forced himself to ask. She wanted to escape to the house; he stopped her. She tried to break free.

"It's all been a lie", she said. "You lied to him and you've lied to me. I heard what you said to him just now in the shed."

Fritz Nettenmaier breathed again. So, she did not know everything. "I had to, didn't I?" he said, scarcely able to look up and meet the purity of her gaze. "I had to, didn't I, to prevent your shame? Do you want old fuss-pot to despise you?" Still her gaze oppressed his own. "Do you know what you are? Ask him what a woman is who forgets her honour and duty? Who are you thinking of with thoughts which should only be for your husband? When you creep around like a love-sick girl hoping to see him. And think people are blind and don't notice. Ask him what he calls a woman like that. Oh, there are some fine names for women like that!"

He saw how frightened she was. Her arm trembled in his grasp. He saw that she began to understand him, she began to understand herself. He had feared her defiance and saw that she had crumbled; the red of anger grew pale on her cheek and the blush of shame quickly replaced it. He saw how her eyes sought the ground as if she felt all men's eyes upon her, as if the shed, the fence, the trees had eyes boring into hers. He saw how in the suddenness of recognition she counted herself one of those for whom there were these fine names.

Pain released its rain down over her cheeks, which were burning and red with shame, and the tears were like oil; and the fire grew as a voice called out from the shed and his step was heard. She wanted to tear herself away and looked up, half-wild, half-pleading, but her gaze sank to the ground again, intimidated by the thousand eyes all round. He saw that his eye, the eye of the man who was just coming through the shed, was the most terrible one to her. He had completely recovered his nerve now.

"Tell him", he hissed, "tell him what you want with him. If he's as you think, he's bound to despise you."

Fritz Nettenmaier held the struggling woman in a victor's grip until he had beckoned to Apollonius, who looked out of the shed to see what was happening. He let her go and she fled o the house. Apollonius stood stock-still in amazement.

"There, you see what she's like", said Fritz. "I told her you wanted to ask her. If you like we'll go after her and she'll have to confess. We'll see whether my wife dares to insult my brother who's so virtuous and honest."

Apollonius had to hold him back. Fritz was not easily persuaded. In the end he said, "You see now, surely, that there's nothing I can do. I'm so sorry!"

There was real pain in these last words, which Apollonius put down to the fact that his brother's attempt at reconciliation had failed. Fritz repeated them, this time more quietly, and now they sounded like a sneer at Apollonius, like scornful regret at some act of trickery that had misfired.

Christiane had rushed into the living-room and bolted the door behind her. She was not thinking of Fritz, but Apollonius might come in. She feverishly turned over in her mind the idea of running away; but wherever she thought of going, the steepest mountain-top, the densest forest, he still met with her there and saw what she wanted and despised her. And what was it she wanted? Did she in fact want anything from him at all? When in her thoughts she fled from him and anxiously sought refuge, was it not to him that she fled? When in her thoughts she longed for a shoulder to cry on, was it not his that she sought? The same moment that taught her she desired something morally wrong also taught her exactly what it was she desired. Annette was in the room; but she had not noticed the child. Her whole being was concentrated on her own inner struggle; Annette did not see what was going on inside her mother. She drew her mother onto a chair and put her arms round her in her own loving way and looked up into her face. Her mother met the look as if it came from Apollonius' eyes.

Annette said, "You know, Mother, Uncle Lonius----" Her mother sprang up and pushed the child away, as if it were Apollonius himself. "Don't say any more ---don't say any more about him!" she said with such angry fear that the child was silent and wept. Annette did not see the fear, only the anger in her mother's sudden agitation. It was anger at herself. The little girl lied when she told her uncle that her mother was angry with him. He did not need to be told. Had he not seen the red cheeks with which she avoided his and his brother's question; the same blush of angry displeasure with which she had received him on his return home?

How sultry and oppressive was the life in that house with the green shutters from then on---- for days and weeks!

The young wife scarcely ever appeared, and if she had to, a burning blush was ever on her cheeks. Apollonius sat up in his cradle hammering from sunrise to sunset. Then he crept quietly along the back alley, through the shed, down the path to his room. He did not want to meet someone who fled from him. Fritz Nettenmaier was hardly ever at home either. He sat from early to late in an inn from where he could see up to the trapdoor and the cradle on the church tower. He was more jovial than ever, bought drinks for all and sundry in order to bask in their false esteem. And yet, whether he laughed, whether he gambled, whether he drank, his gaze constantly flew up round the steep church roof with the ravens. And as if by magic, it happened that Apollonius never slipped home through the shed without Fritz shortly before having entered through the front door.

In the shed and in the quarry the journeyman ruled in his stead. He brought Fritz formal reports on the business. At first that jovial gentleman wrote it all down in thick books, then no longer. Entertainment became more and more indispensable to him; he had no more time to write. Until he got home late at night, the journeyman walked back and forth along the path from the living-room to the shed. There had been thefts in the neighbourhood; the journeyman was on guard; Fritz Nettenmaier had become a worried man at home. Other people were amazed at Fritz Nettenmaier's trust in the journeyman. Apollonius warned him repeatedly. Of course! He had good reason not to want anyone on guard, least of all the journeyman who was not well-disposed towards him. And that was exactly Fritz Nettenmaier's reason for trusting the journeyman and not listening to the warnings. When Fritz had told his brother how really sorry he was, he had caught sight of the journeyman hovering nearby. The grin on his face made it clear that the journeyman saw through him and knew what Fritz was afraid of. So he had gritted his teeth and half an hour later entrusted the journeyman with guarding the property and representing him in the shed and the quarry. He did not need to say much. The journeyman understood what Fritz was telling him to do; he understood also what Fritz was not telling him, but still wanted him to do. Fritz Nettenmaier trusted his honesty in the business no more than Apollonius did. He realised that the journeyman would abuse his trust there, that he knew something which only he and Fritz knew and that nobody else must know. The journeyman's dishonesty in the business guaranteed his honesty where Fritz needed it more. All this showed Fritz's lack of concern, born out of his feverish anxiety, for anything that was not relevant to his main purpose.

The old gentleman in the blue coat had worse dreams than ever; he listened more intently to every fleeting sound, read more into it than was there and laid bigger and bigger burdens on his heart. But he did not ask!

8

It was late one evening. Fritz Nettenmaier had watched from the window of the inn as Apollonius left his cradle and fastened it to the flying scaffold, then he hurried out of the inn as usual in order to get home before Apollonius. He found his wife in the living-room busy with domestic chores. The journeyman came in and made his usual report. Then he whispered something in his master's ear and left.

Fritz Nettenmaier sat down by his wife at the table. This was where he usually sat until the journeyman's shuffling step in the lobby told him that Apollonius had gone to bed. Then he went back to the inn; he knew the house was safe from thieves, the journeyman was on guard.

The feeling that he had his wife in the palm of his hand and that she submitted passively to this, had up to now helped the wine to cast a pale reflection of that old jovial condescension of his, which used to shine so sunnily from every button on his coat. Today this reflection was exceptionally pale. Perhaps because her eyes did not seek the ground as they met his. He asked a few superficial questions and then said, "You've been very cheerful today." She was supposed to feel that he knew everything that happened in the house, even when he wasn't there himself. "You've been singing." She looked at him calmly and said, "Yes, and tomorrow I'll be singing again. I don't see why I shouldn't."

He got up noisily from the chair and walked up and down with heavy tread. He intended to intimidate her. She rose calmly and stood as if expecting an attack, but one that she didn't fear. He went up to her, laughed harshly and made a sudden movement with his hand that was supposed to make her recoil in fear. She did not do so. But a red flush appeared on her cheeks, the only visible sign that she felt hurt. She had become shrewd, suspicious of her husband. She knew that he was having her and Apollonius watched.

"And didn't he tell you anything else?" she asked.

"Who?" said Fritz, taken aback. He drew up his shoulders and thought he looked like 'old blue coat' himself. The young woman did not answer. She pointed to the bedroom door. Annette stood there. "The spy! The go-between!" he hissed. The child came anxiously forward with hesitating steps. She was in her nightdress.

Fritz Nettenmaier did not see the pleading in the child's eyes, begging him to be kind to her mother, for her mother was kind too. He did not see how their domestic strife weighed upon the child and made her pale, as she suffered it with them, though without understanding it. He only noticed how closely she listened in order to be able to pass on what she heard to the one who had taught her to spy. She wanted to cling to his knees, but his look, his raised fist drove her back. Her mother, suffering in silence, picked the child up in her arms and carried her back to bed. She was afraid of what her husband might do to the child. What he might do to herself did not frighten her. She told him so when she came in again and closed the door behind her, as if to shield the child from him.

"I've sorted things out in my mind", she said, and this shone so clearly from her eyes that her husband strode to and fro once more in order not to have to look into them. "I've sorted things out in my mind. I've had certain thoughts, thoughts which I couldn't help and which I certainly didn't encourage. I didn't know they were wicked thoughts. But then I fought against them and I'll never stop doing so as long as I live. I went in my mind to the bed where my dear mother died and I saw her lying there and laid my fingers on her heart. I promised her solemnly that I would not do, nor allow to be done, anything dishonourable and I begged her with tears in my eyes to help me in this. I went on promising and begging so long until all my fear disappeared and I knew that I was a loyal wife and that I shall remain one. And no one can despise me. I'm not afraid of anything you might do to me and I shall not resist. You do it on your conscience. But the child you shall not harm. You have no idea hoe strong I am and what I can do. I won't allow it, I tell you!"

His glance flew warily past her slim figure, avoiding the pale beautiful countenance; he knew it was an angel who stood before him and threatened him. Oh, he recognized, he felt how strong she was; he sensed what a mighty shield the conviction of an honest heart can be. But only against him! He sensed it in his weakness. He felt that she must be believed by anyone capable of believing anything. This right he had lost, had thrown away in the corrupt game he had been playing. He would have had to believe her, had he not known also that what must come, must come. Neither she nor anyone else could prevent it. He was shown one last way out by his guardian angel before he deserted him. What if he made every effort, honestly and unceasingly, to put right all the wrong he had done her? What if he actively showed her his love, the love which the fear of losing her had taught him? Didn't he have helpers? Weren't the children bound to help him? And her sense of duty that was so strong? Her dead mother, to whose bedside she had gone in her thoughts, on whose heart she had sworn? But the very thing he is counting on, her fidelity, frightens him away when he tries to get near her. He has become enslaved by the spectre of his guilt, the thought of retribution, which drives him relentlessly on to do what he really wants to prevent. The constant habit of thinking like this is too deeply engrained. Hope and faith are foreign to this line of thought; Hate is more closely allied to it. He summons it now to his aid. – Outside the journeyman's shuffling step is heard on the sand in the lobby. The house is safe from thieves. He can go out again.

Today Fritz Nettenmaier is as jovial in the inn as only he knows how. His flatterers are thirsty and graciously allow themselves to accept his favours. He drinks, tips the hats of his cronies over their ears, and with his stick and his hand bestows many other such gentle marks of his affection. Then he laughs admiringly at his own skill in making such witty remarks. He does everything he can to forget himself; he does not succeed.

If only he could change places with his wife, who meanwhile sits alone at home. The one thing he is longing for – self-forgetfulness – is the very thing that she must be wary of. What he needs to do, and cannot escape despite his best efforts, is what she is striving for and cannot manage – that is to achieve self-awareness. What is the point of telling the child not to do it, when all her own thoughts speak to her of Apollonius? She thought she was keeping out of his way and now sees that he is avoiding her. She should be glad and yet it grieves her. Her cheeks burn once more. It is strange that she herself views her situation more strictly or more leniently according to how strictly or how leniently she imagines Apollonius will judge her. So, although he is unaware of it, he has become for her the criterion by which to judge everything. Does he know what she is like and despise her? He is so kind and considerate; he did not make fun of Anne, nor despise her; he stood up for her against the contempt and mockery of others. Has she ever, before he came, had thoughts which she ought not to have had and he has guessed them? She imagines herself, with all she knows and desires, as but one single thought in his mind, one thought which he knows like all the rest. And he has felt sorry for her; and was that why he watched her so sadly as she went by? Yes! Of course! And now he avoided her to spare her feelings. The sight of him should not, if he could help it, arouse thoughts in her which would be better left dormant till she slept in her coffin. Perhaps he had told her husband as much, or written it to him; and her husband had chosen this method of curing her - by arousing her aversion.

Was it mere chance that at this moment she glanced at her husband's desk? She saw that he had forgotten to remove the key. She did not remember him having been so careless ever before. Ordinarily she had paid no attention to it; now for the first time it occurred to her, that if he knew she was there, he had never left the room even for a moment without locking the desk and taking the key. In the drawer in the top right corner lay Apollonius' letters; she had always avoided looking there before. Now she opened the desk and took out the drawer. Her hands trembled, her whole body shook. Not for fear her husband might catch her at it. She must find out how things stood between her, Apollonius and Fritz. She would have asked him, not helped herself, if she had been able to trust her husband. She trembled with expectation of what she will find. Does she perhaps suspect what she will find?

There were many letters in the drawer; all lay open and unfolded and all seemed to be copies of one single letter, so greatly did they resemble each other; except that the writing in the earliest ones seemed weaker. The salutation in each was as if marked out exactly on the same spot; exactly at the same number of inches and lines beneath it was the beginning of the letter. The space between the dead-straight lines and from the edge of the paper was the same in all; nothing was crossed out; not the slightest irregularity betrayed the mood of the writer or any change in it; each letter of each word was exactly like the next.

She touched all the letters one after another before she read them; with each a new glowing blush spread over her cheeks, as if she were touching Apollonius himself, and she involuntarily drew her hand back. Now, as she picked up one letter, a small metal box fell back into the drawer; the box came open and out fell a small withered flower, a little blue campanula. Similar to the one she had once laid on the seat for him to find. She shrank back. On that same evening Apollonius had offered that flower around among his friends with scorn and derision, and had asked what they would give for it and then, amidst the general laughter, had ceremoniously knocked it down to his brother. Fritz had brought it to her and told her about while they were dancing and, according to him, Apollonius had watched mockingly through the window. That flower she had pulled to pieces and the young people had danced over the remains. This flower in the box must be a different one. It must say in the letter who it came from or to whom Apollonius had sent it.

But no, it was the same flower. She read it. Imagine her feelings when she read it was the same one! Tear after tear fell on the paper and from them there seemed to rise a rosy haze which veiled the walls of the room. Within this haze there was a stirring like a gentle morning breeze in spring that rolls up the streamers of mist so that the blue sky shines through the gaps and golden heights appear. And the view ever widens and as the veil of billowing mist sinks ever deeper, the rustling woods appear and green meadows with their carpet of flowers, cosy gardens with leafy shade, houses with happy people. Oh it was a world of happiness, a world of laughing and weeping for joy, that sprang from those tears, each one the colour of the rainbow and each one saying 'it was yours' while the last cried 'it was stolen from you'. The flower was the one from her; he carried it next to his heart in longing, hope and fear until she whose memory it preserved belonged to his brother. Then he threw this token of future happiness after the one he had lost. He was such a decent man that he considered it a sin to withhold this poor flower from the person who had stolen the giver from him. It was a man like that she might have clung to, might have passionately hugged and embraced in her longing arms, never to let go. She might have done that, could have done it, should have done it! It would not have been a sin if she had done so; it would have been a sin if she had not. And would it be a sin now, when they had both been betrayed by the one who now tormented her about what he had himself made into a sin? He who forced her into sin; for he forced her to hate him; and that too was a sin, and it was his fault. Who forced her --- who forced her into more than this, into thoughts that were totally sacrilegious, thoughts which sought to justify the love and hate forbidden by God, forced her into terrible, clever, seductive, wild, hot, criminal thoughts. And even if she rejected these with a shudder, she saw other unintentional sins inevitably threatening. With terrible sweet fear, she knew herself to be close to the man who should be a stranger to her, but who was not a stranger to her, and from whom in the fear of her own weakness she saw no escape. She fled from him, from herself, into the bedroom where her children were asleep, where her mother had died. There where she felt a sense of sacred awe she heard the gentle stirring of those innocently slumbering lives to whose protection God had appointed her; heard the calm breathing whisper through the still dark night. Each breath a carefree self-surrender to that unknown power which bears the universe in its maternal arms. She went from bed to bed, knelt down motionless beside each and rested her head against the bed's sharp edge.

From the tower of St George's the bells rang out as the march of time brushed past them; and it did not stop. The clock struck quarter past, half past, quarter to, the hour, quarter past again and half past again. The gentle breathing of the sleeping children stirred around her. She lay there with her hot hands folded for a long time, a very long time. Then the thought came to her from the gentle stirring of the life around her, silvery like the bells on Easter morning. Why are you afraid of him? And she saw all her guardian angels kneeling round her and 'he' was one of them, the handsomest, strongest and gentlest of all. And she dared to look up at him as one looks up to one's guardian angels. She got up and went back into the living-room. She spread the letters out on the table and then went to bed. The person who owned the letters should know when he returned and saw them that she had read them all. Not in order to frighten him, not as an accusation, whatever she might think of him. He was to read into this whatever the consciousness of his guilt should dictate; he was to read into this affront her threat of revenge and her plans for carrying it out. He knew her truthfulness; if he had been as virtuous as she, he would have known she had only obeyed the impulse of her honest nature. It was hard for her tom part with the letters, but they did not belong to her. The little box with the withered flower was all she took, with the intention of telling Fritz next morning that she had done so.

Fritz Nettenmaier still sat all alone in the inn. His head hung down on his chest from tiredness. He was trying to justify to himself his hatred and his actions. She and his brother were false; it was their fault, not his, that he was wasting all the time here that he should be devoting to his children. The person who had stolen their hearts from him could look after them. He had just managed to convince himself of this when the bedroom door opened at home. His wife had got out of bed again and put the little box with the flower back beside the letters. Apollonius had not kept it, so she must not do so either. Her husband was not yet thinking of going home when she pulled the blankets up over her virtuous self once more. With the thought that from now on Apollonius should be her guiding star, and if she acted like him she would remain above reproach and safe, she fell asleep and smiled in her sleep like a carefree child.

9

Life in the house with the green shutters became ever more oppressive. The mutual estrangement of husband and wife increased with every day that passed. Fritz Nettenmaier treated his wife with less and less consideration as his conviction grew that nothing more was to be gained by sparing her. This conviction flowed from the increasingly cool disdain with which she resisted him; he did not realise that it was he himself who was forcing her to this disdain. The effect was a mutual one, making their relationship increasingly unhappy. However seldom Apollonius met up with his brother and sister-in-law, he could not help but notice their strife. It distressed him that he must bear the responsibility for it. In what way he bore it, he did not suspect. While his sister-in-law treated him with loving respect and impressed his features on herself and her whole household, he for his part brooded long on the reasons for her insuperable dislike of him. His brother did nothing to correct this error; he encouraged it rather. At certain times, when by himself, he merely derided him in superior fashion; that was when wine and flattered vanity had their effect and put him in a good mood. But the times when he felt enervated, discontented with himself, were much more frequent. Then he forced himself to see nothing but hypocrisy in Apollonius, and sharpened on the whetstone of his own self-pity his hatred of others, something which always gave him such a sense of well-being.

Apollonius knew nothing of his brother's way of life. Fritz Nettenmaier hid it from him out of some involuntary feeling of compulsion, which Apollonius's very uprightness of character forced him to, but which he would have admitted to no one, least of all to himself. The workmen knew that they dared not come to Apollonius with anything that seemed like tale-telling, especially if it concerned his brother, whom he would have liked to see respected by all, more than himself. But he had noticed that Fritz looked upon him as an intruder into his rights, someone who spoiled his pleasure in the business and everything else he did. Apollonius had not really felt at home since the day of his return; he was a burden to those he loved here; he often thought of Cologne where he knew himself to be welcome. Up to now his moral duty had kept him here, the responsibility he had taken on himself with respect to the repair of the church roof. This was now rapidly approaching completion. So the thoughts of Cologne were now pressing for a decision and he shared this with his brother.

It was difficult for Apollonius at first to convince his brother he was serious about returning to Cologne. Fritz considered it initially as a cunning pretext to lure him into a sense of false security. Fears are just as difficult to give up as hopes. And it would have meant that Fritz would have to confess that he had wronged the two people who he was in the habit of accusing of wronging him, a situation in which he found a kind of comfort. He would have to forgive his brother a second wrong that the latter had suffered from him. He only reconciled himself to the idea when he succeeded in seeing in his brother the old dreamer again, and in his plans an act of folly. When he saw in them an involuntary confession that his brother recognized him as a superior opponent and had decided to go out of despair at ever carrying out his evil plans. At that moment all his old jovial condescension re-awoke as if from a winter's sleep. Once more his boots creaked 'Here he is. Now there'll be fun'; all his old mannerisms proclaimed his triumph. His boots drowned out all that his understanding of the consequences of his extravagance reproached him with, of his fall in general esteem. It seemed to him that everything would be as good as ever again if only his brother were gone. In anticipation he even believed in his own extraordinary magnanimity in forgiving his brother for being there. He was already drawing himself up to his old height in front of his brother and assuming the bearing with which, as sole head of the firm, he had met the newcomer on his return; he indicated with his most condescending laugh that he would soon get his way with 'old blue coat'; for he was the one who must send Apollonius away.

His wife felt differently. Fritz Nettenmaier was too crafty to tell her about it for the time being. But old Valentine was not so crafty and did not see why he should be. Old Valentine was a foolish fellow. He said nothing to the old gentleman. It was strange how conscientiously he carried out his duty; he was the most loyal hypocrite there had ever been. He never betrayed anything to the young people that he had noticed about the old gentleman; out of loyalty to 'old blue coat' he hid it from them as zealously as the old gentleman did himself. But he was also so devoted to the young people that the old gentleman learned nothing about them from him either, except what they themselves wished him to know, even if he did something he in fact never did, namely ask about them.

It seemed to Christiane as if her guardian angel was abandoning her. She felt safer from him in his presence than when she was away from him; for all the magic which prevented her wishes from becoming sinful flowed into her directly from his honest eyes; from his brow that was so pure that even a single sinful glance despaired of dragging her down with it into its vortex of desire, staining her character, but returned whence it had come, cleansed and at the same time cleansing.

Apollonius should not go, especially not through the fault of his brother, who alone in the whole town rejoiced at it. Of course Fritz won't admit his own guilt in the matter; that too he will push onto his brother. Apollonius had also told the architect of his decision. It surprised him that this good man, who normally approved everything Apollonius planned to do in advance, as if Apollonius could do nothing he would not approve, received the news with astonishment and a strange monosyllabic coldness. Apollonius urged him to tell him the reason for this change of manner. The two high-principled men quickly came to an understanding. After expressing surprise that Apollonius was unacquainted with it, the architect told him what he knew of Fritz's lifestyle and was of the opinion that the business and his father's house could not survive without Apollonius's help. He promised to make further inquiries about the matter and was soon in a position to give Apollonius a more detailed account. At various places in the town his brother owed not inconsiderable sums of money, the slate business, especially of late, had been run in such a slapdash and unscrupulous manner that many long-standing customers had already deserted and other were about to do so. Apollonius was shocked. He thought of his father, of his sister-in-law and her children. He thought of himself too, but his strong sense of honour showed him first and foremost what that proud righteous blind old man must suffer at the shame of a possible bankruptcy. He himself would be able to earn his living; but his brother's wife and children? And they were not used to going without. He had heard that Christiane had inherited a considerable sum from her parents. He grasped at the hope that it might still be of help. And he himself wanted to help too. No sacrifice of time and strength and resources would be too great for him. If he could not stop the rot, at least his dependants should not go hungry.

The stout-hearted architect was pleased at the way his protégé's mind worked, had indeed counted on it; it had surprised him that it had not manifested itself earlier. He offered Apollonius his help. He had neither wife nor child and God had been kind to him so that he earned enough to be able to help out a friend. But Apollonius would accept no offer. He wanted to see first how things stood and find out for certain whether he could remain an honest man if he took the friendly offer at face value.

Difficult days now loomed for Apollonius. The old gentleman must not know anything of the matter and if his honour were to be maintained, must also not learn that it had been in doubt. Apollonius needed all his firmness and all his tact in dealing with his brother. He had daily to impress on him the seriousness of the situation and hourly to forgive him. It was difficult enough to get from him the state of his assets, the names of his creditors and the amount of the debts. In vain Apollonius tried to make his good intentions clear, his brother did not believe him; and if he was forced to believe him he would not have hated him any the less. He hated himself in Apollonius and hated him all the more as his own actions appeared more hateful to himself. When Apollonius knew the names of the creditors and the amounts he examined the state of the business and found it in a worse state than he had feared. The books were in a mess. Recently nothing had been entered in them. There were letters from customers complaining about shoddy goods and negligence, others with accounts from the quarry owner who would no longer give credit for new orders since the old ones had not yet been paid for. Christiane's inheritance was for the most part already squandered; Apollonius had to force his brother to give up what was left. He had to threaten him with the courts. One can imagine how such confusion must have told on Apollonius, with his anxious need for orderliness and his great loyalty to the family, in the face of his brother's attitude. And yet the latter saw in his brother's every slight remark, in his every action, only ill-concealed triumph. After endless trouble Apollonius succeeded in gaining an overall view of the situation. It turned out that if the creditors showed patience and the customers could be won back, then with strict economy, hard work and conscientious endeavour the honour of the firm could be saved, and, if his efforts did not slacken, his brother's children could one day take over as their rightful inheritance a business that was at least debt-free.

Apollonius wrote at once to the customers, then he went to his brother's creditors. The former were willing to give the firm another chance. Clearly they were playing for safety for their new orders were little more than a trial run. When he met the creditors he had the pleasure of seeing what trust he had already won for himself in his home town. If he were prepared to stand surety, the sums owed could be retained as capital and paid off gradually at a low rate of interest. Many were even willing to entrust ready money to him as well. He made no attempt to put the truth of these assurances to the test and thus won over even more their full confidence. Now, in his gentle unassuming way he explained to his brother what he had done so far and still had left to do. Reproaches could not help and he considered exhortations useless when necessity alone spoke so clearly. If Apollonius, alone and unaided, now agreed to take over the total management of affairs, both those of the business and those of the household, took control of the money received and the money paid out, then his brother could not possibly see any arbitrary interference in that. In a matter in which his honour alone was the pledge, Apollonius must be able to have a free hand. The smooth coordination of all the activities, by which alone the intended outcome could be achieved, demanded the guidance of a single hand.

The sales side of the business above all must be revived. The quality of the goods delivered by the quarry owner had grown worse and worse. Fritz had had to accept them as satisfactory in order to get any slates at all; so Apollonius accepted the offers of the other creditors to allow the debts to remain as capital and paid off the old debt to the slate-quarry owner with all that was left of Christiane's inheritance that could be turned into ready money. Thus he was able to pay cash in advance for a substantial new order and received once again, and more cheaply this time, slates of good quality which helped him to keep his customers. The quarry owner who had had this opportunity to get to know Apollonius and his knowledge of the material and its handling, made the proposition that, as he was old and tired of work himself, Apollonius could lease the quarry from him. With the conditions that he set, Apollonius could reckon on a good profit, but as long as he was still on his own in a difficult position, he dared not spread his limited assets among any more concerns.

Apollonius drew up his plan for the first year and laid down a fixed amount which his brother should receive from him every week for the maintenance of his household. He dismissed any of the men who could possibly be spared. Old Valentine, in virtue of his honesty, was appointed to be in charge during the times when he himself had to be out on business. There were good reasons for suspecting that the sullen journeyman had committed many acts of embezzlement. Fritz Nettenmaier, who clung on to this guardian of his honour as if it were his last bastion of defence, did everything he could to justify him and so keep him on. For everything of which he was accused, the journeyman had had direct orders from him. Apollonius would have liked to take the journeyman to court, but he had to be content with sacking him and forbidding him the house. Apollonius was inexorable, however tactfully he explained his reasons to his brother. Any impartial person must have said he could do no other, the journeyman had to go. Even Fritz Nettenmaier when he was alone thought to himself with wild laughter, "Of course he must go!" His laughter sounded a bit like satisfaction that he had been right, like schadenfreude with which he derided himself. "Old fuss-pot would be a fool if he didn't get rid of him. A fool like I was, when I believed he would keep him on. I'm too honest, too stupidly honest compared with someone like that. What are my debts to do with him? He wanted to get me in his clutches, so he forced me to run into debt in order to be able to sack the journeyman who was standing in his way. He wanted to be master in the house, so he pushed me from pillar to post in order to intimidate me until I had to put up with whatever he wanted, so that he could get together with her when I wasn't there. And if he's so right, why does he put up with so much from me? Any honest fellow would behave quite differently to me. It's his bad conscience. He wouldn't be like that if he weren't false. He's got me where he wants me. What intimidation can't achieve, servility will. But he isn't clever enough for me. I know the world better than that dreamer does."

However Apollonius might treat him, whether with strictness or indulgence, it only strengthened him in this conviction which became all the more persistent the longer he cherished it, and became all the thirstier for his heart's blood the longer he fed on it. He could no longer see any external means of preventing his brother's evil intent.

From now on his mental state wavered between despairing resignation to what could no longer be prevented, indeed had probably already happened, and feverish efforts to prevent it nevertheless. Accordingly his behaviour towards Apollonius took the form either of unconcealed defiance or cringing wary hypocrisy. If the first mood held sway then he sought oblivion day and night. To his misfortune the journeyman had found work in the local slate quarry and was his companion for whole nights at a time. The 'important people' turned their backs on him and revenged themselves with unconcealed scorn for the need which he had aroused in them and could now no longer satisfy; they paid him back for all the jovial condescension they had suffered at his hands while he treated them to champagne. So he avoided them and followed the journeyman to the places where the latter was more at home. Here he toned down the jovial condescension an octave. Now the grog-shops resounded with his jokes and these took on more and more the character of the new surroundings. Even in better times they had shown a hint of a tendency that way. There came a time when he no longer felt ashamed to fraternize with vulgarity.

While Apollonius hammered away all day on his cradle, working for his brother's family, and sat over his books and letters every night with loving devotion, stinting himself of his well-earned food in order to make up all that his brother had frittered away, this very brother was telling everyone in the grog-shops how badly Apollonius had treated him, because he himself was good and his brother evil. He told them this so often that he came to believe it himself. He expressed his pity for the creditors who had accepted guarantees from that hypocrite who would betray them all, and told all kinds of contrived stories to make his pity creditable. If it were up to him, Apollonius would be hammering away in vain and sitting over his books and letters in vain. But no one believes him; he only undermines whatever respect he still has left. He scornfully opposes all Apollonius's plans. Despite all this Apollonius still hopes that he will remember where his loyalty lies and will make an effort to reform. His hope testifies more to his own feelings than his insight into his brother's mind. If Fritz happens to think of his own corrupt state, it is just one more reason to hate that 'old fuss-pot' and his poor wife has to suffer for it if he happens to come home just as Apollonius is about to go out to work once more.

10

Roofs that are covered with metal or tiles as a general rule only need repairing after some years; with slate roofs it is different. Because of all the scaffolding and the clambering about on the roof while the work is being done, all kinds of damage is unavoidably caused to the slates, damage which does not always show itself immediately. During the first three years after a building has been roofed or re-roofed, more substantial repair work is often required than in the next fifty years. The roof of St George's church was no exception. The slate roof of the spire on the other hand, which Apollonius alone had worked on, gave ample proof of the fanatical conscientiousness of his mastery of his trade. The jackdaws who inhabited it would have long since ceased to be bothered by his cradle if an old master tinsmith had not wanted to demonstrate his interest in the church by donating a piece of ornamental metalwork. It was in the form of a wreath of flowers and had to be fixed round the roof of the spire by Apollonius. It was this that caused him to fasten his ladder once more to the broach post. It was only a little over six months since he had taken it down.

In the meantime his strenuous efforts had not gone unrewarded. He had managed to retain most of the old customers and had won new ones. The creditors had had their interest and a small repayment for the first year; the general trust and respect for Apollonius grew with every day that passed; with them grew his hope and his strength, which he repaid with redoubled efforts.

If only the same could be said for his brother! For the relationship between husband and wife!

It was lucky for Apollonius that he had to devote himself heart and soul to his plans and so had no time left to watch his brother's every move and ponder it in his heart, to see the one he was striving to save sink ever lower. If he was pleased at his own success, it was out of loyalty to his brother and his brother's dependants; his brother on the other hand saw something quite different in his pleasure and thought of nothing but to disturb it.

Things were going from bad to worse with Fritz Nettenmaier.

At first he had handed over to his wife most of the money set aside each week for his household needs. Then he began to keep more and more back and in the end he took it all to wherever his need to buy flatterers with rounds of drinks led him, since he was more of a slave to this need than to that of winning the respect of his fellow citizens.

His experiences with 'the important people' had not wrought any change in him. More and more his wife had to make do as best she could in increasingly wretched conditions. Old Valentine saw her difficulties and from now on the household money no longer passed through her husband's hands but through Valentine's. In the end Valentine became her treasurer and never gave her more than she needed at any particular moment, because the money in her hands was no longer safe from her husband. Of course she had to suffer for this at his hands, as for everything else. He was already accustomed to take out on her all the resentment he felt at the whole world which never ceased to persecute him, at his own nature, at Apollonius's success. Valentine would have long since complained of him to Apollonius if Christiane herself had not stopped him. It was a satisfaction to her to suffer for the sake of the man who was suffering even more for her and her children. If she knew Apollonius to be out in a storm she would wait for hours in the uncovered yard; the weather which afflicted him should also afflict her; she wanted to bear an equally heavy burden if she could not lighten his. That was the extent to which her desire for self-sacrifice drove her.

Otherwise she used the time she had left from her household chores and the children for all kinds of work which Valentine, acting as her agent, put her way. The money from this she used partly - for though she could go hungry herself she could not see her children suffer – to deck out the living-room with all kinds of things that she knew Apollonius liked. And yet she knew that Apollonius never came in there, would never see them. Her husband saw them, though, whenever he came into the room. He missed nothing that could provide a pretext for his anger and his hatred. He saw his sons' hair styled with a curled forelock just like Apollonius wore his; he saw the similarity with Apollonius in the features of his wife and children, watched it start and grow; he saw everything that spoke of his wife's admiration for his brother, everything that her conscious and even her unconscious modelling of herself on his hated brother's most personal characteristics revealed; he hunted this influence down even to the right-angled position of the catch on the window frame. Then he began to be abusive about Apollonius and used such terrible language as if he, too, must now demonstrate how much one could be influenced by others.

If the children were present, then it was his wife's first concern to get them out of the way. They should not know his coarseness and learn to despise their father – not for his sake but for theirs. He did not betray how glad he was to be rid of the 'little spy'. He was not concerned about the children, only about himself; that was how lonely his depravity had already made him. He feared that the children would complain of him to Apollonius. He did not think his wife might do so, despite the fact that he assumed she was meeting regularly with his brother. Violent emotions and a barren life had eaten away whatever small need he had for clear thinking. His assumptions might be contradictory as long as they did not contradict the mood of the moment, the wilfulness of his passionate nature. Everything he saw in the room was a new proof to him of his shame. How could he believe that it had any other purpose than to be noticed by Apollonius!

So when she tells him that he can abuse her but not Apollonius the sharp eye of jealousy shows him what satisfaction she feels in suffering for Apollonius. He reproaches her with it and she does not deny it. She says, "It's because he suffers for me and for my children. He gives up his hard-earned savings to make up for the money my husband robs his children of, money that is put by weekly for their welfare."

"And is that what he tells you? Is that what he said?", laughs her husband, wild with joy at catching her out in this confession that she has been with him.

"No he didn't!", snaps his wife, angry that the man she despises is measuring Apollonius by his own standards. Her husband always disparages what others do for him and constantly exaggerates to their faces all that he is doing for them. Apollonius on the other hand magnifies the extent of what he receives. He does not speak of what he contributes, or else makes light of it in order to make it easier for the other person to accept without feeling unduly indebted. He has no right to think Apollonius had said it! It was old Valentine who had said it. He has even sold on Apollonius' behalf, as if it were his own, the clock he had brought back from Cologne. Apollonius had forbidden him to tell her of it.

"And also to tell you that he's been forbidden?", laughs her husband. And there's something like scorn in his laugh. One could have easily believed the 'old dreamer' capable of something like that; but now he does not want to believe him capable of it. "Of course" he laughs, wilder than ever, "even a bigger fool than that old dreamer knows that nobody does these things for nothing. Even the wickedest woman still thinks herself worth some price. Especially one with hair and eyes and a body like yours!" He grabs her by the hair and looks into her eyes with a look that would have brought a blush to the most innocent and which could only have been laughed off by someone depraved. But he takes her blush as a confession and laughs all the more wildly. "You think I'm worse than he is. That's a laugh! But you're right. I married one of them, he wouldn't have. He's not bad enough for that!"

Every day, every night brought such scenes. If Fritz knew that his brother was out or in his room and the old gentleman was in the garden, then he vented his anger on the tables and chairs. He did not yet dare to do violence to his wife. First his rage must carry him beyond the magic circle drawn round her by her innocence and superhuman forbearance. Once the line is crossed the magic has lost its power and he will then do out of mere habit what at present he still shies away from doing. People don't know what they're doing when they say, "I'll do it just this once". They don't know what propitious magic they're destroying. Their 'just this once' never remains once.

Old Valentine must not have kept his word or else it was chance that led Apollonius past the door when his brother thought him far away. He heard the rumpus, his brother's wild outburst of anger, he heard the pure sound of the wife's voice striving to be heard, even in the commotion sounding clear and melodious. He heard both voices without understanding what they were saying. He was horrified. He had not imagined the discord had gone so far. He felt he must do what he could to improve the situation.

At first his brother stood as if turned to stone in his threatening posture when he saw his brother come in. He felt like a man who has been caught red-handed in some crime. If Apollonius had rebuked him as he deserved, he would have cringed before him. But Apollonius was only concerned to bring about reconciliation and said so warmly, but calmly. He really should have known, having experienced it often enough, that his patience only gave his brother the courage for scornful defiance; he experienced it again now. Fritz taunted him, laughing wildly, for inventing a pretext to come in to where he was already the lord and master. Was that the real reason why he had made himself master of the whole house? He knew he would have acted differently in Apollonius's place. If he knew he had people in his power, he would have made them feel it. He was a straightforward fellow and did not need to put on an act. Anyway he remembered how often he had crept around outside the door in the vain hope of catching Apollonius in their room. And now here he was. He had walked in because he had not expected to find him there. It was Apollonius who should be afraid, it was Apollonius who had been caught in the act, not him. To bring about a reconciliation was only the best available excuse that Apollonius had grasped at. That was why he was being so meek. That was why his wife was frightened, for she wanted to make him believe that Apollonius never came in there. That was why she was looking up at him so beseechingly. The look of contempt she had just been giving him was suddenly torn from her face along with the mask of hypocritical innocence. Now he knew for certain; there was nothing more to prevent, only something to repay in kind. He could now show his brother that he knew him for what he was, knew what he was about, had always known it.

He pointed to his wife. "She's begging me to go. I wonder why? It'll do just as well if I look out of the window. I shan't see what you both get up to."

Apollonius didn't understand what he was talking about. But the wife did without looking at him. All she wanted to do was escape. To be treated like dirt under her husband's feet in Apollonius's presence was more than she could bear. Her husband held her tightly in a wild grip. He grasped her like a bird of prey. She would have cried out if the mental anguish she felt had not consumed the physical pain.

"Don't think she'll run away", howled Fritz Nettenmaier with convulsive laughter, fixing his eyes on his brother just as fiercely as he clamped his hand on his wife's wrist. "You don't need to worry. I'll just turn my back and she'll still be here. Go on. Talk to each other. Tell him, Christiane, tell him you can't stand him. I'll believe you. A man would believe anything from a woman like you. And you, brother, teach her what you learned in Cologne. You seemed to learn everything there. Teach her how to drive a brother out of his house and business in order to----
-in order to----Well, tell her a woman has to be willing. Right? And a woman who's willing is ---tell her what a

woman like that really is. She doesn't know. That little innocent doesn't know!" And he burst out into wild laughter again.

Apollonius understood nothing of what he heard and saw; but the misuse of male strength on a helpless woman infuriated him. Involuntarily he let this feeling run away with him. He redoubled his strength, which was in any case superior to his brother's, as he took hold of the gripping arm, so that it dropped its prey and fell as if paralysed. Christiane tried to escape from the room, but she collapsed in a faint. Apollonius picked her up and laid her on the sofa. Then he stood like an avenging angel before his brother.

"I wanted to win you round by gentleness, but you're not worth it. I've put up with a great deal from you and will do so still", said Apollonius, "for you are my brother. You accuse me of plunging you into misfortune. As God is my witness, I've done everything I could to keep you from it. For who else have I done what you accuse me of, other than for you and to save your honour and your wife and children? Who forced me to be firm with you? Who else do I graft for? Who else do I stay awake at nights for? If you only knew how much it pains me that you force me to bring to your notice what I do for you. God knows you force me to it; I haven't said it before, not to others nor even to myself. You know quite well that you're looking for an excuse to be unbrotherly to me. I know it and will put up with it in future as I have up to now. But that you make out of the dislike your wife feels for me a pretext to torment her too and to treat her as no good man treats a good woman, that I will not tolerate."

Fritz Nettenmaier burst into a horrible laugh. His brother had in every way brought disgrace on him and yet still tried to play the gentleman, one who had been offended in all innocence and who now wished to be the chivalrous protector of all who felt the same. "A good woman! O such a good woman! Of course, that's what she is all right, isn't she? You say so and you're a good man. No one knows better whether a woman is good or not than a good man like you! Haven't you taken enough from me? Now you have to deprive me of my reason, too, so that I'll believe your story. She dislikes you? She can't bear you?" He laughed scornfully. "Oh yes, you don't know how much. I only need to be away from here and she'll tell you herself. Then you'll be for it. She'll keep on at you till you believe her. If I'm there she won't say it. A woman doesn't say that sort of thing in her husband's presence, not if she's as good as all that. Why don't you say you can't stand her either? Oh, my wits have gone completely. I'll believe everything you tell me!"

Fritz Nettenmaier was by now convinced in the forgetfulness of his fevered emotions that the two of them had invented the whole story of her dislike of him.

Apollonius stood there, shaken to the core. He had to admit to himself what he did not wish to believe. His brother read in his face the fear he felt at the light that was dawning on him as well as his resentment and pain at all the misunderstandings. And all that he read there was so true that he himself had to believe it. He was struck dumb with a sudden thought which flashed like lightning through his brain. So there had after all still been something to prevent, there had still been time to put off what must come. And now he was himself once again – But Apollonius, and this he saw despite his confusion, still doubted and could not believe it. So his moment of madness could still be redeemed. Perhaps what must inevitably come could still be prevented, still be delayed if only for today or tomorrow. But how? What if he made the whole thing into some wild joke? Such jokes were not unusual for him, and Apollonius had already become in his mind once again the old dreamer who believed everything he was told. And he himself was once more someone who understood life and knew how to deal with dreamers. He must at least give it a try. But quickly, before Apollonius had overcome the strangeness of the thoughts with which he was wrestling. He burst into laughter, a laughter which was a ghastly caricature of the jovial laughter with which he had previously been wont to reward his own brilliant jokes. It was damned annoying that Apollonius had now allowed himself to be persuaded that he, Fritz Nettenmaier, was jealous. Jovial Fritz Nettenmaier! And what was worse that he was jealous of him, his own brother. Nothing more damnable had ever happened! He read on his wife's face just how much this change of attitude had relieved her. He even dared now to appeal to her to say how damnable it was. Her agreement made him still bolder. He laughed now at his wife who was so perverse as to reproach him angrily for having made her dependant on the favour of the man she hated, and he laughed that that was why these little marital tiffs arose. He laughed at Apollonius for taking such a little tiff so seriously. Was there ever a married couple where such things did not occur? You could see that Apollonius was still a bachelor!

At this moment Apollonius heard from the front door the voice of the architect asking for him; he went quickly out so that the architect should not come in and witness this scene. His brother heard them go off together. He was not a bit reassured. Apollonius's honest face as he went out had still been wrestling with these novel thoughts. Fritz Nettenmaier was full of rage at himself and had to vent it on his wife. He felt at that moment that he was doing everything possible to corrupt a woman. Her glance betrayed to him how much she despised herself for agreeing with him, for allowing herself to be forced into it, how she was saying to herself that now there was nothing else left to be corrupted. He had reason to be afraid, if that was what she was thinking. He dared not let her go so far. He knew that and yet at the same time he sneered that she could lie as cleverly as anyone else. He had never been master of himself; now he was so less than ever.

11

Now within Fritz Nettenmaier one strong desire fought for mastery with another. The dissolute habit of seeking self-forgetfulness in drink drew him out of the house by a hundred chains; jealous fear held him indoors in its thousand clutches. If his brother had not yet thought what could be his if he so wished, he himself had now put the idea into his mind. And even if his brother was as good as he made out, his old love, the love and beauty of his wife – Fritz Nettenmaier had never before felt so vividly how beautiful his wife was - , his own dependence on Apollonius, his wife's hatred of him, the opportunities that inevitably arose from living in close proximity and the consciousness of his guilt -- all these things encouraged and empowered his fear. And even if his brother was as good as he made out, he couldn't trust him with such powerful allies. All day he brooded on his fear and did not let his wife out of his sight. Only when all was calm, the children had been put to bed and his wife herself had retired, only when he could no longer see a light in Apollonius's windows did the clutches of fear grow less and the chains of his need for self-forgetfulness pull all the stronger. He locks the back door which separates Apollonius from the rooms in the main house, he even pushes the bolt across and locks the door of the stairs to the gallery and the door he goes out through. He has reason to hurry, although he does not know it. The journeyman cannot afford to wait much longer. Fritz Nettenmaier has not yet heard; Apollonius has managed to persuade the quarry owner to dismiss the journeyman; and the police to say that he must not let them catch him around from tomorrow onwards. The journeyman is all ready to leave; he's setting off from the inn for pastures new; he only wants to take leave of his former employer and say one last thing to him.

There is not much left in the world which Fritz Nettenmaier is attached to. The way he's going leads further and further away from all that he liked best; it's irretrievably lost to him. He'll never again be admired and flattered. He only remains attached to his wife by the red-hot chains of jealousy. He has never been close to his father; he hates his brother. He hates and knows himself to be hated, or believes he is in his feverish delusion. Little Annie would have clung to him with all the strength of her child's heart, so desperate for love, but he drives her away with hatred; all she is to him is 'the little spy'. He's only fond of one person, the person who deserves it the least. He knows him, yet knows also that he's betrayed him, has helped to destroy him, and still he likes him. He's a man who hates Apollonius, the only man apart from himself who hates Apollonius, and nevertheless Apollonius's own brother admires him!

Fritz Nettenmaier accompanied the journeyman for part of the way. The journeyman wants to walk on faster and begs him not to bother accompanying him any further. When other people part, their last conversation is usually about what they both love; the last conversation between Fritz Nettenmaier and the journeyman is about what they hate. The journeyman knows that Apollonius would have liked to have him thrown in prison if he could. As they now face each other to take their leave, the journeyman looks his companion up and down. It was an evil wary look, a fierce stealthy look which seemed to be trying to judge, without asking directly, whether Fritz Nettenmaier was ready and willing for some purpose which he didn't specify. Then he said, in a hoarse voice which would have struck anyone else as odd but which was familiar to Fritz Nettenmaier, "And what I wanted to say to you was – you'll soon be in mourning. I saw him in a vision recently." He didn't need to name him, Fritz Nettenmaier knew who he meant "There are some people who see more than others", continued the journeyman. "There are people who can tell by looking at a slater whether he's going to fall before the year is out, see him carried home and lying there dead. An old journeyman slater told me the secret of how to get this 'second sight'. I have it. And now farewell. And don't be surprised when they carry his body home."

The journeyman went on his way; his footsteps were already dying away in the distance. Fritz Nettenmaier still stood there looking into the greyish white mist in which the journeyman had disappeared. It hung horizontally above the roadside meadows like a blanket. It rose and thickened into strange shapes, it wreathed up, swirled around, sank lower again and again reared up. It clung in the branches of the willows by the road, one minute cloaking them and the next revealing them, so that it was impossible to be certain whether it was the mist assuming the form of trees or the trees dissolving into mist. It drifted in and out like in a dream and wafted about unremittingly without goal or purpose. It was the very image of what was passing in Fritz Nettenmaier's mind, an image so similar that he didn't know whether he was looking outwards from within or vice versa. There was a shadowy group of people bending down and wringing their hands over a pale shape on the ground, then a slowly winding funeral procession; and one minute it was his enemy and the next his brother who lay there and whom they carried. Now the vision flared up with the harsh light of Schadenfreude and now it died away in compassion and sympathy, now both mingled and one tried to conceal the other. The one who lay there, whom they carried, he now forgave for everything. He wept for him; for in the pauses in the funeral dirge, the strains of a merry dance could just be heard, a dance struck up by the future which announced; 'Here he is! Now things will go with a swing.' And beside the dead man there lay unseen a second corpse, his fear of what must come should his poor brother not be dead. And in the coffin Fritz Nettenmaier's old jovial feeling of good fortune put forth new shoots. Fritz Nettenmaier feels himself to be an angel; he wishes his brother did not have to die because ----but he knows that die he must.

He's still walking along in the mist when the paving stones in the town are once more sounding beneath his feet. His way takes him past the Red Eagle. The windows are still lit up and music can be heard coming from above. Fritz Nettenmaier stops and looks up and involuntarily moves his hand around in his pocket as he used to do when he had money in it to rattle. He has already forgotten the journeyman, his last friend, whom he has just parted from so painfully. "He was a bad fellow; it's a good thing he's gone." He has forgotten the past, he forgets the present, for the future is his once more; it's to be found up there and smiles down on him from above with bright eyes. He's got so used to associating everything that oppresses him with his brother, that he now sees it all buried in the grave with him. He doesn't care to remember the ruination of his prosperity. He doesn't like thinking about unpleasant things till they can no longer be avoided. Isn't it enough that he knows he will lose his brother? And if things get him down and have to be faced, then he always has his devil-may-care attitude to help him. If he thinks about it quickly he can usually come up with a solution to everything, and what he can't think of today will occur to him tomorrow; tomorrow is another day. And he's one of those people who ----. The way in which he turns on his heels works as well and as jovially as it ever did.

A strange feeling comes over him when he thinks that a corpse will be carried out of the door which he has just unlocked. Involuntarily he stands aside to allow room for the coffin and the bearers to pass him. As if rehearsing what he will reply to words of sympathy when that time comes, he says quietly "We all have to bow to the inevitable". And as he shrugs his shoulders at these words he becomes aware of a faint narrow ray of light. Part of it touches his sleeve, another seemingly detached part falls beside him on the pavement. He peers up; the light comes from where the lower section of the shutter does not quite meet the window-sill. There's a light on in the living-room. "So late?" The eavesdropper catches his breath and his nightmare is upon him again. His brother is still alive; and what must inevitably happen if he remained alive can still happen before he dies or – it's already happening! With trembling hands and without wasting a moment he quietly locks the door again Just as quietly and just as quickly he reaches the back door. It's not open but only on half-lock; and Fritz Nettenmaier knows, he can swear to it, that he turned the key in the lock twice as he left. He creeps and feels his way to the living-room door; he finds the latch and presses it quietly; the door opens; a dim light falls out onto the hall. The glow comes from a shaded lamp on the table. Beside it in the shadow stands a small bed; it is little Annie's bed and her mother sits beside it.

Christiane does not notice the door open. She is bending low over the bed; she is singing softly and does not know what she is singing; she is listening anxiously but not to her song; her eyes would be weeping if tears did not blur one's sight. The colour might return to the child's cheeks, the strange tension around the child's eyes and mouth might disappear, and she wouldn't see it and would worry in vain. It seemed to her that the former must return and the latter go away if only she made every possible effort to see clearly. And as she does so she can't help thinking of how suddenly all this that worries her so much has happened; how Annie had suddenly in the bed next to hers cried out in a strange voice and then had not been able to speak again; how she had jumped up and dressed; how in her anxiety she had woken Valentine who in turn had woken Apollonius without her knowledge. Old Valentine had tried all the keys in the house until it turned out that the key to the shed also opened the back door; she didn't know that. She remembered vividly how Apollonius had come in, how she had felt at his unexpected appearance, how despite being full of fear and shame she had nevertheless felt wonderfully relieved. Apollonius had immediately sent for the doctor and then fetched the medicine. He had stood by the bed and leaned over Annie as she was doing now. He had looked at her full of grief

and said that Annie's illness had been caused by the
marital strife and she wouldn't get better unless this
stopped. He had spoken of the miracles a mother could
perform and how people could and must control
themselves. Then he had given Valentine many
instructions about Annie and had left, anxious that his
brother in his delusions should not think he wanted to
drive him from his children's sickbed too. Distress and
anxiety almost drove her into Apollonius's arms; it
seemed to her that everything would come right if only she
could hug him and never let him go. But as he stood there
at the head of the bed and spoke, he appeared to her as
magnificent as a saint before whom she could do nothing
but kneel down. The bed-screen half hid his tall slim
figure in shadow, only his forehead and the high crown of
his head were visible and appeared bathed in the rays of
the light on the table like a halo. If her thoughts flew from
him to her husband, an icy frost clutched convulsively at
her heart and repugnance grew like a giant at the very
thought of him. But Apollonius had said Annie would not
get better unless the strife ended. He'd said people could
and must learn to control themselves; she determined to
control herself because he had said it. A mother could
perform miracles for her child; if she called to mind
Apollonius's face as he said this, she must be capable the
very greatest miracle.

Fritz Nettenmaier came in. He thought of nothing except
that Apollonius must have been there, even if he wasn't
there now. His fury made his eyes swim. He would have
set upon his wife if he hadn't seen old Valentine sitting by
the door. He would wait until he should finally leave the

room and he crept to the chair by the window where he had always sat when quite a different person from now. His wife heard his soft step; she could not see his expression. She thought he knew about Annie's condition and that was why he was walking so quietly. She looked at Annie as much as to say that what she was about to do now she was doing only for the sake of her sick child; a glance at the door through which he had left added "And because he said so!"

"Here is your father, Annie" she said. She was really speaking to her husband who was sitting by the window; but she could not turn her face to him nor direct her words directly at him. "You've been asking for him. You thought that when he came he'd be as he used to be before you were ill. That's what your mother wants too – for your sake."

Her voice spoke from so deep within her that Fritz had to hold back his anger by main force. He thought to himself, "She's being so nice in order to deceive you. They agreed on it together when he was here." And the anger grew even more furious at the tender sound of her voice as she continued, "And you're not going up to Heaven yet, Annie. All right? You're such a good loving child, and you'll stay here with your father and mother, won't you? If only – but you're afraid of your father, you silly sweet girl, just because he shouts sometimes. He doesn't mean anything bad by it."

She paused; she expected the answer from the father, not from the child. She expected him to step over to the bed and speak to the child as she was doing, and through the child to her. Whatever she might think of him, it was still his child and she was ill.

The man said nothing and remained silently sitting on his chair. For the length of time it took to say half the Lord's Prayer nothing could be heard but the ticking of the clock and that became ever quicker like the beating of a human heart when it senses something bad about to happen; the flame in the lamp flickered as if from fear.

Valentine got up from his chair to trim the lamp.

There was a rattle in the child's chest; she wanted to speak but couldn't; she wanted to reach out to her father with her hands, but she couldn't; she could do nothing but reach out to him with the unseen arms of her soul. But the soul of her father did not see these beseeching arms. His hands were convulsively holding in his anger and he did not have a hand free for the child. He heard the rattling but he knew the child had been suborned by his enemies and has no filial love for him; and if she was really ill, it would have been on purpose to help deceive him, and if she died her death would act as some kind of matchmaking service for his enemies. If his own eyes were not so sick that they only saw what he was constantly brooding on, he must have seen by the mother's face, have heard by the tone of her voice, that she was not pretending, that the child is really ill and very ill at that; but he sees her weakness and her fear as merely the fear brought on by her conscience, fear of the punishment she feels she deserves and wants to defend herself against. Valentine steps away from the lamp and goes out in order to weep his fill outside. The man gets up and softly approaches the woman without her noticing. He wants to surprise her and in that he succeeds. She starts up in alarm when she suddenly sees a man's distorted face right in front of her above the bed. She's frightened and he forces out through his clenched teeth, "You're scared? And why is that?"

She had wanted to tell him herself that Apollonius had been in the room, but had not been able to as yet; she dared not do so by the sick child's bed because she knows he will flare up; whenever she could, she had spared the child from having to see his brutality when she was still well; now sheer terror could bring about the sick child's death. So she doesn't reply, but she looks at him beseechingly and glances by way of a hint at the child.

"He was here, wasn't he!?" he asks; not to find out the answer, but to show that he doesn't need to ask. He raises his clenched fist; Annie struggles to sit up. He does not see it; his wife sees it; her fear grows. She clasps her hands imploringly and gives him a look which encompasses everything a wife can promise, everything she can threaten; he only sees her terror that he knows what she has done and his fist smashes down on her face.

A scream rings out; the child thrashes around in convulsions, her mother falls beside her and weeps aloud. Valentine rushes in, Fritz Nettenmaier goes into the next room.

He does not know which emotion has the upper hand, whether it is sweet revenge or horror at what he has done. He sinks on the bed as if the blow he had struck had stunned him and not her; he only half hears Valentine running for the doctor. In the same way he hears the doctor come and go and listens to see if he can hear Apollonius's whispering or the sound of his footsteps. He does not dare to show himself; shame holds him back. He justifies his actions and calls Annie's illness mere attention seeking. "One day children are on the point of death and the next they're livelier than ever!"

This feverish listening and self-justification turns into feverish dreaming. He sees Apollonius tying his ladder to the broach post and says to himself comfortingly as Apollonius climbs each rung, "Now he'll fall! Now!", but Apollonius doesn't fall. At every moment he expects the ropes from which Apollonius hangs in his cradle to break; they don't break. Into this dream intrudes the sound of the door opening; the dream turns this into a fall, the fall of a heavy body from an enormous height. Then he feels easy in his mind as if everything was now all right. Still half asleep he hears people moving quietly about in the room, a stirring and soft weeping, and in between all is still again.

The quiet sobbing which becomes loud and then is brought under control again as if someone asleep nearby mustn't be woken, but then breaks out again, because it is now unable to wake the sleeper, and again grows quiet as if it is startled to be so loud when everyone else is silent; all this is well-known and could not fail to be understood.

Fritz Nettenmaier, too, still half asleep, knows what it is; in the next room someone lies dead. He's been carried home. – "We all have to bow to the inevitable."

For the first time for many months he falls into a peaceful sleep.

And why shouldn't he? The quiet weeping turns into a merry dance tune. "Here he is! Now there'll be fun!" He can hear the words in his sleep coming in the distance from the Red Eagle.

But the quiet movements and whispering was real and went on; and there was a body in the next room, the body of a beautiful child. While Fritz Nettenmaier dreamed of ladders and cradles around the roof, little Annie's soul had gone to a better Father. The body lay stiff in the little bed. The strife between the parents had made the child ill; anguish at the violence the father had perpetrated against the mother had broken her little heart.

Fritz Nettenmaier was still sleeping the sleep of the just as the new day dawned. Apollonius had long been up and about; perhaps he had not slept at all. The wrestling with novel thoughts which his brother had read on his face when he saw him leave the house with the architect, and which the troubles of the day had scarcely suppressed, had in the night driven out any hope of sleep. His brother had been right to see that the jocular turn he had given to the conversation had not achieved its purpose. And if Apollonius leafed back through the pages of his memory he must feel his opinion confirmed that his brother was jealous of him. Many things which he had not understood when he saw them happen now became clear in the light of this revelation and helped to confirm it even more. The wife's dislike of him seemed now a mere pretext of his brother's to keep him away from her. His brother must have thought he could look on her other than with the eyes of a brother-in-law. And that seemed understandable since Fritz knew she had been more to him than that, until she had become his sister-in-law. He would have liked to reproach his brother with that, had he not had to admit to himself that the sympathy his brother's rough treatment of her had aroused in him had given his feelings for her a warmth that caused him some anxiety. He was not afraid that these feelings would run away with him and persuade him to carry out what his brother feared, but his strict scrupulousness made him view this warmth as a crime. But then, he thought, hadn't she in fact shown real dislike of him? And if she felt dislike, how could his brother really be afraid? His brother in a tone of reproach had called it fictitious, so he didn't really believe it himself and thought she was only pretending and did not really feel it. – His cousin in Cologne had often spoken of the nature of jealousy, how it arose from and fed on itself, how its suspicions reached beyond the bounds of reality, even of the possible, and led to deeds only usually produced by madness. It was such a case that Apollonius now saw before him and he felt sorry for his brother and grievous pity for the wife.

He was startled out of such thoughts and feelings by Valentine who called him downstairs. He came back up again even more uneasily than he had gone down. It was not only the condition of Annie, whom he loved like a father, which lay on his mind; also the sympathy with her mother had grown and a new fear had arisen which he would have liked to talk himself out of, if such a procedure had been compatible with his need for clarity and his conscientiousness. When the first glimmer of the new day fell through his window, he got up from the chair on which he had been sitting since he had returned to his room. There was something solemn in the way in which he drew himself up. He seemed to be saying to himself, "If things are as I fear, I must take responsibility for both of us; I'm man enough for that. I promised I would uphold my father's house and his honour and I will carry out that promise in every sense!"

Fritz Nettenmaier finally woke. He could remember nothing of the dream-images of the night; all that remained was the mood of satisfaction they had left. He racked his brains in vain to find what might have brought about this mood, one that had eluded him for so long. All that he could remember of the events of the night was not conducive to explaining it. All he could still recall was that his wife had exaggerated the whining and moping of 'the little spy' into an illness, merely in order to provide an excuse to be with him. With him! Not even when talking to the journeyman, let alone to himself or his wife, did he refer to Apollonius by his name; perhaps because his hatred of the man had transferred itself to his name; perhaps because day and night he only thought about two people and they could not be confused. He had nothing left in the world except his hatred; and 'he' and 'she' were the only two people he knew. He was already thinking of

how he would put an end to this whining when he stepped
through the door and stopped stock still -- in front of him
was a dead body. A shudder ran through him. There was
the dead child in front of him like a warning sign; go no
further down the road you have chosen! There lay the
child, his child, dead. Normally he shooed her away; now
she stayed there and was no longer afraid and asked him if
he could still hate her now, if he could still call her by the
name he used in his hatred. Yesterday he did not see her
when, ignoring her fear, he struck the blow; the father of
the child struck her mother across the bed of her dying
child. Yesterday he did not see her as he stood there
bending over her; but now he sees her wherever he directs
his horrified gaze in order to try not to see her. The child
stands there before him, an accuser and a witness. She is a
witness for her mother. She knew her child was dying and
by the death bed of her child not even the most depraved
of women would do what he believes her capable of. She
accuses him. He has struck a mother by the death bed of
her child. No man could do that even if the wife were
guilty. And she was not guilty; the child is witness to that.
Now he knows what the pale mute expression on the
mother's face was trying to cry out to him, "You'll kill the
child; don't strike!" And yet he did strike. He has killed
his child. That hits him like a bolt of lightning, so that he
sinks down by the child's bed, the same bed across which
he had struck the mother; by the bed in which his child
died because he struck her mother.

He lay there a long time. The bolt of lightning which had
laid him low had shed its light on the events of the past
with a terrible clarity; it had showed him the two he had

been persecuting were innocent. And no guilt could be attached to anyone but himself. He alone has piled up all the misery that lies so heavily on him, burden upon burden, guilt upon guilt. The child's death is at the very top. And perhaps it's not yet the top! The wretched man sees that he must go back. He grasps at any straw, any idea, that might save him. Then he hears once again the gentle voice which yesterday he had hardened his heart against, "You thought that when he came he'd be as he used to be before you were ill. That's what your mother wants too." The sound of the voice was like a gentle hand which the soul of his wife held out to his soul, offering reconciliation; his anguish, his fear hastily grasped at this outstretched hand. He saw the child standing by the bedroom door in her nightie, where she had so often stood when his violence had woken her, her hands folded, her eyes beseeching him so sadly to be kind to her mother and at the same time fearful that he would be angry with her for doing so. Now that it was too late he saw that she wanted to be his good angel. But perhaps it was not yet too late! He heard the soft footsteps of his wife approaching the door. He heard her open the door. If Annie had still been standing by the bedroom door she must have smiled. He wanted to be good; he wanted to be again as he was before Annie was ill. He stretched out his hand to his wife as she entered. She saw him and recoiled. She was as pale as poor dead Annie, even her usually so rosy lips were pale. Her neck, her beautiful arms, her soft hands were pale; the usually so sparkling eyes were dull. All her life force had withdrawn into the depths of her heart and wept there for her dead child. When she saw him, a trembling ran through her whole body. In two strides she went and placed herself between him and the body, as if she wanted even now to protect the child from him. But that was not it. Neither fear nor anxiety trembled round her mouth; it was firmly shut. It was quite a different feeling which caused the beautifully arched eyebrows to crease into a frown and which blazed from her usually so gentle eyes. He saw she was no longer the woman who had spoken the sweet words of peace; that woman had died with her child in that terrible night. The woman who stood before him was no longer the mother who pinned her hopes on him, whose child he could save; this was the mother whose child he had killed. A mother who banished the murderer from the sacred presence of her child. A terrifying angel who drove the tainted defiler away from her sanctuary with great wrath. He spoke – oh, if only he had spoken yesterday! Yesterday she had longed to hear a word from him; today she would not listen.

"Give me your hand, Christiane", he said. She drew her hand back convulsively as if he had already touched it. "I've made a terrible mistake", he continued. "Believe me, I realise it only too well; I won't do it again! You're a better person than I am."

"The child is dead", she said and even her voice sounded pale.

"Don't leave me without comfort in this terrible anguish. If I can be different, I can only be it now, and if you give me your hand and raise me up", said the man. She looked at the child, not at him.

"The child is dead", she repeated. Did that mean that it was of no interest to her what became of him, since his change for the better could no longer save the child? Or had she forgotten him and was speaking to herself? He half drew himself up; he grasped her hand with fearful strength and held it tight.

"Christiane", he sobbed wildly, "I'm lying here at your feet like a worm. Don't step on me! Don't trample me under your feet! For God's sake, have pity! I could never forget what has happened even if I crawled in the dust like a worm in vain. Think about it! For God's sake think; you have me in your hand now. You can make of me what you will. I make you responsible. Whatever happens now is down to you." At last she managed to snatch back her hand; she held it away from her as if it disgusted her because he had touched it.

"The child is dead", she said. He understood this to mean, 'Between me and the murderer of my child there can never again be any association, not on earth and not in Heaven.'

He stood up. A word of forgiveness might perhaps have saved him! Perhaps! Who knows! The lucidity that now drove him to repentance was the lucidity of a lightning flash; all that was having such an influence on him took its power from the shock of surprise. When the child, the very sight of whom had brought him up short, is resting in her grave, her warning presence will gradually fade; every hour will rob the thought of this moment of its power to shock. The old familiar track of his delusions has impressed itself too deeply for him to expunge it permanently. He has gone too far down that dangerous road. The lucidity of the lightning flash would inevitably fade and the old delusion again wrap things in its distorting fog. Fritz Nettenmaier wept aloud or burst out laughing; his wife took no notice what he did; deep revulsion for him blocked her ears, her eyes, her thoughts. He staggered back into the bedroom. She did not see but she felt that his presence no longer desecrated the room where the holy icon of her maternal agony stood. Softly weeping she sank down by her dead child.

12

The repairs to the church roof had begun. Apollonius wanted to finish this first before he undertook the crowning of the steeple with the ornamental metalwork donated by the tinsmith. In addition he had to attend to the burial of little Annie; Fritz didn't concern himself with it at all. So he had to take on this duty of the father of the family too. He felt achingly at home in this role. After all, even these grave duties cost him no sacrifice! He had had no other loving attachments to resist or give up when he had taken upon himself the responsibility for his brother's dependants; he had only followed the most characteristic instincts of his nature. It was at the very core of this nature that he must remain completely what he always was. Since giving up all hopes of the love of his youth and the girl herself, the thought of a household of his own had become alien to him. He knew no other purpose in life than the fulfilment of his duty. But this was not some arid despotic law outside himself, appealing only to his rational mind; it filled his whole being with the fertilizing warmth of real instinctive emotion. It had been like this for months. As he flew round the roof of the spire on his cradle, as he knelt on the cripple-box hammering, the figures of his brother's children, his children, were round him. Faster than his cradle, his imagination flew far ahead into the future. Just as his cradle circled the roof, all his thoughts turned on the time when the sons were grown up and he could hand the business over to them free of debt, when Annie would look like her mother and he would give her away as a bride to some good man. Annie's rosy face was always before him when he looked up from his slabs of slate. When she smiled at him so roguishly, she was the apple of his eye; as her face grew ever sadder and paler, she was so even more; he often saw her double through the water in his eyes. Now --- oh, sometimes he felt as if now he was working to no purpose! And now there was something new which worried him more and more. Out of his sympathy for the tormented wife, tormented on his account, the love of his youth blossomed again and unfolded more and more each day. What his brother's scorn and ingratitude to him had not managed, his behaviour to his wife now succeeded in doing. Apollonius felt his heart grow cold towards his brother. His instinct was to protect the wife, but he knew his interference only exposed her to even harsher mistreatment. He could do no more for her than keep himself as far from her as possible. And not just because of his brother, also for her own sake, if he had seen aright. But had he seen aright? He told himself a hundred times he had not. He said this to himself sorrowfully; but even more often and more insistently he told himself and felt that he must not see her for his own sake too. It pained him when even things of no importance were muddled together and not put straight, and he could not put them in order; here he saw that incongruities and contradictions had invaded the very heart of what was most sacred to him, the core of his family, his own heart too, and he had to watch them grow and his hands were tied!

Life in the house with the green shutters became more and more gloomy and oppressive after Annie's small body was carried out of it. It became more gloomy and oppressive in Fritz Nettenmaier's heart and mind too. He had wanted to turn back when he had been shocked and stopped in his tracks by the vision of Annie dead and the light which this shed on the road he had travelled. He would have turned back if his wife had taken the hand he had offered. At least he had meant to. But she had rejected him and looked at him with revulsion and contempt; he had seen that, in her heart, she considered him the child's murderer; her eye had threatened him with revenge, and then his old nightmare had returned again, his fear born of guilt. Even if she has not yet done what he fears, she will do it now to pay him back for the blow which caused Annie's death. The more he worries away at it in his mind, the more clearly he feels how advantageous for his enemies –and they are his enemies, they've done him a wrong that must be avenged—how advantageous for them was the blow he had struck. Then he realises that his wife could have warned him. She didn't say, "Don't hit me, the child is ill; you'll be the death of her if you hit me!" No! One word from her could have prevented the blow, but she did not speak it. Oh it's clear, crystal clear; she was deliberately provoking him by her silence into doing something wild. But how could that be? Would she have wanted the death of her child? No woman could want that. No, she herself didn't think the child would die; she only wanted a pretext to hate him, to betray him, out of hatred for striking her by the bed of her sick child. She didn't think the child would die; but when it did, she shifted the guilt from herself onto him. And he'd been once more the honest one, stupid enough to fall into this trap in his naivety; he'd grovelled before her like a worm, when she should have grovelled to him. And she'd still rejected him, rejected him with contempt! Whenever he thought of that moment, he made her responsible for everything which could yet happen. Whatever might become of him, she had made him it. He had held out his hand; he was without guilt. Then he brooded about what might become of him and the worst he could come up with was not bad enough to increase the guilt he piled on her. With horror and remorse she should see what she had done when she rejected him. The closer he saw the threat of what must come, the wilder became his love or his hatred, for both were joined in the feeling she kindled in him more and more fervidly. The more attentively his eyes learned to appreciate her every physical charm, the more agonisingly did this beauty stab him to the heart through these same eyes. This damnable beauty that was the cause of all his misery; this cursed beauty for whose sake his own brother drove him out of house and shed and exposed him to the contempt of the

world and even of his wife. He began to mull over ideas of
how he could destroy this beauty so that she would appear
hideous to her lover who, cheated of his purpose, would
have made himself miserable for nothing. And whenever
he thought of that as having been accomplished, he
laughed out loud with such wild and malicious glee that
his strong-nerved drinking companions were taken aback
and any people he met involuntarily stopped in their
tracks. And yet this idea was merely the precursor of one
still more evil. Between times it came into his mind with
second sight that the dream he had had after carrying out
the dreadful deed would come true; for hours at a time he
stood now here, now there, wherever he saw Apollonius
working on the church roof, and looked up and waited and
calculated. Now the planks must surely break beneath him
as he hammered away, now the rope on which the cradle
hung must snap. Now the people just looking indifferently
out of their windows or crossing the street would cry out
in horror. Then he calculated more and more feverishly,
till the cold sweat ran down his face; and the planks didn't
break, the rope didn't snap, the people didn't cry out in
horror. And he laughed to himself ever more wildly when
he finally went on his way, tired and despairing after long
waiting; "If it weren't for my bad luck that he can make
me still more wretched than he has already, he would have
long since been dead. Only because he makes me
miserable by being alive does he still live. He won't die
until he has made me completely miserable!"

This fear would not leave him; it oppressed him ever more
suffocatingly. If he came home obsessed with it late at
night, finding his wife sleeping peacefully enraged him.

She was sleeping peacefully while it was she who was preventing him from sleeping! He sat down by her bed and shook her awake and whispered in her ear what he would do to her lover. They were gruesome things. When her limbs trembled for fear and horror he laughed aloud, content that he had something to frighten away the stupid contempt with which she had armed herself against him, and this made him forget his mental anguish for minutes at a time. Then he laughed almost jovially; he had only wanted to frighten her. It was just one more example of Fritz Nettenmaier's so-called jokes As yet they have not driven him to think seriously about such things. But if she tells Apollonius about it, then he must, and it will be her fault. He watches her every move, she can do nothing that he does not know about. And if she tells a third person, he will read it in his face. O Fritz Nettenmaier is one of those who know ----!"

All day and half the night the wife goes around as if in a fever. Animated by this oppressive fear, her love for Apollonius grows into passion. And she cannot stop this happening, for the passion in turn increases the fear; no one else can have any place in her mind in face of this fear. She longs to run to him, to hug him tightly in her arms and implore him – then again she wants to go to the magistrates to report the threats – but it's only some wild jest and she'll only make him take it seriously if she tells anyone about it. She no longer leaves the living room, no longer walks to the window for sheer terror; she wants to avoid every step, every movement, everything, which might appear to be her looking out for Apollonius. She no longer has the courage to talk to anyone because her husband will find out and might think she is giving them a message to Apollonius. And her husband sees her growing passion, sees how once again his means of holding back what must inevitably come will only speed it up. He calculates and waits ever more impatiently for the planks to break and the rope to snap.

It was a cloudy, sultry night. The night before the day on which Apollonius would begin the crowning of the roof of the spire with the tinsmith's work. Fritz Nettenmaier crept out of the back door and onto the path to the shed in order to look up at Apollonius's window. When he saw the light extinguished, he usually locked the back door and went off to his nefarious pleasures. Since the night when Valentine had opened the back door with the shed key, Fritz had added a padlock to the bolt. Apollonius had not yet gone to bed. Fritz Nettenmaier knew that Apollonius with his excessive caution never put out his candle when he had already got into bed. It stood on his desk a long way from the bed; there he stood it in a dish and blew it out before he went over to the bed. Fritz Nettenmaier shook his fist up at the window. Apollonius was hanging around too long for his liking. He was tired and went to the shed. The key to the back door also opened the shed. It was dark inside.

When a slater trims his slates, he sits astride a work-bench in the middle of which is fixed the prod, his small anvil. Fritz Nettenmaier bumped into one of these and took this as a sign he should sit down. He could look up at Apollonius's window through a small hole in the wall; he would wait here for the light to be extinguished. The slater often has to carry out carpentry so he keeps a small axe among his tools. One of these had been lying on the workbench and had fallen off when he sat down. He picked it up and held it absent-mindedly in his hands, for his thoughts were still back in his room; he was sitting by his wife's bed, tormenting her with threats. His annoyance at Apollonius for keeping him waiting now boiled over; this lingering around was preventing him from seeking oblivion in drink. He has been resting his hand on his wife's bed and felt the trembling of her limbs through the blankets. He puts himself inside her fear, sees how he himself is making her think only of Apollonius; how she is bound to rush into his arms tomorrow when he comes home from work. And even if they were not malevolent fiends but angels, everything he wants to prevent is bound to happen tomorrow. When this beautiful woman, this damnably beautiful woman, holds him in her arms with the ardour of her fear, he would have to have no blood in his veins not to yield to temptation – and even if he had never thought of this, even if it had not been in his sleeping and waking thoughts day after day, he would have to think of it now. It must happen unless--the mere fear of it has made Fritz Nettenmaier the most wretched of men, someone he can despise himself -- unless tomorrow all that his second sight has prophesied takes place. And now he's standing once more at the street corner and looking up and waiting and calculating even more desperately than before; he is bathed in cold sweat, and the planks don't break, and the rope doesn't snap. Oh, he'll assume his vision was a mere fairy-tale, Apollonius will go on living, this year, ten years, a hundred years, just out of hatred towards him. And he keeps on counting "One, two, now it must ------", and he hears the sound of a breaking rope and starts up out of his feverish daydream. His wild feeling of fearful pleasure is in vain; he's not standing at the corner looking up at the church roof. He's sitting in the shed and it's night. But he has heard the sound; that was no delusion of fantasy. And it came from over there. His hair stands on end. There lie the cradles and the pulleys with their ropes. He's heard it said a hundred times, and every slater knows what an ominous sound like that means. But three times it has to sound as if a rope is snapping; and he's only heard it once. He listens, he clenches his fist tightly against his heart. Its beating and the rushing of his blood up and down his veins will prevent him hearing it if it sounds again and again. He listens and listens and the sound is not repeated. Then a thought like a darkly glowing flash of lightning breaks into the tight knot into which all his feelings are concentrated; the thought of giving Fate a hand. He still has the axe in his hands; involuntarily he has been running the palm of his hand along the edge; now he becomes conscious that the axe is sharp, the edge keen. A whole series of thoughts stands ready and waiting; it's as if they've been there a long time and his sudden flash of insight has now made them visible. Tomorrow Apollonius will tie his ladder to the broach post, then the rope with the pulleys and the cradle. Fritz Nettenmaier feels around and has the rope in his hand. Fate needs his help; so it has itself laid the rope and the axe in his hand. Who knows that he was here? Three or four cuts with the axe round the rope, hardly visible, will turn into a single large rent when the weight of a strong man pulls on the rope and the heaving movement of the cradle round the spire adds even more to the man's weight. Who could see that the cuts had been made intentionally? A rope half dragged along on the ground can catch on all kinds of sharp objects. Fate has the slater, hanging up there between heaven and earth, in its hands. It is Fate which holds him up or lets him fall, not the rope or a cut in it. If it wants to hold him, no cut can harm him; should he fall, it's because an intact rope has snapped. And fate has marked him out already. One day earlier, one day later, what does it matter if he is destined to fall? One day later and it will be a criminal who is taken. Wouldn't Fate be doing him a kindness if it took him from this world earlier rather than later?-

All these thoughts drove his first single thought out of Fritz Nettenmaier's mind at a stroke! In an instant he flared up; in an instant this spark from Hell burst into flame. He has the rope in his left hand; he raises the axe – and drops it again with a shudder. There's blood gleaming on the blade; a bloody streak runs the whole length of the shed. Fritz Nettenmaier flees outside. He would have liked to flee from himself; he scarcely has the courage to look up at Apollonius's window. A bright ray of light comes from there, Fritz Nettenmaier retreats from it behind a bush. Now the ray moves too. Apollonius had stood up at his desk and was holding the light high in the air. He had trimmed the wick. A part cut off by the scissors and still alight might have fallen among his papers near the candlestick; it hadn't, so he set the light back down in its place. Fritz Nettenmaier knew all about his brother's anxious scrupulousness; he had seen him raise the light like this hundreds of times; he realised now that it was not blood which had terrified him The reflection of the flame had fallen through the window and through the hole in the wall and had shone red on the blade of the axe and through the darkness of the shed. Nevertheless Fritz Nettenmaier stood trembling behind his bush. The ghastly terror soon left him but his horror at what he had so nearly done and the uncanny feeling that it was as if his brother had intended to give him a light to work by, these feelings did not disappear so quickly. Soon Apollonius' light went out. Fritz could go back and finish his work, nobody else would now disturb him. He did not do so, but pulled his hatred back into line again. He told himself that they wouldn't drive him to go so far. The guilt for the very idea he shifted onto the one he blamed for everything; the fact that he had not carried it out he ascribed to himself. He knows that anyone else in his place would have done the very worst.

Now he locks the back door and the padlock, finally the front door, and goes. He wants to drink until he forgets himself completely. Today he has more to forget than ever. The whole idea goes away. Will it come back again? Not today; but tomorrow or the day after, or the day after that? When the idea has ceased to seem strange to him? Custom and familiarity are well acquainted with the Devil. They shall not bring him to that! Will the time come when he regrets that he has not let himself be brought to this point and does let himself be brought to it? To the point to which anyone else in his place would have been brought?

Ever more gloomy and oppressive became the life in the house with the green shutters. Anyone who looks inside now won't believe just how gloomy and oppressive it once was.

13

From this night on Fritz Nettenmaier no longer struck fear into his wife with threats against Apollonius; he even began to treat her with a certain amount of affability. Between times he lost himself for hours on end in silent introspection, from which he emerged with a start if he thought he was being observed. Then he was even more affable than usual and came out with jokes as in his best times; he even made an effort to go back to work. But his wife became more and more uneasy; she avoided even more than before anything which might give her husband cause to think she wanted to get close to Apollonius. She didn't know why. And even if she was disposed to consider her fear as mere folly, she still could not help being afraid. Apollonius saw the change in his brother with delight and sought to encourage it in every way. He didn't know what interpretation his brother put on that delight!

In the meanwhile Apollonius had begun the crowning of the church spire of St George's with the ornamental metalwork that had been donated. Once again he had pushed out the scaffolding poles and nailed them firmly to the timbers of the roof-frame inside, secured the planks onto them, set up his ladder on the flying scaffold and fastened it firmly to the broach post; once again he had laid the circular rope round the broach post and fastened the pulleys to it and then the cradle. The ornamental metalwork consisted of individual pieces about half the height of a man and which were easy to handle. The whole thing, according to the specifications of the donor, who was himself bearing the costs of the installation, was to take the form of two garlands which would snake round the roof of the spire in parallel circles with hanging festoons. Five, or in the case of the upper garland, three of these pieces made up one of these festoons. At each end they had to be joined with hammered rivets and each one fastened to the underlying wooden battens with strong nails. Since the edges of the slates overlapped everywhere it was necessary to change the slates at the places where the nails were to be driven in for sheets of lead. The same thing happens where the so-called roof hooks, which the slater uses to hang his ladder during repairs, are driven into the woodwork. The area, where the roof hook is firmly nailed to the battens with another two strong nails, after its twisted point has been driven in, cannot be covered with slates. When someone climbs the ladder hung on the projecting hook, the surface vibrates and this would lever up the slates and damage them. That's why it's covered with a sheet of lead. The ornamental garland would move in a similar way when the wind blew through it. There was one other thing to think about. The roof hooks ran at nine and a half feet intervals right round the roof in parallel circles; between every two circles was a space of five feet. It was a matter of fixing the garlands so that they did not cover any of these hooks.

Apollonius worked hard at his task. The master tinsmith, who wanted to see his garland in all its glory as soon as possible, had less cause to complain of Apollonius than the latter had to be content with him. At first it was the master tinsmith who drove him on, but soon Apollonius had to drive the tinsmith.

He was still waiting for the part of the upper garland which was to hang as a festoon above the hatchway. Apollonius could not rest from the work until he received the finished article. He had been sent for from a nearby village to carry out a small repair; he left his cradle hanging on St George's roof till his return and went to Brambach.

It was the following day that old Valentine knocked at the living room door. He had already been to the door once before and gone away again His whole being expressed uneasiness. Something he couldn't stop thinking about was making him so distraught that he thought he must have missed the words, "Come in"; he put his ear to the keyhole as if assuming that he must hear them now if he only tried hard enough. Unease aroused him from his distraction. He knocked for a second time and then a third and when he still didn't get a reply, he plucked up courage, opened the door and went in. Christiane had for some time now been avoiding him. She tried to do it now too, but he simply had to speak to her. She was sitting deliberately away from the window by the bedroom door. Valentine didn't notice that she was just as uneasy as he was and his being here made her even more anxious. He apologized for intruding. When she made a movement as if to depart, he assured her that this would only take a moment; he would not have pushed his way in if he was not driven to it by something that was perhaps very important. He hoped it wasn't the case but it was possible. Christiane listened and looked more and more anxiously, first at the windows and then at the door. If he had to say something to her, could he please be as quick as possible. Valentine seemed to be responding to these anxious glances when he began, "Your husband is up on the roof of St George's. I've just seen him from the yard." "And was he looking over here? Did he see you come into the house?" blurted out Christiane.

"God forbid!" said the old man; "he's working like the devil today. Not even stopping for food and drink. When a man works like that---", the old man broke off and worked out what he was going to say in his head --- "then he's up to something." The woman said nothing. She was struggling to decide whether to confide all her fears to this trusty old man. He noticed none of this. "The neighbour over there, you know who I mean, sometimes can't sleep at night", he continued. "The night before Herr Apollonius went to Brambach, he looked out of his window during the night and saw someone creep along the path at the back of the house and into our shed." The old man didn't say who the neighbour had seen; perhaps he thought the young woman would ask him that. She didn't; she hadn't heard what he said. He continued, "The evening before Herr Apollonius went to Brambach he looked out the things he wanted to take with him; he checked them all over as he always does but he couldn't make up his mind. And that's why it's so strange that your husband has suddenly started working so hard."

Apollonius's name roused the young woman; she listened as the old man continued, "I've only just thought of this in the shed. When the neighbour told me someone had crept into the shed, I thought to myself, 'What can he have wanted creeping in there at night?' And when I looked up and saw your husband working like that, a sense of uneasiness came over me and compelled me to go urgently into the shed. I tried to imagine what anyone who crept in there could possibly have done. First I found the axe which belongs with the other tools lying by the door. So I thought, 'has he done something with the axe?' And again I tried to think what someone creeping in at night could do with that. It occurred to me it might be something with the ladders. But I found nothing wrong there. There was nothing wrong with the cradle still lying there either. Then I began to examine the pulleys and finally the ropes. With one of them it was as if it had come up against something sharp here and there and that had frayed it. So I thought, 'that often happens' and was about to lay it down again. But then I thought about it again. 'There's nothing else; and if someone creeps in here at night he must have wanted something; and if he had the axe he must have done something with it.' So I looked more closely and --- may God forgive me! ---someone had cut into the rope with the axe here and there and again and again. I threw the rope over the beam and put my weight on it and the cuts opened up; I think if a cradle weighed it down it could have broken." Valentine had gone quite pale as he told his story. Christiane had hung on his words more and more anxiously; she had fallen back in the chair and could scarcely speak.

"He threatened it", she groaned. The old man didn't understand what she said. "The evening before there was nothing", he continued. "Herr Apollonius is so thorough, he never misses even a gnat-bite. He would have found it when he checked everything over. So I suspect that whoever made the cuts must have watched Herr Apollonius checking his gear and thought that he wouldn't check it again when he needed it in the morning. So he crept in during the night."

"Valentine", cried Christiane and clasped his shoulders, half as if to compel him to tell her the truth, half in order to stop herself falling. "He surely didn't take it with him? Valentine, for goodness sake tell me!" "No, he didn't", said Valentine, "but he did take the other cradle that was in the shed and the ropes for it and some other things." "And were there cuts in that too?" asked Christiane, her fear visibly increasing. The old man said, "I don't know. But whoever made the cuts can't have known which one Herr Apollonius would take." "If he'd wanted to be on the safe side, he'd have taken both ---and it's all my fault", groaned Christiane. "He's been threatening to do something to him for a long time. He pretended it was only one of his jests. If I told anyone, he said he'd do it in deadly earnest." "Anyone capable of that sort of jest is also capable of putting it into practice", said Valentine.

Christiane trembled so violently all over that old Valentine forgot his fear for Apollonius in his anxiety about her. He had to hold her on to her, to stop her falling. But she pushed him away and begged and threatened in the same breath, "Save him, Valentine, save him! Please do something to help, Valentine! Oh God, otherwise it's my fault." She prayed to God for his deliverance and wept and wailed the whole time that he was dead and it was all her fault. She called Apollonius by the tenderest of names, that he was not to die. Valentine in his anxiety tried to find some comfort for her and in doing so found a modicum for himself. Even if it could not really be of comfort, at least there was hope that Apollonius must already be on his way back. He would certainly have checked the ropes again. If he'd had an accident, they must have heard by now. Ten times he had to repeat it to her before she even understood what he meant. And now she awaited the messenger who would bring the dreadful news and jumped up with a start at every sound. She even took the sound of her own sobbing to be the voice of the messenger. In the end, since her fear and perplexity rubbed off onto him too, old Valentine went to the old gentleman himself to get him to come to her. He didn't know what to do; and perhaps something could still be done to save Apollonius; perhaps the old gentleman would know what to do.

The old gentleman was sitting in his small sitting-room. As he became deeper and deeper enveloped in the mist which cut him off from the world outside, in the end he even avoided the garden. It was especially the often repeated question 'How are you, Herr Nettenmaier?' that drove him from it. He felt people could no longer believe his reply 'I've a bit of a problem with my eyes but it's nothing to speak of ', and since then, whenever he was asked that question, he heard only derision. To Apollonius, however much he empathized with his suffering, this increasing retirement and unsociability of the old gentleman was not unwelcome. The further his brother fell, the more difficult it became to hide the state of affairs in the house from the old gentleman and to keep away potential tale-bearers, from whom it was impossible to shield him in his garden; in fact it seemed impossible. Apollonius, of course, didn't know that the old gentleman in his sitting-room was suffering torments which, even if based on mere delusions, were equal to the ones from which he wanted to shield him. In this room the old gentleman sat the livelong day slumped behind the table on his leather chair, brooding as before on all the possible dishonour which might strike his family, or striding with rapid steps to and fro, when the redness of his sunken cheeks and the violent swinging of his arms showed that he was doing his utmost in his mind to fend off all that was threatening. Only the architect, who was in Apollonius's confidence, was allowed in to see him. The old gentleman, who kept his innermost thoughts and feelings hidden from this guest as he did from everyone else, assumed that he too was dissimulating in the same way, and this only confirmed him in the opinion that he wouldn't find out anything by asking and indeed would only expose his own helplessness. The hotter things boiled up inside him, the cooler he appeared on the outside. It was a state which must have ended in complete madness if the outside world had not thrown him a lifeline and torn him from his isolation by main force.

This was the day when it happened. He was just sitting on his chair brooding when Valentine was driven by his anxiety to enter. Old habit, of which he wasn't aware, caused him to open the door quietly and enter in the same way; but the old gentleman with his abnormally sharpened senses was instantly aware of something unusual. His expectation of what it was naturally followed the same path as all his other thoughts. It was some shame threatening the honour of the house which had changed Valentine's usual so steadfast demeanour; it must be something really bad to have upset his old journeyman to that extent and to have penetrated his practised calmness. The old gentleman was trembling as he got up from his chair. He couldn't make up his mind whether to ask. It was not necessary. The old journeyman came straight out with it unasked. With his heart thumping in his chest he related his fears and what justified them. The old gentleman was shocked, despite his imagination having prepared him so well for the reality; but the old journeyman did not see any of this in the outward demeanour of the old gentleman, who listened to him as usual as if it was the most trivial thing he had to say. When he had finished speaking, not even the sharpest eye could have noticed the slightest tremble in the tall old gentleman. He had the firm ground of reality beneath his feet again; he was the old gentleman in the blue coat once more. He stood before his old journeyman as tall and upright as before, so upright and calm that Valentine took new heart from him. "Fantasies!" he said in his grim persona of old. "Is there no journeyman there?" Valentine found one who was just fetching some slates and called him over. The old gentleman sent him off to Brambach to fetch Apollonius home at once. The journeyman went. "If he's not fast enough for you, you old woman, tell him to hurry so you can speedily find out that you've got yourself in a state over nothing. But there's to be no word about all this fuss you're making! And make sure you include the wife in that so she doesn't do anything silly." Valentine obeyed. The old gentleman's confidence and the fact that now something was really being done had a more powerful effect on him than a hundred sound reasons could have had. He shared his new feeling of encouragement with the wife. He was in too much of a hurry to tell her what he based this on. If he had had the time, he would probably have left her less reassured. And he himself had not the faintest suspicion that the old gentleman was inwardly convinced of the guilt of his elder son and of the danger to, if not of the death of, his younger son, while he sought to persuade Valentine his fears were no more than empty imaginings, and gave the impression that he had sent the journeyman merely to reassure him and the wife.

"Now, you old fool" said Herr Nettenmaier when Valentine had returned to him "I expect you'll have told this whole story you've dreamed up to the neighbours and the wife will have sent at least half a dozen cousins with it round the town."

Valentine did not notice the wrought-up tension with which the old gentleman awaited the answer to his question, disguised as an exclamation. "I certainly have not!" he said vehemently. He felt insulted by the old gentleman's assumption. "I didn't suspect any real harm myself and Frau Nettenmaier has not spoken to a soul!"

The old gentleman gathered fresh hope. During Valentine's absence he had for a moment given way to all the suffering which any father in his position could have felt; but he had said to himself that one must not, through inactivity and despair, throw away with all that was lost what might still be saved. Even if his sons were lost, the honour of the house, his own and that of the wife and children, might perhaps still be saved. Now all the experience he had gained by imagining every possibility stood him in good stead. If his abnormally touchy sense of honour spurred him on not to shrink when faced with the worst, his thoughts now ran along the same feverish lines in this real case as they normally did in the shadowy phantoms of his fear. Keeping secret all that might constitute grounds of suspicion of his elder son seemed to him the first priority. Even if Valentine and the wife had not told anyone what they knew, other similar tales might already be known. Such a criminal idea does not arise by chance. It's the fruit of a poison tree with roots and branches. Valentine must tell him what has been happening in the house since Apollonius's return. Whether Valentine didn't know about Fritz Nettenmaier's jealousy or whether he didn't want to tell the old gentleman, whose suspicious nature he knew only too well, anything about it, the story he told was that of a frivolous ambitious pleasure-seeking wastrel, who despite every effort his better brother made to stop him, had sunk to the level of a common libertine and drunkard; at the same time it was the story of a loyal brother, who out of necessity had taken out of the hands of the wastrel the responsibility for the honour and continuance of the business and the house in order to preserve them and who was being persecuted even to death for doing so by the wretch who had failed.

The old gentleman sat motionless. Only the flush becoming ever more fiery red on his gaunt cheeks was evidence of what he was suffering with the honour of his house. Otherwise he gave the impression of knowing it all already. It was his old way; perhaps he also employed it here because he thought Valentine would then be less likely to suppress anything, or to change it against his better judgement. His inner turmoil prevented him from noticing the incongruity between this pose and his sense of honour. Valentine made no attempt to deepen the shadow that fell on Fritz Nettenmaier's actions; but knowing the old gentleman as he did, he thought it necessary to show the honourable actions of Apollonius in the best possible light. But unfortunately he only half knew the old gentleman. He miscalculated the effect he intended when he praised the filial way in which Apollonius had spared the old gentleman from hearing of the danger. By doing so he undid all that his plain tale had done to depict the son as worthy of the most precious thing the old gentleman knew. The old gentleman saw only that the fear which Apollonius's proficiency had stirred up was more and more justified. Apollonius had kept the danger from him in order to be able to take the credit for the deliverance alone. Or else he considered his father helplessly blind, a man who was nothing any more and could do nothing more than at best get in his way. And the old gentleman could forgive that even less –despite his agony over his son whom he already thought of as dead. He became more and more convinced that he himself would never have allowed things to go so far if he had known about it and taken matters into his own hand, and Apollonius had no one to blame for his death but own presumption. Naturally these thoughts had to take a back seat before what was immediately necessary. What he had learned so far about all that lay behind this idea of fratricide might strengthen the suspicion that had arisen but not have brought it about without something else in addition which he didn't yet know. He must find out from the guilty son himself if there was something else.

His decision was taken whatever the consequences. He demanded his hat and stick. At any other time Valentine would have been astounded at this command, perhaps even shocked. When one is upset by something extraordinary as Valentine was now, the only unexpected thing is what is usually called the routine, something that reminds one of the calm situation of old. While Valentine fetched what had been ordered, the old gentleman got ready to go out, and pointed out to him once again how groundless and foolish his fears were. "Who knows", said the old gentleman grimly, "what the neighbour saw. How could he recognize someone in the dark at such a great distance? And then you with your cuts with an axe! Now if the lad's rope should break in Brambach or he should by chance come to grief in some other way, you'll be totally convinced your imaginary cuts with an axe were the cause and that they were made by the man the neighbour –who is as simple as you are –is supposed to have seen creeping into the shed. And if you say a word of this, or you're clever enough to hint in riddles at whatever delusions you have in your old noddle, it'll be all over the town next day.

Not because anyone would seriously believe what you've cooked up –no sane man could believe it – but because people enjoy thinking the worst of someone and gossiping about him. God will see to it that no harm comes to the boy, but it can happen, perhaps has already happened. How easily even a stay at home can come to grief, let alone a slater who hovers like a bird between heaven and earth, but unlike the bird has no wings. That's one of the reasons why the skill of a slater is such a noble art, because the slater is the most visible symbol of how Providence holds all men in His hands when they work in some honest profession. And if He lets him fall, He knows why; and no man should wrap it all in some complicated web which could
bring calamity on another, or even shame. I'm certain the matter will turn out to be as it is, and not as you have concocted it out of panic. For ----"

The old gentleman had just got this far in his sermon when the sound of a heavy burden being set down was heard outside. The old gentleman stood silent for a moment as if turned to stone. Valentine had seen through the window the tinsmith's journeyman arrive and start unloading. "It's George, the journeyman from the tinsmith's", said Valentine," bringing the rest of the metal garlands." "And there you are, terrified by your delusions, thinking they're bringing you know who. Where's Fritz?" "On the church roof", replied Valentine.

"Good", said Herr Nettenmaier. "Go and tell the tinsmith to come in when he's done." Valentine did so. While they were waiting Herr Nettenmaier went on in an undertone with his severe lecture. He spoke of how people fabricated imaginary events and then worried about them as if they were real; how such thoughts got the better of a man and did not give him a moment's peace if he didn't guard against them from the very beginning. It was as if the old gentleman was having a go at himself. He didn't think that he was lecturing Valentine on what were in fact his own faults. On the other hand Valentine was feeling ashamed of himself as if he had somehow deserved punishment; and he listened to the old gentleman with respect and contrition until the tinsmith came in. Herr Nettenmaier now grasped the stick which Valentine handed him, pulled his hat down low in order to conceal from the world as much as possible any involuntary confession in his lifeless eyes and majestically shook himself straight in his blue coat. Valentine wanted to conduct him, but he said, "The wife needs you; and you know what you have to do in my house". Valentine understood the real meaning of this cryptic way of speaking. The old gentleman was making him responsible for the behaviour of the wife. Now Herr Nettenmaier turned to where the tinsmith's journeyman was respectfully clearing his throat and asked him if he had time to accompany him as far as the roof of the spire of St George's where his elder son was working. The tinsmith agreed. Valentine dared to suggest that it would be better to simply send for Fritz. The old gentleman said grimly, "I must speak to him up on the roof. It's about the repair." Thereupon he turned back to the tinsmith. "I'll take your arm", he said with condescending grimness. "I'm having a bit of trouble with my eyes, but it's nothing to speak of."

Shaking his head, Valentine watched him for a while as he left. When the old gentleman was no longer in sight, all the confidence which he owed to his resolute presence crumbled away again. He clasped his hands together in fear; but since it occurred to him that he was standing at the front door and would be responsible for any gossip that the exhibition of his 'imagined' fears might cause, he acted as if he had clasped his hands merely to rub them in glee.

The journeyman tinsmith had heard that Herr Nettenmaier had been blind for years; but the man himself told him the trouble with his eyes was negligible; he soon noticed, though, that what people had told him was right. Now a man passing quickly by nodded to him and in reply to his "How are you?", the old gentleman smiled back," I'm having a bit of trouble with my eyes, but it's nothing to speak of." At anybody else in Herr Nettenmaier's situation the journeyman would have laughed; but the powerful personality of the old gentleman inspired in him so much respect that he ignored the contradiction between what his senses told him and these words and he believed at one and the same time both what his senses showed him, namely that Herr Nettenmaier was blind, and what the old gentleman told him, namely that it was nothing to speak of.

The appearance of the old gentleman in the street was a wonder and would certainly have caused a sensation and held him up with a hundred hand-shakes and questions, if something else had not diverted attention from him. A rumour, uttered quickly and in an undertone, ran through the streets. People in twos and threes stopped and waited the approach of a third or fourth who showed he knew what was bringing ten other similar groups together. Someone hurrying by passed it on. And always it began with, 'Haven't you heard?' which was often provoked by someone asking 'What's happened then?' Herr Nettenmaier didn't need to ask; he knew what had happened without anyone needing to tell him; but he dared not let it show how he knew that they should really have been asking him; people didn't only want to know what had happened, but also how and why. The tinsmith thought Herr Nettenmaier was about to collapse on him, but the old gentleman had only stumbled, 'it's nothing to speak of'. The journeyman asked a passer-by. "A slater's met with an accident in Brambach." "How come?" asked the journeyman. "A rope broke. Nobody knows anything more." Herr Nettenmaier felt the journeyman recoil, horrified that it was the son of the man he was escorting who had met with the accident. He said, "It will have been in Tambach. People have misheard, that's all. It's not important." The journeyman didn't know what to think of Herr Nettenmaier's lack of concern. The old gentleman said to himself, as the burning flush rose to his cheeks, "Yes, it must be. It must be now". He had thought of a way to avoid all law-courts, all investigations. The way he meant must have been a difficult one for he clenched his teeth as he nodded his head and said to himself, "It must be. It must be now." The journeyman went on as if in a dream, escorting the old gentleman beside him as far as the stairs up the tower of St George's. People were right; Herr Nettenmaier was a very unusual man!

The old gentleman had said he must speak to his son on the church roof – about the repair. He had unintentionally spoken in his old hypocritical way. It must be on the church roof and it was about a repair, but not that of the church roof.

14

The slater's world is high up between heaven and earth. Between heaven and earth, high up on the church roof, Fritz Nettenmaier was hard at work when the old gentleman had himself escorted up the stairs to him. Fritz Nettenmaier had fled up here to get away from the eyes of men which he thought were all turned on him; he had sought to escape from his thoughts up here in hard convulsive work. He had brought up with him all the hell that raged inside him; and however strenuously he worked, the sweat on his brow was not that of warm honest effort, it was the cold sweat of a guilty conscience. He hammered slates into shape and nailed them down firmly, as anxiously and as fast as if he was nailing down the universe, which would otherwise collapse in the next few minutes. But his mind was not on his work, it was far away where ropes continually broke and slaters crashed noisily down to certain death. Sometimes he suddenly paused in his work; he felt as if he must shout down, "Go to Brambach. Tell him not to climb the ladder! Not to sit on the cradle!" But then the hundreds of people running around like ants far below would stop still in shock, as if turned to stone, and so many pairs of eyes filled with horror and disgust would stare up at him, and the court bailiff would come and drive him before him down the stairs; and perhaps it was already too late! Then once he put his hands together on the slate hammer and vowed that if Apollonius didn't die he would be in future a good and honest man. He doesn't think that he's bound to regret this as soon as he knows Apollonius is safe. –But there's someone coming up the stairs –is it the court bailiff already? No. No one knows what he has done. He puts on an obstinate face as if asking, "Who dares bring anything against me?" Now he hears voices and the sound of one of them strikes his tormented heart like the blow of a hammer. It is the one voice he has not expected to hear up here. Will the one whose voice it is ask him "Where is thy brother Abel?" No. It will be telling his son that his brother has had an accident; it's a black day and there's no need for him to work any more. And if nevertheless he does ask the question, the answer is almost as old as humanity itself, "Am I my brother's keeper?" Then it comes to him with an unexpected sense of relief that his father is blind. For he knows there's no way now he could face his all-seeing eyes. He hammers and fastens the slates faster and faster. He would have avoided his father if he could, but the cradle is narrow and the old gentleman is speaking by the hatch in the roof. He determines not to take notice of him till he has to. "That's far enough" he hears the old man say. "Give your master my compliments; and here's something for you. Have a drink on me." Fritz Nettenmaier hears the old man sit down on the plank sticking through the hatch and knows the old gentleman's body fills the entire opening. He hears the thanks of the journeyman and the sound of his footsteps receding in the distance.

"Nice weather we're having" says Herr Nettenmaier. His son guesses the old man is trying to discover whether there's anybody nearby. Nobody answers; speech fails Fritz Nettenmaier; he hammers louder and faster. He wishes the hour, the day, life itself were over. "Fritz!" calls the old man. He calls again and then once more. In the end Fritz Nettenmaier has to answer. He thinks of the cry, "Cain where art thou?" –"Here, father!" he replies and goes on hammering. "That slate's firm enough" says the old man indifferently; "I can tell by the sound; it won't flake." "Yes", replies Fritz with chattering teeth, "it won't let in water." "It's better quality than before" continues the old man; "they've got deeper in the quarry. It looks as if you're on your own." A stifled "yes" comes from his son's mouth. "The deeper the seam, the harder the stone. Is there no more scaffolding here?" "No." "Good. Come over here, here to me." "What do you want?" "Come over here. What I have to say must be said quietly."

Fritz Nettenmaier, trembling in every limb, went over to his father. He knew he was blind but still he sought to avoid his gaze. The old man struggled to compose himself, but no trace of that appeared in his weather-beaten face; only the length of his silence and his breathing, which seemed like a tired echo to follow the heavy wheezing swing of the pendulum of the church clock nearby. Fritz Nettenmaier foresaw from these preparations what was to come. He strove to be defiant. If he suspects something, who's going to prove it? And even if he can prove it, he won't give me away; I'm sure of it. Why else does he want to speak quietly? Let him say what he wants, I know nothing, it wasn't me, I've done nothing. His face struggled to produce from the trembling of all his muscles the wildest expression of defiance. The old gentleman still remained silent. The bustle of the streets sounded muffled up here on the roof; below there were already violet shadows, the last ray of sun quivered on the cradle of Apollonius on the spire. Somewhat further off a flock of doves returning home from the fields swooped past. It was an evening filled with the peace of God. Below stretched the green earth far and wide; high overhead the sky spread above like a glass of blue crystal. Small pink clouds were scattered around like flocks of wool. The noise from below died away more and more. The air carried the individual sounds of a distant bell and bounced them playfully against the roof like recurring waves. There over the nearest green hill, where the sound came from, lies Brambach. It must be the evening bells of Brambach. High in the sky and far below on the earth, everywhere is the peace of God and sweet release for those longing for rest. Only up between heaven and earth do the two people on the roof of St George's not feel its wings. Only over them does it have no power. In one of them burns the madness of an overwrought sense of honour, in the other all the flames, all the torments of Hell.

"Where is your brother?" the words finally issued from the father's mouth. "I don't know. How should I know?" bristled the son defiantly. "You don't know?" The old gentleman only whispered yet each word was like a thunderclap in the son's mind. "Very well, I'll tell you. Over in Brambach he's lying dead. The rope above him broke and you cut it with the axe. The neighbour saw you creeping into the shed. You threatened to do it in front of your wife. The whole town knows it; they're reporting it to the magistrates this very minute. The first person to come up the stairs will be the bailiff to take you in front of the judge."

Fritz Nettenmaier fell in a heap; the scaffolding cracked beneath him. The old gentleman pricked up his ears. If the wretch had collapsed at the edge of the scaffolding, he would fall off into space and all would be over! Everything that had to be done would be done! A lark rose into the air from a nearby garden, its merry warbling filling the air above the trees and houses. Happier men heard its song in the distance; workers rested on their shovels, children dropped their whips and tops and looked up to find the black dot hovering high up in the sky that sounded so sweet and listened with bated breath. But Herr Nettenmaier didn't hear the lark although it was so near; he too held his breath; but he was listening for sounds below, not above. And it was nothing like the song of a lark that he was hoping to hear. It was more the crash of a heavy body on the roof below him and a cry of fear cut short. He listened at first hopefully, then anxiously. No sound reaches him from below From in front of him on the planks of the scaffolding comes the sound of heavy breathing. He listens; Fate which could have come to his aid out of compassion has not done so. He must do it himself, for it must be done. Otherwise people will point at the children and sneer, "Those are the ones whose father killed his brother and was executed or died in prison." And even when it is long forgotten, they will only have to appear for it all to start up again; then people will point at them again and turn away with a shudder. The trust a person inherits from his parents is the capital with which he starts out in life. It must be shown to him before he's had chance to gain it for himself otherwise he will never learn that it has to be earned. Who will show trust to those who are tainted with their father's shame? How will they learn that trust has to be deserved? Living among men but rejected by them, aren't they bound to become like their father was? And his own long life of striving to acquire and maintain honour will be infected retrospectively by his son's shame. The children will be considered capable of doing what their father did; no honest father could have had a son like that!-The flush on the haggard cheeks burned hotter and hotter; the sunken chest heaved convulsively. Involuntarily he made a forward movement with his arm. Fritz Nettenmaier sensed its meaning and tried to struggle to his feet and would have fallen again if he had not supported himself on both hands. So he was lying there before the old man on his hands and knees when he let out an anguished cry, "What is you want of me, father? What's in your mind?"

"I'm waiting to see", replied the old man in a whisper, almost a hiss, "whether you'll do what must be done yourself or whether I must do it. For done it must be.

Nobody knows anything yet which might lead to a judicial enquiry before the magistrates, except me, your wife and Valentine. I can vouch for myself, but cannot guarantee the others won't betray what they know. If you fall from the scaffolding now, so that people think you've been accidentally killed, the greatest scandal is averted. A slater who is killed accidentally is treated with honour like a soldier who is killed on the field of battle. You're not worth a death like that, you wastrel. The hangman should come and drag you off to the place of execution, you villain, for killing your brother and trying to poison the future life of your innocent children and bringing shame on my past life which was so full of honour. You've brought enough shame on your family, but you won't do so any more. They're not going to say of me that my son and my grandsons' father died on the scaffold or in prison. You say an 'Our Father' now, if you're still able to pray. Then you turn round as if you're going back to work and step with your right foot over the edge of the scaffolding. I'll say the shock of his brother's accident made him dizzy; the magistrates and the town will believe me. That's what comes of a life that has been different from yours. If you don't do this willingly, I'll throw myself off with you and you'll have me on your conscience too. People know I've got trouble with my eyes; I stumbled and tried to hang on to you and pulled you down with me. After what I've learnt today my life is finished and worthless; I've reached the end, but the children are only just starting out. And no shame shall attach to the children or my name's not Nettenmaier. Now think how it's to be. I'll count up to fifteen by the swings of the pendulum over there.

Fritz Nettenmaier had listened to what his father had to say with growing horror. The fact that what he had done was not yet generally known gave him hope. The fear of imminent death aroused some of his inner strength again. He fled once more into his attitude of defiance. After the old man had finished speaking, Fritz said hastily, "I don't know what you want. I'm innocent. I don't know anything about cuts with an axe." He expected his father would accept his protests, even if unwillingly at first. But the old man began calmly counting, "One –two --." "Father" he said, interrupting the counting as his fear rose, and the defiance in his voice became more like begging. "Just listen to me for a moment. The magistrates in court listen to what one has to say, but you won't listen to me. All right, I'll jump since you want me dead, I'll die even though I'm innocent. But please just listen to me first!" The old gentleman made no reply; he went on counting. The wretched man saw that his sentence had been passed. His father would not believe anything he might say; and he knew that what the stubborn old man took it into his head to do, he carried out inexorably. He was about to admit defeat when the idea occurred to him that he should beg once more; then again that he could push the old gentleman over backwards, jump over him and flee; then again that he would hold on tight to where he was, if the old gentleman clung to him, so that he didn't fall with him. No one could blame him for that. But at the same time he saw with a shudder what would await him if he fled and the magistrates caught him anyway. It would be better if he died now. But an even more terrible fate awaited him on the other side of Death. He thought back and re-lived his whole life in a flash to try to decide whether the Everlasting Judge would be able to forgive him. His thoughts became confused; he was one moment here and the next there and had forgotten why. He saw the mist thicken as the journeyman disappeared into it, and at the same time he was looking up at the lighted windows of the Red Eagle, from where came the familiar words, "Here he is! Now there'll be fun!" He stood at the street corner counting, and the planks Apollonius was standing on wouldn't break and the ropes above him from which he hung would not snap; he stood again in front of his wife, bending over the bed of poor dying Annie and said, "Do you know why you're frightened?" and swung his fist for the accursed blow; even the fact that he lay there before his father thinking first this and then that in fearful haste came fleetingly into his mind as in a feverish dream. Then it seemed to him as if he came to his senses and endless time had passed between the moment when his father started to count the swings of the pendulum and now. Everything must now come right. He only needed to decide whether he should escape past the old gentleman or hold on tight when his father tried to pull him down with him. But he still lay there and his father still sat there. He heard him count nine and then no more. He lost consciousness completely.

But the old gentleman had really stopped counting and was silent. His sharp ears had heard a footstep hurrying up the stairs. He clutched at his son and held him as if to make certain he did not escape him. By the coldness and the slackness of the arm he had hold of, he felt that it was not necessary to hold his son, because he must be unconscious. This gave him new cause to worry. If his son was unconscious he must if possible stop other people from seeing him. Even this unconsciousness might arouse suspicion or increase it. He got up and turned from the hatch to face the person coming up. He couldn't make up his mind whether to block the hatch with his body or to intercept the person coming up the stairs. The journeyman who he had previously sent to Brambach –for it was the same man now hurrying up the stairs – stopped and coughed. He could keep him away from the scaffolding; he could perhaps prevent him from seeing his son lying there if he went towards him and dealt with him while he was still on the stairs. This was perhaps a surer way than blocking the hatch, since he would probably not cover it completely. Now the old gentleman felt for the first time how all that he had experienced that day had drained his strength. But the journeyman noticed none of this when he saw the old gentleman leaning on a beam blocking his way.

"Shall I fetch him for you, Herr Nettenmaier?" asked the journeyman standing still on the stairs. "Who?", snapped Herr Nettenmaier in response. He had great difficulty trying to preserve his studied calm. If the journeyman had been in Brambach he couldn't have spoken so calmly, whoever the man wanted to talk about.

"I'm sure he'll be home by now" replied the journeyman. The old gentleman did not repeat his question; he had to hang on to the beam he was leaning on. "He was already on his way", continued the journeyman. "I went with him as far as the town gate. Then he sent me off to the tinsmith's to ask whether the metal decoration was finally ready. George said he'd already taken it and had just got back from St George's, where he'd escorted Herr Nettenmaier up onto the roof. Then I thought, 'He'll still be up there'; and because it was so urgent I thought I'd better ask you if you wanted me to fetch Herr Apollonius here as well."

Finally Herr Nettenmaier succeeded in pretending to feel up and down the beam, to which he'd had to hang on tight, as if he'd only got hold of it in order to examine it. Since he felt his hands trembling, he gave up this examination. He said, with as much grimness as he could summon up at this moment, "I'm coming down myself. Wait on the landing till I call you!" The journeyman obeyed. Herr Nettenmaier took a deep breath as soon as he knew no one was observing him, a breath which almost became a sob. Now that the nervous tension which had gripped him since Valentine's disclosures was beginning to dissolve, his paternal anguish came to the fore. With the impassioned efforts to save the honour of the house, this feeling had till now remained unexpressed. Now that it appeared not to have struck him down, he found time to feel sorry for the misfortune of his righteous son. But it occurred to him that this worthy son was still in the very same danger while his wicked brother was anywhere near him. He had taken this eventuality into account too and had planned what he must then do. The strength he had had up to now, and which had barely sufficed, would have left him along with the nervous tension, if the rescue of his worthy son and the honour of his house had not been at stake. He felt his way back to the hatch. Fritz Nettenmaier had in the meantime recovered from his state of insensibility and he'd managed to stand up. The old gentleman told him to come in from the scaffolding and said, "Tomorrow before sunrise you're no longer to be here. See if you can become a better person again in America. Here you're in disgrace and bring disgrace on others. You go home after me; I'll see you have money; you get yourself ready. For years you've done nothing for your wife and children; I'll take care of them. Before daybreak you're to be on your way. Do you hear me?"

Fritz Nettenmaier staggered. He had just been looking certain death in the face; now he was to live! Live where no one knew what he had done, where every chance noise did not frighten him with the phantoms of the court bailiffs after him At this moment he felt that it was a piece of luck that he would be far away from his wife, for whom he had done all that he had done and in whose eyes and look he would see reflected day after day what he had done; who knew what he had done, whose every glance was a threat to deliver him up to retribution. He dreaded being back in the house in which every hour everything would remind him of what he hoped to forget completely out there under the open skies and which he planned to atone for in a new life. He would have preferred to go immediately from this very spot on which he stood to this safe harbour.

"Apollonius has not fallen", continued the old gentleman and Fritz Nettenmaier's whole new Heaven vanished at once. The old spectre had him in its clutches again. Now he once more loved his wife who he had just been looking forward to escaping from. Along with the object of his hatred, love and hate came to life once more and both were flames of Hell. He thought he could have done anything; dying would have been little more than a light-hearted jest if only his rival also lay dead. A dreadful conscience, the fear of the Beyond, everything would have been bearable except one thing –knowing she was in his arms. The old gentleman had expected his son to say 'Yes' to his plan. "You'll go", he said, when no reply came. "You'll go. You'll be on your way to America before daybreak tomorrow or I shall go straight to the magistrates. If there's to be disgrace, it's better to just have disgrace than disgrace and murder. Remember, I've sworn it and now do what you want."

The old gentleman called up the journeyman and had himself taken home.

15

Meanwhile the rumour that the old gentleman had heard on his way to St George's had also reached the street where the house with the green shutters stands. Just outside the windows one passer-by told another. All Christiane heard was "Have you heard the latest? A slater's been killed in Brambach." Then, intending to jump up, she fell onto the floor. Once again Valentine had to exchange his anxiety about Apollonius for concern and care for Fritz's wife. He hurried over. He could not prevent the fall entirely, only protect her head from the hard edge of the chair-leg. He squatted down beside the prostrate woman and held her head and neck in his trembling hands. His grip had pushed her full dark brown hair up over her brow until it covered her pale face. Her hair at the front had a tendency to form natural curls which she could only overcome occasionally by creating a sharp parting. It was as if her hair had taken advantage of its owner's fainting fit to indulge itself. Old Valentine freed his hands by letting her weight slide carefully onto the floor and tried to brush the hair out of her face. He had to see whether she still lived. This caused him much vain effort for a long time; anxiety made his old hands even more clumsy than usual; then there was the shyness which inevitably overcomes an old bachelor in such close proximity to a woman; and also the wilfulness of her hair which would keep falling in curly locks over her face. The pulse in her neck and that in her temple, he saw, were trying to restrain this tendency as they stirred the hair with their beat, and he gained new hope. On the table stood a bottle of water; he poured some into the palm of his hand and sprinkled it on her hair and face. That worked. She stirred; he helped her to sit up and supported her. She now brushed the unruly hair from her face herself and looked round. There was something so strange about the way she looked that Valentine took fright once more. Then she nodded her head and said in a low voice, "Yes". Valentine understood her to be saying to herself she had heard the terrible news and had not been dreaming. By the tone of her voice he heard that she was telling herself what had happened but did not understand it. It was as if what she was saying did not concern her and she was only wondering whom it did concern. She suspected that when she got to the bottom of it there would be horror and grief, but at that moment she did not know what these two meant; a dreamlike presentiment of hand clasping, growing pale, falling to the floor, jumping up, going round wringing her hands, feeling deadly tired, wanting to sit down on every chair she stumbled past and yet driven to go on, of her head constantly jerking back wildly and then dropping dully forward onto her chest again; a dreamlike presentiment of all this stalked the room before her, like her own feint far-off reflection behind a concealing veil. Much closer and more distinct was the dull ache in the pit of her stomach, which grew into a stabbing pain, and the anxious realisation that it would inevitably choke the life from her if she couldn't find the ability to weep which alone could heal everything. So she sat motionless for a long time and heard nothing of all that old Valentine in his anxiety said to her. He tried everything he could think of; he didn't really believe his own words of comfort as he tried to prove to her that Apollonius could not have met with a fatal accident - because he was too cautious and too meticulous for that to happen. To say nothing of the story he recalled from his youth of people now long since dead who had been frightened to death pointlessly by a similar rumour. He didn't believe it and yet he still went on with the story and described the people concerned as if it would without fail calm Christiane if she could see in her mind's eye the old bailiff Kern and his housekeeper as they really were in the flesh. He would have laid down his life to help her; but in his perplexity he didn't know how to. So he sought to help himself get over the anxiety of the moment by telling his story more and more enthusiastically. As he did so he watched for the slightest change of expression on her beautiful pale face; and the more beautiful and youthful it seemed to him, the more grievous seemed her suffering and the more enthusiastic became his story. He had watched her move into the house with the green shutters as a seventeen year old bride, had lived close to her for eight years. Until into her twenty-fourth year she had remained inwardly as innocent as a child happily playing with things, but how she had suffered in the last two years! And how beautiful she had remained in her suffering, how beautifully she had suffered! Now she lay there broken, like a half-opened flower, before his old eyes which had so often wept for her, more at the gentleness and unconscious, unyielding dignity with which she bore her misfortune than at the misfortune itself. There are certain heart-stirring people who are not spoiled by either fear or even anger; people who move us in everything they do, even when they smile or are openly joyful, the mere sight of whom touches us deeply without reminding us of their suffering. It is not something painful we experience; and the very suffering on such a face has a wonderful power both to console us and to lift our spirits as it inspires us to sympathy for the sufferer. Christiane, for as long as he had known her, had been such a person in Valentine's eyes; as such a person she now lay there before him.

Finally she had managed to weep. Old Valentine revived; he saw she was saved. He read it in her face which, just like herself, was too honest to conceal how she felt. He sat and listened to her weeping with such gladness and attention as if she had been singing him a beautiful song.

At moments when a person has to give way unreservedly to his deeper feelings one recognizes most surely his real nature. The fundamental animal-like nature, that lies hidden beneath the customary cosmetic of so-called culture or some deliberate pose, is then revealed unmistakeably in the movements of the body and in the tone of the voice. Old Valentine heard the pure music in Christiane's voice as her tears gushed out, a quality it had not lost since the cry both of pain and anger at the blow that had been struck by Annie's bed. She had now wept her fill and got up; old Valentine wouldn't have needed to help her. She made ready to go out. Her manner had assumed an air of solemn determination. Valentine saw this with astonishment and some concern. He suddenly remembered the responsibility he had been given. He asked anxiously if she was intending to go out. She nodded. "But I can't allow you to go", he said. "The old gentleman has bound me to a solemn promise."

"I must", she said. "I must go to the magistrates. I must say it's all my fault and suffer my punishment. Their grandfather will take care of my children. I'd like to tell the gentlemen to bury him beside Annie; he loved her so much. I would also like to be buried there, but they won't do that. No, I won't say anymore about that."

Valentine didn't know what to reply. He mustn't let her go but saw by her determination that he would not be able to stop her. "If only the old gentleman were here!" he thought. What he said was, "Wouldn't you do something to please old Valentine?"

She gave him a kindly look despite her distress and replied, "How could you ask! You always loved him and I won't forget that as long as I live. He is dead and I must die too. If there's anything I can do for you before I go, you only have to ask. As long as it's in my power and as long as you don't tell me not to go."

"No, not that", said the old man. "But if you would only wait until the old gentleman comes back so that I can be free of my responsibility." The old man was not merely concerned about himself. He hoped the old gentleman would have the presence of mind to find a way to dissuade her from what she planned to do.

Christiane nodded to him. "All right, I'll wait that long", she replied.

Apprehension and hope together drove the old man out of the house to see whether Herr Nettenmaier was coming. Christiane fetched her hymn book from the desk and sat down with it at the table.

Valentine was longer away than he had expected. When he came back in he was no longer the same person who had gone out. He was confused and embarrassed, but confused in quite a different way from before. He seemed to be always on the point of doing something or saying something he was afraid of, and so did something else or said something else and again seemed unsure whether he should be afraid of that too. Always, especially when he had said nothing at all, he thought he had said too much. Sometimes he even seemed to be laughing but then looked all the more sad again. And that had nothing to do with what he was saying, for he talked of the weather. All the while he kept finding lots of things to do by the door, which he kept on opening; in the end he remained standing in the hall from where he could see across to the path to the shed; and they were the most fantastic pretexts he found to justify this activity. The young wife at first did not notice the change, then she observed him in amazement and with increasing presentiment. Eventually he had infected her with his behaviour. Whenever he laughed involuntarily, she brightened up in hope, and whenever he once more adopted his sad expression, she clasped her hands together and went pale again. She followed his eyes and then himself to the door and was terrified whenever he opened it. And all the while they were talking of the weather; if only they had kept calm they would have had to laugh at their own conversation; it was obvious that he was afraid to say something and she was afraid to ask what that something was. In the end she pressed both hands first against her heart which was beating so fast through her bodice and then against her burning throbbing temples. Valentine thought he had now prepared her enough to be able to get off the subject of the weather. "Yes", he said, "today's a day for the dead to come back to life, and who knows ---but please, for my sake, don't agitate yourself." But she was agitated nevertheless. She said to herself, "But it can't be, it isn't possible!" And she was agitated just because it was more than possible, it was true. "Keep looking back there", sobbed the old man who really only wanted to laugh. She looked along the passage; she would have done so even before the old man encouraged her to. Old Valentine hurried out the front door to bring the old gentleman the glad tidings; he was overjoyed and proud of what he had so cleverly done. The young wife held on tight to the door post when she heard steps through the shed. But even the door post was no longer a firm support and she herself no longer on solid ground; she hovered dizzily between Heaven and Earth. And when she saw him coming, nothing existed any more for her except the man for whom she had for weeks suffered more than mortal fear; everything whirled around her, first the walls, the floor, the ceiling, then the trees, the sky and the green earth; it was as if the world were drowning and she would be sucked down in the whirlpool if she didn't hold on tight to him. She felt herself sink down, then nothing more.

Apollonius hurried over and caught her. There he stood and held the beautiful woman in his arms, the woman he loved and who loved him. And she was pale and seemed dead. He did not carry her into the parlour, he did not allow her to slide gently to the ground, he did nothing to revive her. He stood there bewildered; he didn't know how this had come about, he had to think. Old Valentine had not yet spoken to him; he had only learnt from the journeyman who was hurrying to St George's from the tinsmith that Apollonius was just behind him and would soon be here. Apollonius had been delayed at the town gate by the nail maker. Then he'd hurried to obey his father's command. The fact that his father had sent for him had astonished him because he couldn't think why. He had heard of the fall of the slater in Tambach, but he didn't know that the rumour had confused the place names and that people would believe the accident had happened to him. So he had come through the shed completely unprepared for what the next moment would bring. He had been intending to go straight to his father in his room when he had seen Christiane come rushing along the passage, trying desperately not to faint, and had hurried over. And now he held her in his arms. The woman who for weeks he had with the most grievous effort vainly struggled to keep away from, who he only had to picture in his mind's eye for his whole being to be stirred up, who he reproached himself for thinking of sinfully; she now lay cleaving to him in a reality that was distressing in its static intensity, resting her full weight on him, her breast heaving as she breathed. Her head hung backwards over his left arm; he had to look into her face which was more beautiful, dangerously so, than his dreams could paint it. And now a rosy glow spread over the white face as far as the soft brown hair, which rolled down in gentle natural curls over her temples, and the deep blue eyes opened and he could not escape their power. And now she looked at him and recognized him. She didn't know how she came to be there and in his arms, she didn't know she lay in his arms; she knew nothing except that he was alive. How could she think of anything else but that! She wept and laughed at the same time, she put both arms round him to be sure it was really him. And yet she still asked in anxious urgent haste, "And is it you? Is it really you? And you're still alive? You didn't fall? And I didn't kill you? And it's really you? And this is me? But he –he might come!" She looked wildly round. "He wants to kill you. He won't rest till he has." She embraced him as if she wanted to protect him with her body from some enemy; then she forgot her fear in the certainty that he was still alive, and she laughed again and wept and asked him again whether he was still alive, whether it was really him. But she must warn him. She must tell him everything that his brother had done to him and what more he had threatened still to do. She must do it quickly; he might come back at any moment. Warnings, sweet unconscious murmurings of love, tears, laughter; accusations like those a child makes to its father; the need to be loved, with all that she is, with all her joys and cares, to be one of the thoughts in his mind, or feelings in his soul, that he thinks and feels along with his other thoughts and feelings; maidenly confusion and forgetting of everything for the sake of this one moment which is the fulfilment of her existence – for everything that was in the past or is to come is mere shadow – is everything she has talked of, has dreamed and experienced, has felt and now knows for the first time; all that has come before or is to come has only been or will come to pass in order to bring about this moment; before and after this moment time does not exist; -- all this pervaded her mind in confusion, all this trembled in every single note of her rushed, impulsive speech. "He lied to me and to you. He told me you despised me and offered my flower to the other men. You know the one I mean, the little bell-flower that I left for you at the Whitsun ball. And you sent it to him. I saw it. I didn't know why. I felt sorry for you. The fact that you were so quiet, so sad and so alone made me feel sorry for you. Then he told me at the dance that you made fun of me. Then you went away and he told me how you mocked me in your letters; that really hurt. You won't believe how much that hurt as I didn't know the reason for it then. Father wanted me to marry him. And when you came back

I was afraid of you; I still felt sorry for you and still loved you, but just didn't know it. It was he who told me first. Then I tried to keep out of your way. I didn't want to do anything bad and still don't. Certainly not! Then he forced me to lie. Then he threatened me with what he intended to do to you. He would see to it that you fell. He made out it was only a joke, but if I told you, he would do it in earnest. Since then I haven't slept a single night; I've sat up in bed whole nights and have been frightened to death. I saw you were in danger and daren't tell you and daren't save you. And he cut the rope with the axe the night before you went to Brambach. Valentine told me the neighbour saw him creeping into the shed. I thought you were dead and wanted to die myself. For your death would have been my fault and I would have rather died a thousand times over for you. And now you're still alive and I can't understand it. And everything's back the way it was; the trees, the shed, the sky and you're not dead. And I wanted to die because you were dead. And now you're still alive and I don't know whether it's true or whether I'm just dreaming. Is it really true? Tell me again; is it true? I'll believe whatever you tell me. And if you say so I'll die as long as you know. But he might come. Perhaps he's been listening and heard me tell you what he's planning. Send Valentine to the magistrates so that they come and take him away and can't harm you any more!"

So she rambled feverishly on, laughing and weeping in his arms. Forgetting everything, like a child playing on the edge of an abyss she does not see, she is unconsciously invoking a danger much more deadly than that whose passing she rejoices at, much more threatening than that against which she is willing to shield him with her body. She has no idea what the effect of her passionate action, the sweetness of her reckless devotion, her caresses, her warm full embrace must have on the man who loves her; does not suspect that she is doing everything to make the man whose absolute probity and magnanimity she takes for granted forget that very probity and magnanimity in the turmoil of physical desire. She has no suspicion of the struggle she is stoking up in him and how she is making it more difficult, if not impossible, for him to win it. And he knows now that the woman in his arms was really his; his brother has cheated him of her and her of him. Now that the woman in his arms is showing him how great his happiness might have been he knows exactly what his brother has cheated him of. He has stolen her and treated her brutally into the bargain; and despite everything he's suffered or done for him, he's still persecuting him and is plotting against his life. Does she belong with a man who has stolen her from him, who has ill-treated her, whom she hates? Or does she belong with him from whom she was so shamefully stolen, who loves her and whom she loves? But these were not distinct thoughts; a hundred separate sensations carried irresistibly along in a stream of deep turbulent feeling surged through his veins and tightened the muscles in his arms urging him to press to his heart something that was his. But a dark fear flows against the current of this stream and holds back the muscles in a vice-like grip. The feeling that he wants to do something, but isn't clear what it is or where it might lead; a distant memory of having given his word which he will break if he lets himself be carried away; the dark image of standing at a table and if he moves before looking behind him he will knock over something like an inkwell onto some white linen or valuable paper. At the bottom of all this lay the anxious presentiment that he could with one wrong move ruin something that could never be put right again. Through the intoxicating sounds of her voice he had already long been struggling for something before he knew that he was struggling or that this something was clarity, the basic need of his nature. And now this clarity came to his aid reminding him that he had given his word to uphold the honour of the house and that if he did what he wanted it must inevitably destroy it. He was the man and must shoulder the responsibility for himself and for her. Clarity stigmatized what he could bring about with a squeeze of his hand or with a look as a shameful betrayal of that touching absolute trust shown by her devotion to him. Clarity showed him, too, the purity of the face that lay against his heart and looked up to him so adoringly, and how he would corrupt more in himself and in her than he accused their mutual enemy of doing. A solemn shyness still stood protectively between them, but a single squeeze of the hand, a single look could banish it for ever. And so he looked round anxiously for some means of help. If only Valentine would come. Then he would have to let her out of his arms. But Valentine didn't come. But his shame at his own weakness in seeking outside help came to his rescue. He laid the still limp woman gently on the grass. When he let go of the soft yielding limbs his weakness left him for the first time. He had to turn away and could not prevent a loud sob. Then he saw the youngest boy in the yard wondering what was happening. He hurried to him, picked him up in his arms, pressed him to his heart and set him down between himself and

Christiane. It was strange; the very act of pressing the child to his heart had released the pent-up desire, and now the tense muscles relaxed also. It was really her in the person of her son he had pressed to his heart, as only he could press her to his heart.

Christiane saw him set the child down between them and understood him. A burning blush spread over her face up to her wild brown curls. She now realised for the first time that she had been lying in his arms, that she had embraced him and had spoken to him as only permitted lovers might. She now saw for the first time the abyss she had put him and herself in danger of falling into. She got up onto her knees as if she wanted to beg him not to despise her. At the same time it occurred to her that her husband might have been listening and would carry out his threat. Then she would have destroyed him in the very joy of finding him safe. He saw all this and suffered it with her. He had succeeded with a struggle in not showing her what he was feeling; but in his heart the struggle had not yet been won. He nodded to her and said, "You are a good person and my sister. You are a better person than I am. And above us both and above your husband stands God. But now go in, sister, my dear good sister." She didn't dare to look up, but through her lowered lids she saw his gentleness, the deep inexhaustible good will, the steadfast respect on his shining brow and around his soft mouth. And since he was her conscious and unconscious standard, she knew now that she was not a bad person, she could not be; he kept her safe in his strong arms like a mother with her child. As she watched him through her lowered eyelids he grew in her eyes until his head reached up to the sky. She knew that her husband could not harm him. Apollonius put the child in her arms and offered a hand to help her get up. She trembled at his touch and as she was still kneeling, her thoughts rose up to him like a prayer. He led her to the door. From the shed came Herr Nettenmaier with the journeyman. Fritz Nettenmaier, who crept along after them, still managed to see how he led her by the hand.

16

Of all that he had intended and suffered that day nothing could be read on the stony face of Herr Nettenmaier when he came home. Christiane and Valentine had to listen to a sermon on groundless delusions; for the story had turned out the way it had and not as Valentine had concocted in a panic. Fritz Nettenmaier's journey to America he now thought of as a scheme Fritz had long cherished and which he himself had only agreed to that day. Apollonius received the command to report immediately to the old gentleman's room with the account books. The old gentleman gave as a pretext that he wanted to examine the state of the business in detail; but his real purpose was to keep Apollonius in safety by him until his brother had left. Apollonius was able to make available the money for his brother's journey as far as Hamburg, without getting into difficulty with current expenses. In Hamburg he knew a former friend from Cologne who happened to be in good financial circumstances and who to repay him for many services rendered had often, including recently, offered him financial aid. He wrote to him from his father's room. The friend was to obtain a place on a passenger ship for his brother, defray his expenses for accommodation and hand him, but not until immediately before departure, a certain sum of money, all on Apollonius's account. Valentine was sent that very evening to the post to hand in the letter and to book a seat on the mail coach for Fritz Nettenmaier. The coach left an hour before daybreak; one hour earlier than that, Valentine was to be ready and report to the old gentleman.

So life in the house with the green shutters had become even more oppressive. This night with its hushed restlessness was like the anxious stillness in which a storm at sea gathers up its strength before unleashing its full fury. It was a strange ferment. Anyone who could have looked into the house that night, but not into the souls of the people in it, would have stumbled from one source of astonishment to another. Normally when one family member is preparing for a journey from which he may perhaps never return, the others throng around him. The less time he has left to spend with them the more that time will be enjoyed to the full. Years of living together are compressed into it. Every look, every word, every handshake is given, and taken, as an everlasting remembrance. From miles around the friends of the person departing come to see him one last time. But the people in this house did not concern themselves with Fritz Nettenmaier. They shuddered to meet him as if he were a terrifying ghost. And just like a ghost he crept around avoiding people as much as they avoided him. And the people he avoids and who avoid him are not strangers; they're his father, his brother, his wife and his children. He's a traveller who no on sees, who keeps out of sight, who says farewell to no one and to whom no one says farewell and yet who travels of his own free will and whose journey the others know about and sanction!

Apollonius had to read out the accounts to the old gentleman, a strangely purposeless activity! For neither he nor the old gentleman had their minds on the figures. And anyway the old gentleman pretended he knew it all already. The fact that Apollonius had kept from him the danger the firm had been in he naturally did not mention; of the thoughts he had about this he allowed none to be seen. From the things he made the effort to say in his hypocritical way from time to time, in order to give the whole sham a semblance of reality before his son, it was perhaps possible for anyone, who paid more particular attention than Apollonius was able to do, to divine that the old gentleman had let matters go in order to show what a mess they would get into if he took his hand off the tiller, and that he was now once more minded to steer the ship himself from now on. Between times he asked his son once, as if by the way, whether he knew anything more definite about the man who had come to grief in Tambach. Apollonius was able to tell him that he knew the man; it was the unpleasant journeyman who had previously been with them. "Really?" said the old gentleman unfeelingly. "And is the cause of the accident known?" Apollonius had heard that the rope which had snapped above him had been almost new but must have been cut through all round with a sharp tool at the place where it had broken. The old gentleman was shocked. He suspected there was a connection to which other things might be linked. Valentine, he knew, had previously mentioned that the workman who had taken the cart with the tools to Brambach, must have lost a pulley rope on the way back. Apollonius had reassured Valentine that he had himself lent out the rope in Brambach. The old gentleman was now convinced that even Apollonius must suspect some connection, even if suspect it was all he did, and that when answering Valentine he had tried to avoid looking directly at him. He saw that Apollonius was acting in the same spirit as he was. So there was nothing to fear from that quarter. But there might be other circumstances to consider, which despite Apollonius's precautions, might threaten discovery. Hard though it was for him, he now set aside his reserve and after repeated questions Apollonius had to say what he knew. This was it. On the first day in Brambach Apollonius had only used the ladders. The journeyman had been in the inn when he arrived. That same evening he had seen him creeping across the yard. In the morning the rope had been missing. He had immediately suspected the journeyman, but in his conscientious way he had hesitated to accuse him openly. On his way home, just by the town gate, he had heard of the accident that had befallen him; also that the journeyman had not been employed by any master slater but had taken on the small repair to the roof in Tambach off his own bat. One item among the tools he had left behind, an axe, had already been claimed by the rightful owner. Soon afterwards, the warning given him by

Christiane had made him aware that the rope which had caused the journeyman's accident had been his. As matters now stood he naturally dared not now admit ownership of it; he even had to do violence to his own honesty in order by means of fabrications to prevent anyone suspecting the truth.

The old gentleman ordered his son to go on reading out the accounts. Apollonius did so, but both of them again had their minds on other things. Apollonius tried to force himself to go on with it. Not having his heart and soul in what he was doing was quite contrary to his usual way of doing things. He did not succeed. Thus even a well-balanced, well-ordered mind like his was disturbed by outside events. Finally Valentine came in, received the money for the fare for Fritz Nettenmaier and the letter to the friend in Hamburg and the order to take the traveller's luggage to the mail coach office and, waiting in case there were any errands, to stay nearby until Fritz had departed. An hour later Valentine came back and had carried out his orders fully. He told how Fritz Nettenmaier had been looking forward to his new life in America. They would be amazed at him when they saw him again. He could scarcely wait. The old gentleman inwardly took new heart; he said grimly that Apollonius was half asleep and could no longer read so he sent him to bed. They would have to find another time to continue the work they had begun.

And what of Fritz Nettenmaier? What mood was he in during this long night? While he crept restlessly like a tormented ghost, alternately wringing his hands and clenching his fists, along the passage from the house to the shed and back again from the shed to the house? One moment he recoiled in fear from a falling leaf, the next he wished the house would fall on him and bury him. Every time he walked the length of the passage his mind would flare up in the wildest defiance and then sink back again into the most abject helplessness. He had made up his mind to go – yet could he leave her to the man he hated? Could he leave them to scorn him? They'd driven him on in order to get rid of him; then their dearest wish would be fulfilled. No! He would stay! He must stay! – And yet then the magistrates would arrest him – for old blue coat always kept his word – and they would clap him in chains, and –the result would be the same. They would have achieved their purpose again. –Fritz Nettenmaier waved his arms violently in front of him as if he was already rattling the bars of the prison window and breathed so painfully as if the fumes from the damp walls were already stifling him. Then suddenly weary, there came over him the full realisation of his infinite misery, the despair of being completely abandoned. Golden images came into his mind; their vision of the supreme happiness he had lost tormented him more than the bed of nails he had gained. Then he was an innocent child skipping down this self same passage along which he now struggled to drag the heavy burden of his misery; then there were people who loved him. How sweet was his mother's voice as she called him! And now nobody loved him any more. Strangers despised him; those who should have loved him now shuddered when they saw him. If only there was one single heart which would feel sad to see him depart he would go and would be a different man! Now he sees for the first time every friendly glance which he had not noticed when blinded by the violence of his feelings. The smile on little Annie's face as it winced in fear comes into his mind; now he recognizes the inexhaustible love which he rejected and which always returned however often he rejected it, till he broke the vessel that held it; now, when she could have saved him were she not dead because of him; now pity for the child fills him so painfully and so powerfully that he would have forgotten his own misery as a result were it not part of it. Annie's dead, but he has other children; they must love him, for they are, after all, his children. His heart cries out for a word of love. His arms open wide convulsively, ready to press what is his to his heart, so that he knows he is not abandoned; and no one is completely abandoned who has on e other person in the world for him. With powers renewed he hurries along the passage again, through the hall, through the lounge and bedroom door. A nightlight protected by a shade gives the father enough light to see his children. He sinks to his knees by the nearest little bed. A long forgotten sound is whispered through his lips, in a way these lips could never have whispered it before. "Fritz!" He only wants to press the children once to his heart, to see their love and –go. Go and be a different man, a better man, a happier man! The child wakes up; he thinks his mother has called him. He opens his large eyes in a smile and –starts back in fear. He is afraid of the man by his bed. It's a strange man. A man more wicked than strange. An all too familiar man! And yet stranger than strange. It's the man the child has so often seen angry, the man for fear of whom his mother had shut him in the bedroom because he didn't want to see what the man did to her. And on those occasions he had stood trembling at the door listening, then his little fists had clenched in impotent rage. Oh yes, he had taught the child to hate him, not love him.

"Fritz", said his father anxiously, "I'm going away; I'm not coming back. But I'll send you some nice apples and picture books and I'll think of you every minute a thousand times."

"I don't want anything from you", said the boy in a timid but defiant voice. "Uncle Lonius gives me apples; I don't want yours."

"Don't you love me either?" he asked, his voice breaking, by the second bed. Young George fled from him into his brother's bed. There they held on to each other in fear. Nevertheless George too is defiant and his look expresses as much loathing as a child's eye is capable of. "I love mother, I love Uncle Lonius", he says, "but I don't love you. Let us go or I'll tell Uncle Lonius!"

Fritz Nettenmaier laughs wildly for scorn and sobs at the same time for helpless grief. The children are no longer his. He's no longer their father. But **he** is! Apollonius is! He's their father. He's taken everything from him, even the children. The most wretched of men is still left his children. If it was Apollonius who had to leave, the children would be hanging on to him; their little hands would have to be torn away rather than let go of him. And his wife here, this beautiful woman with the angel's face on which the lamp concentrates all its rays so lovingly and which receives more radiance from her than she from the lamp; this woman, no longer his wife, was his brother's! Like everything else which was once mine! She's gone to bed in her clothes; she can't wait for me to go; but if **he** were going, these roses on her cheek would grow pale, she would cling to him and die rather than be separated from him. How she would start up in that dream she is having of him, for she is smiling, if someone in her dream said that he was leaving, he, her ---. No! I won't leave! No! I can't go! A thousand times better to die! And he has already looked Death in the face, only hours before, when he lay on the scaffolding in front of his father. It was child's play, dying, compared with a life like this. It was – for Apollonius too would also be dead. It still would be if Apollonius were also dead. And he would be avenged on her, on her with the infernal angelic smile; and he would be avenged on his father, who had torn him away from Beatrice, his good angel. And on the boys who had rejected him, on dead little Annie, who had helped to destroy him and still tormented him day and night. He would be – but he wasn't. He had to leave; he would be still more miserable than he was now; and those he hated, who had destroyed him, would be happy if he went. Once more he made them all into Demons so as not to be blinded by their radiance. Once more he hated them for what he had done to them; he hated them for the violent effort he had to make to see them as Demons. And were their radiance to break through the darkness in which he fearfully kept them hidden, were they to stand above him as angels, he would hate them still with the envy of the Devil. He had crossed the border-line from which there is no return. As he saw the woman lying there in all her beauty, the thought of destroying this beauty once more entered his mind. But the newly recalled memory of the moment when he lay before his father resigned to death, of what his father had wanted of him, proved more powerful and drove the idea away. The image of that moment remained with him, merely the participants changed. He pictured the scene more and more colourfully. And now it was wild joy that drove him up and down the passage between the house and the shed. His arms waved about as violently as before, but this time it was not prison bars against which they grappled. Meanwhile the moon had risen. The house with the green shutters lay peacefully bathed in its glow. No passer-by would have been aware of the tumult hidden behind its walls; no one would have suspected the thoughts which Hell was brewing up in one irredeemable vessel.

18

Apollonius was tired out from waking and from the struggle which the dangerous presence nearby of the woman he loved and the knowledge of his brother's betrayal and shocking ingratitude had inflamed in him. Alongside this a new struggle had now flared up. His father seemed not to believe his brother's evil intentions. He shrank back from the thought of calling the arm of the law to his support. The shame for the family if what his brother had done was widely known would have killed his father. And perhaps it was still possible to save his brother's soul if only they could convince him that he had done wrong. But how? What if he ---assured him, swore to him, that in future Christiane would be no more to him than a sister? Six months ago, even, he would still have been able to swear that on his honour; today he dared no longer do it, today it would be perjury. If his brother did not give up the invidious threat to his life, he could make it more difficult for him to carry it out, but not prevent it entirely. In the circumstances in which Apollonius found himself, death could well be rather to be wished than feared; then all the struggling, the pangs of conscience, all the cares would come to an end; but what would become of his father, what would become of her and the children? And had he not given his word that he would protect her from dishonour and need? This new struggle was ended by his father's announcement that Fritz was going to America. But it made the old struggle even more difficult by giving the enemy renewed strength. He knew for certain that he was determined not to allow the desires, which he was compelled to condemn as sinful, to come to fruition. But what about the desires themselves? If no external barrier stood in the way of their fulfilment any longer, wouldn't their strength inevitably grow? And with them the pangs of conscience? And the proximity of the inexhaustible source of their daily renewal once again made it impossible to fulfil his word that he had given, the duty incumbent on him even without his word. He was in severe turmoil and needed rest. But this very morning he had to complete the crowning of the church steeple with the ornamental metalwork and then take down the cradle, the pulleys, the ring and the ladder again. His step needed to be firm, his eye clear. For the single hour remaining before the day's work began he did not want at first to undress and lie on his bed. Up to now he had not used the sofa that stood in his room to lie on. He avoided everything that could lead to weakness; an equally strong motive was his need to have things around him which he could lovingly take care of, could brush and polish. Even in the state of bewilderment and tiredness in which he came back from seeing his father, he did not forget this careful treatment of things. Involuntarily he stroked the cover of the sofa with a gentle caressing hand and then sat on the wooden chair where he usually sat for writing. Sleep overcame him before he was expecting it. But it was not the kind of sleep he needed; it was an uninterrupted disturbing dream. Christiane lay in his arms as the day before, he struggled with his desires as before, but this time he did not win; he pressed her to him. Then his brother was standing next to them, and they were no longer in the passage between the shed and the house but up on the roof of the church spire on the flying scaffold. His brother tried to tear the unconscious woman from his arms in order to ill-treat her; with bitter anger he reproached his brother with everything that he had done to him and to her, and in the struggle to hold on to her he pushed his brother from the scaffolding. He woke up. He wanted to stay awake so as not to have to go through the dream again. When he opened his eyes it was already day and time to go to work. He had woken up in a more disturbed state than when he came back from his father. He stood up. He hoped that the fresh morning air as well as the sobering effect of the water which it was his habit to splash over his head and arms would dispel the images from his dream, which could only exacerbate even more the intensity of his old desires and with them the pangs of conscience they caused. But it didn't work; the images from the dream went with him and would not leave him. Not even in his work. All the time he felt the warm breath from her mouth on his cheek; all the time he felt himself in her tightening embrace, all the time he heard pouring from his mouth and his heart the passionate recriminations against his brother who stood beside him. He hardly knew himself any longer. As well as reproaching himself for all this, he was discontented because he knew he was not giving his whole attention to his work. Otherwise he would, as it were, have ingrained his own cheerful efficiency into his work and this would inevitably turn out good and lasting. But today it seemed to him that he was hammering into his work his improper thoughts, hammering into shape some evil magic, and the work might not answer its purpose, might not endure.

The slater must be level-headed and work sensibly. The man who undertakes a repair on a roof today must rely on the professional integrity of those who decades, even centuries, earlier worked here before him. Unreliable workmanship which fastens a roof hook carelessly one day can send to his death the brave man who fifty years later hangs his ladder on this hook. It was not to be supposed that some negligence, some mistake in the work he was completing that day, would have such serious consequences; but his natural cautious accuracy was still one of the factors, along with his other skills, in his abnormal feeling of tension. Behind the struggle of his conscience with the images of his sinful dream there threatened like a dark cloud the suspicion that as a result of his distraction he was hammering into place some future catastrophe.

He had finished. The new ornamental metalwork shone dazzlingly in the sun round the dark surfaces of the slate roof. The ring, pulleys, cradle and ladders were removed; the workmen, who had held the ladders while they were being unfastened and taken down, had gone away again. Apollonius had unfastened the flying scaffold and the poles on which it rested from the roof timbers and stood alone on the narrow plank which formed the bridge between the cross beams and the hatch. He stood there deep in thought. He felt as if he had forgotten to knock in some nails somewhere or other. He looked in the nail box and the slate box on the cradle which hung from a beam beside him. A furtive hasty footstep was heard coming up the tower stairs below him. He paid no attention to it; for just at that moment he noticed in the slate box a sheet of lead that had not been used. He had brought up with him only so many sheets of lead as he needed; so he must have forgotten to fix one of them; in his distracted state he had overlooked one of the fastening points. He looked out of the hatchway up and down the surface of the roof. If the mistake had happened on this side of the tower, it could perhaps be put right without using the cradle. He would perhaps only need the ladder to get to the spot. And so it turned out. About six foot above him, near the roof hook, he had removed the slate but forgotten to replace it with the sheet of lead and to nail down the metal garland to it. Meanwhile the furtive footsteps had come nearer and nearer; the hurrying person had reached the top of the stone stairs and was climbing the ladder up to the roof timbers. The clock beneath him was gearing up to strike. It was coming up to two o'clock. Apollonius had not yet stopped for lunch; if he was on the track of some error in his work he could not rest until he had removed it. He had gone back to fetch the ladder which lay on the beam beside the cradle. As he bent down for it he felt himself seized and pushed with violent force towards the hatch. Involuntarily he grasped with his right hand the bottom edge of a beam that lay laterally above him; with his left hand he sought in vain to stop his forward motion. In doing so he twisted himself round to face his attacker. Horrified he found himself looking into a distorted face. It was the wild, pale face of his brother. He had no time to wonder how he came to be here.

"What do you want", he cried. Whatever he heard he wouldn't be able to believe it. He was answered with a horrible mad laugh; "Either you'll have her all to yourself or you'll go down with me!"

"Get away from me!" shouted Apollonius. With anguished grief and rage all his reproaches against his brother now appeared on his face. With all his strength he pushed back against the man who was pressing him forward.

"So, you're showing your real face at last?" sneered his brother, now even more angry. "You've driven me away from every place I held; now it's my turn. You'll have me on your conscience, you fussy devil! Hurl me down there or you'll go down with me!"

Apollonius could see no escape. The hand with which he was only barely managing to hang on to the sharp edge of the beam was weakening. He would have to grab his brother by the arms with his whole strength, turn him round and send him crashing down or his brother would pull him down with him. Nevertheless he shouted, "Not me!"

"Fine!" grunted his brother. "You'll blame me for that too! You'll bring me to that too! Now all your hypocrisy will come to an end!" Apollonius would have tried to find another handhold if he wasn't absolutely sure that his brother would take advantage of the moment he let go of the old one. And already he was charging wildly forward! Apollonius' hand slipped from the edge of the beam. If he can't find another handhold quickly he's lost. Perhaps he can with a leap grasp the beam with both hands, but then his brother's wild impetus, no longer meeting any resistance would hurtle him down through the hatch. With his mind's eye he sees his proud old father, sees Christiane and the children; he remembers the promise he made; he is the only support for his nearest and dearest; he must stay alive. A swing and he has the beam in both arms; at the same moment his brother hurtles past. The weights on the pendulum far below them rattle and the clock strikes two.

The jackdaws, disturbed out of their slumber by the struggle, swoop wildly down to the hatch and hover there in a flock, cawing loudly. Far below them the sound of a heavy body falling on the pavement is heard. At the same moment an outcry resounds on all sides. Pale living faces look down on an even paler dead one, that lies there on the pavement covered in blood. Then there is a rushing around, exclaiming aloud, gathering of people, wringing of hands which spreads like a whirlwind from the church-yard through the streets to the farthest corner of the town. But high above, the clouds in the sky pay no attention and go serenely on their way. They see so much self-inflicted misery beneath them that a single example can have no effect on them.

Everything that happens in the world has its uses; if not for the one who causes it or whom it affects, then for others. It was the same now; what had brought scandal on the Nettenmaier house became the thing that prevented still greater scandal. Fritz Nettenmaier's habitual drunkenness was well-known throughout the town; everybody had seen him tipsy; so it was no wonder everyone who heard of his death put it down to that weakness of the flesh. Only the first people really had to make the connection, everyone else learnt it as an established fact. It was a good thing no one outside the immediate family knew that he had planned to go to

America and that he had got into the mail coach in his work clothes, with just an overcoat thrown over them, in order to be less conspicuous on his return. His coat had been dumped somewhere en route and those who were expecting him naturally did not report him missing. He had returned wearing merely his work clothes. Anyone who knew he was leaving assumed he had first gone home and changed; anyone who met him on the way back thought he was coming from the slate quarry or from some other job or professional consultation. It occurred to no one to lay any store by the barely noticed circumstances that had relevance to this, since there was no point in trying to reconstruct a story which had come to them already complete. Moreover, before the fatal act he had been drinking hard in his usual locals and had been boasting in his daredevil way. As was his nature he had always seen this as the highest characteristic of an ideal slater and during the time when he was active he had given sufficient proof of this which had not remained unnoticed by the authorities. Then he had said in a loud voice that now he was going to carry out his masterpiece and, very much the worse for wear, he had gone from the ale-house straight to Saint George's. All these circumstances got about and only confirmed the generally accepted opinion. By a lucky chance all the workmen had left St George's; the only ones who knew of the struggle before the fall were Apollonius and the jackdaws who lived there. The architect had gone to find his protégé immediately he had heard what had happened and had brought this already fully-developed account with him to where he found him sitting, completely exhausted, at the base of the tower. So it occurred to no one to question

Apollonius. They told him, instead of letting him tell them. In his grief at what his father must be suffering he had been pleased that no one knew the true facts of the case; his brother's dishonour, and with it that of the whole family, could help no one and could be the death of his father. He kept silent, therefore, about everything they didn't ask him directly. The old gentleman suspected that his lost son had intentionally sought his own death. He found that it was well it should be so. Everything he heard proved to him that his unfortunate son had wanted to save the honour of his house. Nevertheless he was bothered by the possibility that circumstances might still come to light which would correct the general erroneous opinion. Naturally, though, he did not allow what he thought or feared to be seen. He did not even reveal it to Apollonius who, in the belief that the old gentleman shared the sentiments of the whole town, also kept quiet about what he was afraid would unnecessarily shock and worry his father. So the initial opinion of the matter remained undisputed, the magistrates found no cause to take any steps to investigate, and the danger threatening the family honour happily went away.

So one evening the black bier was seen outside the house with the green shutters, which kept its eyes closed to it, in order to vindicate its rose-pink exterior. A little further off, groups of women and children gathered, sometimes quietly whispering, sometimes with a keen attention which on occasions almost amounted to impatience. The same stir and the same sensations with which the more educated stratum of the population wait for the moment when the curtain goes up on some moving scene in the theatre; the same need has drawn these blue aprons here as that which assembles those wearing the most beautiful dresses there. From time to time a black coat and tricorn hat comes down the road in the most austere solemnity and steps behind the bier into the house. Finally the double-door opens wide. The coffin stands on the bier, the shroud covers both; quietly and steadily the black swaying shape is raised; now it's in place for the bearers straighten their hats. And now it's on its swaying unsteady way. On the top gleams the slate-hammer which Valentine has polished and which is meant to show that the man they are now giving up to the earth has worked honourably between Heaven and Earth. The old women with their sweet tears wash away anything that besmirches his memory. Inwardly they promise themselves not to let anyone in their family become a slater if they can help it. Working as a slater up there between Heaven and Earth is a dangerous profession; that is the sermon preached with most moving eloquence, although so silently, by the man lying there beneath the fluttering black cloth between the boards. Then they look over the old gentleman who is supported by two mourners. He looks the very Spirit of a proper funeral. Yet at the sight of the tall slender figure of Apollonius alongside the worthy architect they forget the leniency they have shown so far; in their minds they bury the dead man again without his borrowed pomp, without the wet funeral wreaths which cover his human, all too human nakedness. If it were merely up to the dead man himself the hammer on the coffin would be covered in the dark rust of shame, it's Apollonius he has to thank for the fact that the tool that lies on his last bed is so spotless. And has he deserved it of him? No one will say that he has. If only the dead man could hear this through the planks and the black drapery he would have had yet one more thing to forgive his brother for. Or not to forgive; he had forgiven him nothing, not what Apollonius had done to him and not what he had done to Apollonius. And if he could see fully into the heart of his brother, from which his death had washed all trace of a resentment, which had only been full of reproach because it saw a wicked man when it should have felt sorry for a sad unstable man, he would have steeped himself still further in devilish envy. Then it's the turn of the young wife, and as is the wont of their sex the female mourners change suddenly into matchmakers. And with some truth! They are not wrong; a more perfect couple, one that was better matched, where each was worthy of the other, could not be found in the entire town by even greater connoisseurs in this field. The procession went past the Red Eagle. There was already a dance upstairs there at which Fritz Nettenmaier was absent, a very dull dance obviously! "Here he is! Here he is!" rang out on all sides towards the procession and accompanied it tirelessly the entire length of the street. But nevertheless there was no way it was fun. It was the same road Fritz had returned along after he had accompanied the journeyman. On that occasion he had envisioned his brother beneath the slate hammer and the flowing black drapery and he himself walking along behind him in mourning. Now in the real world the situation had been reversed, but Apollonius genuinely felt what his brother merely put on for the sake of appearance. And so the procession went on through the streets along which Fritz Nettenmaier had come then. And outside the town gate again the willows dissolved into mist or mist thickened into willows. On both sides figures in the mist carried misty coffins alongside the real one. At the crossroads where Fritz Nettenmaier had then watched the journeyman disappear into the mist, he now disappeared into it himself. Would he be pleased if someone told him he would see his friend again? Would accompany him again? – but where to? They are just engaged in burying him in Tambach too. They have a lot to say to each other. Fritz Nettenmaier can tell the journeyman how carefully he has carried out the germ of the idea the latter gave him, even to the extent of cutting the rope and the journeyman can tell his former boss that he was killed thanks to the very cut in the rope which the latter had made. The clergyman who gives the funeral sermon – for Fritz Nettenmaier is buried with all the honours befitting his status and obtainable by money –does not know what a fruitful subject for a moral hominy he is missing.

The last word of the sermon had died away, the last handful of earth had fallen on Fritz Nettenmaier's coffin, the mourners had gone home; night had come and then day again and again night, and again and again night and day; other things had driven Fritz Nettenmaier's accident from the minds of the town and other things again had driven out these. On his grave a stone had been placed and on this his respectable death had been once more attested and enjoined upon neglectful posterity by the monumental mason with his chisel. One would have thought that the dark clouds looming over the house with the green shutters must have burst in the thunderclap which had dashed the elder son to the ground from the tower of St George's, and that the life in that house must now become as cheerful as its outward appearance seemed to promise. Yes, one would have thought so if one saw the young widow or her children! These three resilient people once more raised their downcast heads as soon as the burden which had depressed them, was lifted. The young widow did not look as if she had already been a wife, still less that she had been an unhappy wife; every day she appeared more and more like a girl about to marry or a girl bride. And why not? Didn't she know that he loved her? Did she not love him? Did not the teasing of others inevitably remind her, if she did not think of it herself, that her love was now sanctioned? How often did she have to put up with questions about whether she was already preparing her trousseau? And hearing the children asked whether they would like a new papa? Could she answer in any other way than with a silent blush and by quickly beginning to speak of something else? And that's how girls about to marry and girl brides behave; everyone knows that. And the marriage was such a natural thing, so necessary according to conventional ideas, that the more serious people and those who were beyond mere teasing, took it for granted and did not speak of it simply because it was self-evident to them. Even the old gentleman in his hypocritical way of speaking did not omit to drop hints to that effect. Christiane saw the man, whom everybody thought could or must surely marry her, still far above her; in this respect as in all others it was to her a need, a duty and an almost sensual pleasure to devote herself to his will which she knew to be the purest and the most saintly. If, despite this devotion, she cherished other hopes and wishes, who would not have thought it natural? Who would have blamed her?

The old gentleman was convinced that if he had kept the reins in his own hand things would have turned out differently. Yet he had managed to carry on what Apollonius had ruined to the best conclusion that was possible. Necessity had forced him to take the reins back into his own hands and he was not going to let them go again. The heightened opinion of himself, which had come about thanks to his fortunate success, had caused him to forget that he had already twice before been forced to the conclusion that taking control in his old blue-coat style was only possible if one did not have to brook any opposing views. He was now to learn it for the third time. It was no wonder that he put a false construction on Apollonius's motives for acting the way he had up to now. Already, even while he had been rejoicing at his son's ability, he had felt a certain fear which Valentine's confession that matters had been concealed from him had only confirmed. Behind his son's alleged careful treatment of him he saw only highhandedness and a desire not to show his hand, a view that was all the more natural because he was judging him by his own standards. It was the most natural thing for him to assume his son had the same propensities as himself. Even then he had felt a kind of jealousy that, as against his son's youth and ability, he himself in his blindness was no use any longer, could be no use. The suspiciousness his helplessness had taught him inevitably told him that, despite his efforts to conceal it, Apollonius had seen through this fact, and so he saw contempt as part of the motivation for his son's actions.

Since that night before his eldest son's violent death, Herr Nettenmaier had once again become the head of the firm. Apollonius reported to him each day on the progress of the current work and received his orders. Once a piece of work is running on the right tracks it continues without further direction and all it needs is supervision and occasional encouragement from the man in charge. But if a new piece of work should be undertaken then it is important first to try to find the tracks on which it can run and to choose from these the shortest, the safest and the most profitable. The employer often makes the task more difficult because he wants to interfere himself or has particular secondary desires which the master craftsman is to fulfil at the same time. The place, the time and the material all make their individual claims and assert their particular needs. Not every piece of work can be entrusted to every workman; the master craftsman must not neglect the current work for the sake of the new. Choice, proper employment of time and division of labour have their difficulties. Distance and the weather also have their say. All of this needs to be overcome and overcome in such a way that the wishes and interests of the contractor do not conflict with the reputation and the interests of the craftsman. For that an open mind and clear eye that can quickly obtain an overview of the problem are necessary. The old gentleman recognised that Apollonius possessed these from the very first time he gave his report. This concerned a particularly difficult job. Apollonius described it with such clarity that the old gentleman could almost see things with his own eyes. It was a case where the old gentleman's experience failed him. It was no problem to Apollonius. He pointed out three or four different ways in which the job could be carried out and caused a confusion in the old gentleman's mind that he could scarcely conceal. Over the bony forehead, beneath the covering eye-shield, passed a wild profusion of the most contradictory feelings; pleasure and pride in his son, then pain that he himself was no longer any use, could be no more use; then shame and anger that his son knew this and triumphed over him; the desire to cut him down to size and show him that he was still lord and master. But if he tried to assert his authority, would his son obey? He could think of nothing better than what his son had proposed; if he ordered something different he only strengthened his son in his lack of respect for him; and in any case he would merely give the appearance of carrying out his father's orders while really doing exactly what he wanted himself. And he could not prevent that, could not compel him. He had perforce to believe what his son, what other people told him. Had he not for eighteen months already had to believe what his son, helped by others, told him? And if he appointed a third party to keep watch on his son, could he be sure of the loyalty of that third party? And even if he could be, was he not exposing his helplessness to the light of day, so that the whole town learned he was a blind man who was no longer any use, could no longer be of use and who could be toyed with as one wished? He no longer had any means of even appearing to be in control, except for his ability to simulate confidence. He now gave his orders in a grim voice, orders which were not really necessary because they concerned things which were obvious and which would have been done without an order anyway. With new work which had first to be set in motion, he angrily rejected Apollonius's proposals; but the order which he finally gave amounted after all in the main to the acceptance of the proposal which had seemed to Apollonius the most practical. On the quiet he tried to build himself up again as far as possible; if he found out something which he considered more sensible than what Apollonius proposed; if he convinced himself that if he still had his sight everything would go quite differently, then he could freely indulge in the pleasure and the pride of having such an able son, until he once more found himself in the angry necessity of having to use his hypocritical skills again. Apollonius had as little idea of the pressure he unintentionally put on the old gentleman as of the latter's pride in him. He was pleased that he no longer had to keep anything about the business secret from him and that his obedience did not stand in the way of the fulfilment of his promise. Even for this side of things the sky above the house with the green shutters was becoming ever more blue. But the spirit of the house still crept around inside wringing its hands. Whenever the clock struck two in the night it stood in the gallery by the door to Apollonius's room and raised its pale arms to Heaven as if in supplication.

19

Apollonius, when he was at home, kept himself to himself in his room. Old Valentine brought him his food there as usual. No one could be surprised at that. The business had grown in his hard-working hands; compared with before it was now worth more than twice as much on paper. The postman brought whole bundles of letters to the house. In addition Apollonius had recently accepted the advantageous offer of the quarry owner and had leased the slate quarry. From his time in Cologne he had learnt how to run a slate-quarrying business and had sent for a former acquaintance from there who he knew was well-versed in the business and was generally reliable. His choice turned out to be a good one; the man was hard-working; but nevertheless Apollonius had a significant increase in work from taking on the lease. The old architect sometimes looked at him with concern and thought Apollonius had taken on more than he could chew. It did not surprise the young widow that Apollonius only rarely came into the sitting-room. The children, whom he often called to him to do small services for him from which they might learn, maintained communications. And they could testify that Apollonius had no spare time. She herself was more often in his room; but only when he was not at home. She decorated the doors and walls with everything she had and which she knew he liked, and stayed working there sometimes for hours on end. But she too noticed the paleness of his face which seemed to have got worse each time after she had not seen him for a while. As she had now become a complete mirror of him, she too reflected this paleness. She would have gladly cheered him up, but she did not seek to be near him; it seemed to her as if her presence near him had the opposite effect from the one she intended. He was always friendly and full of gallantry towards her. That at least reassured her against the fear which concerned her most, that of his complete withdrawal into himself. Just as she had endowed him with every virtue she knew, as if he were some sort of shrine, she had not neglected to include truthfulness which was the greatest of all to her. And so she knew he would not make the effort to show his regard for her if he did not feel it. He sometimes laughed at himself, especially if he saw her looking anxiously at his ever paler face; but she noticed that, despite this, her company did not make him any brighter or any healthier. She would have loved to ask him what was wrong. Whenever he stood before her she did not dare; whenever she was alone she asked him. For whole nights she racked her brains to find words which would coax a confession from him, and spoke to him in her thoughts. Of course, if he had heard her weeping, heard how she cajoled and begged him in ever sweeter and more ardent terms, heard the sweet names she used for him, he would have had to say what was wrong with him. Her whole life was poised then between her heart and her mouth; but if she once heard the words come out, heard what she said, then she blushed and her blush fled from her own self and from the listening night deep under the blankets.

She confided her worries to the friendly architect. "Is it any wonder", he said forcefully, "when he spends every day for a year and a half exerting himself excessively and sitting up every night over books and papers? Then, on top of that there were the increasing worries caused by –God forgive him, he's dead and one should not speak ill of the dead –caused by his brother; and the last straw the fear, which even made me ill for three days, that --, and even though I'm saying it in the presence of his widow, I have to admit that I never really liked him, least of all at the end. Still, that's youth for you. I must have warned him a hundred times, the determined young man. And now the damned slate quarry! Conscientiousness indeed! But he's not being conscientious if he doesn't consider his own health!" The old architect gave the young widow a severe lecture, but one that was really meant for the person who didn't hear it. Then they came to an agreement that Apollonius should see a doctor whether he wanted to or not; and the architect went immediately to the best doctor in town. The doctor promised to do his best. He called on Apollonius who submitted to the attentions of the doctor, but only because those he loved wished it. The doctor took his pulse, came again and again, prescribed this and that; Apollonius merely became paler and paler and more and more gloomy. In the end this experienced and highly-qualified doctor had to admit that there was some malady here against which all his science was of no avail, an illness so deeply engrained that none of his remedies had any effect.

Apollonius had therefore refused to see the doctor any more. He knew well enough that there was no cure for his sickness. Its cause was only partly what the architect thought it was. Overexertion had merely prepared the ground for the parasitic plant which was eating away at Apollonius's inner core. Its roots lay in his emotions but not in those the architect thought. Not in the shock of his brother's accident, but in the situation he was in when the shock occurred. The first symptoms of the illness seemed to be of a physical nature. At the very moment when his brother plunged past him to his death, the clock below them had struck two. From then on any clock striking filled him with terror. What caused him even more concern was an attack of vertigo. All the horrors of that day had not been able to obscure his anxiety when he found an inaccuracy in a piece of work and it never left him until it had been put right. Every time a clock struck it seemed to him a reminder of that. The very next morning he had opened the hatch with the roof ladder in his hand. He had already noticed how unsteady his foot had been on the step-ladder up the tower; now when he saw through the opening the distant mountains, which he had scarcely noticed before, swaying towards him and the solid tower beneath him began to rock, he was frightened. This was vertigo, the slater's worst and most insidious enemy when it attacks him suddenly on the unsteady ladder up there between heaven and earth! In vain he strove to overcome it; but for that day what he had intended to do had had to be given up. Never had he found a climb more difficult than that down the step-ladder of the tower of St George's. What was going to happen! How was he going to fulfil his promise if the vertigo stayed with him! The same day he had to see to something on the tower of St Nicholas's. Here he had to do something more dangerous than at St George's; the clock struck when he was standing at the most dangerous part but he felt not the slightest trace of vertigo. Full of joy he hurried back to St George's; but once again the step-ladder trembled beneath his feet and as he looked out the mountains swayed and the tower again rocked. He was already on the lowest rung of the ladder when the clock began to strike above. It rang and resounded through to the very core of his being; he had to hang on tight to the hand-rail until the last vibrations had died away. He tried again and again; he climbed up all the other roofs and towers with his old confidence; only at St Georges's did he suffer from vertigo. There he had hammered his wicked thoughts into the work; he had felt even at the time that he was hammering some magic spell into shape, was putting the finishing touches to some future disaster. He was haunted day and night by the image of the place where he had forgotten to insert the sheet of lead and to fasten the metal garland. The gap was a bad spot, a place where a crime is planned or carried out, where no grass grows and there are no shadows; like an open wound which does not heal until it has been avenged; like an empty grave which does not close until it has taken in its dead. If only the gap was closed the magic spell would have no more power. He could have given the job to a journeyman, but the thought of leaving someone else to put right his neglected work caused a blush of shame to suffuse his pale cheeks. And in any case if the sheet of lead was nailed on by someone else it would be bound to fall off again; the gap cried out for him and only he could close it. Or the journeyman would be caught up by the rottenness which he had hammered in, by the vertigo which was built into it, and which would plunge him to his death.

Since his brother's wife had lain in his arms, he led a double life. He worked long hours every day out of the house, and spent his nights sitting in his room over his books; all that went on quite mechanically; despite his financial worries he only had half his mind on the job; the other half had its own life, for ever hovering with the jackdaws around the gap in the spire roof and brooding on what coming disaster he had hammered home that morning. Again and again he dreamed through his sinful dream, fought through the terrible fight with his brother. Was it his brother's headlong fall that he had been hammering in place? Then he began to wonder whether it had not been possible to save him in his madness. Then he began to rack his brains anxiously to discover the means by which he might have been saved and shrank back in horror if he thought he should and could have found one. This was how guilt over his brother's death had unhinged him. But even in the way he brooded he revealed a nature totally opposite to that of his brother, where selfishness and an evil disposition predominated. In Apollonius's nature all that was good in him manifested itself in abundance; his conscientiousness, his loyalty and devotion and his innate need for neatness and integrity. He did not shift his guilt from himself onto his brother; rather he lovingly took his brother's guilt onto himself. For it became ever clearer to him that he could still have saved his brother before he fell. He would inevitably have found some way or other if his heart and mind had not been full of wild forbidden desires; if he had not been enraged by the mad fool whom he should have felt sorry for. Yes, he had hammered out his brother's downfall with his wicked thoughts. Without these thoughts he would have finished his work earlier and his brother would not have found him still up in the tower; his brother would have come too late and would have gained the time to repent of his decision. And even if he had still been up on the tower he was still the stronger of the two, the more sensible and was bound to have found some means of preventing the disaster. Even in outward behaviour this contrast with his brother was evident. While his brother had become more and more selfish, wilder and more reckless, Apollonius's mental suffering made him ever quieter and gentler. Despite his own situation he did not lose his compassion for the suffering of others. He did not feel sorry for himself. If he thought of the people who were lovingly close to him, his pain was more a kind of sympathy with their sympathy. He did not even forget to stroke his sofa with his hand; he did it in the same way one consoles a servant who feels his master's misfortune as his own. Naturally people also teased him about a marriage which they saw as necessary. He had to tell himself that he thought as they did and that his desires were no longer forbidden. But that they had once been so in the past cast a shadow over the irreproachable present. His love, his claim on her seemed somehow besmirched. Whatever reason and love might say he still felt guilty about such a marriage. So it came about that Christiane's presence did not cheer him. There were moments when his gloominess seemed even to him a kind of sickness and he hoped it would pass. But even so he did not come any closer to Christiane however much his heart drew him to her. He remained the same towards her as before, when he had set the boy down between them. The slightest of advances he interpreted in this fashion as a commitment, and if he thought marriage had been decided, the feeling of guilt once more weighed heavily on him. He put off any thought of it to some indeterminate future and only then did he feel his situation was bearable. And he was the man who normally could not bear any unclear relationship! But in this respect he was still entirely consistent, that in his thoughts he always felt any possible guilt was his alone. In all circumstances she remained saintly and pure.

To the old gentleman with his concept of public reputation, Apollonius and Christiane living together under the same roof without the sanction of the church in marriage was a serious scandal. Apollonius could only be the guardian and supporter of the beautiful young widow and her children without reproach if he was her husband. In his usual style he issued a peremptory order. He decreed when it should be. The necessary six months of mourning had now passed; in a week's time the betrothal would take place and three weeks after that the wedding.

Life in the house with the green shutters once again became more and more oppressive; the new clouds which had blown up unseen threatened a still sharper storm than that which the earlier ones had caused. The young widow was now able to appear as a bride-to-be. She did what she had been teased about before; she completed her trousseau. She sat up half the night cutting and sewing, bent over her white linen and brightly-coloured bed clothes. Tears fell on it, but less and less did joy form any part of these tears. She saw the condition of the man she loved get hourly worse, and could not doubt that the marriage was responsible. The paler and weaker he became the more did his behaviour towards her become more gentle and respectful. Indeed there was something in it which seemed like aching pity and an unspoken apology for some wrong or insult which he thought himself guilty of inflicting on her. She did not know what to think of it; she only knew that she couldn't think anything unworthy of the man whose image she bore in her very soul. In his presence she was as quiet as he was. She saw his silent, agonised brooding; but only when she was alone with her children asleep beside her did she have the courage to ask him. For hours she begged him, just like a child, to tell her what was wrong. She would bear it with him; she had no choice; was she not his?

And what of Apollonius himself? Until now he had managed to lessen the pressure of the guilty feelings which all thoughts of the marriage caused him by postponing having to make any decision to some indefinite future. In this he was helped by the hope that the feeling was just a morbid sickness which would pass. Now that the old gentleman had given his orders, that strategy had been taken from him. The goal was set; every day, every hour it was coming nearer. He must decide. He could not. The open division in his deepest feelings still yawned as widely as ever. If he gave up all ideas of happiness then the spectre of guilt receded, but the hope of happiness still stretched out its ever more enticing arms towards him. It used his sense of honour as its ally. What if his father were to send him away; how would he then be able to fulfil his word? Who could blame him if he took his happiness with open arms? His father wanted it; she loved him and had always loved him and only him; everybody approved it, even demanded it of him. Then he had a vision of her, before she was stolen from him, as she left the little flower for him, her rosy complexion beneath her curly brown hair which always refused to stay in place; then again pale-faced from the mistreatment of his brother who had stolen her from him, pale for his sake; then again trembling at his brother's threats, trembling for his sake; then again laughing, weeping, full of happiness and fear in his arms. And since she belonged to him, was his, he should be able to hold her in his arms like that without reproach! But despite her ever closer embrace, despite all the images of quiet tender happiness, the old terror still sent shivers down his spine. That had already been there in his earlier dream when he had fought his brother for her and pushed him down from the flying scaffold to his death. He told himself it was only a dream; what one did in a dream one had not done in reality. But even when awake the tempestuous feelings of his dream still reverberated. His wicked thoughts had made him incapable of saving his brother. His brother's fall left his wife free. He had known that when he had let his brother fall. In the dream that was why he had pushed him to his death. Now everything was as it had been in his bad dream, his brother was dead and his brother's wife was his. If he took his brother's wife who had been freed by the fall, then he had as good as pushed him to his death. If he accepted the reward for what had happened, then he must accept responsibility for it too. If he took her for his wife, this feeling would never leave him; he would be unhappy and would make her unhappy with him. For her sake, as well as for his, he must not do it. And if he makes that decision, he must recognize how untenable it seems when he considers it clearly with his mind's eye, yet if he grasps at happiness once more the dark feeling of guilt again hangs like some icy frost on the flower and his mind can do nothing against its destructive power. In addition to all that the clock in St George's tower kept on uttering its warning louder and louder as it struck the hours. His agitation at not having put right the fault on the roof became ever more frenzied. External forces only increased the urgent desire to get it done. It had rained continuously, the gap in the roof let in the water, the planking soaked it up greedily; the wood was bound to rot. If the winter frost got any worse, the water in the wood would freeze, the planking would warp and damage the slates. The town, which had put its trust in his professional integrity, would suffer because of him. Every night he was woken by the clock striking two. The shadows mingled together in the burning heat of his fever. The reproaches caused him by his obsession with cleanliness, both within and without, merged with each other. The open wound, that in the roof as well as that in his mind, demanded justice with ever more irresistible force, the open grave cried out for the man to close it. And he was the one whom the striking of the clock called to judgement, who must close the grave before the misfortune he had hammered into place fell on some innocent head. It was he himself who had hammered into place the coming misfortune. He must go back up to put the mistake right. And when he was up there and the clock struck two he would be seized by vertigo, and thrown down after his brother.

The friendly old architect tried to get to the bottom of what Apollonius was suffering; he had won the right to demand his confidence. Apollonius smiled sadly; he did not refuse what he asked, but put off fulfilling it from day to day. From day to day, from hour to hour, the beautiful young widow watched him grow paler and paler and grew pale herself in sympathy. Only the old gentleman in his blindness did not see the cloud which threatened the worst possible storm. The life in the house with the green shutters had again become oppressive and it now became so even more. Nobody looking at the rose-pink house now sees how oppressive it once was within.

20

It was during the night before the day appointed for the formal betrothal. Suddenly it snowed, then a great frost set in. For several nights already the so-called St Elmo's fire had been seen arcing from the tip of the spire up into the starry sky. Despite the dry cold the inhabitants of the district felt a strange heaviness in their limbs. There was not a breath of wind. People looked at each other as if enquiring whether they too were experiencing the strange uneasiness. Peculiar prophecies of war, sickness and famine went the rounds from mouth to mouth. The more intelligent ones smiled at this but could not themselves resist the urge to clothe their inner anxieties in suitable images of something external threatening them imminently. The whole day dark clouds had been building up, of more varied shapes and colours than was normal in the winter sky. Their blackness would have formed an unbearably sharp contrast to the snow, which covered mountains and valleys and hung like icing on the leafless branches of the trees, had not their reflection deadened the white glare. Here and there the firm outline of the dark bank of clouds extended downwards in loose soft loops. These had the appearance of usual snow-bearing clouds and their dull reddish grey served as a midway point between the leaden blackness of the higher layer of clouds and the dirty white of the earth with its darkish gleam. The whole mass of clouds stood motionless above the town. The blackness grew. Already two hours after noon it was already night in the streets. The people who lived on the ground floor closed their shutters; in the windows of the upper storeys light after light came on. In the town squares, where a larger section of the sky could be seen, groups of people congregated together, looking first up at the sky in all directions and then into each others' long anxious faces. They told each other about the ravens which had come into the suburbs in great flocks, pointed out the restless fluttering of the jackdaws round St George's and St Nicholas's, spoke of earthquakes, avalanches, even about the Day of Judgement. The braver ones thought it would just be a severe storm. But even that seemed disquieting enough. The river and the so-called fire pond, a reservoir whose water could be instantly directed through underground channels to any part of the town, were both frozen. Many hoped the danger would simply pass. But every time they looked up the dark mass of clouds had not moved from the spot. At two o'clock in the afternoon it had already been there and around midnight it still remained there unchanged. Only, it seemed, it had become heavier and had sunk lower. How could it have moved when there was not a breath of wind; and to scatter and drive away such a mass of clouds would have needed a gale.

It struck twelve from St George's tower. The last stroke seemed unable to die away. But the deep echoing vibration which went on so long was no longer that of the clock chimes dying away. For now the storm began to grow; it came rushing and rising as on a thousand wings and struck angrily against the houses which stood in its way, and whistled shrilly in through every opening it came to; it rattled around in the houses until it found another opening it could go out through; it tore open shutters and banged them furiously shut again; it forced itself with a moaning sound between neighbouring walls; it whistled angrily round street corners; it dispersed into thousands of separate gusts; it crashed together again into a veritable torrent of wind; it swept up and down with fierce joy; it shook all fixtures; it played with wild fingers on the rusty weather vanes and flags and laughed shrilly at their groaning; it blew the snow from one roof to another and swept it from the streets, chasing it up steep walls until for fear it crept into all the crevices of the windows and drove gigantic shapes of snow in a swirling dance before it.

Since a storm had been foreseen, everyone had remained fully dressed. The town and district storm wardens as well as the firemen had already been mustered for hours. Herr Nettenmaier had sent his son to their headquarters in the town hall to deputise for him in the role of official master slater to the council. The two journeymen were with the tower wardens, one at St George's and the other at St Nicholas's. The rest of the council workmen set themselves up as best they could in the headquarters. The town architect watched Apollonius with some concern as he sat there brooding. He, though, felt his friend's eye on him and got up in order to conceal how he was feeling. At that very moment the storm once more raged and roared through the air. The clock on the tower of the town hall struck one. The sound of the clock became shrill as the force of the storm tore it away with it in its wild rout. Apollonius stepped to the window as if to see what was happening outside. Then a gigantic sulphurous blue tongue of flame shot in, twitching and darting up the stove, the walls and the people, and then disappeared into itself leaving no trace. The storm roared on; but just as it seemed born out of the last stroke of the clock on St George's so now something grew out of its raging violence which in power as greatly exceeded it, as it exceeded the striking of the clock. A whole invisible world seemed to be being smashed to pieces in the wind. It roared and howled around with the rage of a tiger that could not destroy what it had caught; the deep majestic rumbling of the thunder which drowned it out was the roaring of a lion which has his foot on its prey, a triumphant expression of satiated power.

"That was a strike" said someone. Apollonius thought to himself; what if it struck the tower of St George's, in that very gap I left, and I had to go up and the clock struck two and --. He could not imagine it. A cry for help, a cry of "Fire!" rang out through the storm and the thunder. "The lightning's struck" cried someone out in the street. "It's struck the tower of St George's. Everyone to St George's! Help! Fire! To St Georges! Help! Fire at St George's!" Horns blew, drums rolled. And amidst it all the storm and clap after clap of thunder. Then there was a shout, "Where's Nettenmaier? If anyone can help, it's

Nettenmaier. Help! Fire! To St George's! Nettenmaier!
Where's Nettenmaier? Help! Fire! To St George's tower!"

The architect saw Apollonius's face go pale, his frame
slump even deeper into himself than before. "Where's
Nettenmaier?" came the call from outside once more.
Then a dark flush spread over his pale cheeks and his slim
figure rose to its full height. He quickly buttoned up his
coat, tightened the straps of his cap under his chin. "If I
don't come back", he said to the architect as he turned to
go, "please look after my father, my brother's wife and his
children". The architect was surprised. The young man's
words 'If I come back' sounded more like 'When I come
back'. His friend had an inkling that there was something
here to do with Apollonius's mental anguish. But the
expression on his face showed no more sign of anguish; it
was neither anxious nor wild. Through all his worries and
fears the good-hearted architect felt something like joyful
hope. It was the old Apollonius again who stood before
him. The old calm, modest determination, which had won
him over to the young man's cause from the very first, had
returned in full. "If only he would remain like this!"
thought the architect. He did not have time to make any
reply to Apollonius. He pressed his hand. Apollonius
sensed everything that this handshake intended to convey.
An expression of pity for the good old man showed for a
moment on his face, as if he regretted the fact that he had
given the old man pain and would probably cause him still
more. But he said with his old smile, "I am always ready
for situations like this. But haste is of the essence. I'll see
you again soon!" Apollonius was faster than the architect
and was soon out of sight. On the whole way to St

George's, amidst the horns and drums, the storm wind and the thunder, the architect kept repeating to himself, "Either I shall never see the brave lad again or he'll be quite well again when I next see him." He did not seek to account for how he came to that conclusion. Even if he had been able to there was no time for it. His duty as Town architect demanded his whole attention.

The cries of "Nettenmaier! Where's Nettenmaier?" followed Apollonius all the way to St George's and still rang out behind him. The trust of his fellow citizens awoke in him once more the feeling of his own worth. When he returned from foreign parts and saw his home town lying there before him, he had dedicated himself to it and its service. Now he had the chance to show how serious his vow had been. He ran through in his mind the different forms the danger might possibly take and how he could tackle them. A fire-pump stood ready inside the roof with pieces of cloth which could be soaked in water and used to protect endangered spots. The journeyman had been instructed to keep some hot water prepared. He had fastened ladders everywhere to the roof timbers. For the first time since he had come home from Brambach his whole mind was on his work. Faced with this real emergency and its demands, the images he had been brooding on receded like fading shadows. All his old resilience and delight in work had come back, and the feeling of relief increased it even more. One can always fight thoughts with other thoughts, but they are a weak weapon against feelings. In vain had his mind sought a way out; it, too, had been affected by his general state of prostration. Now a much stronger, healthy feeling had sprung up to combat the strong sick feeling and had consumed it in its flames. He knew without any special thought that he had found the decision that would save him, and this was the source of his renewed existence. He knew he would not get vertigo and if things remained so he could only fall victim to his duty but not to his guilt and God and the gratitude of the town would take over his responsibility for keeping his promise to his loved-ones.

The square around St George's was filled with people all looking up anxiously at the roof of the spire. The enormous old building stood like a rock amidst the battle being tirelessly fought all around it by the lightning with the blackness of the night. Now it was encircled by a thousand blazing white-hot arms with such force that it seemed itself to flare up beneath the flames; they surged up it like breakers on a beach and fell back again defeated, then the dark flood-tide of night closed over it again. Just as frequently the crowd of pale faces pressing close together round its foot could be glimpsed before they sank back again into the general darkness. The storm tugged at the bystanders' hats and coats and lashed them with their own hair as well as that of others and with the loose ends of their clothing, and showered them with a fine drizzle of snow which drifted down on them in the gleams of the lightning like an incandescent rain of sparks, as if it wanted to take out on them its frustration at battering in vain against the stone framework of the church. And as people appeared and disappeared again, all talking at once, what they said was drowned and swept away again and again by the storm and the thunder.

Then someone trying to take what little comfort there was, cried out, "At least it was a cold strike. There's no sign of fire." Someone else was of the opinion that the flames caused by the lightning strike could still break out. A third person was angry; he thought this opposing view was tantamount to a wish that the lightning had not been cold and that the flames would break out yet. He had already taken comfort from the first remark and was getting his own back for the alarm that had now been roused in him again. Many people, trembling with fear and cold, were looking up with dull blinded eyes and no longer knew why. A hundred voices, on the other hand, clamoured to point out what a misfortune the town might suffer, indeed must suffer, if the lightning had indeed caused a fire. Someone spoke of the nature of slates, how they melted in the flames and, flying through the air like burning cinders, often for a distance of many streets, had often before spread a conflagration instantly over a whole town. Other people complained that the storm favoured any possible conflagration and that there was no water on hand to put it out. Still other people said that even if there was water on hand it would freeze in the hoses and pumps from the cold. Most people with anxious eloquence described the course the blaze would take. If the burning roof timbers collapsed the storm would drive the flames to where a thick mass of houses butted almost up to the tower. Here was the part of the town most at risk of fire. Numerous wooden galleries in narrow courts, wood-slatted gables, shingle-covered sheds, all packed so close together that it would be impossible to bring in a fire pump anywhere and no fire-crew could be used with any success. If the burning roof timbers fell in this direction, as was ever likely, this whole district which lay down wind would be lost without the slightest chance of being saved what with the storm and the lack of water. These predictions so disconcerted the most anxious of the people that every new flash of lightning seemed to them to be the flames breaking out. That they could each only see one side of the spire roof fostered the spread of false information. It was remarkable, but now was heard on all sides simultaneously, "Where? Where?" The storm and the thunder hindered communication. Everyone wanted to see for himself; thus a wild jostling throng occurred.

"Where was the strike?" asked Apollonius who had just arrived. "On the side facing Brambach" said several voices in reply. Apollonius cleared a path through the crowd. With long strides he hurried up the tower stairs. He was a fair distance ahead of the men following him who were slower. At the top he asked again, but in vain. The tower wardens were of the opinion that it had been a cold strike and there was no fire, yet they were nevertheless in the process of collecting together their most valuable possessions in order to flee from the tower. Only the journeyman, whom he found busy at the stove, was still keeping his head. Apollonius took a lantern and hurried to hang it up from the roof timbers. The stepladder no longer trembled beneath his feet; he was in too much of a hurry to notice it. Apollonius could find no sign of a fire beginning in the roof timbers. There was no reek of sulphur that usually indicates a lightning strike, nor any trace of smoke. Apollonius heard the others following him up the ladder. He called to them to tell them where he was. At that very moment there was a blue flash which came in through every opening in the roof, accompanied by a rattling clap of thunder. Apollonius stood there at first as if stunned. If he had not automatically clung onto a beam he would have fallen over from the shock. The dense fumes of sulphur almost took his breath away. He sprang to the nearest opening to draw in some fresh air. The workmen, who were further away from the strike, had not been stunned, but for fear had stopped on the top step of the ladder. "Up here!" shouted Apollonius. "Bring the water. Quickly! Bring the pump! It must have struck on this side –that's where the blast and the reek of sulphur came from. Quickly with the water and the pump to the hatch!" The carpenter already coughing on the ladder called out "But the fumes!" –"Quickly!" replied Apollonius. "The hatch will give us more air than we want!" The mason and the chimney-sweep followed the carpenter who carried the hose, bringing the pump as quickly as possible up the ladder. The others brought buckets of cold water, the journeyman a container of hot water which could be poured on to stop the water freezing.

At such moments a person who exhibits composure inspires trust and the others subordinate themselves without question to the calm man of action. The planking that led to the hatch was narrow; nevertheless, thanks to Apollonius's directions everything instantly fell into place. Next to Apollonius at the hatch stood the carpenter, then came the pump, then the mason. The pump was so placed that the two men had the pump-handles in front of them. Two strong men could operate the pump mechanism. Behind the mason stood the journeyman slater in order to pour some of the hot water from over their shoulder whenever it was necessary. Others took over the journeyman's former task; they melted snow and ice and kept the resulting water in the heated warden's room so that it didn't freeze up again. Yet more stood ready to carry water from the room to the roof frame and they formed a kind of bucket-line. While Apollonius was outlining this plan with quick words and gestures to the carpenter and the mason who then put it into execution, he was already holding the roof ladder in his right hand and was reaching for the bolt on the hatch with his left. The men were filled with hope; but when the storm whistled in through the open doorway, tore the carpenter's hat from his head, and dashed masses of fine snow against the timbers and roared and rumbled and howled up and down the roof space, and flash after flash of lightning broke blindingly through the dark opening, then even the bravest wanted to abandon the futile task. Apollonius had to turn his back to the doorway in order to be able to breathe. Then, with both hands pressed against the slates above the doorway, he bent his head back so that he could look up the outside of the roof surface. "We can still save it!" he shouted strenuously so that the men could hear him over the storm and the continuous rumbling of the thunder. He got hold of the nozzle of the shortest hose, while the carpenter screwed its bottom end to the pump, and wound it round his body. "When I tug on the hose twice in succession, turn on the water pressure! Master, we'll save the church yet, perhaps the town!" Pressing his right hand against the slates he ducked out of the hatch; in his left hand he held out the light roof ladder in order to try and hang it from the nearest roof hook above the door. It seemed quite impossible to the workmen. The storm was bound to sweep away the ladder and –only too likely – sweep way the man with it. It stood Apollonius in good stead that the wind pressed the ladder against the roof surface. There was no lack of light to find the hook; but the fine snow swirling around and rolling off the roof got in his eyes and hindered him. Nevertheless he felt that the ladder hung firmly. There was no time to lose; he swung himself out. He had to rely more on the strength and sureness of his hands and arms than on secure footholds as he climbed; for the storm swung the man as well as the ladder backwards and forwards like a bell. Above and to one side of the top rung of the ladder bluish flames with yellow tips leapt out from beneath the fatal gap he had left and licked from under the edges of the slates. It was two foot below the gap that the lightning had struck. Only an hour before he had been frightened by the mere thought that the lightning might strike here and he would have to go up –a whole series of dark deadly images had been associated with it in his feverish state –now it had all turned out exactly as he had imagined; but the gap he had left now seemed no different from any other place on the roof. He stood on the ladder quite free of vertigo and he was only filled with a new intrepid feeling – the impulse to avert the danger threatening the church and the town. Yes, something which had before heightened his dark fears with worry, now turned out to be even beneficial and auspicious. He realized that it was only the water which had soaked through the gap into the woodwork all week and had now frozen, which was preventing the flames from spreading more quickly. The area where the fire had taken hold so far was quite small. The frost in the planking for a long time held back the stubborn little flames which leapt up again and again before they took a permanent hold and could spread from the seat of the fire. If they had once managed to combine into a larger flame and this had then jumped the space beneath the gap, which was proof against it because of the frost, then the fire must have enormously shot up and enveloped the top of the spire and the church and perhaps the town would have succumbed to the combined forces of storm and fire. He saw that the situation could still be saved; and he needed the strength which this thought gave him. The ladder no longer merely swung from side to side, it heaved up and down at the same time. What was wrong? Even if the roof hook was loose – but he knew that couldn't be – this movement was impossible. But the ladder was not hanging from the hook; he had hooked it on a projecting oak leaf of the metal garland near to one of the fastenings; but the other end of the section of the garland from which the ladder hung was the very one he had forgotten to fasten. His weight on the ladder hung heavily from that section, pulling it down more and more and bending it over on the side the ladder hung from. Another inch and the oak leaf would be horizontal and the ladder would slip from the garland sending him crashing down to the ground an immense distance below. Now his newly-won optimism and courage must prove its worth, and it did. The actual hook was only six inches away from the oak leaf on the garland. Three more light steps up the swinging ladder and he grasped the hook with his left hand, held on firmly and lifted the ladder with his right hand from the garland over to the hook. It now hung on it. With his left hand he let go of the hook and grabbed the first rung of the ladder which was still in his right; his feet followed and he was standing on the ladder again. And now the slates beneath the gap began to glow red-hot; it wouldn't be long before they would melt and roll down and the burning ash and cinders would fly into the air spreading the destruction far and wide. Apollonius drew the claw-hammer from his belt; a few blows with that and the slates he had stripped off fell far below. Now he could clearly see the small extent of the burning surface; his confidence grew. Two tugs on the hose and the pump began to work. First he directed the jet at the gap in order to make the planking above the fire more able to retard the flames. The pump proved to be powerful; where the jet of water forced its way beneath the edge of the slates they split away from the nails with a sharp report. The flames crackled and hissed angrily as the water flooded down; at first only the jet of water directed straight at them, and that more through its ability to stifle them rather than its inherent nature, succeeded in subduing their stubborn persistence.

The burnt area lay there black in front of him, no hissing any longer answered the jet from the hose. Then the mechanism of the clock startled to rattle far below him. It struck two. Two strikes! Two! And he was still standing and did not fall! How differently the reality had turned out to be from what his feverish forebodings had threatened! Then he had been up on the roof, it had struck two and vertigo had gripped him and caused him to fall in order to atone for some dark guilt. That's what his oppressive waking dreams had shown him. And here he was in reality up on the roof, and the ladder was swinging in the storm, snow flakes were swirling round him, flashes of lightning were flickering round him; with each one the covering of snow on roofs, mountains, the valley, the whole district lit up in an enormous flame, and now it struck two below him, the sound of the bells, distorted by the wind, added their drone to the uproar, and he stood there, stood there without dizziness and did not fall. He knew that no guilt attached to him; he had done his duty when thousands would not have done; he had saved his town to which he was totally devoted, saved it unaided from the most frightful danger. But any pride in this became in his mind only a prayer of thanksgiving. He did not think about the people who would praise him, only about the people who would now be able to heave a sigh of relief, about the misery that had been prevented, about the prosperity that had been preserved. And he himself for the first time in months felt what it was to breathe freely again. This night had brought back his sense of enjoyment, his love of life. He remembered with pleasure once more the promise he had made. To people like Apollonius the highest blessing is to do a good deed for this gives them the strength to do more good deeds.—

The crowds of people below had still been shouting out "Where? Where did it strike?" and were milling around when the second bolt of lightning had struck. For a moment they had all stood stock-still, paralysed with fear. "Thank God! It was a cold strike again!" cried a voice. "No! No! This time it's burning! God have mercy!" replied others. When there were intervals of darkness between the flashes sharp eyes saw the small flames dancing like little lights over the slates. They sought to join up with others, and when they did, they flared up convulsively into one larger flame; then they danced apart and sprang together again. The storm bent them and stretched them backwards and forwards; at times they seemed to go out but then licked up again higher than ever. They were growing, everyone could see that; but they weren't growing quickly. Much more quickly and more powerfully the cry of "Fire!" rang out through the whole town. Anxious and strained, all eyes peered up intently at the small burning area. "If we get help now it can still be put out!" And once again the cry "Nettenmaier! Where's Nettenmaier?" was heard above the storm and the thunder. A voice cried "He's up in the tower". Everybody felt reassured by that. And most people didn't know him, including most of those who shouted out. And those who didn't know him shouted the loudest. At moments of general insecurity the crowd always puts its trust in one particular name, often just a word. Some of them use this means to deflect the demands of their conscience that they should personally get involved and risk their lives; and these are the ones who criticize unmercifully any person who does help and find fault with what he has done and what he has not done. The others are merely glad if they survive the next few moments by deluding themselves. "What can he do?" cried one. "Help to save the town!" cried others. "Even if he had wings nobody would risk it in this storm". "Nettenmaier would for sure!" At the bottom of their hearts even those with the most confidence in him knew that he wouldn't risk it. The thought that the flames could still be put out if one could only get access to them made this general impression all the more painful, since it prevented the apathetic sense of resignation which unavoidable necessity forces on one with unfailing rigour. When the hatch opened and the ladder was seen being pushed out, when it appeared that someone was willing to take the risk after all, it had the same alarming effect as the lightning strike itself. The ladder hung there and swung back and forth high in the air with the man climbing up it, with the snow swirling and the lightning flashing all round him. The ladder seemed made out of matchsticks and swayed with him like a bell at a frightening height. Everyone held their breath. Hundreds of the most diverse faces looked up at the man with the same expression. Nobody had believed anyone would risk it and yet here was someone doing just that. It was like something that was both a dream and reality at the same time. No one had believed it possible yet each one of them felt he was standing on the ladder himself, with the flimsy support swaying beneath him in the storm, the thunder and the lightning, high up there between heaven and earth. But they were back standing below on terra firma and only looking up; and yet if the man were to fall, then it was they who would fall. The people below on terra firma clasped their hands convulsively, held on to their hats, their sticks, their clothing so as not to fall from that dreadful height. So they stood there quite safe but at the same time on the edge of the precipice of Death, stood there for what seemed years, a whole life time, for the past had never been; and yet they had only been hanging there a moment. They forgot the danger to the town, even their own danger for the danger to the man up there, which was yet their danger too. They saw that the fire was extinguished, the danger to the town over; they knew it as if they were in a dream where one knows one is dreaming; it was a mere thought without living content. Only when the man had climbed down the ladder and had disappeared through the hatch and the ladder had been pulled back in, only when they no longer hung up there, when they no longer had to clasp their hands or hang onto their hats and sticks, only then did amazement struggle with the fear which stifled any jubilation in the cries of "Go on, Lad!" and in the anguished cry "He's fallen!". A voice trembling with age began to sing "Now thank we all our God!" When the old man came to the line "And free us from all ills", they saw in their mind's eye all that they might have lost and which had been preserved for them. Even the greatest of strangers fell into each other's arms embracing in the other person the loved ones he could have lost and which had been preserved for him. Everyone joined in the hymn; and the sounds of thankfulness rang through the whole town, through streets and squares where people had stood in fear and trembling, and passed into the houses even as far as the innermost chamber and climbed to the highest attic. The sick man in his lonely bed, the old woman in the chair to which she had been confined through weakness, they all joined in from afar; children joined in who did not understand the hymn nor the danger which had been averted. The whole town became a single great church in which the storm and the thunder were the gigantic organ. And once again came the cry, "Nettenmaier! Where's Nettenmaier? Where's the man who's saved us? Where's the brave lad? Where's the plucky fellow?" The storm and the tempest were forgotten. All ran in confusion looking for him; the tower of St George's was stormed. The carpenter came to meet them and said that Nettenmaier had lain down to rest for a moment in the wardens' room. So now they urged the carpenter to tell them whether he was hurt. Had his health suffered? The carpenter could tell them nothing except that Nettenmaier had done more than any man in the normal course of events was capable of. On an occasion like today's the man had surpassed himself; afterwards he himself had been amazed at the strength he had had. But it would all take its toll. He –the carpenter –would not be at all surprised if Nettenmaier slept for three days and nights at a stretch after the exertions he'd endured. The people seemed prepared to wait that long on the stairs just to get a glimpse of the brave man immediately after he woke. In the meantime on the market square nearby a man of some standing in the town had begun a collection of money. Of course money is no reward for a brave deed like the one our hero had carried out that day; but they could at least show him that they knew how much they had to thank him for. In the mood of the moment, which found an echo in every individual, some well-known skinflints even ran home to fetch their contribution, not bothered in the slightest that they would regret it an hour later. Few of the better-off people failed to join in; the poorer people all contributed. The collector of the money was himself astonished at the success of his efforts and the amount collected.

Apollonius had been lying down for a good half hour. Before lying down he had made sure that the lanterns were all carefully extinguished. He had had the hatch closed, the pump emptied and the hoses brought back to the wardens' room, so that the frost could not damage them. He could scarcely stand up any more. The architect, who had come up in the meantime, had nevertheless had to almost forcibly bring him down to the wardens' room.

Then he had bolted the door from the inside, made Apollonius take off his frozen clothes and then sat like a mother by his protégé's bed. Apollonius could not sleep; but the old man did not allow him to speak. He had brought rum and sugar with him; there was no lack of hot water; but Apollonius, who never took heated drinks, refused the grog with his thanks. The journeyman had in the meantime fetched fresh clothes. Apollonius assured them he felt completely strong again, but hesitated to get out of bed. The old man laughed and gave him his clothes. Just as before Apollonius had undressed under the covers, so now he dressed again in the same way. The architect turned his back and laughed through the window at the storm and the lightning; but he wasn't sure whether he was laughing at Apollonius's bashfulness or just for sheer pleasure in his protégé. He had often regretted that he had remained a bachelor; now he was almost glad. For he had a son, and as brave a one as any father could wish.

On the way home great agony began for Apollonius. He was pulled about from arm to arm; even respectable distinguished ladies embraced and kissed him. His hands were pressed and shaken so much that he lost all feeling in them for three days. He did not lose his natural noble demeanour; the embarrassed modesty when faced with effusive expressions of gratitude, the blush in response to admiring praise, these became him just as well as his courageous resolute bearing when facing the danger. Those who didn't already know him were astonished; they had thought he was different from that, brown, bold-eyed, daring, overflowing with strength, perhaps even wild. But they had to admit that his appearance nevertheless did not contradict his deeds. The maidenly blush on such a tall manly figure had its own charm, and the embarrassed modesty on such an honest face, which did not seem to know what it had done, won everyone's approval; his gentle presence of mind and simple calmness only set what he had done in a better light; one could see that vanity and ambition had had no part in it.

21

We now jump forward in our minds three decades and come back to the man who we were talking about at the beginning of our tale. We left him sitting in the arbour in his garden. The bells of St George's were calling the inhabitants of the town to the morning service; the sound of their chimes could be heard also in the garden behind the house with the green shutters. There he sits every Sunday around this time. When the bells call the people to the afternoon service, he can be seen walking up to the church with his silver-topped cane in his hand. There is no one who meets him on the way who does not greet him with the greatest respect. It is now almost thirty years ago but there are still people who were there on that night, the memorable night we have just described. They can tell those who don't know already what the man with the silver-topped cane did for the town that night. And the stones can still be seen that bear witness to what he set out to establish the next morning. Just outside the town on the road to Brambach, not far from the clubhouse of the shooting club, there rises an imposing building amidst a pleasant garden. It's the new public hospital. Any stranger who visits the building learns that the impetus for building it came from Herr Nettenmaier. He has to listen to the whole story of that night, the brave deed of Herr Nettenmaier, who at that time was still young; then, how a considerable sum of money had been collected for him which he had given to the Council to form the core of the funds needed for the building; how his example had borne fruit and rich citizens had donated and bequeathed greater or lesser sums to it, until at last after many years a grant from the city treasury had made possible its construction and completion.

When Herr Nettenmaier gets back from church he spends the rest of Sunday in his room – for he stills lives there -- or he goes for a walk as far as the slate quarry which is not far away. It now belongs to him, or rather to his nephew. The fulfilment of the promise he gave has remained the guiding principle of his life. All that he provided and achieved, he provided and achieved for his brother's dependants; he saw himself merely as their trustee. If he should meet a pretty young girl on his walk, she would remind him of little Annie. His memory was as conscientious as he was himself. He would call the child to him, pat her on the head and it would have been very strange indeed if he didn't happen to have in the pockets of his blue coat something carefully wrapped up in clean paper which he could give in order to earn a word of thanks from her pretty mouth. But the child could only begin to enjoy it when he had gone by. Despite all his friendliness, his tall figure was so serious and solemn that the child out of sheer respect was unable to get any pleasure from the meeting. During the week Herr Nettenmaier sat over his books and letters or supervised in the shed the loading and unloading, the dressing and sorting of the slates. On the dot of twelve he had his lunch and on the dot of six his dinner in his room; he took about a quarter of an hour over it, then he brushed his hand over the old sofa and if it was summertime walked about in the garden for the other three quarters of an hour. Just as the clock began to chime one and seven o'clock, he would close the gate in the fence behind him. On Sundays it's different; then he sits for a whole hour in the arbour and looks up at the roof of the spire of St George's. There's no need to repeat what goes through his mind then as he contemplates the roof, for the reader knows it already. Just as he now knows whose face it is, the face of an elderly but still beautiful woman, who from time to time peeps through the fence and the trellis for the beans at the man sitting there. The now white curls over her brow, which still have a tendency to come loose, were still dark brown and full and hung over her smooth unwrinkled brow, her cheeks were still full with youthful vigour, the lips still rosy red, and the blue eyes sparkling, when she came hurrying towards the man who had just saved the town. He kissed her gently on the brow and called her 'Sister'. She understood at once what he meant. Even then she looked up to him with the same deference, even devotion with which she now eavesdrops on his musings, but then a quite different feeling showed itself on her transparent face.

The old gentleman had flown into a rage when Apollonius told him his decision not to marry. He gave his son the choice either to do the right thing for the honour of the family or return to Cologne. It was more difficult in his heart than in his head to convince his father that he was the only one who could uphold the family honour and that he must stay. He knew that only by remaining true to his decision could he continue to be the man to keep his promise. He could not say this to his father, for if he were to learn of the real relationship between the two young people he would push even harder for the marriage. Then he would also have had to tell him how his brother had met his death. He would have had to worry him even more. He did not know that his father was in his heart convinced his elder son had taken his own life. These two men, so closely related, just did not understand each other. Apollonius assumed his father shared the profound nature of his own sense of honour, and the old man saw in his son's refusal and belief that only he could deal with their difficult situation the old defiance of his father's indispensability which it was no longer worthwhile concealing; in fact his father was in his eyes no more than a helpless old blind man. And what caused and encouraged these misunderstandings was reticence, the very family trait that they both shared. That same morning a deputation of the Town Council had brought Apollonius the official thanks of the town, and the most eminent citizens had competed to show him their respect and attention. Cause enough to tempt an ambitious person to become arrogant, reason enough for the old gentleman, who considered Apollonius to be such an ambitious person, to believe in his arrogance. The old gentleman was forced to recognize the indispensability of his defiant son and was not in a position to assert any right or power against him. The emotion and mental overexertion on the day before the death of his elder son had undermined what remained of his strength; now it collapsed completely. From day to day he became more and more eccentric and irritable. He no longer expected deference from Apollonius; he found a perverse pleasure in reproaching his son in his hypocritical way for his want of filial affection, while at the same time constantly expressing his fierce regret that the capable son of an old domineering father, who was of no consequence any more, had to put up with him so much. Everything his son tried to do was in vain; his father simply refused to believe in his sincerity. At the same time in his eccentric way he was nevertheless able to enjoy both his son's capability and increasing honours as well as the growing prosperity of his firm, as long as he did not allow himself to take note of it. He lived long enough to see the purchase of the slate quarry which Apollonius had previously leased. The son put up with his father's eccentricity with the same loving untiring patience as he had shown to his brother. He lived only to carry out as best he could the promise he had made; and in this his father was also included. The thriving of his work gave him the strength to cheerfully put up with all mortifications.

The day after that stormy night he had shared with the old architect all his deepest feelings and thoughts. The old architect, who was attached to him heart and soul until his death, remained the only person he associated with, the only one whom Apollonius could befriend without having to betray his true nature.

Some days after that night Apollonius had had to take to his bed. A severe fever had gripped him. The doctor declared the illness at first very grave, but it was really the body fighting the battle against his general distress which his mind had already fought that night and won, finding salvation in the decisions he had made then. The sympathy of the whole town for Apollonius as he lay sick expressed itself in many touching ways. The old architect and Valentine were his nurses. The woman whom nature had destined through love and gratitude to be his most caring nurse was not asked to come to his bedside by Apollonius, and she dared not come unasked. For the duration of his illness she set up her bed in the narrow gallery outside his door in order to be as close to him as possible. When he slept the old architect beckoned her in. Then she stood with folded hands by the bed-screen accompanying the sleeper's every breath with concern and hope. Involuntarily her quiet breathing took on the same rhythm as his. She stood there for hours watching the sick man through a rent in the bed-screen. He knew nothing of her presence and yet the architect noticed how much lighter his sleep became on those occasions, how much more smiling his face. He did not drink from a single glass which, unknown to him, he did not receive from her hand; not a plaster or poultice which she had not prepared; not a sheet touched the sick man which she had not warmed at her breast, which she had not kissed. When he spoke of her to the architect, she saw that he was more concerned for her than for himself; when he sent friendly consoling greetings to her, she trembled for joy behind the bed-screen. She spent hardly any time in bed and if the cold winter wind blew cold snow flakes through the loosely-fitting shutters into her warm face at night, if her own breath froze on the blanket and came into contact with her icy neck, chin and bosom, then she was happy to suffer a little for him who suffered everything for her. During these nights her mortal love was suppressed and transformed into a spiritual, unworldly love; from the pain of her unrequited desire of possessing him, his image once again obtained the unapproachable height of glory in which she had beheld him before.

Apollonius quickly recovered. And now began the strange family life of these two people. They saw each other rarely. He remained living in his room and Valentine brought him his food there as before. The children were often with him. If the two of them chanced to meet he greeted her with friendly reticence and she replied in the same way. If they had something to discuss it happened that each time as if by chance the children and old Valentine or the housemaid were present. Not a day went by without some unspoken sign of loving esteem. If he came in from the garden on Sundays, he always had a bunch of flowers for her which Valentine had to deliver. He could have made several good matches and many impressive suitors asked for her hand. He declined all proposals and she rejected all the suitors. So days, weeks, months, years, decades went by. The old gentleman died and was buried. The old architect followed him and old Valentine followed the architect. In exchange the children grew up into young men. The unruly curls over the widow's brow and the curled forelock on Apollonius's faded; the children had become men, strong and gentle like their champion and tutor; hair and locks went white; life remained the same for both of them.

Now the reader knows the whole history of what is going through the old gentleman's mind as he sits in his arbour looking up at the tower of St George's as the bells ring out on Sundays calling the faithful to the morning service. Today he looks forward more into the future than back into the past. For his elder nephew is about to lead the daughter of Anne Wohlig to the altar in St George's and then home; but not to the house with the green shutters, but to the large house next door. The pale pink house has become too small for the now much larger business and there is no room for the new household in it; Herr Nettenmaier has bought the large house on the other side of the lane. His younger nephew is going to Cologne. Their old cousin there, whom Apollonius has so much to thank for, has long been dead and the son of the cousin has also died. He had left the large business to his only child, now the fiancée of the youngest son of Fritz Nettenmaier. Both couples will be married together in St George's. Then the two old people will live alone in the house with the green shutters. The old gentleman has for a long time wanted to hand over the business; the young men have so far found ways to turn this down. In fact the eldest nephew insists the old gentleman will remain head of the firm. The old gentleman does not want this. He has set aside part of the legacy he inherited from the old architect to last him the rest of his life; all the rest –and we're not talking of a small amount, for Herr Nettenmaier is known to be a rich man –he hands over to his nephew; all that is left after his death will be left to the new public hospital. He has carried out his promise; the slate-hammer on his coffin will be irreproachable as is the case on few others.

The young bride at first resists accepting everything her future mother-in-law wants to give her. But even if she gives her everything, there is one thing she will always keep; it's a little tin box containing a withered flower; she keeps it next to her bible and prayer book and to her it is as sacred as they are.

The bells still ring out. The roses on the tall-stemmed bushes still exhale their scent, a warbler sits on the bush beneath the old pear tree and sings; there is a silent stirring in the whole garden and even the thick-stemmed box hedge around the circular beds moves its dark leaves. Lost in thought, the old gentleman looks up at the roof of the spire of St George's; the beautiful but now ageing face of a woman listens out for him through the bean trellis. The ringing of the bells proclaims it, the warbler sings it, the roses exhale it in their scent, the soft stirring throughout the garden whispers it, the handsome elderly faces say it, you can read it from the roof of St George's spire – their message is the same. Men talk of the good luck or the bad luck that Heaven brings them! But what they call good luck or bad luck is only the raw material; it's up to men themselves to make of it what they will. It's not Heaven that brings good luck; man makes his own luck and creates his Heaven in his own breast. Men should not be so anxious to get into Heaven, but rather that Heaven should get into them. If you do not have it within you, you will seek it in vain in the entire universe. Be guided by your understanding but do not offend against the sacred precepts of feeling. Do not turn your back in scorn on the world as it is; seek to do justice to it and then you will do justice to yourself. And in this sense your path through life will be 'Between Heaven and Earth'.

 GA
CEN(

Drama for Students, Volume 6

Staff

Editorial: David M. Galens, *Editor*. Tim Akers, *Contributing Editor*. James Draper, *Managing Editor*. David Galens and Lynn Koch, *"For Students" Line Coordinators*. Jeffery Chapman, *Programmer/Analyst*.

Research: Victoria B. Cariappa, *Research Manager*. Andrew Guy Malonis, Barbara McNeil, Gary J. Oudersluys, Maureen Richards, and Cheryl L. Warnock, *Research Specialists*. Patricia Tsune Ballard, Wendy K. Festerling, Tamara C. Nott, Tracie A. Richardson, Corrine A. Stocker, and, Robert Whaley, *Research Associates*. Phyllis J. Blackman, Tim Lehnerer, and Patricia L. Love, *Research Assistants*.

Permissions: Maria Franklin, *Permissions Manager*. Kimberly F. Smilay, *Permissions Specialist*. Kelly A. Quin, *Permissions Associate*.

Sandra K. Gore, *Permissions Assistant*.

Graphic Services: Randy Bassett, *Image Database Supervisor*. Robert Duncan and Michael Logusz, *Imaging Specialists*. Pamela A. Reed, *Imaging Coordinator*. Gary Leach, *Macintosh Artist*.

Product Design: Cynthia Baldwin, *Product Design Manager*. Cover Design: Michelle DiMercurio, *Art Director*. Page Design: Pamela A. E. Galbreath, *Senior Art Director*.

Copyright © 1999
The Gale Group
27500 Drake Rd.
Farmington Hills, MI 48331-3535

This book is printed on acid-free paper that meets the minimum requirements of American National Standard for Information Sciences—Permanence Paper for Printed Library Materials, ANSI Z39.48-1984.

ISBN 0-7876-2755-0
ISSN 1094-9232
Printed in the United States of America

10 9 8 7 6 5 4 3

The Bacchae

Euripides

405 B.C.

Introduction

Euripides was more than seventy years old and living in self-imposed exile in King Archelaus's court in Macedonia when he created *The Bacchae*, just before his death in 406 B.C. The play was produced the following year at the City Dionysia in Athens, where it was awarded the prize for best tragedy. Ever since, *The Bacchae* has occupied a special place among Greek dramas and particularly among the eighteen surviving plays of Euripides. It was a favorite of the Romans in the centuries following the decline of the Greek Empire. It persisted through the "dark ages" of Medieval Europe and was among the first classical plays translated into vernacular languages during the Renaissance. Alongside *Medea* and Sophocles's *Oedipus the King* (also known as *Oedipus Rex*) it is one of the most produced ancient plays of the twentieth century.

The simple plot of *The Bacchae* mixes history with myth to recount the story of the god Dionysus's tumultuous arrival in Greece. As a relatively new god to the pantheon of Olympian deities, Dionysus, who represented the liberating spirit of wine and revelry and became the patron god of the theatre, was not immediately welcomed into the cities, homes, and temples of the Greeks. His early rites, originating in Thrace or Asia, included wild music and dancing, drunken orgies, and bloody sacrifice. Many sober, conservative Greeks, particularly the rulers of the many Greek city-states, feared and opposed the new religion.

Pentheus, the king of Thebes, stands as a symbol in the play for all those who opposed the cult of Dionysus and denied the erratic, emotional, uninhibited longings within all human beings. He confronts the god, faces him in a battle of wills, and is sent to his bloody death at the hands of his own mother and a frenzied band of maenads, female worshipers of the god.

In half a century of playwriting, Euripides tackled many difficult and controversial topics and often took unconventional stands, criticizing politicians, Greek society, and even the gods. *The Bacchae*, however, has proven frustratingly ambiguous in its treatment of gods and men. Writing the play in exile, while watching the glory of Athens disintegrate near the end of the Peloponnesian War, Euripides explores the disintegration of old systems of belief and the creation of new ones. He questions the boundaries between intellect and emotion, reality and imagination, reason and madness. At the end of it all, however, it is not quite clear whether the tragic events were meant to glorify the gods and reinforce their power and worship among the Greeks, or condemn the immortals for their fiendishness, their petty jealousies, and the myriad sufferings they inflict on humankind.

Author Biography

The life of Euripides, one of the great tragic playwrights of Classical Greece, spans the "Golden Age" of 5th century B.C. Athens. This single stretch of a hundred years saw the reign of Pericles, the great Athenian statesman and builder of the Parthenon; the final defeat of the Persians at the Battle of Salamis; the philosophical teachings of Anaxagoras, Protagoras, and Socrates; the construction of the Theatre of Dionysus; the playwriting careers of Aeschylus, Sophocles, and Aristophanes; and, ultimately, the decline of the Greek Empire following the devastating Peloponnesian War.

Although accounts of Euripides's life differ, some elements seem relatively certain. He was born on the island of Salamis in 484 B.C. but spent most of his life on the Greek mainland, in Athens. Based on the education he received, and the personal library he reportedly owned, his family was likely at least middle-class. His father, upon hearing a prophecy that his son would one day wear many "crowns of victory," led him to begin training as an athlete. Later, he studied painting and philosophy before finally turning to the stage and producing his first trilogy of plays in 455 B.C., just after Aeschylus's death.

Third in the line of great Greek tragedians, behind Aeschylus and Sophocles, Euripides's plays were quite different from his traditional-minded predecessors and stirred much controversy when they were presented at the annual theatre festivals (called the Dionysia) in Athens. To begin with, Euripides shared a healthy intellectual skepticism with the philosophers of his day, so his plays challenged traditional beliefs about the roles of women and men in society, the rights and duties of rulers, and even the ways and the existence of the gods. He had been influenced by the Sophists, a group of philosophers who believed that truth and morality are matters of opinion and by the teachings of Sophocles, who sought truth through questioning and logic. His own doubts, about government, religion, and all manner of relationships, are the central focus of his plays.

Additionally, Euripides did not adhere to accepted forms of playwriting. He greatly diminished the role of the chorus in his plays, relegating them to occasional comments on his themes and little or no participation in the action onstage. Furthermore, he was criticized for writing disjointed plots that didn't rise in a continuous action and for composing awkward prologues that prematurely reveal the outcome of plays. When seeking a resolution for the conflicts in his work, he often turned to the *deus ex machina*, or "god from the machine," and hastily ended a play by allowing an actor, costumed as a god, to be flown onto the stage by a crane to settle a dispute, rather than allowing the natural events of the story to run their course.

Perhaps most importantly, Euripides provided characters for his plays that seemed nearer to actual human beings than those of any of his contemporaries. Figures like Medea, Phaedra, and Electra have conflicts rooted in strong desires and psychological realism, unlike the powerful, but predictable, characters in earlier tragedies. It has been said that Aeschylus wrote plays about the gods, Sophocles wrote plays about heroes, and Euripides wrote plays about ordinary humans.

During his fifty year career as a dramatist, Euripides wrote as many as ninety-two plays, yet won only five prizes for best tragedy in competitions. In contrast, Sophocles wrote more than 120 plays and won twenty-four contests. During his lifetime, Euripides was not always appreciated by his audiences or his critics—he, in fact, found himself the object of ridicule among writers of comedies like Aristophanes, who lampooned the tragedian and his techniques in his satire *The Frogs*. Time, however, has proven Euripides's merits. While Aeschylus and Sophocles are each represented by only seven surviving plays, eighteen of Euripides's tragedies still exist, along with a fragment of one of his satyr plays. They have been preserved over the centuries as admirable models of classical tragedy and helpful examples of spoken Greek. Due largely to his progressive ideas and realistic characters, the same qualities that once earned him scorn, he is now one of the most popular and widely-produced writers of antiquity.

Plot Summary

The setting of *The Bacchae* is the royal palace of Thebes, where Pentheus has succeeded his grandfather, Cadmus, as king. The play begins with a prologue spoken by Dionysus, the great god of wine and revelry himself. He announces that he has successfully spread his cult throughout Asia and returns now to the land of his mother, Semele, in order to teach the Greeks how to worship him through dancing, feasting, and sacrifices.

Some of the women of the city, including his own mother's sisters, have denied his status as a god, claiming he is simply a mortal and that the great Zeus killed his mother for lying about her lover. In threatening tones he describes how he has already driven the women of Thebes mad and sent them to the hills around the city, where they wear the animal skins of bacchants, priestesses of Dionysus, carry the ivy-entwined thyrsus (a symbol of his worship), and dance and sing hymns of praise to the new god. Now he is ready to turn his attention to King Pentheus, who opposes his worship and denies his existence.

To accomplish his task, he has come to Thebes disguised as a mortal and brought with him a chorus of his Asian followers. Together, he claims, they will try to persuade the Thebans to accept him into their rites of worship, even fight them if necessary. Then he will leave Thebes and spread his cult throughout Greece.

Dionysus leaves to join the bacchants on Mount Cithaeron as his Chorus enters to sing and dance for the people of Thebes. The Chorus' song explains the origins of the god and describes how the Greeks can become worshipers themselves. They sing about Dionysus's mother, Semele, who conceived the god with Zeus, ruler of all the immortals on Mt. Olympus; and how she was tricked into asking Zeus to reveal himself to her in all his godlike glory. Zeus complied, appearing to Semele as a lighting bolt and killing her instantly in his flame. Zeus himself plucked the unborn Dionysus from the fire and sealed him up in his thigh, later giving birth to his half-human, half-divine son.

To worship Dionysus, the Chorus sings, followers need only to crown themselves with ivy, wear deer skins lined with goat hair, carry the branches of oak and fir trees, delight in the bounty of the vine, and make ritual animal sacrifices. If they do, the land will overflow with natural beauty and riches—fawns and goats, wine and honey.

The women worshipers of Dionysus are interrupted in their revels by the arrival of Tiresias, the famous blind prophet. Tiresias has come to collect Cadmus; the two elders have rediscovered their youth in the worship of Dionysus, and they are headed to the hills around Thebes to dance and sing the god's praises. Before they can leave, however, King Pentheus returns to the city from a trip abroad. He heard about the flight of women from his city and hurried back to contain the madness. He proclaims the worship of Dionysus false and immoral, reveals he has already caught and jailed many of the mad women, and soon will have them all captured and safely imprisoned.

Although both Tiresias and Cadmus try to convince Pentheus not to spurn the new god, on peril of his life, the king is unconvinced. He has heard about the arrival of a mysterious stranger in Thebes, a sorcerer with golden curls who is always surrounded by women. Not knowing the man he seeks is actually the god Dionysus himself, he orders the stranger caught and brought back to the palace in chains, to face death by stoning. As a further insult, he orders Tiresias's home—where he divines his prophecies—destroyed and even threatens his grandfather, Cadmus, before rushing off in search of Dionysus.

After a brief interlude by the Chorus, which chants a warning about human pride and men who will not give in to the pleasures of life, Pentheus returns and is met by a Servant, leading the disguised Dionysus in chains. The Servant reports that the stranger turned himself in willingly, but that all the women Pentheus had captured have escaped from their jails by some miracle of the gods. In a brief exchange, Pentheus accuses the Stranger of worshiping a false god and undermining the morals of women and orders him imprisoned, to await his death. The Stranger (Dionysus) warns Pentheus that he will free himself and that the god's wrath will fall heavily on the king and his city, but Pentheus, filled with arrogance, doesn't listen and leads the god away to his punishment.

The Chorus provides another interlude, this time worrying about the fate of Dionysus. They wonder if the god has forsaken them in Thebes. Suddenly, in the midst of their chanting, the Chorus is startled by a roar of thunder and the brilliant flash of lightning that engulfs the palace and the nearby tomb of Semele. When the blaze dies, the Stranger appears again and tells the bacchants how he escaped by tricking Pentheus into shackling a bull, tearing down the prison, and fighting phantom images.

Worn down by his struggles, Pentheus reappears in pursuit of the Stranger. They are met by a Herdsman from Mount Cithaeron, who describes a terrible battle he has just witnessed between Dionysus's frenzied female worshipers, the maenads, and the villagers on the mountain. Stumbling upon the bacchants in the forest, the villagers hid and saw the women perform strange miracles. They seemed to communicate with the wild animals and draw water from rocks and wine from the earth itself. Among the crazed women was Agave, Pentheus's mother, and they decided to help their king by capturing her and bringing her home again. When the women saw the villagers, however, they attacked them ferociously. Weapons could not harm the bacchants, but with simple branches or their bare hands Dionysus's priestesses wounded their attackers, then turned on their cattle, ripping the cows and bulls to pieces and feeding on the raw flesh.

Though the Herdsman and the Chorus implore Pentheus to accept the fearsome new god, the king is more resolute than ever. He orders his soldiers called to arms in preparation for an attack on the bacchants in the hills. Dionysus, still in the guise of the Stranger, again warns Pentheus not to tempt fate by taking arms against a god, but it is too late to change his mind: Pentheus, like all tragic figures, is blind to his errors, and stumbling inexorably toward his doom.

Seeing no way to deter the king, Dionysus instead begins to prepare Pentheus for his punishment. He offers to lead the hapless man to the forest to spy on the women in their revels. To prevent him from being discovered, Dionysus convinces Pentheus to dress himself as a woman. Thus, attired in women's robes and deerskins, and carrying the Thyrsus of Dionysus, Pentheus is led, in a hypnotic trance, through the streets of Thebes and into the hills where the bacchants dance. The Chorus, knowing the fate that awaits him, sings a song of celebration, cheering the impending death of the foolish king and exalting the name of Bacchus—Dionysus—the god of wine and revelry.

Soon afterward, a Messenger arrives to relay the news of Pentheus's grisly destruction: When the king and his soldiers arrived near the grassy glade occupied by the maenads, the Messenger tells the Chorus, Pentheus complained he could not see the women through the trees. The Stranger reached up and pulled down the top of a tall fir tree, set

Pentheus in its branches, then gently straightened the trunk again, sending the king upward to the top of the forest. As soon as he was aloft, the Stranger disappeared and the voice of Dionysus boomed across the hillside, calling the women to attack the non-believer perched helplessly atop the tree.

The Messenger watched while the women pulled the tree from the ground, roots and all, sending Pentheus plummeting to earth. They descended upon him like animals with Agave, his own mother, in the lead. Pentheus tore off his disguise and pleaded with his mother to recognize him and spare him, but in her madness she thought he was a mountain lion and helped tear him apart, limb from limb, taking his head as a trophy of the hunt.

Finishing his tale, the Messenger hurries away as Agave approaches, bearing Pentheus's head on her thyrsus. Still in a Dionysian frenzy, Agave boasts that she was the first of the maenads in the hunt to reach the lion, whose head she claimed as a prize. Cadmus enters with servants, carrying some of Pentheus's remains on a bier. Sorrowfully, the founder of Thebes forces his daughter, Agave, to shake off her trance and recognize her own son's bloody head in her hands. He laments that it was her own blindness, and that of Pentheus and the women of Thebes, that led to this disaster. Because they mocked the god and dishonored his name, Dionysus has punished them all.

Dionysus himself returns and pronounces their final punishment: Cadmus will be driven into exile, later to be turned into a serpent with his wife Harmonia. Agave, too, will be banished from Thebes and forced to wander as an outcast for the remainder of her days. As father and daughter bid each other a tearful goodbye, the Chorus delivers the play's final lesson—that the gods may appear in many forms and accomplish wondrous, unexpected things. Let mere mortals beware.

Agave

Agave is daughter to Cadmus, the founder and former king of Thebes, and mother to Pentheus, the city's current ruler. As revealed by Dionysus in the play's prologue, Agave insulted the god by saying he was not the son of Zeus; that Semele, Dionysus's mother and Agave's own sister, lied about her lover, who was actually some mortal. For her heresy, Dionysus has driven Agave, and all the women of Thebes, mad and sent them into the hills where they have been wearing animal skins, dancing, and singing hymns of praise to the god of wine and revelry. Near the end of the play, Agave, still in a mad frenzy, leads the women in a bloody attack on Pentheus, her own son, who she mistakes for a mountain lion. She returns to Thebes triumphant, carrying her son's head as a trophy. Cadmus finally breaks the spell she has been under, bringing her back to sanity and the painful realization of what she has done. She and her father are both condemned to exile by the angry Dionysus.

Cadmus

In Greek mythology, Cadmus was the ancient founder of Thebes. He populated the city by sowing the teeth of a dragon he and his brothers had slain. The planted teeth grew into soldiers called Spartoi, who became the Theban nobility and helped Cadmus build the city's citadel. Interestingly, because one of Cadmus's daughters, Semele, was Dionysus's mother, Cadmus is actually the god's uncle. In *The Bacchae*, Cadmus appears in his old age, after he has resigned the throne to his grandson, Pentheus. Cadmus and his friend, the blind prophet, Tiresias, have discovered the joys of the worship of Dionysus and thereby discovered a second youthful spirit. Try as he will, however, he cannot convince the headstrong Pentheus to accept Dionysus into the pantheon of gods in Thebes. At the end of the play, he is banished by Dionysus and told he and his wife, Harmonia, will become serpents before perishing in another land.

Chorus

The Chorus is a group of Asian "Bacchae," women followers of Dionysus who wear deer skins and crowns of ivy, carry the thyrsus wand and fennel stalk, drink, dance, and sing hymns—or "dithyrambs"—in honor of the god of wine and revelry. They watch all the action of the play, never becoming direct participants but providing, through their songs, important background information about the life and worship of Dionysus. As with most choruses in Greek tragedies, they often address the audience directly, moralizing about the actions of the play's characters, as when these Bacchae warn the onlookers that the gods punish mortals who do not honor them properly. Their pure spirit and beneficent actions contrast with the view

Pentheus has of Dionysus and his cult.

Dionysus

The Greek god of wine and revelry, Dionysus was also known as Bacchus to the Romans. In Greek myth, he is said to have been the son of the immortal king of the gods, Zeus, and Semele, the mortal daughter of Cadmus, founder of Thebes. When jealous Hera, Zeus's Olympian wife, tricked Semele into asking Zeus to show her his real identity, the hapless woman caught only a glimpse of the god in his glory before she perished in his divine fire. Zeus plucked the unborn baby Dionysus from her womb and concealed him in his thigh, until his proper birth.

Media Adaptations

- *The Bacchae* has inspired a handful of operas, including at least three that are available on CD: Szymanowski's *King Roger* (1926) and Hans Werner Henze's *The Bassarids* (1966), each available from the Koch Schwann label; and Harry Partch's *Revelation in the Courthouse Park* (1961), available on the Tomato label. Other operatic versions include Egon Wellesz's *Die Bakchantinnen* (1931); Daniel Bortz's *Backanterna* (1991); and John Buller's *Bakxai* (1992).

- Italian director and writer Giorgio Ferroni produced a filmed adaptation of Euripides's play in 1961 called *Le Baccanti*. The film stars Taina Elg as Dirce (a character Ferroni introduced to his version of the story), Pierre Brice as Dionysus, and Elberto Lupo as Pentheus. An English version, called *Bacchantes* is available on video.

- In 1968 the avant-garde American theatre producer Richard Schechner formed his own company called the Performance Group. Their first production, staged in a converted garage, was *Dionysus in 69*, a reworking of *The Bacchae* that explored sexuality, freedom, and societal repression through a series of ritual vignettes.

As a young god, Dionysus did not receive the recognition he deserved in Greece, so he left for Asia, where he gathered his power and his followers before returning to conquer his homeland and spread the worship of the vine. It is at this point in the god's life where the play begins. He has returned to Thebes, the home of his mother, Semele, leading a chorus of "Bacchae," his female followers. He wants the Thebans to be the first among the Greeks to learn the songs, dances, and rites of the Dionysian cult. He has encountered difficulty, however: While the old founder and ruler of Thebes, Cadmus, and the wise seer Tiresias have chosen to honor him, the people of Thebes, and especially their new king, Pentheus, deny his name and refuse his worship.

A jealous but patient god, Dionysus has driven the women of Thebes mad and sent them into the hills where they have been dancing and singing his praises. Disguising himself as a mortal, a priest of his own cult, he tries to convince King Pentheus to accept the new god into Thebes. Pentheus, however, doubts Dionysus's existence and finds the drinking and dancing associated with his worship immoral, especially among women. He orders the Stranger (Dionysus) placed in chains and led off to prison to await his death. Dionysus escapes, wreaking havoc on the king and his court. Unable to reason with Pentheus, he finally devises a gruesome punishment for the prideful mortal: He places Pentheus in a trance, then convinces him to dress as a woman and spy on the Bacchae dancing Dionysus's rites in the hills. When the women discover him, they tear Pentheus limb from limb, and his own mother carries his head back into the city. In the end, Dionysus banishes what is left of the royal family of Thebes and declares his cult newly established in Greece.

First Messenger

Messengers in Greek drama are typically minor characters whose principal function is to relay important information about plot developments offstage, so the action of the play can continue unabated. The First Messenger in *The Bacchae* is a herdsman from Mount Cithaeron, who appears halfway through the play to describe a terrible battle he witnessed between the "maenads" (another name for Dionysus's female followers) and the villagers of the mountain. During the battle, he claims, the women were impervious to the villagers' weapons but were themselves able to wreak terrible havoc with simple branches and reeds. Furthermore, they tore cattle apart with their bare hands and caused wine to flow from the earth. Like others before him, the First Messenger encourages King Pentheus to accept Dionysus and his cult before it is too late.

Pentheus

Pentheus is the son of Agave and grandson of Cadmus, making him cousin to the god, Dionysus.

He has inherited the throne of Thebes from Cadmus, and early in the play he is abroad on business of his realm. He returns quickly, however, after hearing that the women of his city have been driven mad and are cavorting in the hills around Thebes, dressed in the manner of Dionysian priestesses. Though Cadmus and Tiresias each try to convince him to accept the new god and his rituals, Pentheus is, in the manner of all Greek tragic protagonists, too filled with pride and blind to his errors to see the folly of his ways.

Even when he is confronted with the god himself, disguised as a priest of his cult, Pentheus calls Dionysus a false divinity, sends him off to prison, and orders soldiers to attack his Bacchae in the hills. As punishments for his crime, Pentheus is entranced by Dionysus, who convinces him to don women's clothes and suffer humiliation walking through the streets of his city out to the forest, to spy on the women worshiping the god. He is placed atop a tall tree to see the women dancing and singing but once there they see him and, in their frenzy, pull the tree up from the roots, tumbling the ill-fated king to the ground. The women fall on him, led by his own mother, Agave. They tear him limb from limb, and Agave, thinking he is a mountain lion, claims his head as a prize.

Second Messenger

For the most part, scenes of death and destruction in Greek tragedy occur offstage. It is usually left to messengers to report the bloody deeds to the other characters and the audience, using words that often describe the scene as vividly as if it were taking place before their eyes. The Second Messenger in *The Bacchae* is given the task of reporting the grisly death of Pentheus. He was part of Pentheus's retinue of soldiers who followed the king to the forest and witnessed him being torn to pieces by the maenads. Near the end of the play, he arrives back in Thebes just ahead of Agave and tells the Chorus about the tragic events on Mount Cithaeron.

Servant

Playing only a small part in the play, the Servant is one of King Pentheus's men. He leads the group that captures the Stranger (actually Dionysus in disguise), and he reports the escape of the captured Bacchae from their jail cells.

Tiresias

In Greek mythology, Tiresias was the famous blind prophet of Thebes, and he appears in many stories, including Homer's *Odyssey*, Sophocles's *Oedipus* cycle, and another play by Euripides, *The Phoenician Women*. He was a descendant of the Spartoi sown by Cadmus, and he was given the gifts of prophecy and long life by Zeus, after being struck blind by the goddess Hera.

In *The Bacchae*, Tiresias appears briefly at the

beginning of the play, as the voice of wisdom and experience. Along with Cadmus, he tries to persuade the headstrong Pentheus to accept Dionysus and his worship, telling him he is wrong to rationalize about the gods, whose ways cannot be known by mere mortals such as himself.

Rational vs. Instinctual

The Greeks of the 5th century B.C. prized balance and order in their lives. Their art and architecture, laws, politics, and social structure suggest a culture that sought equilibrium in all things, including human behavior. Even their gods aligned themselves with opposing aspects of human essence. Apollo was the Greeks' god of prophecy, music, and knowledge. He represented the rational, intellectual capacity of the human mind and its ability to create order out of chaos. As the god of wine and revelry, Dionysus represented the opposite but equally important feature of human instinct: the emotional, creative, uninhibited side of people that balances their daily rational, structured, law-abiding behavior. The main conflict in *The Bacchae* is between these two conflicting behavioral patterns, the rational and the instinctual, disciplines often referred to as the Apollonian and the Dionysian.

Topics for Further Study

- Research the agriculture and economy of Greece in the 5th century B.C. What products did the Greeks export? Which did they import? How was trade within the country, and outside the country, managed? How was the worship of Dionysus conducted to coincide with important phases of agriculture throughout the year?

- When writing his plays, Euripides seems to have concentrated his efforts mainly on characters and themes and often appears to have ignored important elements of plot. Sophocles, on the other hand, has been called the greatest constructor of plots in the ancient world, and

Aristotle called his *Oedipus the King* the finest example of Greek drama. Research *Oedipus the King* and compare it to *The Bacchae*. Consider the similarities and differences between each play's plots, characters, and themes.

- By the end of the 5th century B.C., Greek theatres had developed a distinct shape and very particular elements of scenery, costuming, and special effects that affected the way plays such as *The Bacchae* were produced. Research the physical properties of Greek theatres in the age of Euripides, then choose a scene from *The Bacchae* and describe how it might have been staged. As a group project, you may wish to actually recreate the scene you have chosen.

- In his time, Euripides was widely known as skeptic, someone who questioned authority and doubted traditional beliefs. His ideas were influenced by, among others, the *Sophist* philosophers, who believed that truth and morality were relative to the individual and largely matters of opinion. Who were some of the Sophists? What were their beliefs? How did they influence Western culture?

- In his *Poetics*, Aristotle suggests that the ideal tragic protagonist is someone who is highly renowned and prosperous, basically good, and suffers a downfall not through vice or depravity but by some error or frailty—a "tragic flaw" as it has often been called. Does this description suit Pentheus? Why/why not?

The fruits of Dionysus's worship are extolled by Cadmus, the former king of Thebes; Tiresias, the elderly blind prophet of the city; and by the Chorus of Bacchae, the god's followers. Never too old to learn a new lesson, Tiresias and Cadmus have discovered the joys of the Dionysian rites and in them a new youth. "I shall never weary, night or day, beating the earth with the thyrsus," Cadmus boasts, "In my happiness I have forgotten how old I am."

The Chorus, who explain the history of the god and describe how to worship him, also warn about his dual nature, and the peril of crossing him. "The deity, Zeus's son, rejoices in festivals," they sing. "He loves goddess Peace, who brings prosperity and cherishes youth. To rich and poor he gives in equal measure the blessed joy of wine. But he hates the man who has no taste for such things—to live a life of happy days and sweet and happy nights, in wisdom to keep his mind and heart aloof from over-busy men."

Pentheus's error in the play is his distaste for the simple pleasures Dionysus offers. He is totally dedicated to reason, and he refuses to acknowledge the need of his citizens, or himself, to occasionally release inhibitions—to dance, to sing, to eat, drink, and be merry. Ever the conservative moralizer, he warns Tiresias, "When the sparkle of wine finds a place at women's feasts, there is something rotten about such celebrations, I tell you." His sin is excessive pride, or *hubris* to the Greeks. He doesn't believe in Dionysus, a god of wine and celebration, and his fanatical obsession with order proves his downfall, in spite of the warnings he is given.

Individual vs. God

The struggle between individuals and their gods, whether actual or metaphorical, has been depicted countless times in literature, from the biblical stories of Moses and Job to modern plays like Peter Shaffer's *Amadeus* (1985) and Tony Kushner's *Angels in America* (1993). Each of these stories recounts the difficult, delicate relationship between mortals and the higher powers that may have created them—and possibly provides them their life force, their sustenance, and their inspiration. In spite of the love/hate relationship they often share in these stories, however, humans rarely encounter their divine nemeses directly, the way Pentheus battles Dionysus in *The Bacchae*.

At stake in the struggle is Dionysus's right to exist and to expect homage from the mortals of Greece, whether they wish to honor him or not. "This city must learn, whether it likes it or not, that it still wants initiation into my Bacchic rites," the god explains in the prologue to the play. "The cause of my mother Semele I must defend by proving to mortals that I *am* a god, borne by her to Zeus." Dionysus's jealous behavior is similar to that of God in the Old Testament, who tests his human creations, ravages entire cities, and floods the earth to purify it for his worshipers.

Pentheus, Dionysus's mortal opposition, is a cynical realist, unwilling to believe in the god or his fantastic powers. He believes he can shackle Dionysus, contain his followers, and stop the spread of his worship through sheer physical force, even though everyone near him warns against his folly. Cadmus and Tiresias encourage Pentheus to allow Dionysus's worship into the city. The Chorus sings the god's praises. The Herdsman from Mount Cithaeron declares, "If *he* exists not, then neither does Cypris, nor any other joy for men at all." In spite of all the warnings, however, Pentheus stays his course, and only experiences the mystery of Dionysus's powers when the god himself hypnotizes the hapless king and sends him to his death.

The result of the struggle between individuals and gods is often the same, though with different lessons to be learned. After battling his creation for centuries, the Biblical God is reformed in the New

Testament, following the life and martyrdom of his son, Jesus. Free will is offered to humanity, along with the freedom to suffer or prosper at the hands of others. In *Amadeus*, Shaffer's Salieri is consumed by his hatred for God and destroys himself. The characters in Kushner's *Angels in America* fight divinity to a draw. Pentheus, of course, learns a valuable lesson much too late.

Sex Roles

Of all the Greek tragedians, Euripides provided the most leading roles to women (although, in keeping with the theatrical conventions of the time, the parts would have been played by men). His plays also often seem to sympathize with the plight of women in Greek society. Medea, scorned by Jason, becomes an almost sympathetic figure, in spite of the fact that she murders her own children. Hippolytus's stepmother, Phaedra, is driven by a passion she cannot control and, like Pentheus, Hippolytus is a fanatical extremist who may deserve his grisly fate. In *The Bacchae*, the playwright's analysis and criticism of the Greeks' treatment of women may not be immediately obvious, but it exists in the portrayal of the Dionysian rites, the sympathetic Chorus of Bacchae, and Agave's suffering at the end of the play.

During Euripides's lifetime, women were mainly prohibited from politics, the arts, and many religious ceremonies. Dionysus's cult offered women an outlet for worship, equal or greater to that afforded to men. In the spirit of the wine and revelry he represented, women could become priestesses of Dionysus, or "Bacchae," simply by drinking, dancing, singing, and releasing their inhibitions. Although Pentheus, the conservative voice of male-dominated Greek culture, objects to women drinking and participating in religious ritual, Tiresias notes that women's own nature, not a god, will determine whether they are moral or not. "Even in Bacchic revels the good woman, at least, will not be corrupted," he claims. The Chorus of Bacchae in the play prove Pentheus wrong. They have followed the god from Asia minor, where he first established his cult, and now exist only to worship him and share in his peaceful bounty. "The ground flows with milk, flows with wine, flows with the nectar of bees," they sing.

Agave's punishment at the end of the play proves that women are equal candidates for suffering as well as for pleasure. It was Agave who originally denied Dionysus's divinity, claiming her sister, Semele, lied about her amorous relationship with Zeus, the king of the gods. Agave's false claims brought the wrath of Dionysus down on the women of Thebes, driving them mad and sending them into the hills around the city. Because her son, King Pentheus, chose to compound her mistake by denying the worship of the god to the people of Thebes, they both suffered horribly: The mother was forced to kill her own son and carry his severed head among the stunned Thebans.

Style

Climactic Plot Construction

Classical Greek tragedians were the creators of climactic plot construction, a form of playwriting that condenses the action of the story into the final hours or moments of the protagonist's struggle and places the most emphasis on the play's climax. This is quite different from an episodic plot, such as those created by Shakespeare or those used by most modern films, in which the protagonist, or hero, of the story encounters many harrowing episodes in a story that may take place across many days, months, or even years. Aristotle recognized the appeal of climactic plots in his *Poetics* when he suggested that "beauty depends on magnitude and order." In the case of a climactic plot such as *The Bacchae*, magnitude and order emerge from the simple structure of the plot: One man struggles against one overwhelming force, a god, and is defeated in the course of a single day.

In a climactic plot, the "point of attack," or starting point, of the play is relatively late in the entire story, requiring a great deal of exposition up front. In other words, a number of things have already occurred to propel the action to the point it is at when the play begins and all that is left is for the protagonist to make the fatal error that plunges him into tragedy. In *The Bacchae*, for example,

Dionysus presents a prologue at the beginning of the play that sums up what has already taken place: He has been to Asia and successfully started his cult of worship there and now has returned to Greece to offer his homeland the rewards of his divinity. He has learned, however, that his own mother's sisters have denied his origins, and King Pentheus refuses to worship him. In retaliation, he has already driven the women mad and sent them into the hills. Almost immediately, Pentheus returns from abroad to confront the new menace, and the play's struggle begins in earnest. A few hours later, the battle has ended and, through his pride, Pentheus has suffered a grisly death.

Dialogue

One interesting convention of the Greek stage required playwrights to carefully structure their tragedies in short, distinct episodes and forced actors to be extremely versatile in approaching their parts. When Thespis, a dramatist and performer long credited with being the first "actor" (thus the term "thespian"), won the award for the best tragedy at the City Dionysia in 534 B.C., he alone played all the parts in his plays. For at least the next sixty years, tragedies were limited to a chorus and one actor. According to Aristotle, Aeschylus introduced the second actor, sometime around 470 B.C., and Sophocles is credited with adding a third. By the time Euripides began writing plays, dramatists were limited to no more than three principal actors to play all the parts.

To the dramatist, this means the plot of the play must be divided into distinct episodes in which the important characters of the story can confront one another in groups of two or three, with the chorus standing near, observing the action. Playwrights manufactured reasons for characters to leave the stage, so other characters (played by the same performers) could appear. To accommodate scene and costume changes, the chorus provided interludes consisting of song and dance that usually commented on the action of the play. A quick glance at the episodes in *The Bacchae* will reveal that three separate actors must play the parts of Pentheus, Cadmus, and Tiresias, since these characters all appear on stage at the same time; but the actor playing Tiresias might also portray Dionysus and the Stranger, while the actor playing Pentheus may double as his mother, Agave, since these combinations are never seen together on the stage.

Chorus

One of the most unique and recognizable features of the construction of classical Greek tragedies is the use of a chorus. Some historians have speculated that the very origins of Greek tragedy lie in the appearance of the chorus on stage. Before there was actual dialogue and characters in conflict in drama, performances consisted of large groups of men, perhaps as many as fifty, representing each of the various tribes in the hills around Athens, who would gather at festivals honoring Dionysus and dance and sing hymns (or dithyrambs), honoring the god of wine, revelry, and the theatre. After 534 B.C., the year of the first competition for tragedies at the City Dionysia festival in Athens, the role of the chorus began to diminish as the individual characters in the plays became increasingly important.

By the time Sophocles wrote *Oedipus the King* in the late 5th century B.C., the conventional size of the chorus had been fixed at fifteen. The chorus continued to sing, chant, and dance and occasionally interacted with the principal characters, but most often, as in *The Bacchae*, they stand outside the action and provide the audience with important background information, sometimes commenting on what they see happening or even warning characters that their choices may prove dangerous. Typically, the singing and dancing of the chorus occur during choral interludes that divide the episodes of the play. These interludes may help suggest the passing of time, as when the Chorus of Dionysus's followers in *The Bacchae* chant an appeal to the god for justice while Pentheus goes off to face his death. Practically speaking, they also may help delay the action in the play while scenery is replaced or actors change costumes to appear in other roles. Of the three Greek tragedians whose work has survived, Euripides used the chorus least, preferring instead to allow his individual characters more time to develop his themes.

Historical Context

Greece in the 5th century B.C. was a collection of many small, independent city-states, each called a "polis." While these tribal communities would occasionally band together in a common cause, as the Athenians and Spartans did to overthrow Persian control of Greek colonies early in the century, they remained, for the most part, separate, autonomous entities, constantly suspicious of each other and forever questing for greater wealth and control in the realm.

The 5th century B.C. has been called the "Golden Age" of Greece, and for most of the era, the polis of Athens was the centerpiece of a burgeoning culture that has left an indelible imprint on more than two thousand years of science, religion, philosophy, and the arts. Golden Age Athens produced the philosopher Socrates and his pupil, Plato. Phidias, the famous sculptor, lived in the same community as the great dramatists Sophocles and Euripides. Pythagoras, Protagoras, and Herodotus, some of the greatest scientists and thinkers of all time, lived in the shadow of the famous Parthenon, perched atop the city's Acropolis.

Politically, Athens accomplished what has been called the world's first democracy nearly 2,500 years ago. Beginning with the "tyrannos," or popular leader Pisistratus, who fought against aristocratic power in the 6th century B.C., Athens was led by a series of governors who included its citizens in the creation and enforcement of its laws, even though those citizens did not include women, foreigners, or slaves, which the Athenians took from various wars and kept as household servants and tutors for their children. The democratic system established by the Athenians divided the society into ten tribes, each of which provided fifty men for the city's "boule," a legislative body that was on duty year round, night and day, with each tribe on duty for thirty-six days at a stretch, working three daily shifts. Additionally, all eligible Athenians were expected to participate in the "ekklesia," a meeting of at least 6,000 citizens held about every nine days, during which the entire city would debate issues raised by the boule.

Between them, the boule and the ekklesia created laws, empowered a police force, established a law court, the Helaia, and developed a trial by jury system. Interested as they were in fair, impartial decisions, the Athenians demanded a minimum jury size of 201 citizens, with larger juries of 501, or even 1001 or 2001 not uncommon.

As presented in *The Bacchae*, ancient Greek religion was "polytheistic." The Greeks believed in a "pantheon" of twelve main gods, along with a host of lesser deities, heroes, and local, household gods. Each of the gods represented a different facet of human knowledge and experience, though they were recognized as something superior, or at least different from, earthly mortals. Stories about the gods often depict them interfering in human affairs, though no god was ultimately viewed as entirely good or entirely bad. Each was capable of helping, or harming, humans.

Religious ritual was extremely important in the daily lives of the Greeks. Their cities were often set up around the various temples to Zeus, Hera, Poseidon, Demeter, Apollo, and the other immortals who were thought to live atop Mount Olympus; many days in the Greek calendar were set aside for the worship of these gods, which included prayer, sacrifice, and divination.

Compare & Contrast

- **5th Century B.C.:** The Athenian democracy which evolved during the 5th century B.C. is considered to be the first of its kind in the world. Matters of the state are decided by a vote of the citizen assembly, known as the *ekklesia*.

  Today: The United States is considered the world's leading democratic nation, though American democratic practices are quite different. Officials of the state are elected to one of three branches of the government: the executive, the legislative, or the judicial. Each branch is given different responsibilities and authorities to act on behalf of the citizens of the country, all of whom, men, women, and naturalized citizens included, may vote, or choose to run for office, during periodic public elections.

- **5th Century B.C.:** Education in Athenian society is reserved for boys, who learn reading, writing, arithmetic, and music. Once the boys reach age twelve, physical education becomes a priority, and they are taught gymnastics and sports such as wrestling, running, the discus and javelin toss, which will serve them well during their mandatory military service at age eighteen. Middle and upper class girls, expecting to marry well, may learn to read and write, and perhaps play the lyre, from a female tutor at home. They rarely, if ever, participate in physical education or sports.

  Today: Equal education for women, in both academic subjects and sports, is recognized as important in a majority of the world's industrialized nations. In the United States, some type of formal education is required of all children and public education is available for everyone from kindergarten through the twelfth grade. A limited amount of music and physical education may be required of students but intense training in these areas is largely elective. Military service is not mandatory for young men, though American boys must still register to be drafted when they turn eighteen.

- **5th Century B.C.:** Theatre in Greece is associated with religious worship and the cult of Dionysus, the Greek god of wine and revelry. Plays are produced each March during the Dionysia. Production of the plays is financed by rich and public-spirited citizens, known as *choregoi*, who are assigned a playwright and up to three actors and charged by the state with employing a chorus, hiring a trainer for the group, and providing costumes, scenery, and props.

  Today: Most theatre is no longer associated with religious worship, though "Passion Plays," commemorating the lives of Jesus and the saints, are common in American Christian churches. Plays are performed year-round, mainly for recreational and entertainment purposes. In the United States, professional play production is concentrated mainly in larger cities, such as New York, where individual financiers or groups of wealthy investors provide the funds necessary to pay large groups of performers and buy often extravagant sets, costumes, and lighting effects, which may cost millions of dollars.

- **5th Century B.C.:** Many of the most popular Greek tragedies impart a lesson that is central to Athenian society: the gods are all-knowing and all-powerful and human beings should not allow hubris to let them think they are equal or superior to the deities.

  Today: The European Renaissance of the fifteenth and sixteenth centuries encouraged exploration and experimentation in the fields of science, geography, philosophy, and the arts. As a result, in the twentieth century, a variety of mainly monotheistic religions offer the opportunity to worship at will, while individual human endeavors and accomplishments are regularly recognized for superior achievement, and pride in ability, within reason, is encouraged as an important feature of personal development.

Greek theatre emerged from the worship of one of the minor gods, Dionysus, who was thought to be the son of Zeus and Semele, a mortal, and was associated with wine, fertility, and celebration. Although Dionysus had been worshiped in Thrace and Asia Minor since at least 700 B.C., it wasn't until the 6th century B.C. that his cult reached into Athens. Worshiping Dionysus involved the sacrifice of animals and feasts, accompanied by wine drinking, dancing, and singing dithyrambs, ritual hymns honoring the god. Eventually, a contest for dancing and dithyramb singing evolved among the tribes of Athens and from this singing and dancing, it is believed, drama developed. The first contest for tragedies was held in Athens at the City Dionysia, an entire festival honoring Dionysus, in 534 B.C. During the next hundred years, through the play-writing careers of Aeschylus, Sophocles, and Euripides, the great stone amphitheatres of Greece, some seating as many as 17,000 people, were built and production practices involving costuming, masks, and machinery evolved.

Throughout its Golden Age, Athens's great rival was Sparta. While Athens assembled a confederacy of city-states in the North through peaceful agreements and trade negotiations, Sparta, known primarily for its military might, built a minor empire to the South out of smaller territories it conquered. While the two rivals found a common interest in defeating the Persians early in the 5th century B.C., old jealousies and new affronts stirred renewed animosity and led to the Peloponnesian War. This terrible series of battles between Spartan and Athenian forces lasted from 431 to 404 B.C., eventually destroying Athens and elevating Sparta to supremacy in mainland Greece. At the end of the war, to avoid having all their soldiers killed and their women and children sold into slavery, the Athenians agreed to Spartan terms of peace, which included government of Athens by thirty pro-Spartan aristocrats, who became known as the Thirty Tyrants. Athens's democracy was dead, and though it would struggle to its feet again in the fourth century, the glory of Greece belonged next to the Thebans, the Macedonians, and, finally, the Romans.

It was in the historical context of Athens's decline, just before its defeat at the hands of the Spartans, that Euripides chose to leave the city he had called home for so many years and journey into self-imposed exile to King Archelaus's court in Macedonia. There, he wrote *The Bacchae* and, according to popular account, was accidentally killed by the king's hunting dogs while walking in the woods—just two years before the fall of Athens.

Critical Overview

While the original productions of classical Greek tragedies were not reviewed for potential audiences the way theatrical performances are today, some measure of their critical success may be determined by the awards they received (or did not receive) during the festivals at which they were produced, and by the subsequent number of times the plays were revived over the years.

Euripides spent most of his playwriting career pursuing the elusive top prize at the City Dionysia, Athens's famous annual festival honoring Dionysus, the Greek god of wine and revelry. While Aeschylus, Sophocles, and dozens of other tragedians whose work has not even survived the ages received many honors and a great deal of popular acclaim, Euripides took only four first prizes during his lifetime and, as often as not, his plays came in last. Whether it was his own death in 406 B.C. or the radical departure in subject matter from his earlier plays, he achieved a new level of fame and appreciation by the time *The Bacchae* was produced in Athens in 405 B.C. The avant-garde playwright was posthumously awarded the top prize for that year's festival.

Scattered references to the play suggest that it was revived continuously on Athens's stages for the next hundred years and that it continued its popularity during the period of the Roman Empire, when it was translated into Latin and performed across Italy. There is evidence that the work was familiar to Horace, Virgil, and Ovid. During the Middle Ages, it is commonly known, Euripides received more attention than either Aeschylus or Sophocles as a first-rate tragedian and brilliant writer of spoken Greek. *The Bacchae* and other plays by Euripides were among the first to be translated into Latin prose and Italian during the Renaissance and seventeenth and eighteenth century writers from Milton to Goethe praised the play's singular purpose and intense depiction of man's conflict with his god.

In the modern era, criticism of *The Bacchae* has largely been divided between scholarly commentary on the text and history of the play and popular reviews of occasional performances. In *Dramatic Lectures*, a collection of his scholarly analyses of dramatists and their plays, the nineteenth century German critic August W. Schlegel wrote, "In the composition of this piece, I cannot help admiring a harmony and unity, which we seldom meet with in Euripides, as well as abstinence from every foreign matter, so that all the motives and effects flow from one source, and concur towards a common end. After the *Hippolytus*, I should be inclined to assign to this play the first place among all the extant works of Euripides."

In his autobiographical *Life of Macaulay*, the famous English historian G. M. Trevelyan praised Euripides, writing,"*The Bacchae* is a glorious play.

I doubt whether it be not superior to the *Medea*, it is often very obscure; and I am not sure that I fully understand its general scope. But, as a piece of language, it is hardly equaled in the world. And, whether it was intended to encourage or to discourage fanaticism, the picture of fanatical excitement which it exhibits has never been rivaled."

Twentieth century productions of *The Bacchae* are not as common as stagings of Euripides's other masterpiece, *Medea*, and they tend to meet with mixed or unfavorable reaction. In his review of Michael Cacoyannis's adaptation of the play, which Cacoyannis himself directed for Broadway in 1980, *New York* magazine critic John Simon wrote, "There is serious doubt in my mind about whether Greek drama can be performed today." Simon complained about the artificial, melodramatic qualities of classical tragedies, Cacoyannis's translation of the play, which he deemed embarrassing and accidentally comic, and the problems inherent in staging plays that were originally meant to be performed in enormous outdoor amphitheatres before crowds of several thousand.

In his review of the same production for *Newsweek* magazine, critic Jack Kroll observed that mounting modern productions of classical tragedies is a difficult feat, requiring immense creativity and, often, radical reinterpretation for contemporary audiences. "Euripides's *The Bacchae* is a stupendous, searing play," Kroll noted, "but like most productions of Greek tragedy, Michael Cacoyannis's staging at Broadway's Circle in the Square can't really break through the centuries-old crust to the white-hot life beneath. Directors have gone to great lengths to solve this problem. In America, Peter Arnott used marionettes instead of actors. In Italy, Luca Ronconi used one actress... to speak the entire play as the audience moved with her through a series of rooms and spaces. In Germany, Klaus Michael Gruber used nudity, horses, glass walls and 100,000 watts of neon lights."

In the *Nation*, reviewer Julius Novick echoed Kroll's comments, and asked, "Am I alone in having difficulty with the elaborate passages of woe in which the Greek and Elizabethan tragic playwrights so frequently indulged themselves? If my sensibilities are typical at all, modern audiences are conditioned to be moved obliquely, by irony, or poignant understatement, rather than by lines like 'O Misery! O grief beyond all measure!'"

At least part of the reason *The Bacchae* has been applauded as a literary text and dismissed in performance during the twentieth century may lie in Greek tragedy's original purpose: religious ritual. Several critics have observed that, since modern audiences do not feel the same ritual impulses as the ancient Greeks, their plays do not have the same effect on us in performance. In 1969, the avant-garde theatre producer Richard Schechner assembled a group of performers and created a modern version of *The Bacchae* they called

Dionysus in 69. In his collection of criticism called *God on the Gymnasium Floor*, Walter Kerr explained his objections to the production this way:

> Mr. Schechner has gone all the way back—as far as our literary history permits—in his search for a religious impulse capable of breeding a fresh form of drama. He really does wish us to act on the impulse he has attempted to borrow: to get up from our places on the floor and to enter, to *feel*, the interior Dionysiac pressure toward abandon that the Greeks felt and that exists as a record in Euripides's play. We do not in fact feel this specific religious impulse today, however; we do not bring it into the theatre with us as a deposit or guarantee. The specific religious impulse is dead. It has been dead for a very long time. Because it is dead, the gesture dependent upon it must, for the most part, be empty, effortful, artificial. We can try to let ourselves go, but there is nothing genuine pushing us.

What Do I Read Next?

- Eighteen of Euripides's plays have survived, each of which contains elements of the dramatist's non-traditional style that raised criticism from his contemporaries and earned him the respect and admiration of later generations of play readers and theatergoers. One of his most popular works is *Medea*, Euripides's 431 B.C. retelling of the myth of the sorceress who, faced with abandonment and exile in a strange land, murdered her own children and cursed her unfaithful husband. *Hippolytus* (428 B.C.) is the story of King Theseus's bride Phaedra, who falls in love with her stepson, Hippolytus, leading them both down a path toward destruction.

- Classical historian Michael Grant has written several books about the ancient Greeks and Romans, including *The Rise of the Greeks* (1987), which largely examines the political and military history of the Greek Empire; *The Classical Greeks* (1989), which provides a profile of Greek society through brief biographical essays about prominent Greek writers, philosophers, and leaders; and *A Social History of Greece and Rome* (1992), an exploration of the roles of women and men, slaves and citizens in Greek society.

- *The Mask of Apollo* is a novel of historical fiction by Mary Renault. Niko, the story's protagonist, is an actor in the 4th century B.C. who travels the Greek Empire, performing for kings and tyrants and befriending Plato, the famous philosopher, and Dion, a great soldier and statesman. The book draws on Renault's lifetime of classical research and presents an engaging glimpse into the life of the Greeks thousands of years ago.

- Much of what is known of classical Greek tragedy is recorded in Aristotle's *Poetics*, a 4th century

B.C. treatise in which the philosopher attempts to describe dramatic poetry (tragedy). Aristotle suggests the six essential ingredients of good tragedies are plot, character, theme, diction, music, and spectacle; and he refers specifically to the plays of Aeschylus, Sophocles, and Euripides as examples. While several translations and editions of the *Poetics* exist, S. H. Butcher's version, which first appeared in 1902, is one that is often used in the classroom and appears frequently in literary anthologies.

- For nearly 150 years, students and teachers alike have relied on *Bulfinch's Mythology* as a dependable and entertaining way to learn about the great heroes, gods, and myths of the world. In this great collection of legends, originally published in 1855 but readily available in recent editions, Thomas Bulfinch has carefully researched and retold some of the greatest stories the world has ever known, including tales about the full pantheon of Greek gods and the mortals who dared to cross them.

- Peter Connolly's *The Ancient City: Life in Classical Athens & Rome* is an introduction to the history and culture of two of the world's greatest empires. Filled with original drawings, suggesting what ancient theatres, temples, and homes may have looked like, as well as photographs and helpful maps, Connolloy's carefully researched text is simple, straightforward, and entertaining.

Sources

Kerr, Walter. *God on the Gymnasium Floor*, Simon and Schuster, 1971, p. 42.

Kroll, Jack. Review of *The Bacchae* in *Newsweek*, October 13, 1980, p. 135.

Muller, K. O. *A History of the Literature of Ancient Greece: Volume I*, Parker, 1858, p. 499.

Novick, Julius. Review of *The Bacchae* in the *Nation*, October 25, 1980, pp. 417-18.

Sandys, John Edwin. *The Bacchae of Euripides*, Cambridge University Press, 1880.

Schlegel, Augustus Wilhelm. *A Course of Lectures on Dramatic Art and Literature*, translated by John Black, H. G. Bohn, 1861.

Simon, John. Review of *The Bacchae* in *New York*, October 20, 1980, p. 101-02.

Further Reading

Arnott, Peter. *The Ancient Greek and Roman Theatre*, Random House, 1971.

> An accessible, basic introduction to the drama and stagecraft of the classical Greeks and Romans that includes theories about the origins of tragedy, suggestions about the evolution of the Greek performance space, a handful of illustrations, and a helpful bibliography.

Bieber, Margarete. *The History of the Greek and Roman Theatre*, Princeton University Press, 1961.

> An in-depth, scholarly look at the evolution of the classical Greek and Roman theatres, including many photographs, illustrations, and conjectural drawings.

Foley, Helene P. "The Bacchae" in her *Ritual Irony: Poetry and Sacrifice in Euripides*, Cornell University Press, 1985.

> In this essay, Helene suggests one of the things Euripides accomplished with *The Bacchae* was an investigation of the relationship between ritual and theatre and between the spirit of festival and the society that creates it.

Grube, G. M. A. "The Bacchants" in his *The Drama of Euripides*, Barnes and Noble, 1961.

> A careful episode-by-episode examination of the plot of *The Bacchae*, with running commentary by Grube explaining terminology and the possible historical and cultural significance of words and deeds in the play.

Hamilton, Edith. *The Greek Way*, W. W. Norton, 1993.

> Hamilton's research and writing about the minds and culture of the ancient Greeks have been popular reading for decades. This relatively slim volume includes references to Euripides.

Segal, Charles. *Dionysiac Poetics and Euripides's* Bacchae, Princeton University Press, 1982.

> In this exhaustive, scholarly tome, Segal examines many of the popular questions about *The Bacchae*, including whether or not Euripides approved of Dionysus's worship himself, the importance of the Dionysiac cult to Greek society, and sex roles in the plays of Euripides.

Stapleton, Michael. *The Illustrated Dictionary of Greek and Roman Mythology*, Peter Bedrick Books, New York, 1986.

A helpful collection of brief descriptions of some of the most famous Greek gods, heroes and myths, arranged alphabetically.

Winnington-Ingram, R. P. *Euripides and Dionysus: An Interpretation of the Bacchae*, Cambridge University Press, 1948.

A careful examination of *The Bacchae* that explores each action of the play, setting it in its literary and historical context, with special emphasis on Euripides's possibly negative opinion of Dionysus and the Greek gods.